About

Kate Hewitt has wor
from drama teacher
worker, but writing r
also writes women's fi
the healing and redemptive powe
in a tiny village in the English Cotswolds with her
husband, five children, and an overly affectionate
Golden Retriever.

Maya Blake's writing dream started at 13. She
eventually realised her dream when she received The
Call in 2012. Maya lives in England with her husband,
kids and an endless supply of books. Contact Maya:
www.mayabauthor.blogspot.com   www.twitter.com/
mayablake www.facebook.com/maya.blake.94

Caitlin Crews discovered her first romance novel at
the age of twelve and has since conducted a life-long
love affair with romance novels, many of which she
insists on keeping near her at all times. She currently
lives in the Pacific Northwest, with her animator/comic
book artist husband and their menagerie of ridiculous
animals.

The Gorgeous Greeks

COLLECTION

Seductive Secrets

KATE HEWITT

MAYA BLAKE

CAITLIN CREWS

MILLS & BOON

First Published in Great Britain 2020
By Mills & Boon, an imprint of HarperCollins*Publishers*
1 London Bridge Street, London, SE1 9GF

GORGEOUS GREEKS: SEDUCTIVE SECRETS © 2020
Harlequin Books S.A.

Bound to the Greek © 2008 Kate Hewitt
What the Greek Wants Most © 2014 Maya Blake
The Billionaire's Secret Princess © 2017 Caitlin Crews

ISBN: 978-0-263-28140-8

MIX
Paper from
responsible sources
FSC C007454
www.fsc.org

This book is produced from independently certified FSC™ paper to ensure responsible forest management.

For more information visit: www.harpercollins.co.uk/green

Printed and bound in Spain
by CPI, Barcelona

BOUND TO
THE GREEK

KATE HEWITT

CHAPTER ONE

'COME right this way, Mr Zervas. You're going to meet with Eleanor, our top planner.'

Jace Zervas stilled his stride for no more than a second as the word reverberated through him. *Eleanor.* He hadn't heard that name in ten years, hadn't let himself think it.

Of course, it had to be a coincidence. There were certainly more Eleanors in the United States—in New York City—than the one who had broken his heart.

The assistant who had led him through the elegantly sparse lobby with its designer sofas and modern art now stopped in front of a door of tinted glass, gave a perfunctory knock, then pushed it open.

'Eleanor? I'd like to introduce you to—'

Jace didn't hear the rest. For as the woman in the office swung round to face him, his mind buzzed, blanked. It *was* Eleanor.

His Eleanor. Ellie.

He knew she was as surprised as he was that he was here, that *they* were here, face to face. Although her expression didn't really change, he was aware of the slight widening of her eyes, the parting of her lips.

Then she drew herself up, gave him a professional smile that managed to irritate him with its coolness, and said, 'Thank you, Jill. That will be all.'

The assistant, surely aware of the current that crackled through the air, glanced speculatively between them. Jace ignored her, his gaze fixed on Eleanor Langley, so utterly, appallingly different from the Ellie he'd once known. 'Shall I bring coffee?'

A tiny pause. 'Certainly. Thank you.'

The assistant left, the door clicked shut, and Jace's mind kicked back into gear.

Of course he should have expected this might happen. He'd known Ellie was from New York, and her mother was an event planner. Why shouldn't she have followed the same career path?

Because the Ellie you knew hated her mother's career, her mother's world. The Ellie you knew—or at least thought you knew—wanted to open a bakery.

Clearly much had happened in the last ten years.

'You've changed.' He didn't mean to say it, yet it was impossible not to notice it. The Ellie he'd known ten years ago had looked nothing like the shiny, polished woman in front of him.

His Ellie had been relaxed, natural, *fun*, so different from this woman with her tailored black power suit, her high-lighted hair barely brushing her cheekbones in an elegant chestnut bob. Her hazel eyes, once warm and golden, now seemed darker, sharper, and were narrowed into assessing slits. As she moved back around to her desk Jace saw her shoes: black three-inch stilettos. His Ellie had never worn heels. His Ellie had never worn black.

Yet why was he even thinking this way? *His* Ellie hadn't been his at all. He'd realised that all too terribly when he'd last seen her…when she'd lied to him in the worst way possible. When he'd walked away without another word.

Eleanor Langley stared down at the burnished surface of her desk and took a deep breath. She needed the moment to regain her poise and control. She'd never expected this moment to happen, although she'd fantasised about it many times over the last decade. Coming face to face with Jace

Zervas. Telling him just what she thought of him and his cowardly creeping away.

She'd envisioned herself slapping his face, telling him to go to hell, or, in her more dignified moments, sweeping him with one simple, disdainful glance.

She had not pictured herself trembling, both inside and out, unable to think of a single thing to say.

Stop. She'd worked too hard for too long to let this moment defeat her. Taking another breath, Eleanor lifted her head and settled her gaze coolly on the man in front of her.

'Of course I've changed. It's been ten years.' She paused, letting her gaze sweep over him, although she had a feeling it wasn't as disdainful as she might have wished. 'You've changed too, Jace.' It felt strange to have his name on her lips. She never spoke of him. She tried not to think of him.

He *had* changed; his ink-black hair was now streaked with grey at the temples and his face looked leaner, longer. Harder. Eleanor noticed new lines from nose to mouth, and the faint fanning of crow's feet by his eyes. Somehow those lines didn't age him so much as give him an air of dignity and experience. They even emphasised the steely grey of his eyes with their silvery glints. And his body hadn't changed at all, it seemed: still long, lithe, and powerful. The grey silk suit he wore only emphasised his muscular shoulders and trim hips; he wore it, as he had the cashmere sweatshirts and faded jeans of his college days, with ease and grace.

He looked, she thought a bit resentfully, great. But then, she reminded herself, so did she. She spent a lot of time and effort making sure she looked great; in her job a professional and even glamorous appearance was a must. She was grateful for it now. The last thing she wanted was to be at a disadvantage. She straightened, smiled even, and flicked her hair back from her face in one quick movement. 'So you're my two o'clock.'

Jace smiled back, faintly, but his eyes were hard. He looked almost angry. Eleanor had no idea what *he* had to be angry about; he was the one who had left. If anyone should be angry— She stopped that thought before her resentful mind gave it wings. She wasn't angry. She was over it. Over him. She no longer cared any more, at all, about Jace Zervas.

She turned to her planner, still open on her desk, and trailed one glossily manicured finger down the day's appointments. 'You're here on behalf of Atrikides Holdings?' she asked. 'It says Leandro Atrikides was supposed to have been coming.' She looked up, eyebrows arched. 'Change of plans?'

'Something like that,' Jace agreed, his voice taut. He sat down in one of the leather armchairs in front of her desk and crossed one leg over the other.

'Well.' She made herself smile and sat down behind her desk, hands neatly folded. 'How can I help?'

Jace's lips tightened, and Eleanor wondered if that was going to be it. Ten years of anger, bitterness, and overwhelming heartache reduced to nothing in a single sentence. *How can I help?* Yet what other choice was there? She didn't want to rake over the past; it would be messy and uncomfortable and far too painful. She wanted to pretend the past didn't exist, and so she would. She'd treat Jace Zervas like a regular client, even though he was far from one, and she hardly wanted to help him. She didn't even want to talk to the man for another second.

The sane thing, of course, would be to respectfully request a colleague to take Jace as her client, and step away from what could only be an explosive situation. Or if not explosive, then at least angrily simmering. She could see it in the hard steel of his eyes. She could feel it bubbling in herself.

Yet Eleanor knew she wouldn't do that. Her boss wouldn't be pleased; Lily Stevens didn't like changes. Messes. And Eleanor could certainly do without the gossip. Besides, there was another, greater reason why she'd face Jace down in her own office. She didn't want to give him the satisfaction of making her run away. As he had.

'Well,' Jace replied after a moment, 'obviously I'm here because I need you to plan an event.'

'Obviously,' Eleanor agreed, and heard the answering sharpness in her tone. This was not going well. Every little exchange was going to be pointed under the politeness, and she didn't think she could take the tension. The trouble was, she didn't know what else to do. Talking about the past was akin to ripping the bandages off old wounds, inflaming the scars that still remained on her heart. Her body. Even remembering it hurt.

She clamped her mind down on that thought. Jace Zervas was just another client, she told herself again. Just a regular client. She let her breath out slowly and tried to smile.

'What I meant,' she said evenly, 'was what kind of event are you hosting?' She gritted her teeth as she added, 'Some details would help.'

'Isn't there some form that's been filled out? I'm quite sure my assistant did this all on the telephone.'

Eleanor glanced through the slim file she had on Atrikides Holdings. 'A Christmas party,' she read from the memo one of the secretaries had taken. 'That's all I have, I'm afraid.'

A knock sounded on the door, and Jill came in with a tray of coffee. Eleanor rose to take it from her. She didn't want her assistant picking up on the tension that thrummed angrily through the room. God knew how she'd try to use it; Jill had been jockeying for her position since she arrived, fresh from college, two years ago.

'Thanks, Jill. I'll take it from here.'

Surprised, Jill backed off, the door closing once more, and Eleanor set the tray on her desk, her back to Jace. She still heard his lazy murmur.

'You didn't used to drink coffee. I always thought it was so funny, a girl who wanted to open a coffee shop and yet didn't drink coffee herself.'

Eleanor tensed. So he was going to go there. She'd been hoping they could get through this awkward meeting without referencing the past at all, but now Jace was going to talk about these silly, student memories, as if they shared some happy past.

As if they shared anything at all.

A single streak of anger, white-hot, blazed through her. Her hands shook as she poured the coffee. How dared he? How dared he act as if he hadn't walked—run—away from her, the minute things got too much? How dared he pretend they'd parted amicably, or even parted at all?

Instead of her going to his apartment building, only to find he'd left. Left the building, left the city, left the country. All without telling her.

Coward.

'Actually, I think it was enterprising,' she told him coolly, her back still to him. Her hands no longer trembled. 'I saw the market, and I wanted to meet it.' She handed him his coffee: black, two sugars, the way he'd always taken it. She still remembered. Still remembered brewing him a single-serve cafétière in her student apartment while she plied him with the pastries and cakes she was going to sell in her little bakery. While she told him her dreams.

He'd said everything was delicious. But of course he would. He'd lied about so many things, like when he'd said he loved her. If he'd loved her, he wouldn't have left.

Eleanor poured her own coffee. She took it black now, and drank at least three cups a day. Her best friend Allie said so much caffeine wasn't good for her, but Eleanor needed the kick. Especially now.

She turned back to Jace. He still held his mug, his long, brown fingers wrapped around the handle, his expression brooding and a little dark. 'That's not how I remember it.'

Disconcerted, Eleanor took too large a sip of coffee and burned her tongue. 'What?'

Jace leaned forward. 'You weren't interested in meeting a market. You weren't even interested in business. Don't you remember, Ellie?' His voice came out in a soft hiss. 'You just wanted to have a place where people could relax and be happy.' He spoke it like a sneer, and Eleanor could only think of when—and where—she had said that. In Jace's bed, after they'd made love for the first time. She'd shared so many pitiful, pathetic secrets with him. Poured out her life and heart and every schoolgirl dream she'd ever cherished, and he'd given her—what? Nothing. Less than nothing.

'I'm sure we remember quite a few things differently, Jace,' she said coolly. 'And I go by Eleanor now.'

'You told me you hated your name.'

She let out an impatient breath. 'It's been ten years, Jace. Ten years. I've changed. You've changed. Get over it.'

His eyes narrowed, the colour flaring to silver. 'Oh, I'm over it, Eleanor,' he said softly. 'I'm definitely over it.'

But he didn't sound over it. He sounded angry, and that made Eleanor even angrier despite all her intentions to stay cool, not to care. He had no right, no right at all, even to be the tiniest bit furious. Yet here he was, acting as if she'd been the one to do something wrong. Of course she *had* done something wrong, in Jace's eyes. She'd made the classic, naive mistake of accidentally getting pregnant.

Jace stared at her, felt the fury rise up in him before he choked it all down again. There was no use in being angry. It was ten years too late. He didn't want to feel angry; the emotion shamed him now.

Yet even so he realised he wanted to know. He needed to know what had happened to Eleanor in the last ten years. Had she kept the baby? Had she married the father? Had she suffered even a moment's regret for trying to dupe him so damnably? Because she didn't look as if she had. She looked as if she was angry with him, which was ridiculous. She was the guilty one, the lying one. He'd simply found out.

'So.' She sat down again, behind the desk, so it served as a barrier between them. Not that they needed one. Time was enough. Putting her coffee carefully to one side, she pulled out a pen and pad of paper. Jace watched the way her hair swung down in a smooth, dark curtain as she bent her head. Everything about her was so different from the Ellie he had known, the Ellie he remembered. The woman in front of him was no more than a polished, empty shell. She gave nothing away. She looked up, her hazel eyes narrowing, her mouth curving into a false smile. 'Can you give me a few details about this party?'

Damn the party. Jace leaned forward. 'Did you have a boy or a girl?' God only knew why he wanted to ask that question. Why he even wanted to know. Surely there were a dozen—a hundred—more relevant questions he could have asked. *When did you cheat on me? Why? Who was he? Did he love you like I did?*

No, he wasn't about to ask any of those questions. They all revealed too much. He had no intention of letting Eleanor Langley ever know how much she'd hurt him.

His voice was no more than a predatory hiss, an accusation, yet Ellie's expression didn't change. If anything it became even more closed, more polished and professional. The woman was like ice. He could hardly credit it; the Ellie he'd known had reflected every emotion in her eyes. She'd cried at commercials. Now Ellie—Eleanor—simply pressed her lips together and gave her head a little shake.

'Let's not talk about the past, Jace. If we want to be professional—' Her voice caught, finally, and he was glad. He'd almost thought she didn't feel anything and God knew he felt too much. So this icy woman could thaw. A little. Underneath there was something, something true and maybe even broken, something *real*, and for now that was enough.

He leaned back, satisfied. 'Fine. Let's be professional. I want to hold a Christmas party for the remaining employees of Atrikides Holdings.'

'Remaining?' Ellie repeated a bit warily.

'Yes, remaining. I bought the company last week, and there has been some unrest because of it.'

'A corporate takeover.' She spoke the words distastefully.

'Yes, exactly,' Jace replied blandly. 'I had to let some of the employees go when I brought in my own people. Now that there is a new workforce, I'd like to create a feeling of goodwill. A Christmas party is a means to that end.'

'I see.'

Yet Jace could see from the flicker of contempt in her eyes, the tightening of her mouth, that she didn't see at all. She was summing him up and judging him up based on very little evidence—the evidence he'd given.

Yet why should he care what she thought of him? And why should she judge at all? She'd been just as ruthless as he was, as enterprising and economical with the truth.

And he'd judged her with far more damning information.

Eleanor wrote a few cursory notes on the pad of paper on her desk. She wasn't even aware of what she was writing. Her vision hazed, her mind blanked.

Was it a boy or a girl?

How could he ask such a question now, with such contempt? His *child*. He'd been asking about his child.

She closed her mind on the thought like a trap, refusing to free the memory and sorrow. She couldn't go there. Not now, not ever. She'd kept those emotions locked deep inside herself and even seeing Jace Zervas again wouldn't free them. She wouldn't let it. She drew in a deep breath and looked up.

'So what kind of Christmas party are we talking about here? Cocktails, sit-down dinner? How many people do you anticipate coming?'

'There are only about fifty employees, and I'd like to invite families.' Jace spoke tonelessly. 'Quite a few have small children, so something family-friendly but elegant.'

'Family-friendly,' Eleanor repeated woodenly. She felt her fingers clench around the pen she was holding. She could not do this. She could not pretend a moment longer, even though she'd been pretending for ten years—

Was that all her life had been? Pretending? Pretence? And she hadn't realised it until she'd come face to face with Jace Zervas.

Stop, she told herself yet again. *Stop thinking, feeling.*

Another breath. Somehow she made herself nod as she wrote another note on the pad of paper. 'Very well. Now—'

'Look,' Jace exhaled impatiently, 'I don't really have time to go over every detail. I came here as a favour, and I have a lot to do. I'm only in New York for a week.'

'A week—'

'I need the party to be this Friday,' Jace cut her off.

Eleanor's mouth dropped open before she quickly closed it. *That* hadn't been on the memo. 'I'm afraid that's impossible. Venues are booked, I have a complete client list—'

'Nothing is impossible if you throw enough money at it,' Jace replied flatly. 'And I chose your company because I was assured you could make it happen.' His gaze, cold and contemptuous, raked over her. 'I was told the top event planner would see to me personally. I suppose that's you?'

Eleanor merely nodded. She didn't trust herself to speak.

'Then email me a list of details to go over by tomorrow morning.' Jace rose from his chair. 'You've done very well for yourself, Ellie,' he said softly. 'I wonder how many people you had to climb over to get to this lovely little spot.' He glanced out of the window at her view of Madison Square Park, the leafless trees stark against a grey winter sky.

His comment was so blatantly unfair and unwarranted that Eleanor could only gasp. And fume. What right did he have to make such a judgment? If anyone should be *judging*—

Jace headed for the door. 'I don't think I'll need to see you before the party,' he said, and somehow this bored dismissal stung her more than anything else had.

He was going to leave, just like that, after raking up the old wounds, after asking about her baby—their baby—

'It was a girl,' she burst out, the words like staccato gunfire. Her chest burned, and so did her eyes. Her fingers clenched into a fist on her desk. Jace stilled, his hand on the door. 'A girl,' she repeated tonelessly. 'Since you asked.'

He turned around slowly, lip curled in an unpleasant sneer. 'So I did,' he replied. 'But actually I really don't care.'
And then he was gone.

CHAPTER TWO

'ELEANOR? Did Jace Zervas just leave the office?'

Eleanor jerked her head up to see her boss, Lily Stevens, standing in her office doorway. Under her glossy black helmet of hair her eyebrows were drawn together sharply, her mouth a thin red line. The elegantly disapproving look reminded Eleanor of her mother, which was unsurprising since Lily and her mother had been business partners until five years ago.

'Eleanor?' Lily repeated, more sharply, and Eleanor rose from her desk, trying to smile. How long had she been lost in her own miserable reverie? 'Yes. We just concluded our meeting.'

'That was fast.'

Eleanor moved around her desk to put Jace's coffee cup—barely touched—back on the tray. 'He's a busy man.'

'Jill said things seemed tense when she came in here.'

Of course Jill would run to her boss, Eleanor thought with resentment. What a frenemy! This business could be cut-throat, and everyone was trying to claw a way in or up. She gave a little shrug. 'Not really.'

'I don't think I need to tell you,' Lily said, her tone making it clear she thought she did, 'that Jace Zervas is a very important client? His holdings are worth over a billion—'

'You don't need to tell me.' She didn't need Lily telling her how rich and powerful Jace was. She'd known that already. When she'd met him as a twenty-two-year-old exchange student in Boston, he'd been from money. Rich, entitled, spoiled.

Except he'd never seemed spoiled to her…until he'd left. Then he'd seemed rotten right through.

'I want you to do everything in your power to make this party a success,' Lily told her. 'I'm releasing your other clients to Laura for the week.'

'What?' Eleanor heard the outrage in her voice, and strove to temper it. She had several clients she'd been working with for months, and she knew Laura—another frenemy—would be eager to scoop up the contacts and run with them. Eleanor gritted her teeth. This business could be brutal. She'd toughened up a lot in the last ten years, but it still made her weary. She also knew there was nothing she could do about it.

If Lily was going to make that kind of executive decision, so be it. He wasn't worth her jeopardising her career; he wasn't worth *anything*. She would work on Jace's damn party for a week. And then she would forget—again—that she'd ever met him.

Lily's eyes narrowed. 'Is that going to be a problem, Eleanor?'

Eleanor bit the inside of her cheek. She hated that tone, that silky, dangerous, warning tone that her mother had always taken with her as a child. Funny, how she'd ended up in a job just like her mother's, with a boss just like her mother.

Except there was nothing remotely funny about it, or even coincidental. Every choice, every decision had been intentional, a way of distancing herself from everything she'd been or believed in. A way of reinventing herself.

And it had worked.

Now she turned to smile sweetly at her boss. 'Of course not. I'm absolutely thrilled—and honoured, Lily—to be working with Mr Zervas. Getting his account is a coup for the agency.'

Lily nodded, seemingly satisfied. 'So it is. Are you meeting with Zervas again?'

'I'll email him the particulars tomorrow.' Eleanor shuddered inwardly to think what that meant. She'd be tied up in begging calls for the rest of the day, recalling favours and currying some more so she could make this thing happen.

The idea that she would have to slave away all for Jace burned in her gut, her heart. It was just *wrong*.

But she wasn't about to lose her job over this, or even her cool. And, Eleanor told herself, there could be some sweet, sweet satisfaction in showing Jace how he hadn't hurt her at all.

Even if he really had—and horribly at that.

She spent the rest of the day immersed in work, planning Jace's party while refusing to think of the man himself. A call to Atrikides Holdings yielded some interesting—and unsurprising—information.

'It all happened so fast,' gushed the staff member Eleanor had been connected to when she asked to speak to someone about details. Eleanor leaned back in her chair and prepared to hear some gossip. 'One minute everything was fine—it's a family business, you know—and the next he swooped in and took over. Fired half the people.' The woman—Peggy—lowered her voice to an awed hush. 'They had to leave that very day. Pack their stuff in boxes. Even Talos Atrikides—the CEO's *son*!'

'Well, hopefully this party will go some way to smoothing things over,' Eleanor replied. She could listen to the gossip, but she wouldn't indulge in it herself. She knew better.

Still, as she hung up the phone, the conversation left her a little shaken. She'd fallen in love with Jace Zervas when he'd been just twenty-two years old, charming, easy-going, carefree and careless. She hadn't realised just how cold—and cold-hearted—he'd been until he'd walked away.

And hearing about his actions with Atrikides Holdings today confirmed it. He really was that man.

The other one—the one she'd fallen in love with—had been nothing more than a mirage. A lie.

It was nearly midnight by the time Eleanor finally

stumbled out of the office, exhausted and eyesore from scanning endless sheets of paper with their myriad details. Still, she had the basis of a party to propose to Jace—via email—tomorrow. Massaging her temples, she headed out into the street, the only cars visible a few off-duty cabs. It looked as if she would have to walk.

It was only a few blocks to her apartment in a high-rise condo on the Hudson River, a gleaming testament to glass and steel. Eleanor didn't particularly like the modern architecture, or the building's fussy, high-maintenance residents, but she'd bought it because her mother had said it was a good investment. And she didn't spend much time there anyway.

Sighing, Eleanor nodded hello to the doorman on duty and then headed in the high-speed lift up to the thirtieth floor.

Her apartment was, as always, dark and quiet. Eleanor dropped her keys on the hall table and flicked on the recessed lighting that bathed the living room with its modern sofa and teakwood coffee table in soft yellow light. Outside the Hudson River twinkled with lights.

Her stomach rumbled and she realised she had skipped dinner. Again. Kicking off her heels, she went to the galley kitchen and peered in her near-empty fridge. It held half a carton of moo shoo pork and a yogurt that was—Eleanor peered closer—two weeks past its sell-by date. Neither looked appetising.

Dispiritedly Eleanor closed the fridge. It was hard to believe she'd once baked cookies and muffins by the dozen, had dreamed of owning her own café. She'd been unbearably, determinedly domestic, and now she could barely feed herself.

She grabbed a handful of rather stale crackers from the cupboard and went back to the living room. Funny, she hadn't thought of her old café dream in years, yet when she'd known Jace she'd spent hours embroidering that daydream, how it would be a little bit of everything: coffee shop, bakery, bookstore, gallery. Warm, cosy, bright, and welcoming. The home she'd never felt she'd had. It—everything—had seemed so possible then, so bright and shiny.

And now having Jace back in her life so suddenly, so surprisingly, brought it all back. The dreams, the disappointments.

The despair.

Eleanor thrust the thought away as she munched another cracker. Her stomach rumbled again. Perhaps sleep was better. She was exhausted anyway, and at least when she was asleep she wouldn't feel hungry. Neither would she have to think—or remember.

Dropping her uneaten crackers in the bin, Eleanor turned towards her bedroom.

Yet as she lay in the darkness of her room, the duvet pulled up to her chest, sleep didn't come. She was exhausted yet her eyes were wide open and gritty. And despite her best effort for them not to, the memories came, slipping into her mind, winding around her heart.

Lying there in the dark, she could almost feel the late autumn sunshine slanting onto the wide-planked wooden floors of her college apartment. She saw herself, tousle-haired, young, laughing, holding out a cupcake to Jace. They weren't lovers then; they hadn't even kissed. Yet. He'd invited himself over to taste the treats she'd been telling him about when he'd come into the café where she worked for his morning latte. And high with anticipation, Eleanor had invited him in, revelling in the charged atmosphere as he took a bite of the cupcake right from her hand, and then, laughing, pulled her close for a kiss.

It had been so easy, so right, and she'd gone without even considering another option, a different choice. He'd tasted like chocolate.

She closed her eyes, her throat tight and aching. She didn't want to resurrect these memories. She worked hard never to remember them. Yet they came anyway, so sweet and yet so bitter for what came afterward.

The empty apartment. The disconnected cellphone. The

bounced emails. The cold, cold despair when she'd realised just how alone she was.

Groaning alone, Eleanor turned on her side, tucking her knees up to her chest, and clenched her eyes shut as if that could keep the memories from coming and consuming her.

The blip of her baby on the monitor. The hard, sharp edge of the examining table, the cold slime of the gel on her tummy, and the endless silence of the technician, frowning, as she stared at the scan.

What's wrong?

Eleanor bolted up in bed and went to the bathroom for a herbal sleeping pill. She might have faced down Jace today, but she couldn't face the memories at night. They tormented her in a way even he never had. Their stark truth remained lodged in her gut, in her heart, like a stone. Nothing would remove it, or take away the bleak knowledge that she could never—

Eleanor closed her eyes again, tightly, and to her relief she finally slipped into a sleep made sweet by its absence of memories or dreams.

Despite her bad night, Eleanor was at her desk by eight o'clock in the morning. She saw Lily walk past her office door, nodding grimly, and she knew she'd been right to hurry to her desk that morning. She'd email the party plans to Jace, and then she'd put him out of her mind for ever. Or at least until he emailed back.

It took her nearly an hour to compose the email; it was aggravatingly difficult to strike the right tone, professional yet personable. She didn't want Jace to think for a second that she was affected by him. That she'd been hurt. Yet she hardly wanted to seem too friendly, either; that smacked of desperation.

Too tired to tweak the email any more, Eleanor just ended up sending a rather boring list of details, explaining in dry terms the choice of venue, the seating plan, the floral arrangements, the menu.

Then she determinedly pressed send.

Two minutes later her phone rang.

'This is completely unacceptable.'

Dumbly Eleanor stared at her computer screen, with its 'your message has been sent' confirmation still visible. It seemed impossible that in the approximately one hundred and twenty seconds since she'd pressed send, Jace had read her entire email and deemed it all unsuitable. Unacceptable, even.

'Excuse me?'

Over the phone Eleanor heard Jace exhale impatiently. 'This is all very standard, Ellie—'

'Don't call me that,' she said sharply. He ignored her.

'If I wanted a run-of-the-mill upscale do, I could have gone elsewhere. I came to Premier Planning because I was told you'd give me something extraordinary.'

Eleanor closed her eyes and prayed for patience. For mercy. She counted to ten, all the while listening to Jace's impatience, hearing it in those short little exhalations of breath, and then said coolly, 'I assure you there will be nothing run-of-the-mill about this party.'

Jace made a sound of disbelief that came close to a snort. 'Salmon pâté? Gardenias? Champagne? Standard luxuries.'

'That's an oxymoron, if ever I've heard one—'

'All of it is run-of-the-mill, Ellie.'

'I told you, don't call me that,' she snapped.

'Then impress me.'

That was the last thing she wanted to do. Why would she want to impress the man who had treated her like dirt, who had ground her heart into dust? Was her job really worth that much, worth her own dignity and pride?

Of course it was. It had to be. For the last ten years her job had been just about the only thing she had valued, the one thing she'd poured herself into. She wasn't risking it for Jace. He'd already done enough damage in her life.

'You gave me less than twenty-four hours to come up with

an entire event,' she finally ground out. 'Of course I haven't worked out all the details yet—'

'I expected better than this.'

'Funny, I said that ten years ago,' Eleanor snapped. Then she closed her eyes. The last, the very last thing she wanted was to drag the past—their past—into this mess. And from the taut silence crackling along the phone lines, she had a feeling Jace felt the same.

'You have no idea,' he said coldly. 'Meet me at my office building for lunch, twelve o'clock sharp.' And then he hung up.

Eleanor cursed aloud, just as Lily poked her head in her office door and smiled narrowly.

'Everything all right, Eleanor?'

'Fine,' Eleanor replied thinly. 'I just got a paper cut, that's all.'

Jace hung up the phone, massaging his knuckles as if he'd been in a fight. That terse conversation had not been a satisfactory outlet for his anger, for from the moment he'd walked into Eleanor Langley's office and seen her cool little smile that was what he'd been feeling. *Rage.*

He was furious that she seemed so unrepentant, that she'd attempted to foist another man's baby on him and didn't even possess the decency now to admit it or apologise. Yet what had he really expected of a woman who was willing to sink so low, to lie to someone she'd said she loved?

He didn't want to feel so angry, hated how it made the control he'd guarded carefully these last ten years slip away, so he hardly even knew what he was going to say or do. Or feel.

He'd never expected to feel so angry. He'd thought he'd got over Eleanor Langley and her betrayal, had put it far, far behind him. Now it felt fresh and raw and that made him even angrier. He didn't want Eleanor to affect him this much. He didn't want her to affect him at all.

Sighing impatiently, Jace turned back to the papers on his

desk. Atrikides Holdings was a mess and he had plenty to occupy both his mind and his time. He didn't need to waste either on Eleanor Langley, not even for a second.

All he wanted from her was a party. That was the only reason he was inviting her to lunch, why he was even bothering to see her again. He'd make it clear just what kind of high standard of service he expected. He'd put her in her place. His lips curved in a humourless smile as his sense of calm return to cloak him in reassuring coldness. All he wanted from her was a party, and by God he'd get one.

Three hours later Eleanor stood in front of the dark gleaming skyscraper that housed the offices of Atrikides Holdings. She took a deep breath and let it out slowly, and then resolutely headed for the door.

After she was cleared through security she took the lift to the building's top floor and stepped out into a room of elegant, old-style luxury with a stunning view of Central Park. She stared at the yawning rectangle of green, surrounded by concrete, the trees stark and bare above, as the elderly assistant pursed her lips before pressing a button on her telephone.

'Mr Zervas, I have Eleanor Langley for you.'

The reply was sharp, terse. 'Send her in.'

'You may go in,' the assistant said, nodding towards the wood-panelled double doors at the far end of the room.

Eleanor nodded back, swallowing down the sudden flutter of nerves that had risen to flurry wildly in her throat. She hated that she was nervous, almost as if Jace scared her. She would not let herself be cowed by him, not when he had been in the wrong ten years ago, not when *he* had been the coward then.

She certainly wouldn't be the coward now.

Squaring her shoulders, she knocked once, perfunctorily, before opening the doors and striding into the room.

The office was elegant, huge, and clearly not his. In one quick glance Eleanor saw the portraits of several Atrikides men on the walls, a side table cluttered with family photos. Children. She averted her eyes from the pictures. This had to be the office of the former CEO of Atrikides Holdings, Eleanor surmised, whom Jace had ousted along with half of the company's employees. A cold-blooded, corporate take-over. Should it really surprise her at all?

Jace stood behind the desk, his back to her. He didn't turn around even though he must have heard her come in.

Faintly annoyed, Eleanor cleared her throat. He turned, and in that moment—a single second, no more—her breath dried and her heart beat fast and she remembered how good it had been between them, how she'd lain in his arms as the sun washed them in gold and he'd kissed her closed eyelids.

She forced the memory—so sweet and painful—away and smiled coolly. 'You've taken over the CEO's office, I see.'

Jace waved a hand in dismissal. 'For the time being. It's convenient.'

'And he was fired along with most of the employees, I suppose?'

'Most is an exaggeration,' Jace replied, his eyes narrowing, flashing steel.

Eleanor wondered why she was asking. It was almost as if she was trying to pick a fight—and perhaps she was, for the anger and resentment still simmered beneath her surface, threatening to bubble forth. She wanted to hurt him, and yet she knew she wouldn't succeed with these silly little jabs. She'd only hurt herself, by revealing her own vulnerability. The fact that she was making them at all spoke of how hurt she had been and still was. She drew in a steadying breath and managed a small smile. 'You'd like to talk about the plans?'

Jace didn't smile back. 'I'm not sure they're worth discussing.'

Eleanor bit the inside of her cheek. 'Fine,' she said when she could be sure her voice was level, 'let's discard them if you find them so unsuitable. But you could at least make an effort to be civil.'

To her surprise, Jace acknowledged the point with one terse nod. 'Very well. Let's have lunch.'

He led her to a table hidden in the alcove, a tiny little table set intimately for two. Eleanor swallowed hard. She didn't know if she could do this. Every second she spent with Jace strained the composure she'd been working at maintaining for the last ten years, the air of professionalism that had become her armour. Just one sardonic look from those steely eyes—she remembered when they'd softened in pleasure, in love—made her calm façade crack. It crumbled, and she was defenceless once more, the cracks in her armour letting in the memories and pain.

She hated that she was so weak.

Jace drew her chair for her, the epitome of politeness, and with a murmured thanks Eleanor sat down. Her hands trembled as she placed her napkin in her lap. Jace sat in the chair opposite, his fingers steepled under his chin, his dark eyebrows drawn together. He looked so much the same, Eleanor thought with a lurch of remembered feeling, and yet so different. His hair was cut closer now, sprinkled with grey, and his skin looked more weathered. That glint of laughter in his eyes was gone, vanished completely. Yet he still possessed the same compelling aura, like a magnetic field around him. He still drew her to him, even though she hated the thought. Even now she could feel her body's traitorous reaction to his—the shaft of pleasure deep in her belly, the tingle of awareness as he reached for his own napkin, his fingers scant inches from hers. Eleanor made herself look away and a staff member came in to serve them.

'Would you care for a glass of wine?' Jace asked.

'I don't normally—'

'Half, then.' He held up the bottle, one eyebrow arched in silent challenge, poised to pour. Jerkily Eleanor nodded. This felt like a battle of wills, a contest over who could be the most professional. And she'd win. She *had* to. If he was so unaffected, well, then, she could be too, or at least seem as if she were. *Pretend.*

She could pretend to Jace and perhaps even to herself that the room didn't seethe with memories, that her heart wasn't splintering along its sewn-up seams. She *could*. It was the only way of getting out of here alive.

'Thank you.' She stared down at her salad, the leaves arranged artfully on a porcelain plate with an elegant little drizzle of vinaigrette. She had no appetite at all. Finally she stabbed a lettuce leaf with her fork and looked up. 'So why don't you tell me what kind of party you'd prefer?' She strove to keep her voice reasonable. 'If I have a few more details, we can brainstorm some ideas—'

'I thought that was your job. I already gave you a list of requirements—'

'You gave me less than twenty-four hours to mock up a plan,' Eleanor returned, her voice edged with anger, 'and a week to put it all together. Those are impossible conditions.'

Jace smiled thinly, his voice smooth and yet still conveying contempt. 'Your boss assured me your company was up to the task.'

Eleanor looked away and silently counted to ten. Breathe. In. Out. In. Out. 'I assure you, I am up to the task. But since the original plans were so unsatisfactory, perhaps I need a little more information about what you're looking for.' She hated this, hated feeling as if she had to kowtow to Jace, hated knowing he was baiting her simply because he could. At this moment it was hard to believe that they'd ever felt anything for each other but bitterness and dislike.

Jace exhaled impatiently. 'I want something unique and elegant, that shows the employees of this company that they will be cared for.'

'Except for the ones who were fired, you mean,' Eleanor retorted, then wished she could have held her tongue. Why was she so hung up on that? Who cared how Jace did business? She certainly couldn't afford to.

He arched one eyebrow, coldly disdainful. 'Are you questioning my business practices?'

'No, I just object to the idea of a party that makes it look like you care about these people when you really don't.' Jace stilled, his face blanking, and too late Eleanor realised how she had betrayed herself. Who she'd really been talking about.

Me.

She let out a slow, shuddery breath and reached for her wine. 'Just give me some details, Jace.'

Jace's mouth tightened, his eyes narrowing. 'I believe I mentioned yesterday that many of the employees here have families. The party needs to be family-friendly. Children will be invited.'

Eleanor's hand tightened around the stem of her wine glass. She didn't expect it to hurt so much to hear Jace talk of children. She realised, with a sudden laser-like dart of pain, that he could be married. Maybe he had children of his own. Maybe he just hadn't wanted *her* children.

The children she'd never have.

She had to stop thinking like this. She'd got over Jace and his betrayal—unbearable as it had been—years ago. She *had*. She'd even accepted her own loss, the heartache that she'd always carry with her. She'd moved on with her life, had made plenty of friends, developed an exciting and successful career—

'Family-friendly,' she repeated, trying to keep her mind on track. She'd forgotten that rather crucial detail in her flurry of plans. Conveniently. She preferred not to think about families—children—at all. They no longer figured in her life. At all. They couldn't.

'Yes,' Jace confirmed, and his voice held an edge now. 'As I told you yesterday. Weren't you taking notes?'

Finally goaded past her emotional endurance, Eleanor set her wine glass down with an undignified clatter. 'Perhaps I just had trouble believing a man like you could be interested in anything family-friendly,' she snapped. 'The image doesn't really fit.'

'Image?' Jace repeated silkily. 'What are you talking about, Eleanor?'

'You, Jace.' The remembered pain and hurt was boiling up, seeping through the barely healed-over scars. She stood up from the table, surprised by this sudden, intense rush of feeling. Suddenly she didn't want to keep her composure any more. She wanted it to slip, wanted Jace to see the turbulent river of emotions underneath. Even to know how much he'd hurt her. Perhaps she'd regret the impulse later, but now it was too overwhelming a need to ignore. 'You're not "family-friendly".' She held up her hands to make inverted commas, her fingers curling into claws. 'You certainly weren't when I knew you.'

Jace stood up too, his hip bumping the table, sloshing wine onto the pristine white tablecloth. With a jolt Eleanor realised he was just as angry—and emotional—as she was. Maybe even more so.

'*I* wasn't family-friendly?' he repeated in a low voice that was nearly a growl. 'And just how and when did you draw that ridiculous conclusion?'

Eleanor nearly choked in her fury and disbelief. 'Maybe when you left your apartment, left the damn *country* when I told you I was pregnant!' There was a buzzing in her ears and distantly she realised she was shouting. Loudly.

Jace let out an ugly snarl of a laugh. 'Oh, I see. How interesting, Ellie.' On his lips her name was a sneer. 'So I'm some monster that doesn't like children simply because I didn't want to take on another man's bastard.'

Eleanor's mouth dropped open. The buzzing in her ears intensified so she couldn't hear anything. Surely she must have misheard him. 'What did you say?' she asked numbly, still slack-jawed.

Jace's lip curled in contempt. 'You heard me. I knew that baby wasn't mine.'

CHAPTER THREE

THE room was silent save for the draw and tear of their own ragged breathing. Numbly Eleanor turned away from Jace, from the table with its jostled dishes and spilled wine, and walked on wooden legs to the window.

Outside the sky was the ominous grey-white that promised a storm, the world below a winter palette of browns and greys.

Another man's bastard. Jace's words echoed in his ears, over and over, so Eleanor could not frame another thought or even a word. *Another man's bastard. Bastard. Bastard. Bastard.*

She closed her eyes.

'So you have nothing to say,' Jace said coldly, and that too was an indictment.

Eleanor shook her head. Her heart was thudding sickly and her knees nearly buckled. She'd never had such a physical reaction to a single piece of information, except when—

Tell me what's wrong.

No. She wasn't going to open up that Pandora's box of memories. Not with Jace in the room, with his ugly words still reverberating through the air.

And she wasn't going to defend herself either. There was so clearly no point.

Slowly she turned around. 'No,' she said quietly. 'I have nothing to say.'

Jace nodded in grim acceptance, and Eleanor knew she'd

just confirmed the worst he'd ever thought about her. Judged again. She hadn't even realised, ever known, that she'd been judged in the first place. All these years she'd had no idea Jace had been thinking that. Believing the worst. And why? What reason had she ever given him?

She walked back to the table and reached for the attaché case she'd propped against her chair.

'I'm going to go now,' she said steadily. She was grateful her voice didn't tremble or break. 'I'll make sure Lily assigns someone else to your party.'

'What are you talking about?' Jace demanded, and Eleanor almost laughed. Did he actually think she'd work with him now? Considering what had just happened—what he thought—

She shook her head again. 'Clearly, Jace, we can't move on from the past, and it's affecting our—our work relationship.' What a ridiculous idea, as though they could have any relationship at all. 'There's no point continuing this way. Someone else will serve you better.'

'So you expect me just to forgive and forget,' Jace surmised, his voice sharp with sarcasm.

Now Eleanor did laugh, a short, humourless bark. 'No. I'm the one who can't. Forgive *or* forget.' She hoisted her bag on her shoulder and gave him a grim little smile. 'Goodbye, Jace.'

And somehow, *somehow* she managed to walk from the room with steady legs, her head held high.

Jace watched Eleanor walk away from him in stunned disbelief. He heard the click of the door shutting, the surprised murmur of his PA, the whoosh of the lift doors. And he still didn't move.

I'm the one who can't forgive or forget.

What the hell had she been talking about?

Muttering an angry oath, Jace whirled towards the window. What could Eleanor Langley possibly have to forgive? All right, perhaps he'd been ruthless in the way he'd cut her out of his life, leaving Boston—leaving her—so abruptly and absolutely. But he'd done it because the realisation that she'd been deceiving him all along had been too terrible to bear. He'd felt quite literally gutted, empty and aching inside. And meanwhile she—*she* had been trying to foist another man's child on him. Living a lie all along. She'd never really loved him.

Yet apparently Eleanor did think she had something to forget. To forgive.

What?

Impatiently Jace turned away from the window where a few random snowflakes had begun to drift down onto the asphalt. He felt restless, angry, uncertain. The last was what bothered him the most; he'd never felt doubt before. How could he? He'd known since he was fifteen years old that he was infertile.

Sterile. Like a gelded bull, or a eunuch. As good as, according to his father. For what good was a son who couldn't carry on the family name? Who had been unmanned before he'd even reached his manhood?

What use was a son like that?

Jace already knew the answer, had known the answer since his test results had come back and his father's dreams of a dynasty had crumbled to dust. Nothing. A son like that—like him—was no use at all.

He'd lived with that grim knowledge for half of his life. Felt it in every quietly despairing stare, every veiled criticism. His own infertility had consumed him before he'd even been ready to think of children, had dominated him as a boy and become part of his identity as a man. Without the ability to have children, he was useless. Worthless.

And yet now, with Ellie's words, doubt, both treacherous and strangely hopeful, crept into his mind and wound its tendrils of dangerous possibility around his thoughts. His heart.

What did Ellie have to forget? To forgive? What had she been talking about?

Half of him wanted to ignore what she had said, just move on. He'd get a different event planner, forget Eleanor Langley even existed. Never question what she said.

Never wonder.

Yet even as these thoughts raced through his brain, Jace knew he couldn't do that. Didn't even want to. Yes, it was saner, safer, but it was also aggravating as hell. He didn't want to doubt. Couldn't let himself wonder.

He needed to know.

Eleanor walked all the way back to Premier Planning's office near Madison Square Garden, oblivious to the cold wind buffeting her face and numbing her cheeks. She was oblivious to everything, every annoyed pedestrian, cellphone clamped to an ear, who was forced to move around her as she sleep-walked the twenty-three blocks to her office. She felt numb, too numb to think, to consider just what Jace had said. What he'd thought all these years.

She stood in front of the building, still numb, still reeling, and realised distantly that she couldn't return to work. Lily would be waiting, anxious for a report—or worse. Perhaps Jace had already rung. Perhaps her job was already in jeopardy.

Either way, she couldn't face it. She turned her back on ten years of professionalism and went home.

Back in the apartment she dropped her bag on the floor, kicked off her heels, and slumped into a chair, staring out into space. She didn't know how long she stayed like that for, without moving, without thinking, but the sky darkened to violet and then indigo, and her stomach rumbled. She hadn't eaten since breakfast, and that had been no more than half a bagel as she hurried to work. Yet she still couldn't summon the energy to eat. To feel. Anything. She hadn't felt this numb—the pain too consuming to allow herself to feel it—for a long time. For ten years.

Finally she stirred and went to the bathroom. She turned both taps on full and stripped off her clothes, leaving her savvy suit crumpled on the floor. Who knew if she'd need it any more?

Twenty minutes into a good soak she felt her mind start to thaw. So did her heart. So Jace assumed she'd been unfaithful, had been labouring under that unbelievable misapprehension for ten long years. No wonder he was so angry. Yet how could he be so *wrong*?

How could he have thought that of her, considering what they'd been to one another? Even the logistics of infidelity were virtually impossible; she'd spent nearly every waking moment working, at school, or with him.

Yet he'd believed it, and believed it so strongly that he'd judged her without trial, without even a conversation. He'd been so sure of her infidelity that he'd left her, left his entire life in the States, without even asking so much as a single question.

Somehow it was so much worse than what she'd thought all these years: that he'd developed a case of cold feet. In her more compassionate moments, she could understand how a twenty-two-year-old man—*boy*—with his whole life in front of him might get a little panicked at the thought of fathering a child. She understood that; what she didn't understand, had never understood, was the way he'd gone about it. Leaving so abruptly. Abandoning her without a word or even a way for him to contact him. Cellphone disconnected. No forwarding address.

It hadn't been merely a slap to the face, it had been a stab wound to the heart.

And he'd done it not because of his own inadequacy, but because of hers. Infidelity. He actually assumed she'd cheated on him.

The bath water was getting cold, and Eleanor rose from the tub. There was no point letting herself dwell on the recriminations, the regrets. If Jace Zervas had been able to believe something so atrocious and impossible about her so easily, obviously they'd never had much of a relationship at all.

And *that* was a truth she'd lived with for ten years.

She'd just slipped on her comfort pyjamas—soft, nubby fleece—when her doorbell rang. Eleanor stilled. She lived on the thirtieth floor in a building with two security personnel at the front door at all times, so no one made it to her door without her being alerted. The only option, she supposed, was a neighbour, although she'd never really got to know her neighbours. It wasn't that kind of building, and she didn't have that kind of life.

Cautiously Eleanor went to the door. She peered through the eyehole and felt her heart stop for a second before beginning a new, frenetic beating. Jace stood there.

'Eleanor?'

He sounded impatient, and it was no wonder. Eleanor realised she was hesitating for far too long. Resolutely she drew a breath and opened the door.

'What are you doing here, Jace?'

'I need to talk to you.'

She folded her arms and didn't move. She didn't feel angry now so much as resigned. 'I told you in your office I had nothing to say.'

'You may not, but I do.' He arched an eyebrow. 'Are you going to let me in?'

'How did you get my address?'

'Your boss gave it to me.'

Eleanor gave an exasperated sigh. *Of course.* Lily would do just about anything for a client, especially a rich one like Jace. 'How did you get past security?'

'I sweet-talked him.'

Eleanor snorted. 'You?'

'Andreas is manning the door tonight. He has six grandchildren back in Greece.' Jace smiled thinly. 'He showed me pictures.'

Eleanor slowly shook her head. She'd been on the end of Jace's charm once; she knew how forceful it was. And how false.

Sighing in defeat, she turned away from the door. 'Fine. Come in.'

He entered, shutting the door carefully behind him. Eleanor moved to the window, her arms creeping around her body despite her effort to maintain a cool, composed air. She felt vulnerable, exposed somehow, as if from the stark modernity of her apartment Jace could somehow guess at the emotional barrenness of her life.

Stop. She couldn't think like that. She had a job, friends, a life—

She just didn't have what mattered.

Love.

Stop.

'What do you want?'

Jace stood in the centre of her living room, seeming too big, too *much* for the space. He glanced around, and Eleanor saw him take in all the telltale signs of a single life. No jumble of shoes or coats, no piles of magazines or books. Just a single pair of heels discarded by the door. In the galley kitchen she saw her lone coffee cup from this morning rinsed and set by the sink. 'You live here alone?'

She lifted one shoulder in a shrug that couldn't help but seem defensive. 'Yes.'

He shook his head slowly. 'What about—the baby?' He spoke awkwardly, the words sounding stilted. They felt stilted to Eleanor. She didn't want him to ask. She didn't want him to know.

She didn't want to tell.

'What about the baby?' she asked evenly.

'He—or she, rather—doesn't live with you?'

'No.'

'The father retained custody?'

She gave a short, abrupt laugh. The weariness was fading away and the anger was coming back. Along with the hurt. She was tired of feeling so much, so suddenly, after ten years of being comfortably numb. She dropped her arms to her sides. 'What do you really want to talk about, Jace?'

'You said you were the one who couldn't forgive or forget. And I want to know why.' He spoke flatly, yet she saw something in his eyes she hadn't seen in ten years, something that hadn't been there yesterday or this morning. Need.

Hunger.

Why did he want to know? Why did he care?

'Because you may have felt you had just cause, but the fact that you abandoned me the very day I told you I was pregnant was a hard thing to get over.' She smiled thinly. 'Surprisingly, it seems.'

Jace shook his head, the movement one of instinctive denial. 'Ellie, you know that baby isn't—wasn't—mine.'

Anger, white-hot, lanced through her. '*I* know?' she repeated, her voice rising in incredulity. '*I* know? I'll tell you what I know, Jace, and that is that the only bastard I've ever met is you. First-class, A-plus, for thinking that.'

He took a step towards her in an action both menacing and urgent, his features twisted with what looked like pain. 'Are you telling me,' he demanded in a low voice, 'that the baby was mine? Is that what you're actually saying, Ellie?'

She lifted her chin. 'That's exactly what I'm saying, Jace. And the very fact that you could think for a moment—'

'Don't.' He held up one hand, and Eleanor saw to her shock that it trembled. 'Don't,' he repeated rawly, 'lie to me. Not now. Not again. Not about this.'

For a second Eleanor's anger gave way to another powerful emotion: curiosity. Jace faced her, his expression open and hungry. She'd never see him look so…desperate. There was more going on here than she understood.

'I'm not lying,' she said quietly. 'What makes you think I ever was?'

Jace didn't speak for a moment. His gaze held hers, searching for a truth he seemed hell-bent on disbelieving. 'Because,' he finally said, his voice little more than a ragged whisper, 'I can't have children. I've known it since I was fifteen years old.' He let out a long, slow breath before stating flatly, 'I'm infertile. Sterile.'

Eleanor stared. *I can't have children.* Such a stark and sorrowful phrase; she knew just how much. And yet coming from *Jace*…the words didn't make sense. They couldn't. Then in a sudden flash of remembrance she recalled the moment she'd told Jace she was pregnant, and how he'd stared at her so blankly, his jaw slackening, his eyes turning flat and then hard. She'd thought he'd been surprised; she'd had no idea just how stunned he must have been. Infertile. *Impossible.* It had to be. 'You must be mistaken.'

'I assure you I'm not.'

Eleanor shook her head, speechless, disbelieving. 'Well, neither am I,' she finally said. 'Mistaken, that is. I was a virgin when we got together, Jace, and I didn't sleep with another man for—a long while.' She swallowed. Years, in fact, but she wasn't about to tell him that. 'You were the only candidate.'

Jace smiled, the curving of his mouth utterly without humour. 'The facts don't add up, Ellie. Someone's lying.'

'I've told you not to call me that.' She turned away from him and stared blindly out at the Hudson River, its murky black surface just visible under the city lights. 'Why does someone have to be lying, Jace? What if you're mistaken?' She turned around. 'Did you ever—even once—think of that?'

'I'm not!' The words came out in a roar, and she stilled, surprised by the savagery.

'How can you be—?'

'Trust me,' he cut her off, the two words flat and brutal. 'I am. And if I can't have children, there must be another—' he paused, his mouth curving in an unpleasant smile '—candidate.'

Eleanor cocked her head, curiosity and anger warring within her. 'Is it easier for you to believe that?'

'What the hell do you mean?'

She shrugged, a little unnerved by Jace's anger but still refusing to be cowed. 'You prefer believing I was unfaithful to you rather than the idea that you could be wrong, that it's a mistake—'

'It's not a mistake!' Jace leaned forward, lowered his voice to a savage whisper. 'It's *impossible*.'

Eleanor blinked, discomfited by his intensity. 'How did you find out you were infertile at such a young age?' she asked slowly. 'Most men don't find out until they're married and run into trouble with conceiving, don't they—'

'I had mumps. A lingering infection, and it made me sterile.'

'And you were tested—?'

'Yes.' He bit off the word, his lips pressed together in a hard line.

'But…' Eleanor shook her head, genuinely bewildered. 'Why? Why would you be tested at such a young age?'

Jace turned away from her. He drove his hands into his pockets, his shoulders hunched, the position one of defensive misery. 'My father wanted to know,' he said gruffly, his back still to her. 'I'm an only son, as was he. The male line dies out with me.'

Eleanor didn't reply. She couldn't think of a single thing to say, for suddenly everything was making horrible sense. No wonder Jace was so sure he couldn't be the father. No wonder he'd been so hurt. No wonder the whole idea of a pregnancy—a baby—that wasn't his would be an affront, an abomination.

The male line dies out with me.

For a boy from a traditional Greek family, that had to be very hard indeed.

Regret replaced anger, and it hurt far more. She swallowed past the tightness in her throat. 'Well, perhaps you should get yourself tested again. Because I assure you, Jace, the baby was yours. Why would I lie now? What point would there be?'

Jace was silent for a long, tense moment. 'I don't know,' he finally said. 'God help me, I don't know.' Eleanor stared at him, his back to her, his head bowed, and she wondered what he must be feeling now. Could he accept he wasn't

infertile, that he'd been living with an incorrect diagnosis
for his entire adult life?

Would he?

It would be hope and tragedy mixed together, for what
was lost, for what now could be—

But not for her. Eleanor swallowed past the tightness in
her throat, closing her eyes as if that could blot out the pain.
The memory. Never for her.

Jace drew in a ragged, desperate breath, his head still bowed,
his back to Eleanor. He felt the rage course through him,
consume him, and he didn't trust himself to speak.

The baby was his. *Could* be his. Except in his gut—perhaps even in his heart—Jace knew the truth. He saw it in
Eleanor's eyes, dark with remembered pain. The baby was
his.

He wasn't infertile.

And all he could feel was anger. All he could think of
was the waste. His life, his family, his father. Everything
had pointed to his failure as a son, as a man. He'd lived with
it, let it cripple him, let it guide and restrain his choices, and
for what?

For a lie? A *mistake*?

The realisation made him want to shout to the remorseless
heavens, to hit something, to hurt something. Someone. *It
wasn't fair.* The cry of a child, and yet it bellowed up inside
him, the need so great he clamped his lips together and drew
another shuddering breath.

Eleanor, he knew, would never understand. How could he
explain how utterly sure he'd been of his own infertility, so
that he'd been able to walk away without once considering
that she'd been telling the truth? He'd always been so certain
that even now he wondered. Doubted.

It can't be.

And yet if it was…

Too many repercussions, too many unspoken—un-
thought—hopes and fears crowded his mind, his heart. He

pushed them down, unable to deal with them now, to consider what they meant, what changes to both the present and future—and, God help him, the past—they would require.

The baby was his.

The baby was his.

He had a child.

Jace whirled around again, the movement so sudden and savage that Eleanor gasped aloud and took a step towards the window.

He crossed the room in three long strides and grabbed her by the shoulders, his face thrust near hers. 'Where is the baby? If it *is* my child—'

Eleanor closed her eyes. She didn't want this. She didn't want Jace here, stirring up memories, regrets, *pain*, and for what? Yet she knew he had a right to know. She swallowed again. Her throat was so very tight. 'Was,' she whispered. 'It was.'

'What—what are you talking—?'

'It *was* your child,' she explained very quietly, and the fierce light that had ignited in Jace's eyes winked out, leaving them the colour of cold ash.

'You mean…' his hands tightened on her shoulders '…you had an abortion.'

'No!' She jerked out of his grasp, glaring at him. 'Why don't you just leap to yet another offensive assumption, Jace? You're good at that.'

He folded his arms, his expression still hard. 'What are you saying, then?'

'I had a…a miscarriage.' A bland, official-sounding word for such a heart-rending, life-changing event. She turned away from him so he wouldn't see the naked pain on her face. She felt the thickness of tears in her throat. 'I lost the baby.' She swallowed. *My little girl,* she thought, *my precious little girl.*

Jace was silent for a long moment. Eleanor stared blindly out of the window, trying not to remember. The screen, the silence, the emptiness within. 'I'm sorry,' he finally said, and she just shrugged. The silence ticked on, heavy, oppressive. 'I'm sorry,' Jace said again, the word raw, and Eleanor felt again the thickening of tears in her throat. She swallowed it down, reluctant to let Jace enter her sorrow. She didn't want to rake it up again; she didn't even want him sharing it. She was still angry. Still hurt.

'I'll still have to be tested,' he continued, 'to make sure—'

'That the baby was yours?' Eleanor filled in. 'You still don't believe me?' She shook her head in disbelief. 'Just when would I have had this other affair, Jace? I spent every waking—and sleeping—moment with you for six *months*.'

'You don't understand—' Jace began in a low voice, but Eleanor didn't want to hear.

'No, I don't. I don't understand how you could think for a moment that I was unfaithful to you. But even if you did, because I suppose you must have had some kind of *trust* issue, I don't understand how you could walk away without a word.' Her voice shook; so did her body. 'Without a single *word*.'

'Eleanor—'

'It doesn't matter. I don't want to hear your explanations now. They don't matter.' She took a deep, shuddering breath and forced herself to sound calm. To feel it. 'It's ten years ago, Jace. Ten years. It really is time we both moved on.'

He was silent, and when she looked at him she saw how drawn and tired and *sad* he looked. Well, too bad. She hardened her heart, because she didn't want to feel sorry for him. She didn't want to feel anything; it hurt too much. 'If only I'd known,' he murmured, and she shook her head.

'Don't.' She didn't want him to open up the painful possibilities of what if, if only... No, they were too dangerous. Too hard even to think about now. 'And it doesn't even matter anyway,' she continued, her voice sharp. 'You didn't trust me enough to tell me any of this, or give either of us a chance to explain. That's what this was really about.'

Jace's brows snapped together, his body tensing, and Eleanor knew he was poised to argue. Again. She couldn't take any more, didn't have the energy for another round. 'Go get tested or whatever it is you need to do,' she told him. 'Satisfy your own curiosity. You don't need to tell me about it.' She paused, her voice sharpening again in spite of her best efforts to sound reasonable. '*I* know who the father was.'

Jace stared at Ellie's hard face, derision in every line, her eyes dark with scorn. He felt a scalding sense of shame rush through him. This hard, polished woman, this glossy professional who lifted her chin and dared him to feel sympathy or compassion or dreaded pity, was a product of his own judgment. His own failure.

If he'd stayed with Ellie…if he'd seen her through the miscarriage…would she be a different woman? Would she have stayed the same?

It was a pointless question. As Eleanor herself had said, this was all ten years too late. They'd both moved on. They'd both changed. He certainly wasn't the same foolish boy who'd let himself be besotted, who had eagerly fallen in love because the experience had been so intoxicating, so vital, so different from what he'd known.

Who had a heart to be broken.

No, he wasn't that same man. He'd changed, hardened, and so had Ellie. *Eleanor.* They were different people now, and the only thing they had in common was loss.

The loss of their baby. A sudden, new grief threatened to swamp him, and to his shock he felt the sting of tears in his eyes, the ache in the back of his throat. He forced the feeling down, refusing to give into such an emotion. He never cried. In the fifteen or so years since his life had changed for ever—or at least until now—he'd developed a foolproof way of dealing with his father's disappointment. He never acted as if he cared. Whether it was a flat, emotionless response, or a carefree, laughing one, either way he kept his heart off-limits. He remained detached. He *had*, until Eleanor.

Somehow Eleanor had slipped through the defences he'd erected—that charming, laughing exterior—and found the man underneath. He wondered if she even knew how much she'd affected him.

And how had he affected her? In a sudden, painful burst of insight he pictured her in his apartment building, twenty years old and pregnant, realising he'd gone. He'd abandoned her utterly, and she'd been innocent.

Innocent.

He'd never, for a moment or even a second, considered that the child—their child—might have been his. This infertility was so much a part of him, a weight that had been shackled to him for so long, he'd never considered existing without it. He'd never even hoped for such a possibility.

And yet now for it to be given to him, and taken away, virtually in the same breath was too much to consider. To accept. He was left speechless, his mind spinning in dizzying circles, his heart thudding as if he'd just finished a sprint.

He didn't know what to think. To feel. And he was afraid—yes, afraid—to open up the floodgates of his own heart and mind to all the possibilities, all the realisations, all the regret and guilt and hope and fear. They would consume him; he would have nothing left. Nothing he could count on or control. He couldn't do that. Not yet, maybe not ever.

He needed to get this situation back under control, Jace knew, and there was only one way to do that.

'So,' Jace said, and was glad to hear how even his voice sounded. 'Let's talk about this party.'

CHAPTER FOUR

'WHAT?' Eleanor heard the screech of her own voice and briefly closed her eyes. She opened them and shook her head. 'No.'

Jace arched an eyebrow in challenge. 'Why not? You didn't seem to have a problem with planning the party before.'

'You can't be serious. After everything—'

'We're professionals, Eleanor.' Jace's voice was hard, and Eleanor saw a bleak darkness in his eyes. She felt its answer in herself, and she wondered if Jace was trying to prove something to himself, just as she was. *The past is finished. It doesn't matter. I'm not hurt.*

But she was. And she was so tired of pretending she wasn't. Yet even so she couldn't admit that to Jace. She felt exposed enough, considering all she'd already revealed. She wasn't about to say anything more. 'Of course we're professionals, Jace. But I simply think it would be sensible—not to mention more productive—to have a colleague plan your event.'

'I don't.'

Why was he doing this? She shook her head again. 'I told you at your office—'

'That you were quitting? Lucky for you I didn't communicate that to your boss. I don't think she would have been pleased. And somehow I had a feeling you might change your mind.' His mouth twisted sardonically, his eyes glinting.

Eleanor didn't answer. She knew just how displeased Lily would have been. She might have thrown her entire career away in a single, emotional moment, and Jace at least had had the presence of mind not to let her do it.

She supposed she should be grateful.

Eleanor walked slowly back to the window. It had become her place of retreat; either that or she was simply backed into a corner. 'I don't understand why you want to do this,' she said quietly. 'Or what can be gained—for either of us.'

Jace shrugged one powerful shoulder. 'You're the best planner. Or so I was told.'

'You didn't even like my ideas,' Eleanor protested numbly. What she really wanted to say was, *Why doesn't being with me hurt you?* She felt his presence like an agony, exquisitely painful. And he wanted her to plan his *party*?

'I just know you can do better.'

She shook her head, even as she acknowledged that he was right. She *could* do better. She'd fought long and hard to get to where she was in her business and stay there. And she wasn't about to throw it all away simply because Jace had come back into her life—however briefly—and stirred up some old memories. She could shove them down again. She could handle this party. She could handle Jace. Doing it would help her feel more in control, and God knew she needed to feel that again.

She felt as if she were spinning out of it, and she couldn't stand the sense of powerlessness. She'd felt that before, when Jace had walked out of her life. When the ultrasound technician had sorrowfully shaken her head, and the doctor had come in to give her lots of important-sounding words and clinical, medical terms.

She wasn't going to feel it now.

She turned around. Jace gazed at her, waiting, assessing. She had no idea why he still wanted her to plan his wretched party, what he hoped to gain or prove. Or was the past nothing more than a finished chapter of a sad story? Could he actually move on so quickly, *minutes* after she'd told him the truth? She made herself not care. She'd done that before, plenty of times, starting when she was a little girl and her mother had worked late again and again, missing plays and soccer matches and anything important. When Jace had walked away, when she'd lost her little girl, when life had seemed empty and endless and without hope—she'd survived by making herself not care. By blanking her mind to any thought—any possibility—that was too painful. Too hard. And she could keep doing it. Keep surviving. Keep not caring.

Eleanor smiled coolly. 'Fine, Jace. I'll plan your party. Satisfied?'

'Getting there.'

'And it's late. I'd like to go to bed.' Too late she realised how laced those words were with innuendo—and remembrance. And so did Jace. She saw it in the subtle flaring of his eyes, the way they turned to sleepy silver. And before she could stop herself, her mind flashed images from a lifetime ago—a lifetime with Jace. Lying in his arms, tracing circles on the bare, bronze skin of his chest. Laughing, stretching like a cat, sleepy and secure. Sated. Loving every moment of being with him, because she'd been young and naive enough to think it was real and that it would never end.

Eleanor swallowed. 'I'm tired,' she said as an explanation, but it came out in a whisper. Jace smiled.

'So am I.'

Was she imagining the current that suddenly seemed to run between them, alive and electric? She must be, because surely, *surely* there was nothing between them. After everything that had happened—after everything she had endured—there could be nothing between them now.

Yet that didn't stop her from remembering just how good it had once been.

'Goodnight, Jace,' Eleanor said, and her voice, to her relief, sounded flat and final and almost cold. Jace ignored her.

He took a step towards her. Eleanor held her breath. She didn't speak, didn't move. Didn't protest. Another step, and he was only inches away. He lifted his hand and she braced herself for his touch, welcomed it even, wondering what it would feel like after all these years. What he would feel like.

And even as she stood there, still and silent, *waiting* for him to touch her, he dropped his hand, smiling almost sadly. 'Goodnight, Ellie,' he said, and this time Eleanor didn't try to correct him.

She watched him leave, not realising until the door had shut that she was still holding her breath. She let it out in a long, shuddery rush.

She could do this. She had to.

Jace strode from Eleanor's apartment, his body filled with a restless energy, his mind teeming with both possibility and fury. He was angry at himself, at fate, at life itself.

So much waste. So much wrong.

Guilt rushed into the corners of his mind, the empty spaces in his heart. He could hardly bear to think what Eleanor must have felt, what she'd endured alone.

If only—

Two desperate and dangerous words.

If only he'd known. If only he'd waited and said something, asked her—

If only. If only.

There was no such thing as *if only*. There was only regret.

And hope.

Jace shook his head in silent disbelief. Hope had long since become an unfamiliar concept. What on earth could he hope for? Love, family, children—he'd turned his back on them all. Was he now actually thinking that he could change that? Change himself? It would not be so easy.

For years work had been his only respite, his only comfort. He'd come to New York as a favour to Leandro Atrikides, and as a favour to his father. He'd clean up the family mess and then he'd go home to Greece.

And forget about Eleanor Langley...just as he had once before.

Except he'd never forgotten her, not really. She'd always lurked on the fringes of his consciousness, memories drifting and dancing through his mind even when he tried to push them away. She lingered there now.

He recalled her scent, something young and girlish and flowery. He didn't think she used the same perfume now. And her hair had been wild and curly and artless, not her current glossy bob. He remembered the feel of those curls bouncing against his chest as she laughed in his arms.

Now Eleanor Langley looked totally different from the young woman he'd fallen in love with. He wondered if the changes were intentional. Had she transformed herself into this hardened career woman on purpose? Or had it happened gradually, without her even realising, the product of ten years' ceaseless striving in this heartless city?

And what about underneath?

Had her heart changed?

Ten years ago he'd judged her heart. He'd thought her cold and scheming and had walked away without ever finding out the truth. He'd thought he'd known it. He'd been so sure...

Now every certainty had been scattered, leaving him both hopeful and afraid. He didn't know what the future could hold, for him or Eleanor. He didn't even dare think, or question or wonder.

If only...

Jace left Eleanor's building, clamping his mind down on that thought as he walked down the dark, empty street.

Eleanor woke slowly, swimming upwards through consciousness from a deep and dreamless sleep. She blinked slowly; her room seemed to be obscured by a soft white haze.

As she sat up in bed, pushing her tangled mass of hair out of her eyes, she realised why. It was snowing. She scrambled out of bed and hurried to the window, pressing her hand against the cold glass. Outside the city's skyscrapers were lost in a snowstorm. Huge white flakes drifted down and the streets were already covered, the parked cars no more than white humps.

Snow. She smiled, suddenly feeling as excited and hopeful as a child when she'd had a rare snow day. There had been a blizzard once, when she was nine, and her mother had been forced to stay home from work. Eleanor still remembered that magical moment when her mother had decided to stay home for the day. The telephones hadn't been working, and, according to the television, no one was going anywhere. For a moment that pinched look had left her mother's face and she'd smiled and shrugged. 'I guess we'll have a snow day,' she'd said.

They'd trudged to Central Park through several feet of fluffy whiteness armed with a metal baking sheet—all the sledges had been sold out at the shop—and gone sledging on Cedar Hill near Seventy-Ninth Street. The feeling of flying down the hill, the world no more than a blur of muted colour, her mother's arms wrapped around her, was one Eleanor had never forgotten. She carried it with her like a treasure.

Snow. This sudden snowstorm felt like a treasure, a promise, a gift. Snow covered up all the grime and grit and hard concrete of the city, all the memories and regrets. It was a new beginning. A new hope. She didn't have to think about what had happened before, didn't have to carry the heavy, unbearable weight of ten years of memories or last night's conversation with Jace. She'd let the snow fall over it, cloaking it in whiteness, hiding it from herself.

Suddenly, certainly, Eleanor knew how to make this party just what Jace wanted. What she wanted. Smiling with a new determination, she turned away from the window.

She soon became immersed in organisation, making calls, checking facts and details, and arranging the most amazing party Jace Zervas could ever imagine. The party of her career.

She loved the buzz of creating something, seeing it emerge from her own imagination, and this party in particular was both a challenge and a dream. She had just days to conjure something spectacular.

The amount of work also kept her from thinking. Remembering. She was grateful for the activity that kept her from dwelling on the pain Jace had raked up, the regrets that still lingered on the fringes of her mind.

If only I'd known...

In her mind she never let Jace finish that sentence.

Every night she fell into bed, too exhausted to think or wonder, yet even so in that vulnerable moment before sleep overtook her she found herself picturing Jace's face, both as it had been ten years ago, young and smiling, and as it was now, determined and harsh. She remembered that shiver of electric awareness when he'd been in her apartment, when she had thought—perhaps even hoped—that he might touch her, and the memory carried her into the cocoon of sleep and insinuated itself into her dreams.

The day before the party Eleanor spent the afternoon making sure everything was in place at the event site. So much of planning an event like this was simply getting on the phone, putting in orders, cajoling and commanding at turns. Now the real fun began: making the magic.

'It's so unusual to have a party here at this time of year,' Laura, the woman who managed the boathouse in Central Park, remarked as Eleanor went over the party details with her. 'Especially with a request for the outside terrace. We're completely booked for spring and summer, but December...'

'I know,' Eleanor agreed. It was part of the reason she'd just chosen the park's boathouse as the venue; most other places had already been booked. And it was perfect for the kind of party she had planned. She surveyed the room, taking a mental count of the chairs and tables. 'My client is looking for unusual,' she explained, satisfied with the arrangements so far.

'It won't be too cold?' Laura asked dubiously. Although

the boathouse had inside seating, its most spectacular feature was the pillared terrace overlooking the park's lake. Now the lake was frozen solid, and in the distance Eleanor could see the Angel of Bethesda fountain still shrouded in snow.

'I hope not,' she said cheerfully. 'Of course, we're working on that.' She'd ordered electric heaters to be placed on the terrace in strategic spots, to warm up cold little hands and feet.

'Well, all right,' Laura said, still sounding doubtful, and Eleanor pushed away the thought that perhaps she was in fact crazy. Ever since she'd first seen those few fat flakes drifting down, she'd been gripped by a vision, a *memory*, and she'd let it drive her through one of the most intense working weeks she'd ever experienced.

It left little time or room for doubt. Yet now as Laura went back to her office and Eleanor was left alone in the boathouse's Lake Room, she wondered if Jace would think this party was impressive enough. *Suitable.*

And she wondered why she should even care.

Sighing, Eleanor shook her head and walked over to the glass doors that led out onto the terrace. It was too late for doubts or regrets; the party was tomorrow night. Everything had been ordered, prepared, paid for. The invitations, in the shape of snowflakes, had been sent out to all the employees. All that was left was the doing.

Eleanor turned the door handle and pushed it open; a gust of freezing air hit her in the face. Drawing in a deep lungful of the cold, frosty air, she stepped out onto the terrace.

The sky was just darkening to violet, the sun disappearing behind the stark, bare branches that fringed the park. Eleanor stood by the railing, surveying the silent, frozen lake, the park empty of tourists or pedestrians on this cold evening. It never ceased to amaze her that she stood in nearly the exact centre of a city of eight million people, and the only sound was the creak and crack of shifting ice.

It's going to be okay.

She let herself relax, unloosen all the tensed, tightly held parts of herself. She didn't let herself relax too often; she knew from experience it was too hard once you let go to get it all back together again. Yet now, just for a moment, she let herself be still, serene—or as close to it as she could be.

It's going to be okay.

She wasn't even sure what was going to be okay: the party? The future? Something more nebulous that she couldn't yet name? Eleanor had no answers.

'They told me I'd find you here.'

Eleanor tensed, all the loosely held parts of herself coming together in a cold, hard ball. She turned slowly around to survey Jace.

He stood in the doorway, dressed in a navy suit and wool overcoat, a briefcase in one hand. His cheeks were reddened with cold, emphasising the silvery glint of his eyes and the inky blackness of his hair.

'On the terrace?' Eleanor said a bit stupidly, for despite her cool smile her mind seemed to have slowed down, only able to process how amazing he looked.

Jace smiled crookedly. It reminded her of the way he used to smile, back when they were students. Lovers. He hadn't smiled like that in the last week; all his smiles had been cold or calculated, a cruel curving of the lips. This one was real, lopsided, and yet somehow sad. The memories still lay between them, heavy and unspoken. Eleanor wondered if they would always be there. 'Actually, in the restaurant. But the door was open, so I figured you came out for a breath of fresh air.'

'Very fresh,' Eleanor agreed, and Jace smiled again. Her heart turned right over, a flip-flop that was both exciting and a little alarming. She didn't want to respond to him, not physically, not emotionally. She didn't want to feel anything at all. Yet somehow, even now, after everything they'd been through, after everything she'd endured, she still did.

He set his briefcase down by the door and joined her at the railing. 'How's it going?'

'Good.' She gave a quick little laugh; it sounded sharp.

She knew what that laugh was: a defence mechanism. She inched away from him. 'You haven't been checking up on me all week. I expected an email or phone call to make sure the arrangements were *acceptable*.' Her emphasis on the word, Eleanor knew, sounded petty.

'I thought it best,' Jace said after a second's hesitation, and Eleanor saw his fingers tighten on the railing.

And before she could stop herself, Eleanor whispered, 'Why didn't you just get someone else, Jace?' Her voice sounded little and lost.

'I don't know.' He stared out at the frozen lake, his features harshening once more. 'I didn't want to walk away from you…like that.'

Like before. Her heart turned over again. It was, she thought ruefully, as desperate and flailing as a dying fish. She averted her face as she replied, 'It would have been easier.'

Jace turned away from the railing and the lake, and Eleanor knew that the conversation—*that* conversation—was over. 'It looks like you've done a fabulous job, at any rate,' he said, his voice brisk and light. Eleanor felt equal and infuriating amounts of disappointment and relief. She really didn't want to talk about the past, about *them*, yet here she was, ripping off scabs, opening wounds.

'It's cold out here.' The lake, she saw, was now cloaked in darkness. Above the trees lights winked on in the elegant apartment buildings lining Fifth Avenue. 'I should go back inside, check on the details before I return tomorrow.'

'All right,' Jace agreed, and he followed her back into the Lake Room. Eleanor didn't look at him as she consulted her list, mindlessly scanning the endless items she'd assembled for the party. She felt rather than saw Jace, still standing by the door, watching her. Even though he stood halfway across the room, she imagined she could feel the heat emanating from his body, winding around her own heart and warming her from the inside.

'There's still a lot to do,' she told him, her eyes fixed

firmly on her list. She felt a strange new tension crackling between them, snapping inside her. A sexual tension, and she wasn't prepared for it. She'd spent ten years being angry at Jace Zervas; she wasn't ready to feel anything else. She didn't want to. 'I'll have to be back here early in the morning,' she told him brightly, at least half aware that she was starting to babble. 'Setting up. There's a lot of outside work—'

'Outside?' Jace asked, taking a step closer. 'What's outside?'

'Snow,' Eleanor said simply, and looked up.

Mistake. Jace was looking at her so intently, yet it was an intensity she felt rather than saw, as if his gaze reached right down into her soul and touched it. Held it, even. In that moment she remembered—she *felt*—the power he'd held over her ten years ago, when she'd given him everything. Her body, her dreams, her very life. Her happiness. And for a little while he'd kept them, treasured them, or seemed to. For such a short, sweet time life had seemed so wonderful.

Somehow she found a way to drag her gaze from his. She didn't want to feel that way again. It *was* wonderful, it was captivating, and it was also extremely dangerous. If you gave someone your happiness, you might never see or feel it again.

'Snow?' Jace repeated, the word a question. 'What does this party have to do with snow?'

'Everything.' Eleanor looked back at her list, although the words blurred in front of her. She was tired, exhausted, and she probably couldn't do much good here. Yet the thought of going home made her feel a little sad. A little lonely. She could call Allie, go out for a drink—

'Eleanor?' Jace broke into her thoughts. 'You look a million miles away.'

She looked up, distracted, discomfited, because she knew why she didn't want to go home, or out, or anywhere but where Jace Zervas was.

He still held this awful, awful power over her; she was still captive. The thought was utterly aggravating.

'Sorry.' She forced herself to give him her sunny, and rather impersonal, smile, falling back on professional ploys she knew well. 'Snow, yes. When it blizzarded the other day, I thought how much fun snow is for children, especially city children, who don't see all that much of it. Winter for us— them—usually just means cold and a lot of grey slush.'

'And?'

'So I thought a party centred around snow—building snowmen, sledging, that sort of thing—would be fun. Family-friendly,' she reminded him, the stress on the word only slightly edged. Even now, it hurt. She summoned her professional smile. 'Some of my happiest childhood memories have to do with snow.'

'Really.' Jace took a step towards her. Even though he was still a good ten feet away, Eleanor felt he was too close. She made herself not move. 'I never knew that,' he said quietly.

'Well, snow days, you know. No school.'

'You didn't like school?'

She shrugged. 'What kid doesn't want a snow day?'

'Did you build snowmen? Go sledging?' He arched an eyebrow. 'Somehow I can't see your mother doing that.' He paused. 'Based on how you described her to me, of course.'

Did he remember, after all these years? Eleanor did. She remembered lying in Jace's arms, probably boring him with the silly little details of her life, her family. How she resented her mother for working so much, for being so hard and stern, for never giving her a father. She'd had an anonymous sperm donor instead, the easy, convenient way for a career woman to have a child. She'd even told Jace how she'd always insist on her own child knowing its father—

Ironic, that.

'Once she did—' She stopped. She wasn't ready to share that memory. 'Anyway, you don't know everything about me, Jace.'

'Once,' he repeated softly, moving towards her, 'I thought

I did.' He took another step closer to her. She saw a dark urgency in his eyes, felt its desperate answer in herself.

Why was she thinking like this? Feeling like this? Breathless and buzzy and so achingly aware?

'No, you didn't,' Eleanor informed him, keeping her voice curt. *Focus.* Focus on what Jace was saying, rather than how wonderful he looked. How close he was. How she could take one step—maybe two—and be in his arms.

Eleanor turned away, busying herself with the already fastened clasp of her attaché case. 'Admittedly, I made a fool of myself,' she continued in that same curt voice, 'telling you every empty thing that came into my head, but there was plenty you didn't know about me.'

'Like what?' Jace challenged softly. He'd moved even closer and she could feel him again, his heat and his strength, the sheer power radiating from him, making her, absurdly, want to lean on it. Lean on him. Already she could imagine his arms enfolding her, his chin resting on her head as he used to do—

Eleanor straightened. 'Like the fact that I wouldn't lie,' she said shortly.

Jace stilled, and the room crackled with a new kind of tension. A chilling remoteness that made Eleanor feel as cold as she'd been on the terrace.

'Right,' Jace said, and his voice sounded distant. 'Of course.' Eleanor forced herself to say nothing. No apologies, no excuses. No regrets. 'You've changed,' he said after a moment, and she tensed.

'I've been saying that all along.'

'You're the kind of person you never wanted to be,' Jace told her quietly. Eleanor froze, her mind shocked into numbness, and then she whirled around.

'That's a rather arrogant statement,' she said, her voice coldly furious. 'Not to mention incredibly rude.'

'You told me,' Jace replied steadily, 'that you never wanted to be like your mother.'

'You've never even *met* my mother—'

'You told me she was an event planner, the best in her field. Never missed a day of work. Never made a softball practice.'

Eleanor's breath came out in a slow, surrendered hiss. '*Stop*—'

'Consumed by her career, hardened and weary and lonely,' Jace finished. Each word was an indictment, delivered in a terrible, matter-of-fact tone. 'I could be looking right at her.'

Eleanor felt her face drain of colour. Her fingers, clutching the strap of her attaché so tightly, were aching and numb. She hated that Jace had assessed her so thoroughly, so damningly. She hated that he was right.

'You don't know anything,' she said, the words forced out of a throat that had closed in on itself, tight with tears. She hated too that he'd made her so emotional, when for ten years she'd managed to be as cool and professional and feelingless as ice. As snow.

'Don't I?' Jace took a step closer. Eleanor saw compassion on his face, softening those taut lines, turning his eyes to a soft, sympathetic grey. 'What made you change so much, Ellie?'

A single stab of fury streaked through her, startling her out of numbness. 'Even now you don't know the answer to that question?' she demanded, her voice harsh with accusation. 'I'll tell you what changed me, Jace. You did.'

His eyes widened, his jaw slackening for the briefest of seconds. 'Ellie—'

'And I told you, don't call me that. I stopped being Ellie the day I went to your apartment building and nobody was there.' She saw him give a little shake of his head, and she wanted to scream at his arrogance. He had no idea what she'd been through. No idea at all. He'd chosen to damn her and miss it all. 'So don't call me that again,' she informed him brutally, 'because that Ellie? The one you think you knew so well? She no longer exists. She hasn't for ten years.'

And with that, leaving Jace still shocked and speechless, Eleanor turned and left the room.

CHAPTER FIVE

EVERYTHING was ready. Or, Eleanor amended silently, as ready as it ever would be. She glanced around the dining room; the first guests were scheduled to arrive in just ten minutes.

She'd spent the entire day at the boathouse, arranging centrepieces and party favours, checking to make sure the sound system worked and the band, who had arrived an hour ago, had everything they needed. She'd visited the kitchen several times to check on the food, and just fifteen minutes ago she'd finally retired to the Ladies to freshen up and change into her cocktail dress. She'd bypassed her standard LBD, classic but boring, in favour of a spangled silver sheath dress that glittered when she moved. By the time the party rolled round, event planners were meant to fade into the background, not take centre stage. Yet Eleanor hadn't been able to resist this dress. It made her feel like a snowflake. And she needed to feel good, craved that little pleasure because ever since she'd seen Jace last night she'd been out of sorts, emotionally edgy and drained at turns. He'd thrown her completely off balance, and she hated it. One minute she felt coldly furious, the next aggravatingly aware. She hated the flip-flop of her moods, her own body. She hated that Jace had caused this, that he was the source of her weakness.

She straightened a few napkins, moved a few of the freshly cut pussy-willow branches that made the stark yet elegant centrepieces for the table. The colour of the soft grey buds reminded her of Jace's eyes.

Forcing her mind away from that train of thought, she glanced outside at the terrace, where snow had been carted in to make playful mounds, ready to be turned into snowmen and igloos. A special kids' cocoa bar with four different kinds of hot chocolate and several flavours of marshmallows and whipped cream had been set out by the electric heater.

Family-friendly.

She didn't normally do parties with children, and she'd been surprised how much she had enjoyed it. Surprised and a little sad, for children surely were not in her future. She'd accepted that long ago, had had years to live with it, yet now, with Jace back in her life—for however short a time—the pain was fresh again. Did you ever *truly* heal?

She heard a sound at the door, and with both relief and a little anxiety she realised the first guests were arriving. The party had started.

Jace stood at the threshold of the Lake Room, gazing in amazed wonder at the transformed space. The dining room was the epitome of understated elegance, strung with fairy lights, everything silver and white and crystalline. Like snow. He took in the long, graceful branches of pussy willows in their crystal vases, the snowflake ornaments at every child's place, and then glanced outside where children were delighting in playing with the mounds of snow, their faces already happily smeared with chocolate.

It was perfect.

He was only sorry to have missed the beginning, both for Eleanor's sake and that of Leandro Atrikides. Already he saw the speculative, sideways looks employees slid him, wary and uncertain. It had been Leandro's damn son Talos who had kept him from being prompt; the greedy bastard was still angling for a bigger payout.

Jace suppressed a sigh. Sometimes he wished he'd never involved himself in this unholy mess; Leandro's avaricious children had made a near ruin of his company. Jace's buyout had been little more than a mercy mission.

Yet if he hadn't come to New York, he wouldn't have seen Eleanor again…

And he was glad he had.

Wasn't he?

He realised he was searching for her through the crowds, had in fact been doing so since he'd arrived. He'd been thinking about her since he'd seen her last night, since she'd damned him with those words:

That Ellie? The one you think you knew so well? She no longer exists.

And it was all, utterly his fault. He was to blame for making Eleanor Langley the woman she was now.

You're the kind of person you never wanted to be.

Harsh words, and he knew he'd hurt her by saying them. But he couldn't take them back. He wouldn't. Yet what could he do about it? How could he help her?

And even if he did help her, somehow, wasn't he just doing it to make himself feel better? Still selfish.

Jace moved through the crowds, scanning the throng for a glimpse of Eleanor.

And then he saw her, and his head emptied of thoughts. She stood by the window, surveying the party scene with a preoccupied air, and yet despite the tiny frown between her brows she looked lovely. Breathtaking in a shimmery dress that moved like liquid silver, encasing a slender body Jace remembered and knew so well. His palms suddenly itched to slide along that silky material and find the curve of her hip, the dip of her waist. To pull her towards him, to have her·come to him, unresisting, unrepentant.

To feel Ellie in his arms again.

'Eleanor!'

Eleanor turned, nerves fluttering low in her belly as she saw Jace coming towards her. It was a feeling that was both familiar and strange, for the nerves were not caused by anxiety, but anticipation. Even though they'd parted on such harsh terms last night, her body still leapt when she saw him. Almost as if she were *glad* to see him. Even though she shouldn't be.

He stopped in front of her, reaching out with both hands to clasp hers. Eleanor accepted his touch—his hands were warm, dry, and strong, his fingers folding over hers—without even thinking about what she was doing. Part of her brain knew she should step back, smile coolly, and remain safely distant. Yet that part of her had fallen silent and still. She did nothing.

He was smiling at her with warm admiration, his gaze sweeping her from the top of her elegant chignon to the tips of her rhinestone-encrusted stiletto sandals, and it did something rather pleasant and shivery to her insides. It also kept her from forming a single coherent thought.

'You look magnificent.'

'So do you,' Eleanor blurted, and then blushed. But he did, she couldn't deny it. He wore a dark grey silk suit, his crimson tie a festive splash of colour, the expensive material emphasising his powerful frame, a body she knew and remembered. A body she had once loved.

'And this party is wonderful,' Jace continued in that same warm voice, a voice she also remembered, low and honeyed, sliding over her senses.

'Thank you,' she murmured, and slipped her hands from his. Her brain was reminding her why this wasn't a good idea. Why she needed to remain poised, polished. Professional.

'Very unique.'

'That's what you wanted.' She realised she sounded a little sharp; she felt sharp, as if she were nothing but edges. She softened her words with a smile even as she took a step away. 'Everyone is about to sit down for dinner, so I should go see to a few things—'

Jace nodded his acceptance. 'I'm sorry I was late.'

'You can be late to your own party if you want.' Damn, she still sounded defensive. Why did Jace still affect her in so many ways? Her hands tingled from his touch. Her heart hurt. And the fact that he had been late hurt too. It shouldn't matter. She shouldn't care. She'd spent ten years making sure she didn't care.

Yet apparently she still did.

'I'd better go,' she said, and turned quickly away before Jace could say anything more.

A minor dilemma in the kitchen—a shortage of vegan meals—kept her occupied for the next while, and she managed to avoid Jace as she moved around the room, making sure everyone was happy and fed. Yet even so her gaze kept sliding to him of its own accord. He was seated at the head table, his head bent as he chatted and laughed with the guest on his right, a curvaceous brunette poured into an emerald-green cocktail dress. She was, Eleanor knew from the guest list, Leandro Atrikides's daughter, Kristina. She looked as if she wanted to gobble up Jace in one delicious bite.

And, Eleanor told herself, so what if she did? She was *not* jealous. Jealousy would be both pointless and absurd. She didn't *care* what Jace did, or with whom he did it. She couldn't. Eleanor turned away, smiled and chatted with a young couple five tables away from Jace and made sure not to look at him again.

At the end of the meal, just before Eleanor was about to cue the music for dancing, she heard the sharp, crystalline clang of a fork tapped against a wine glass and the room fell warily silent.

Jace rose from his seat.

Eleanor held her breath.

'Thank you all for coming,' Jace began in a melodious voice that flowed over her and the rest of his audience. 'It is a pleasure and an honour to be among you today.' He let his gaze rove over the room, warm and smiling. Eleanor stepped back away from the table, into the shadows. She wasn't sure why she didn't want Jace to see her—or if he even would—but she felt safer against the wall, away from the light. 'I'm very grateful for your presence,' Jace continued, 'especially in this difficult period of change.' Eleanor saw people shift in their seats, heard a few murmured whispers. Jace must have felt the sudden, palpable tension in the room, although he gave no sign of it. He smiled easily and kept talking.

'I want to assure you that I will do everything in my power to ensure a smooth transition, and that it is my first concern to uphold the integrity of this company, which Leandro Atrikides instilled nearly half a century ago.' He paused, letting his gaze linger on a few faces, then looked up to scan the entire audience. Eleanor retreated even further, so her back came up against the wall. 'But this evening is a time for celebration, and I am delighted to see all of you—' here he smiled at a sleepy child lolling against her mother's arms '—enjoying yourselves. So let me take a moment to thank the person who made it all happen, and in the space of a single week. Eleanor?' Her name was a question, and Eleanor blinked, stunned, speechless.

She'd been thanked before, although not very often. Event planners were meant to be invisible, as if the party magically put itself together. That was the goal. Yet here was Jace, extending his hand, smiling warmly, and looking right at her.

Somehow, even though she was skulking in the shadows like some shamed wallflower, he'd found her. And under the admiring heat of his gaze, Eleanor felt as if she'd stepped straight into the spotlight.

She heard people shift and murmur yet again, and knew her silence was becoming ridiculous. And so unlike her. She was professional. This was professional.

Even if it didn't feel like it.

Clearing her throat, she stepped away from the wall as a patter of applause fell around her like rain. She gave a little nod of acceptance. 'Thank you, Mr Zervas.' His name stuck in her throat.

'And thank you,' Jace replied. 'This couldn't have happened without you.'

She nodded again, jerkily this time, and stepped back into the shadows. To her relief the conversation resumed, and she was forgotten. Yet when she looked up she saw Jace was still gazing straight at her, and the look in his eyes—something both fierce and primal—made her legs so weak that she sagged helplessly against the wall once more.

She managed to avoid him for the next hour, although why she was avoiding him at all, Eleanor had no idea. What was she scared of? They'd parted so harshly last night, and while her mind reminded her of that painful conversation, her body tingled with awareness and memory. Desire, even.

Eleanor stopped in mid-stride on the way to the kitchen and blew out a long, slow breath as she acknowledged her attraction to Jace. Her aggravating and overwhelming attraction. It shouldn't even surprise her, really. Ten years ago she'd been overwhelmed by desire for him from the moment he'd entered the coffee shop where she'd been a barista and asked for a latte in that delicious Greek accent. Even after they'd been dating for several months, he'd still had the power to leave her speechless and desperate with longing in a matter of minutes. Why should that change?

As long as she reminded herself that her body's reaction to Jace was purely biological, chemical, nothing more than hormones or pheromones or whatever those things were—

'I'm almost starting to think you're hiding from me.'

Eleanor stiffened. Ahead of her the kitchen loomed, bustling, bright, safe. The hallway was narrow, dark, and empty. Except for her and Jace.

She turned around slowly, taking in his powerful frame, his immaculate suit. He smiled, that sleepy, suggestive smile she knew so well. She'd teased him that he knew it, and he always acted innocent and even affronted. Now she had no doubt: he knew. He knew the power of that smile, how it made her feel. What it had once made her do. And perhaps what it could make her do again. That was why she was avoiding him.

'Hiding from you?' she repeated, forcing a light little laugh. 'Hardly, Jace. Just busy.'

'Of course,' he murmured, still smiling, and Eleanor had

a feeling he wasn't fooled. Even if it was true; she *was* busy. Although maybe not quite that busy. 'Still,' he continued, making Eleanor tense again, 'surely you have a few moments for me? For a dance?'

'A dance?' she repeated blankly, and his smile deepened, revealing a dimple in his cheek. She'd forgotten about that dimple; he hadn't smiled widely enough in the last week for her to see it.

Yet even though he was smiling now, even though he was looking at her with that seductive sleepiness she remembered so well, she sensed something underneath. Something deeper and darker, marred by sorrow. He hadn't forgotten. The past still loomed between them. No matter how light he kept his voice, Eleanor sensed he was pretending—hiding—perhaps as much as she was.

'Yes, you know? Dance?' He held out his arms as if he were leading an imaginary dance partner and did a quick box-step in the hallway. Eleanor folded her arms, trying to be resolute and regretful and failing. She was actually smiling, although perhaps not as widely as Jace. Yet it felt good to smile, felt right to leave the cares and regrets behind, if only for a night.

'I don't really dance.'

'Good thing I do. And I'm a good teacher.'

'Really?' She arched an eyebrow. 'We never danced before.'

He stopped mid-step and dropped his arms. 'We were too busy doing other things, I suppose.'

Eleanor's cheeks heated and she was grateful for the shadowy dimness of the hallway. Why had she mentioned the past? Why had she referred to anything about their old relationship, their old selves?

'One dance, Eleanor.'

He made it sound like a challenge. And it *was* a challenge; suddenly Eleanor wanted to show Jace Zervas that she could dance with him and remain unaffected. She could walk away. She was desperate to prove to him—and to herself—that he really didn't affect or matter to her at all. And she'd enjoy it at the same time. One dance.

'Fine.'

She walked past him, stiff with resolution, back out into the crowded light of the party. She heard Jace walk behind her, felt the heat of his hand on the small of her back. The band she'd chosen herself was playing a lively swing tune and all around her couples were happily cutting up the floor. Eleanor wasn't much of a dancer—she was usually working behind the scenes, not *in* them—but she thought she could manage a brisk shuffle.

Jace's hand pressed against her back, steering her through the crowd to a spare space on the dance floor. Eleanor turned to face him, firm smile in place. Jace smiled lazily back—as if he knew exactly what she was thinking, that she was simply trying to prove something. Just as he was.

'Shall we?' Eleanor asked brightly and Jace reached for her hand, his fingers threading through hers.

'Oh, yes.'

He pulled her to him, and when Eleanor resisted that sensual tug he murmured so only she could hear, 'Come on, Eleanor. We're dancing.'

'Right.' She let him draw her closer, knowing it was dangerous, feeling that awful desire leap in her belly as she inhaled the woodsy musk of his cologne.

'You're dancing like a twelve-year-old boy,' he chided as Eleanor started an awkward box-step. 'And you're leading.'

'I can't help it,' Eleanor said, laughing reluctantly.

Jace placed his hand on her waist, his fingers splayed across her hip, and drew her close enough so she could feel the heat of him. 'This is how you do it,' he said mock sternly, and began to move her around the dance floor in a lively jitterbug.

Eleanor wasn't sure how she did it. Somehow Jace put enough pressure on her waist to guide her along, twisting and whirling her with such a natural ease that Eleanor was left breathless, amazed at her own gracefulness.

The other dancers had cleared a space around them, and several couples had stopped to watch, clapping their hands in time to the music.

'You're making a scene,' Eleanor hissed when she came close enough to Jace to have him hear. His arm slid along the length of hers before he grabbed her hand and whirled her in a neat, fast circle so her dress spun out around her in a silver arc.

'Isn't that the point?' he challenged with a wicked smile, and Eleanor felt her insides melt.

This was so dangerous. This was the Jace she'd once known, the Jace she'd fallen in love with. The Jace who had broken her heart. She preferred the harsh, hard man she'd met in her office; there had been no danger of falling in love with *him*.

'Where did you learn to dance?' she asked breathlessly as Jace spun her around yet again.

'I have five older sisters. How could I not learn how to dance?'

'Five?' she repeated in surprise. She'd had no idea.

'Now for the finale,' Jace said and Eleanor stiffened in alarm.

'I can't—'

'Yes,' he told her as he pulled her closer, 'you can.'

And before Eleanor knew what he was doing he'd flipped her right over so her legs had gone over her head until she was on her feet again, dazed and incredulous. Around them people clapped and cheered.

'*Jace!*'

'Wasn't that fun?'

'That doesn't matter—' she blustered. How many people had seen her underwear?

'Don't worry,' he murmured, drawing her close again, 'no one saw anything.'

'How did you—' She didn't finish that question and shook her head. It *had* been fun, yet she couldn't quite keep herself from still acting annoyed and defensive; those postures were her armour. They kept her safe. She wasn't ready to unbend entirely.

The song had ended, replaced by a slow jazz number. Distantly Eleanor recognised the sexy, mournful wail of a single saxophone as Jace lazily pulled her even closer so their hips collided and his hands slid down to her lower back, his fingers splayed across the curve of her bottom.

'Jace—' Eleanor hissed, trying to move out of the all-too-close contact. Around them couples swayed to the music.

'Relax. It's a slow dance.'

Relax? How on earth was she supposed to relax with her body pressed against Jace's, his hands moving lazily up and down her spine? She was conscious of how thin her dress was, how little separated their bodies—

Eleanor clamped down on that thought. Fine. She could endure this. She could still walk away with her head held high—except, there was no *enduring* about it. It was far, far too pleasant to let her body relax into Jace's, to enjoy the feel of his hand on her back, his fingers burning her through the thin material of her dress. Too wonderful to let him pull her closer, to lean her head against his chest so her lips hovered less than an inch from the warm skin of his neck.

They'd never danced before. There had been no opportunities. Their love affair had been conducted in the café where she'd worked, walks in the park, and the big double bed in Jace's apartment. Eleanor hadn't even known Jace could dance just as she hadn't known he had five older sisters. He'd never told her, just as he'd never told her so many things. She'd been in love with him, yet in some ways she'd barely known him. It made her wonder if you even could be in love with someone you hardly knew. Had it simply been infatuation?

'See how easy this is?' Jace murmured. His lips brushed her hair and his breath tickled her cheek. Eleanor closed her eyes.

Yes, it was easy. Far, far too easy. She'd wanted to cling to the knowledge that they were two different people now, that even if she could forgive and forget what had happened between them—which she didn't even know if she could—a relationship was impossible. Unwanted on both sides.

Yet in Jace's arms all those resolutions fell away, as insubstantial as smoke, or the snow that had already started to melt into slushy puddles. In Jace's arms, she was conscious only of how everything felt so wonderfully, painfully the same.

The song ended and they remained swaying for a heartbeat before Eleanor found the strength to break away. Her face was flushed and she could feel a rather large strand of hair against her cheek, falling down from her professional, sleek chignon. Her image was falling apart. *She* was falling apart.

'I need to go. There are things to do.'

'Okay.' She risked looking up, saw how shuttered Jace's eyes looked, his jaw taut. This dance had cost him something too. Why were they doing this? Flirting with the past? Flirting with each other? Surely it could only lead to heartache...for both of them.

'Thank you for the dance,' she said, and hurried away without waiting for Jace's reply.

Jace watched Eleanor weave her way through the crowd. His body tingled where he'd touched her. He felt alive, more alive than he had in years, and yet restless and edgy as well.

What was he doing? What was he trying to prove? Dancing with Eleanor was dangerous. There could be nothing for them now, not with the past still lying so heavily between them. Not when he was leaving in less than a week. He didn't even *want* there to be anything between them; he wasn't interested in love, and learning he might actually be fertile couldn't change that.

Could it?

The best thing—the wisest and safest—would be to leave Eleanor alone. To walk away right now, and let them both get on with their lives. Yet even as he made this resolution, Jace realised he was still looking for her. Waiting for her.

Wanting her.

* * *

Eleanor avoided Jace for the rest of the night, feeling ridiculous as she skulked in the corners of rooms, hurried
down hallways, and kept an eagle eye out for his appearance. Yet avoiding Jace had become necessary for her sanity,
her safety. That dance had broken down the barriers she'd
erected between them, barriers between the past and the
present. Barriers she needed. She didn't want to get close
to Jace, couldn't let herself love him or be infatuated with
him. Whatever it was—had been—she had no desire to feel
it again. Not with a man she still couldn't trust. Not with
Jace.

Still, she couldn't avoid him for ever. He found her after
the party had finished, the last guests trickling out into the
night, and the staff starting to clear the party's debris.

'Always busy,' he murmured.

Eleanor didn't turn around, though she could feel him
behind her. 'I have a lot to do. It's a party to you, Jace, but
for me it's work.'

He propped one shoulder against the wall of the Lake
Room where she'd been going over her list of rented equip-
ment on one of the cleared tables. 'It was a great party. And
great work.'

'Thank you.' Needlessly she ticked an item off on her list.
One of the staff hoisted a tray of dirty wine glasses and left
the room, making Eleanor tinglingly aware of how alone she
and Jace were. The last guests had gone into the park and the
darkness, and, now that the room was cleared, all the staff
seemed to have vanished. She ticked another item off on her
list, eyes fixed firmly upon it.

'I'm leaving for Greece in three days,' he said quietly. He
sounded sad. Eleanor tensed.

'I see.'

'I'd like to think…' He paused, clearing his throat.
Eleanor looked up, surprised by the naked vulnerability in
Jace's eyes. The list fell from her hand, forgotten. 'I'd like,'
Jace started again, 'to return home knowing things are—
resolved—between us.'

Resolved. The word echoed through her. What did that mean? How did you find resolution, that oft-touted closure? Eleanor wished she knew. 'Fine,' she said after a moment. 'Consider us resolved.' She picked up her list again and stared at it blindly.

'Eleanor—'

'I don't know what you want, Jace. Whatever it is, I don't think I can give it to you.' She swallowed, stared at her list. 'I'm sorry.' She might have danced with him, had even *wanted* to dance with him, but it meant nothing. She knew that, she felt it now. Her body might betray her again and again, but her mind and heart remembered just what Jace had done. Her mind and heart wouldn't forget. Couldn't forgive. She slipped her list into her bag and met Jace's troubled gaze. Even now her body reacted to his nearness, both with wanting and remembrance. Even now she remembered how she'd felt in his arms, both an hour ago and a lifetime ago. From somewhere she summoned the strength to move past him, making sure they didn't even brush shoulders. 'Goodnight, Jace.'

She walked out of the room without looking back, fumbling for her coat by the front door. She usually stayed for longer after a party, making absolutely sure everything was cleaned up and taken care of. But she couldn't tonight, couldn't handle another moment of being near Jace, of enduring the temptation of being near him.

She hated that her body was so weak, that she still desired the man who had betrayed her. At least she'd been strong enough to walk away.

Jace stood alone in the Lake Room, everything empty and silent around him. In the distance he heard the door click open and shut. Eleanor had gone.

He let out a long, slow breath. It was better this way. It really was. It had to be. Yet even so, the restlessness didn't leave him; the regret still weighed heavily on his heart.

It might be better this way, but it didn't feel like it. Too many things still lay between them, words unspoken that needed to be said.

Consider us resolved.

He didn't.

His body taut with grim purpose, Jace strode from the room.

Outside the park was dark, the last guests already long gone. Eleanor dug her hands deep into the pockets of her coat and walked resolutely towards Fifth Avenue. There should be plenty of cabs there, even at this hour.

She'd only been walking a few minutes, skirting the edge of the Sailboat Pond, afloat with model boats in the spring and summer but now drained and empty, when she heard footsteps behind her. Eleanor's heart stilled even as she quickened her pace. The park was generally safe at night these days, but this was New York and she knew to be careful.

'Eleanor, I'm sorry.'

It was Jace. Eleanor's heart resumed its normal thump for only a second before it began beating all the faster. It was *Jace*. She slowed her pace and turned around.

'What did you say?'

'I'm sorry.' She could barely see him in the darkness; the only light was from a high, thin crescent of moon just emerging from behind the clouds. She couldn't make out the expression on his face, but she could hear the contrition and regret tearing his voice and it startled her.

She hitched her bag higher up on her shoulder. 'What for?'

'For hurting you so badly.' Jace took a step closer to her, and now the moon cast a pale, silvery glow over his features, etched in regret. Eleanor's breath dried in her throat. 'For walking away so utterly. For not being there when you must have been going through a very difficult time.'

'Don't—' Eleanor whispered. He had no idea just how difficult a time she'd been through. He had no idea how much she'd needed to hear these words, and yet how afraid she was to hear them, because an apology required a response. It meant things would change. *She* would have to change.

'Don't say sorry?' Jace smiled, that wonderful crooked smile Eleanor knew and had once loved. 'But I have to. For my sake, as well as your own. We can't be—resolved—until I say it. I know that.'

'I don't need—' Eleanor began, roughly, for her throat was already clogged and tight. Yet she couldn't even finish the sentence. It was a lie. She *did* need. She needed Jace to apologise. She needed to be able to forgive him. For ten years she'd managed to move on without it, but her heart had stayed in the same place. She hadn't realised just how much until Jace had come back into her life.

He was right in front of her now, so close she could reach out and touch him if she wanted to. She didn't move. 'Will you forgive me, Eleanor?' Jace asked softly. 'For hurting you so much?'

Eleanor wanted to shake her head. She wanted to cry. She wanted to tell him she wouldn't, because she was still angry and hurt and afraid, and yet she wanted to say she would because she needed the closure, the redemption. She nodded jerkily, unable to offer him more.

It didn't matter. Jace closed the small space between them, pulling her into his arms. She felt the soft wool of his coat against her cold cheek as she remained in the circle of his embrace, unresisting, unable to move or push away as she surely should do. 'I'm sorry,' he said again, his voice rough with emotion, and the shell around Eleanor's hardened heart finally cracked and broke.

'I forgive you,' she whispered, the words barely more than a breath of sound. Her throat was so tight. She tilted her head up to look at him, meaning only to offer absolution, yet there must have been too much yearning in her eyes—too much desire—for Jace's own expression darkened and after a second's hesitation—a second that seemed to last for ever—he lowered his mouth to hers.

The first brush of his lips against hers was a shock,

electrifying her from the tips of her fingers to the very centre of her soul.

Then her senses sweetly sang to life as both body and mind and even heart remembered this, remembered Jace. How he felt. How he tasted. How right she'd always been in his arms and under his touch.

Her lips yielded to his, parting, inviting, and Jace took full advantage, deepening the kiss so Eleanor felt that plunging sensation of helpless desire deep in her belly, so she craved more, and *more*, her hands sliding over his coat, across his shoulders, down his back, bringing her closer to him.

She didn't know how long the kiss went on. And it was more than a kiss. Jace's hands had slipped under her coat, under her dress, cold against her skin and yet still enflaming her with his touch so that both their breathing was ragged and Eleanor's mind was as hazy and high as a cloud.

Her head dropped back, her back arching, a moan escaping her lips as his hands roved over her body and his mouth moved on hers. It had been so long. It had been ten years.

She couldn't think past this moment, couldn't register anything but the onslaught of her senses…until she heard two teenagers' raucous laughter from across the pond, the ugly sound jolting her out of that desire-induced haze and right out of Jace's arms. She jerked away, her chest rising and falling in shock, in shame, while she stared at him with dazed, disbelieving eyes. He looked back at her, his expression just as stunned. Neither of them spoke.

Eleanor could hardly believe what she'd just allowed. What she'd done. He said sorry and she melted into his arms? She'd practically begged him to touch her, *take* her? Jace looked as if he hadn't even meant to kiss her, and maybe he hadn't. Maybe she'd kissed him without realising—

'Eleanor—'

'No.' She couldn't hear what he was going to say, no matter what it was. Anything Jace said now was sure to break her. 'This shouldn't have happened.'

'I know.' Those two sorry words almost made her cry.

Somehow she didn't want him to admit it was a mistake, even though she knew it was. 'Even so—'

'No,' Eleanor said again. There was no *even so*. There couldn't be. She shook her head, backing away, and then with a stifled cry she fled into the night.

Jace watched Eleanor run through the darkness as if the very demons of hell were on her heels. Perhaps she felt they were. She had clearly been shocked by that kiss, and frankly so had he.

He'd meant only to say sorry, to make up for the past, and instead he'd reopened it, ripped the scabs off their scars. His heart ached with remembered pain. His body ached with unfulfilled desire.

What was he doing? Why couldn't he just leave Eleanor Langley alone? Jace realised he was still walking towards Fifth Avenue, following her fleeing footsteps. He slowed his stride.

Ever since Eleanor had come back into his life—ever since he'd discovered she'd been telling the truth—he hadn't been able to stop thinking of her. Thinking about the what ifs, wondering if life could give them a second chance.

Jace stopped in his tracks. A second chance at what? At *love*?

Did he really want that?

The last ten years he'd been hardening his heart against love, against any messy emotion. He'd focused on his business, building an empire instead of a dynasty.

And yet now...now he wanted more. He wanted Eleanor.

Ellie.

He wanted to reawaken the woman he'd lost when he'd walked out ten years ago. He wanted Ellie to find herself again, her true self, the self whom he'd loved and who had loved him. He wasn't even sure why; he didn't know what he even wanted with that woman. He'd lost her once, and he'd spent the intervening years making sure he never lost—anything or anyone—again.

Did he really want that change? That risk?

Did Ellie?

And how the hell could any of it happen, when he was leaving in a few days?

Jace stopped walking. The past was better buried. He knew that, felt it. No matter how these if onlys and what ifs might torment him, he knew they were only that. Possibilities, not realities. Not even hopes.

Distantly he heard the teenagers move off, still laughing raucously, and the laboured chug of the Fifth Avenue bus as it headed downtown. Letting out a long, slow breath, Jace slowly turned around and walked in the other direction.

CHAPTER SIX

ELEANOR didn't go back to her apartment. She didn't want to be alone, so she took a cab to the West Village, where her best friend Allie had a studio on the top floor of a brownstone. They'd both been interns at Premier Planning nine years ago. Allie had lasted two weeks. Eleanor had stayed for ever.

Even though it was now after midnight, she knew she could trust Allie to welcome her with open arms—and an open heart.

Still, she had to press the buzzer for a good thirty seconds before Allie came to the intercom.

'Who is it?' she demanded in a voice that sounded both sleepy and irritated.

Too emotional and fragile to explain, Eleanor just said, 'Me.'

Allie pressed the buzzer.

She was waiting outside the door in her pyjamas, hugging herself in the cold of the corridor, as Eleanor made her way up the six narrow flights of stairs.

'Eleanor, what on earth happened? You look terrible.'

'Thanks,' Eleanor managed wryly, and Allie shrugged this aside, taking in Eleanor's up-do and silvery dress.

'Actually, you look fantastic. You *sound* terrible. What's wrong?'

'Everything, it feels like,' Eleanor replied, her words wobbly. Now that she was finally here with Allie, safe, loved, the reality of her confrontation with Jace—and that wonderful, awful, confusing kiss—was slamming into her, leaving her more than shaken. Leaving her shattered.

Allie ushered her inside the cosy apartment, plonking the kettle on the stove before Eleanor had even asked.

'You want to talk about it? Didn't you have an event tonight?'

Eleanor sank onto the worn futon and kicked off her heels, nodding wearily. Allie's apartment was so different from her own modishly sterile condo; it was colourful and cluttered and shabby, and Eleanor loved it. Now it made her ache just a little bit for the kind of apartment she'd once had, the kind of life she'd once had. The kind of person she'd once been.

You're the kind of person you never wanted to be.

Eleanor pushed the thought away. Allie sank onto the futon across from Eleanor, flicked her long braid over one shoulder and propped her chin on her fist. 'So?'

'He came back.'

Allie's eyes widened, her breath coming out in a slow hiss. Eleanor knew she didn't need to explain who *he* was. One night long ago, when they'd both had too much wine, she'd told Allie her whole sordid story. Or most of it, anyway. She'd left out some of the heartache, the consuming loss that was too private to share.

'He did?' Allie finally said. 'How—?'

Eleanor didn't want to explain it. She didn't have the strength or will. 'Party,' she said simply, and Allie nodded. It was enough.

'What happened? Did the bastard finally apologise, I hope?'

Eleanor let out a choked laugh. 'Yes,' she managed, and covered her face with her hands.

'And isn't that a good thing?' Allie asked cautiously. Eleanor was prevented from answering by the shrill whistle of the kettle. Allie got up to make their tea, and Eleanor sagged against the futon. It *was* a good thing. At least, she'd always thought it would be. Yet when someone asked for forgiveness, you were meant to give it; you were meant to let go. And Eleanor wasn't sure she could. She might have told Jace she forgave him, but those were only words. *Could* she forgive him? What would happen if she did?

Allie returned, handing Eleanor a mug of tea before settling back onto the futon. 'So it doesn't seem like a good thing,' she remarked wryly. 'Why not?'

Eleanor let out a hiccuppy laugh. 'Well, I suppose it's not so much the apology, as the kiss that came after it.'

There was a second's silence and then Allie nodded. 'Ah.' She took a sip of tea. 'Was it nice?'

Eleanor burst out laughing, nearly spluttering her tea. It felt good to laugh, despite the pain and regret still tearing at her. 'That was the last thing I expected you to say.'

Allie shrugged. 'For all the apparent heartache it's causing you, I hope it was.'

'Very nice,' Eleanor admitted after a moment. She gazed down into the milky depths of her tea. 'Very nice,' she repeated quietly. Even now she could remember how good Jace had felt, how *right*, which was ridiculous because there had been nothing right about it all. It had been very, very wrong.

'So why exactly did he kiss you?' Allie asked after a moment. She tucked her knees up to her chest and looked at Eleanor over the rim of her mug. 'Was he just caught up in the moment?'

'I don't know,' Eleanor said slowly. Why *had* Jace kissed her? Had it been a spontaneous gesture, as Allie had said? He had seemed so surprised, as stunned as she had…yet she could hardly believe that Jace would be so out of control. Had he been proving to her that she was still attracted to him? Had it been a mere amusement? Or worse—far worse—a *pity* kiss?

'Eleanor, stop whatever you're thinking. You're looking way too freaked out.'

Eleanor groaned. 'I'm feeling freaked out. You know I haven't had much time—or inclination—for relationships, Allie. I can't *do* this—'

'Does he want a relationship?'

Eleanor groaned again. 'No, of course not. That is—I don't think so. I shouldn't even care.'

'But you do,' Allie filled in quietly and Eleanor bit her lip, nipping hard.

'No,' she finally said, firmly. 'I don't. I can't. Ten years ago he broke my heart and—more than that.' She twisted the mug, her tea barely touched, around in her hands. 'My whole life collapsed, Allie. Everything. I never told you how—how bad it was, but it was. Bad.' She tried to smile wryly, but her lips trembled instead. 'Really bad.'

'Oh, Eleanor.' Allie reached over to place a hand on top of hers. 'I'm sorry.'

'So am I. And that's why this kiss—for whatever reason—was a bad idea. I'm not going to ever let myself feel that way again. Be used that way. And,' Eleanor finished, her voice turning hard and flinty, 'the simple fact is, I may have changed a lot in ten years, but Jace Zervas hasn't.' Not enough. Not in ways that mattered. She smiled grimly at her friend. 'I don't think he's changed at all.'

Eleanor spent the night on Allie's futon, and slept deeply and dreamlessly. By the time she swam to consciousness the next morning, the sun was high in the sky and Allie had already gone out for the coffee and croissants.

'I feel like I've been hit by a truck,' Eleanor muttered as she pushed her hair out of her face and blinked in the sunlight flooding the room. She hadn't even washed her face before going to bed, and her eyes felt sticky both with sleep and dried mascara.

'You basically were,' Allie replied cheerfully. 'The Jace Zervas Express.' She handed Eleanor a paper cup of coffee and a flaky croissant. 'Here. Sustenance.'

'You're amazing.'

Allie grinned. 'I know.'

Eleanor sat cross-legged on the sofa and ate the buttery croissant, licking the crumbs from her fingers, before she started on her coffee. She hadn't eaten much last night, as busy as she'd been with the details of the party, and she was starving.

Her cellphone beeped just as she took her first sip of coffee.

'My boss,' she explained when she'd located the phone and listened to Lily's brief message. She sounded her usual terse self, and simply asked her to call, which made Eleanor feel a flutter of panic. Had Jace talked to Lily? Had the party *not* been a success after all?

Had that kiss changed everything?

She ended the message and dropped her cellphone back into her bag. Leaning back against the sofa she took a sip of coffee, determined to forget Lily, forget Jace, forget everything, if just for a day. It was Saturday; she was with Allie. And she needed a break. She turned to Allie, smiling with bright determination. 'Let's go out. Do something fun. Go to the Greenmarket in Union Square and buy funky jewellery at St Mark's Place.'

'Funky jewellery?' Allie repeated, eyebrows arched. 'When have you ever worn funky jewellery?'

Eleanor bit her lip, her smile wobbling just a little bit. She used to wear funky jewellery. She used to look and feel and *be* so different.

She simply wasn't that person any more, and she didn't think she ever could be again. After she'd lost both Jace and their baby, she'd ruthlessly gone about becoming someone else…the person she was now.

The kind of person you never wanted to be.

Shrugging away the sorrow this thought caused, she smiled once more at Allie. 'Well, let's go to a museum, then. The Met or the MOMA.' She took her last sip of coffee, her voice taking on an edge. 'You're right, I'm really not a funky jewellery kind of person.'

Monday morning came soon enough, and as Eleanor walked through Premier Planning's office she was uncomfortably aware of the curious looks of everyone on the office floor, the sideways glances, the open speculation. Her skin prickled. What had happened? What had Jace done?

Then she stopped in the doorway of her office, for there in the centre of her desk was the most enormous, most outrageous bouquet of flowers she'd ever seen. She dropped her bag on the floor and approached the arrangement of creamy white lilies and small, violet blooms that a card tucked in among the leaves told her was glory-of-the-snow.

Snow.

Her heart constricted. A little envelope had been taped to the crystal vase, and Eleanor took it with trembling fingers. She slipped the stiff white card out and read the two words printed on it: *Sorry. Again.*

Her fingers clenched on the card. Sorry for what? Sorry for the kiss? Sorry for—

'Well, well.'

Eleanor turned around, the card still clutched in her fingers. Lily stood in the doorway, as sharp and freshly pressed as ever, the expression on her thin face impossible to read.

'Good morning, Lily.'

'I'd say from those flowers that Zervas was pleased with the party.'

'I hope so.'

'I know he was pleased because he called me Saturday morning to tell me so. I knew we could do it,' Lily told her in a smug voice that made Eleanor wonder if her boss was taking credit for pulling off the event.

'That's…wonderful?' she said numbly.

Lily narrowed her eyes. 'It is, isn't it? You don't sound too thrilled, though. And you look terrible.'

Leave it to Lily not to sugarcoat it, Eleanor thought sourly. She moved the flowers to a side table. 'I'm just exhausted. Organising a party like that in just a week takes it out of even me.'

'You're right,' Lily conceded grudgingly. 'You can take a half-day, if you like.'

Eleanor shook her head. She didn't need more time to think, to dwell, to wonder. Nor did she need people like Jill or Laura eager to keep her clients or steal more while she was away. She needed to be here, at work, where she was needed and useful and busy. 'No, thanks. I'm fine. I need to catch up on all my other accounts anyway.'

Yet even as Eleanor worked solidly throughout the day, she found it still gave her mind plenty of time to wonder. To remember. She relived every second of that kiss with Jace, how unbearably good it had felt to be held by him again. How she realised her body had been waiting to be held again—by him—for ten long years.

How infuriated and frustrated and *scared* it made her feel. She didn't want to want him.

She was just about to leave for the day when her phone rang. Thinking it was a callback from a client, she reached for the phone quickly, her voice brisk and professional.

'Eleanor Langley.'

'Hello, Ellie.' A pause, and she heard a wry note of laughter in his voice as he corrected himself. 'Sorry. Eleanor.'

Her fingers clenched on the phone. Blood drained from her face, raced to other parts of her body. 'Hello, Jace.'

'I'm leaving for Greece tomorrow.' He spoke quietly, almost sadly. 'I just wanted to say I'm sorry. For the other night. I know me kissing you wasn't on either of our agendas.'

Agendas. She pictured herself pencilling in *kiss Jace*. No, that had definitely not been on her agenda. And obviously not on Jace's either, Eleanor acknowledged bleakly. 'The flowers did the job admirably,' she said after a moment, her voice sounding constricted.

'I'm glad you liked them.'

Eleanor didn't answer, couldn't, because her throat had tightened so terribly. The silence ticked on between them, punctuated only by the soft sound of their breathing.

Finally Jace spoke again. 'So I suppose this is goodbye. I don't intend to return to New York.'

'Not even to manage Atrikides Holdings?'

'I've appointed a CEO,' Jace said. 'Leandro Atrikides's nephew. That was the plan all along.'

'Whose plan?'

'Leandro's.' He sounded weary, and Eleanor realised with a jolt that the corporate takeover might not have been quite as ruthless as she'd thought. *Jace* wasn't as ruthless as she had thought.

But it didn't matter, because he was leaving New York. And there could be—would be—nothing between them anyway, which was how she wanted it. How it had to be. The past could be forgiven, maybe, but not forgotten. Not undone.

'I see,' she managed. Her voice sounded distant and polite despite the ache in her throat and even in her heart. 'Well, goodbye, then.'

Jace was silent, long enough for Eleanor to wonder what he was thinking. What he wanted to say. What *she* wanted him to say.

'Goodbye, Eleanor,' he said, and then he put down the phone.

Staring into space, Eleanor realised that Jace had just left her a second time. At least this time he'd said goodbye.

Jace stood up and walked over to the floor-to-ceiling window of Leandro Atrikides's office, the view of Central Park now shrouded in shadows.

Tomorrow morning he'd take his private jet back to Athens. He had plenty of work to keep him busy, meetings to attend, companies to control, decisions to make. A life.

Yet right now it all felt empty, meaningless, and all he could think of was the woman he'd left, the woman he was leaving again. The life he'd lost a decade ago.

Irritated, Jace shook off his maudlin thoughts. They were not worthy of him. Regret was a useless emotion. The best option, the only option, was to move on. To forget. As they both surely should do.

And that was what he *wanted* to do, anyway. He wasn't interested in resurrecting some youthful affair that had most likely been doomed from the start. He wasn't interested in becoming that carefree young man again, the man with a heart to break, even if he grieved the loss of the woman he'd once known. He'd wanted to bring that woman back last night; he thought apologising would help. Kissing her wouldn't. Didn't.

That kiss, Jace knew, had been a mistake. Even if it hadn't felt like one at the time.

That kiss had unearthed memories, desire, regrets—all of which Jace wanted to keep buried, and he had no doubt that Eleanor did too.

Sighing, shrugging off these thoughts, he told himself he should return to his penthouse hotel suite. He'd order in and go to bed early, take a morning flight back to Athens. He was neither needed nor wanted here.

Yet still he remained, hands in his pockets, staring out at a darkening sky.

Three months later

'Why do you work so hard?'

Jace looked up from the financial newspaper he'd been scanning as he drank his morning coffee. 'Sorry,' he said, giving his sister Alecia a still-distracted smile. 'Habit.' He reached for one of the rolls on the table. They were sitting in one of the cafés off Kolonaki Square, in one of Athens's best neighborhoods.

Across from him Alecia made a face and reached for a roll herself. 'I don't mean reading your newspaper, Jace. It's everything. Ever since you came back from that trip you've been like a grumpy bear, growling at everyone who sees you. And you've missed three family dinners—that's at least two too many. I know you try to miss them anyway, but still…' She smiled teasingly as she said it, but even Jace could see the shadows of worry in her eyes.

He broke his roll in half. 'What trip do you mean?'

'The one to the States. New York, wasn't it?'

Jace shouldn't have asked. He already knew what trip, knew what lay behind his sister's concerned comments.

Eleanor. He couldn't get her out of his mind. He hadn't been the same since he'd seen her. Since he'd left her. Again.

Sighing, he reached for his cup and took a small sip of the strong, syrupy Greek coffee.

'I'm worried about you, you know.'

'Don't be.' The words came out harshly, too harshly, for he and Alecia had always enjoyed a close relationship. She was older than him by only eighteen months, and the only one of his sisters still to be unmarried. She understood him perhaps better than anyone else did, and she was the only person he'd told about Ellie. Yet he hadn't told her about Eleanor, or what had happened in New York three months ago.

'Jace? What's going on?'

'Nothing.' His throat constricted and his fingers tightened around the coffee cup. He wasn't ready to share everything he'd learned in New York: that he'd made a mistake, that he wasn't infertile, that he'd ruined what might have been his only chance at happiness and perhaps even love. He could barely voice those sentiments to himself. For the last three months he'd been working as hard as he could to keep from thinking about them. To keep from thinking about anything.

Yet it obviously hadn't worked, for Alecia had seen that something was amiss, and Eleanor never really left his thoughts. She invaded his dreams. He felt her like a constant presence, a mist over his mind, even though she was thousands of miles away.

'Is it a woman?' Alecia asked playfully, and Jace's head jerked up.

'What?'

'A woman.' Alecia smiled, her chin resting on her laced

fingers. 'If I didn't know you better, I'd think it was a woman. You seem almost lovesick.'

Lovesick. What a terrible expression. Love. *Sick*. And he didn't love Eleanor; he didn't even know her any more.

'Alecia, that's ridiculous.'

'Is it?' Alecia cocked her head. 'I know you haven't given any women a chance since that conniving slut back in Boston—'

'Don't.' Jace bit the word off, heard the tension and anger in his voice. Alecia blinked in surprise. 'I don't want to talk about her.'

'I know how much she hurt you, Jace. Even if you've never wanted to admit it.'

'Don't,' he said again, and barely managed to get the word out. He turned his head, not wanting Alecia to see the naked emotion and pain on his face. Not wanting to feel it himself. He missed her, he knew. He couldn't hide from it. He missed Ellie. *Eleanor.* Since seeing her in New York, he hadn't felt complete or whole or happy.

He *needed* her.

He just didn't want to.

'All right, then,' she said after a moment. 'Let's talk about something else. Papa is going to be seventy next month, and no one's done a thing about it.'

Jace tensed, as he always did when his father was mentioned, but then he made himself relax. 'And what,' he asked Alecia with a bland smile, 'are we supposed to do about it exactly?'

'A party, Jace! I know Elana usually organises such things, but she's busy with her four—Lukas is applying to university this year—and Tabitha is pregnant with her third—'

'Her third?' Jace murmured. 'Already?' He could never keep track of his sisters and their growing brood. Admittedly, he didn't try very hard. He sent expensive presents and occasionally he showed up. For so long he'd felt separate from all of them, with their busy lives and their bands of children. He'd felt so *other*.

Yet now he didn't need to; he'd gone to a fertility specialist as soon as he'd returned to Athens, and the results had come back two weeks ago. He had, the doctor told him, limited fertility. It would still be possible to have a child; it would have been possible ten years ago.

It had been. He thought of the daughter he'd had and never known, and then closed his mind off from the memory-that-wasn't.

He'd avoided thinking about the implications of the doctor's news because it hurt too much. It hurt to realise he had wasted so many years of his life; it hurt even to think how glad his father would be at the news now. His existence would finally be validated. Jace hadn't told him—or anyone—yet. It wasn't as if he were about to run off and make that oh-so needed heir. Unlike his father, he had no desperate urge to create a dynasty. He refused to be defined by either his inability or ability to have children.

'Jace, are you listening to a word I'm saying?' Alecia asked, good-natured impatience edging her voice, and Jace smiled in apology.

'Sorry. Go on. Tabitha's pregnant and Elana's busy.'

'And Kaitrona is hopeless at organising these things, and Parthenope isn't speaking to Papa—'

'Parthenope isn't? Why not?'

Alecia waved a hand in dismissal. 'Oh, who knows? Someone's always in an argument with him. He said something rude to Christos once—'

'Ah.' Christos was Parthenope's husband, a charming city type that his father didn't trust. And, Jace knew well, his father had always been a plain speaker.

You're sterile. You cannot have children. What use is it to me, to have no more Zervas men to follow me? What good are you?

'What about you, then?' he asked, pouring them both more coffee.

'I just started a new job and it has crazy hours,' Alecia replied. 'Which you'd know, if you listened to me for more than five minutes. Honestly, Jace, you're hopeless. Who is she?'

'*She* is no one,' Jace replied, an edge to his voice. 'Don't start assuming things and spreading rumours, Alecia.'

'Who, me?' She blinked innocently. 'Anyway, since none of us can do it, that only leaves one person.'

'Mother?' Jace guessed, and Alecia rolled her eyes.

'You, Jace, you! You can organise a party. I thought we could have it out on that island villa of yours. You hardly ever go there, and it's the most amazing place I've ever seen.'

Jace stilled, his face blanking. Give his father a party? A celebration thrown by the son who had been nothing but a disappointment? Such a party could only be an insult, a mockery, especially considering how strained and distant their relationship had been and still was. 'I don't think that's a good idea, Alecia.'

'I know you and Papa have your differences, Jace, but you're his son—'

'I'm not the right person to do this,' Jace cut her off flatly. He knew his sisters didn't understand the tension between him and his father; Aristo Zervas had wanted to keep his son's infertility—his family's shame—a secret.

'Fine, then hire someone to do it,' Alecia replied. A steely look that Jace knew well had entered her eye. She wasn't going to let go of this.

'Alecia—' He stopped as her suggestion sank in. *Hire someone to do it.* The words echoed in Jace's mind, reverberated in his heart. He felt, bizarrely, as if everything had just slid into place. As if everything suddenly made sense. It was as if he'd been waiting for this opportunity, and now that it had fallen into his lap he knew just what to do. What he wanted to do, what he needed to do.

'So?' Alecia asked, sipping her coffee, her smile turning just a little bit smug. 'What do you think?'

'I think,' Jace said slowly, 'that it's a good idea. And I know just the person to do it.'

* * *

Eleanor picked up another stone, worn silky smooth by the endless tide, and, aiming carefully, threw it into the Long Island Sound. Satisfied, she watched it skip four times before sinking beneath the waves. She heard the crunch of footsteps on the sand behind her.

'You've been doing that for hours.'

Eleanor reached for another stone, offering her mother a quick smile. 'It's therapeutic.'

'You need therapy?'

'I live in New York. Doesn't everyone there need it?'

'Probably.' Her mother sighed and sat down on the hard, cold sand. It was almost April, and, although the trees were starting to bud and daffodils lined the drive up to Heather Langley's beach cottage, the wind and waves were still cold. 'You want to tell me about it?' she asked eventually and Eleanor skipped another stone across the water. She'd arrived at her mother's place last night, and she'd leave tomorrow. They hadn't spoken much beyond pleasantries; her mother knew better than to press.

'Not particularly,' she replied lightly. She knew her mother—and her mother knew her—too well to dissemble or pretend there wasn't anything going on. Yet she didn't trust her mother with the truth.

Their relationship had always been a strained one, marred by ambition and yet marked with moments of intimacy and caring. Still, it wasn't enough to make her want now to unburden her heart and reveal her vulnerabilities.

'Lily says you're doing well at work. Amazing, really.'

'Thanks.' It seemed like the only thing in her life that *was* going right. Since Jace had left, she'd poured herself into work more than ever before. It grated on her nerves that her mother and her boss talked about her, checked up on her. It was ridiculous and even inappropriate, yet Eleanor knew she couldn't tell either of them that. They were best friends, competitors and colleagues until a minor heart attack had forced Heather into early retirement. She'd left her job and the city and taken this cottage out on Long Island. Once in a while she planned someone's beach party in the Hamptons, but her career was essentially finished, and Eleanor thought it was the best thing that had ever happened to her mother—and to their relationship.

She sighed, sinking onto the sand next to her mother, her elbows resting on her knees. 'It's nothing, really. I'm just restless.'

'You've been at Premier Planning for a long time,' Heather said after a moment. 'Maybe you should think about something else.'

Eleanor rounded her eyes in mock horror. 'Give up my job? That's the last thing I'd expect you to say.'

Heather shrugged. 'A job doesn't have to be everything. I know it seemed like it was for me, but—' She stopped, uncertain, and Eleanor smiled to help her out.

'I know.'

Her mother smiled in apology. There was still so much that hadn't been said between them. From her fatherless childhood and her mother's workaholic schedule, to the whole mess of Jace and her pregnancy—an entire language of loss and hurt that neither of them knew how to speak.

'Well,' Heather said finally, 'a sabbatical maybe.'

Eleanor shook her head. 'I'm okay.' She couldn't give up work; it was all she had. Yet she didn't know *what* she wanted to do. Ever since Jace had left New York—ever since he'd kissed her—she'd been feeling restless and edgy and uncertain. Wanting something different. Something more. Maybe even wanting Jace. Yet she wasn't about to abandon her senses or her job for some impossible dream, some distant fantasy that was never meant to be real.

Smiling, she stood up and stretched her hand out to her mother. Heather took it. 'Come on. It's pretty cold out here. I've got one more afternoon before I have to head back to the city, and I fully intend to beat you at Scrabble for once.'

Laughing, Heather let her change the subject. 'I'd like to see you try.'

* * *

Monday morning came soon enough, and Eleanor arrived at work a bit weary from her three-hour journey on the Hampton Jitney the night before.

Shelley, the receptionist, rose from her desk as Eleanor entered the office. 'I have your nine o'clock waiting in your office.'

'My nine o'clock?' Eleanor repeated. She'd gone through her schedule that morning while sipping coffee at the sink, and her first appointment was at ten.

'Yes, he said he'd like to wait there.' Shelley, all of twenty-two years old, made a swoony type of face that caused Eleanor a ripple of unease.

'All right,' she murmured, walking down the hallway. Her office door, she saw, was closed. Lily poked her head out of her own office.

'I pencilled him in,' she told Eleanor briskly. 'Apparently he was *very* impressed. Would only have you for this project, and this time there's no rush.'

Eleanor's unease increased to foreboding as she reached for the knob of her door and turned.

'Hello, Eleanor.'

Jace Zervas stood in the centre of her office.

CHAPTER SEVEN

'WHAT are you doing here?'

Eleanor closed the door quickly behind her before her boss could hear any more of the conversation. Her heart was thudding heavily and her palms felt slick. Even more alarming were the sudden nerves that fluttered through her, making her tingle in—what? Annoyance? Anticipation? *Excitement?*

She sidestepped Jace to move behind her desk, where she felt safer. Slipping off her coat, she felt a flicker of gratitude that she was wearing one of her smarter outfits: a cream silk blouse and a cherry-red pencil skirt, with nails freshly manicured to match. Her hair was pulled up in a sleek twist, and her appearance felt like both her armour and her ammunition. She used it; she hid behind it.

'A party, of course.' He smiled, but Eleanor thought she saw a shadow of something in his eyes—uncertainty? Fear? This was foreign territory for both of them. He'd shed his cashmere trench coat and wore a charcoal-grey suit that matched his eyes perfectly. His silver-grey silk tie emphasised their metallic glints, and Eleanor had trouble tearing her gaze away from him.

'A party?' she repeated, looking down to reshuffle a few random papers on her desk. 'I hardly think I'm an appropriate candidate for—'

'You're the best.'

She looked up. 'I'm not that good.'

Jace took a step closer, one finger to his lips. 'Shh. Don't let Lily hear you.' He smiled, teasingly, and Eleanor felt those wretched nerves flutter through her again, as flighty and feather-brained as the pigeons crowding Central Park, fighting over a few paltry crumbs. 'She's quite a dragon,' Jace continued. 'She was business partners with your mother?' At Eleanor's sharp intake of breath he looked up and smiled. 'We had a little chat while I was waiting for you.'

'I really think it's better, Jace, if someone else organises this party. Anyway, I didn't think you were even coming back to New York.'

'This party's not in New York.'

Eleanor's breath came out in a rush. 'Then I'm certainly not the right person to plan it. Everything I've done is New-York-based—'

'You organised a birthday party in the Hamptons.'

'Still city-based,' Eleanor countered firmly. 'The client lived year round in Manhattan. Anyway, it's not worth arguing about. I don't care if your party is in Times Square, I don't want to organise it.' Brave words. Brave sentiments. She wished she sounded stronger. Felt surer. In truth she felt horribly uncertain. Half of her wanted to leap at the chance of spending more time with Jace; half of her wanted to run away.

The contradictory nature of her own emotions was ridiculous. And annoying.

'Actually,' Jace said, smiling faintly as he watched her, 'the party is in Greece. It's my father's seventieth birthday party.'

'What?' The word was more of a squawk. Jace's smile deepened so Eleanor saw his dimple. She wished she didn't. That dimple made him look friendly, approachable. Desirable.

'Have you ever been to Greece?' he asked as he started to stroll round her office, gazing at the rather pedestrian artwork on her walls.

'No,' she replied flatly. 'In fact, I've tried to avoid the whole country.'

'I think you would enjoy it. It's beautiful this time of year. Not too hot.'

'I'd hardly be relaxing,' Eleanor countered, then wished she hadn't. She didn't even want to discuss this. She was not going to Greece.

'Well, I don't want to run you ragged like last time,' Jace replied. 'The party's not for nearly a month.'

'Doesn't matter. I can't organise a party like that from here, and I can hardly go to Greece for a month.'

Jace stopped strolling and turned around to face her. He was smiling, but his face still looked grave. 'Can't you?' he asked softly.

Suddenly the atmosphere in the room changed, a different kind of tension tautening the air between them. Suddenly Jace seemed very close, even though he hadn't moved. Eleanor drew in a deep, shuddery breath.

'Don't, Jace.'

'Don't?' he repeated, the word a question, and Eleanor shook her head. She didn't want to explain. She didn't even know what to explain. She just knew that seeing him again was both a joy and agony, the emotions tangled so closely that she could not separate one from the other, or from herself. She wished he hadn't come, yet she'd been waiting for him to come.

He must have sensed something of her turmoil, for he took a step closer and said with a little smile, 'A couple of weeks in Greece. Can't you think of worse things?'

A couple of weeks in Greece *with you*, Eleanor amended silently. 'I can't leave my other clients for that long,' she began, trying to stay professional.

'Lily said someone else could take them. Laura or someone?'

Laura. Of course. She'd snagged her clients last time. Eleanor sagged into her chair as she felt the first flickers of defeat. 'You've already spoken to Lily,' she stated flatly and Jace shrugged.

'How could I not?'

She looked up, her eyes wide and meeting his own directly, daring him to be honest. 'Why me?'

'Why not you?' Jace countered quietly.

Eleanor swallowed, her gaze sliding away. 'You know why.'

Jace was silent for a moment, and when he spoke again his voice was light. 'I don't know any other event planners, and I think you're the best for the job.'

He didn't want to talk about the past. Fine, she didn't either, so she'd stick with the present. There was enough trouble with that. '*Me*? How about someone Greek for starters?' Eleanor drew in a breath, ready to launch into a tirade of how she couldn't go with Jace, she couldn't plan his party. She didn't want to. She was afraid to. She *wouldn't*.

'Actually, Eleanor, you'd be doing me a favour,' Jace cut her off, his voice quiet and a little sad. Eleanor closed her mouth with a surprised snap. 'My relationship with my father has never been—what it could be. What it should be.' He glanced away, his expression turning distant, shuttered. 'I'm afraid I've been a disappointment to my father, in many ways,' he confessed in a low voice. 'This party could help in healing our rift.'

This was more than Jace had ever shared with her before. About his life. About himself. She felt as if she'd been given a tiny glimpse into his mind, his heart, and it left her aching and curious and wanting to know more.

She cleared her throat, striving to keep her tone professional. 'I still don't know if I'm the right person for this, Jace…considering.' It occurred to her that perhaps he'd never told his family about her. Perhaps he'd walked right back into life in Greece without a single backward glance or thought at all. Strange—and stupid—that it hurt to think that, even now.

'You'd be helping me out,' Jace told her. 'Although I recognise that might not be a point in my favour.'

Eleanor flushed. 'I don't have some kind of—vendetta,'

she told him. 'Really, Jace, the past is forgotten.' It was a lie, but she said it anyway.

'Do you really think so?' Jace queried softly. 'I know I can't forget that easily.'

Eleanor's flush deepened. She didn't know what Jace was talking about, but she knew there were plenty of things she couldn't forget. Like the first time he'd kissed her, after she'd given him a chocolate cupcake she'd baked, so that she couldn't eat chocolate even now without thinking of that wonderful, breathless moment. Like how wonderful it had been to lie in his arms, the sun bathing them in gold. How he was the only person who had ever made her cry with joy.

'I don't know,' she said slowly, yet as the words came out of her mouth she realised she already knew, she'd known from the moment she'd walked in and seen Jace in her office. She might have offered a few paltry protests for form's sake, but in her heart she'd already agreed to go to Greece.

The question she had no intention of answering or even asking herself was *why*. Was it simply pressure from work—Lily would undoubtedly insist she go—or a deeper, more dangerous reason? A reason that had nothing to do with business and all to do with pleasure?

With Jace.

'Two weeks,' Jace told her, his tone turning brisk and reasonable. 'Not that long, but long enough to plan a small family party. And the weather will be fabulous. I'm sure you could use a break.'

Eleanor nodded jerkily and pulled a fresh pad of paper towards her. 'Where exactly is this party going to be?'

She saw triumph gleam in Jace's eyes, turning them silver, and his mouth curled upwards in a smile of victory. 'At my villa. I own a small island in the Cyclades.'

Her head jerked up. 'Your private *island*?'

'It's very small.'

'Sure it is,' Eleanor muttered, and uselessly scribbled 'island' on her notepad. She could hardly believe she was agreeing to this so readily, so easily, and yet she knew how little choice she really had. If Lily wanted Jace's business, and Jace wanted her to plan the party, she was left with very few choices.

But why does he want me to plan the party? And why do I want to go?

Eleanor forced the questions aside and turned to smile with sunny professionalism at Jace. 'Can you give me a few details?'

'I don't think that's necessary,' Jace replied easily. He rose from his chair, and after a second's hesitation Eleanor rose as well. 'I'm returning to Greece on Friday, and I'd like you to come with me. That should give you enough time to wrap up things here for a bit, and it will also leave enough time on the other end to plan the party.'

'Right,' she replied, her mind spinning. Friday. Greece. *Jace.*

'If you have any questions, don't hesitate to contact me,' Jace continued, matching her best, brisk and professional tone. 'Otherwise, I'll see you Friday morning. I'll send a car to pick you up at your apartment at nine o'clock?'

Eleanor nodded her acceptance, and, with an answering nod, Jace picked up his coat and was gone.

Eleanor sank back into her chair just as Lily poked her head round the door.

'Well?'

'I guess I'm going to Greece.'

'Good.' Lily nodded with smug satisfaction. 'I told him it wouldn't be a problem.' She paused, eyes narrowing. 'You did seem a little reluctant to work with Zervas before, Eleanor, which surprised me. I trust you've got over it?'

Eleanor nodded wearily, too overwhelmed to offer a defence. 'It's fine,' she said, and almost believed it.

The days between Monday and Friday flew by and crept along at the same time. Eleanor immersed herself in work, transferring clients, wrapping up details, and yet it still left her with far too much to think about.

She alternated between wondering if she was making the biggest—or perhaps the second biggest—mistake of her life, and convincing herself that this was nothing more than a business trip. It wasn't like the *biggest* mistake she'd made, which had been to fall in love with Jace Zervas in the first place.

She had no intention of doing that again.

Neither her mother nor Allie were convinced.

'I just don't see why you're going,' Allie said for the third time as they shared a Chinese takeaway in her apartment on Wednesday night. 'Or, more importantly, why he's taking you.' She lowered her chopsticks to regard Eleanor severely. 'Do you think he's interested in you again?'

'No,' Eleanor said firmly. 'It's nothing like that.'

'How can you be so sure? He kissed you, didn't he?'

'Yes, but…' She shook her head, realising she couldn't answer the question. She didn't know why Jace had kissed her. She had no idea why he wanted her to go to Greece. 'We're different people,' she stated, rather uselessly, for Allie just narrowed her eyes.

'Not that different. I just don't want this jerk to hurt you again, Eleanor. That's all.'

'He's not a jerk,' Eleanor whispered. She felt herself flush as Allie stared at her in disbelief. 'At least, not as much of one as I once thought,' she amended, and Allie snorted.

'Well, that's reassuring.'

'I suppose I'm realising that I never really knew him,' Eleanor explained slowly. 'I know we were supposedly infatuated with one another, but Jace never really talked about himself. I only realised that later—when I saw him again, and he said things…' She paused, helpless to explain. 'I never knew he had five sisters. Or he didn't get along with his father. Or—'

'Oh, help,' Allie cut her off, her eyes widening in horror. 'You're in love with him already, aren't you?'

'No!' The word was a yelp. Eleanor scrambled off the sofa and stood there, chest heaving in denial. 'No,' she said more calmly. 'Of course not. But I suppose seeing him again—for real—is important to me. Necessary. I need the closure.'

'But didn't you get that when he apologised?'

She took a breath and let it out slowly. 'Not really. I need to know that I can't fall in love with him again. That there really is nothing between us, and that we're just too different. Too changed.' She sighed, the truth coming to her as she spoke it. 'Then I'll finally be able to move on.' Why did that idea make her feel sad rather than hopeful? Was she *still* fooling herself?

'Maybe,' Allie allowed, her voice laden with doubt. 'What if you find out you can fall in love with him, Eleanor? What if you *do*?'

That was another question Eleanor couldn't answer, and didn't even dare ask.

Her mother was just as doubtful of the wisdom of Eleanor's decision, but they didn't discuss love or anything close to it. They never had.

'I wouldn't get within a hundred feet of that man,' Heather said darkly when Eleanor called her to tell her she'd be out of town, 'but if it really is just business…'

'Of course it is.' She sounded far more certain than she felt.

'I'm sure you know what you're doing,' Heather said briskly. 'And in any case, it's wonderful that Lily thinks so highly of you.'

Eleanor didn't want to argue that it was actually Jace—and his money—that Lily thought highly of. She was too tired and she had too much to do to argue the semantics. 'I'll talk to you when I get back,' she said, and after exchanging a few more pleasantries she hung up the phone.

Surveying the mess of her bedroom, the contents of her wardrobe spilled across her bed, she wondered just what to pack—and what to wear when she saw Jace tomorrow.

She settled on a pair of tailored tan trousers and a petal-pink cashmere sweater set that would have made her feel like a granny save for its hugging fit. Paired with a pair of kitten-heeled open-toed sandals, they made her feel professional and just a little bit sexy, which gave her confidence a needed boost as she waited in her building's lobby for the car Jace had sent.

The limo came promptly at nine. As the driver opened the door and Eleanor slid into the car's luxurious interior, Eleanor felt a flicker of disappointment that it was empty. Jace wasn't there.

'Mr Zervas will meet you at the airport,' the driver told her as he pulled away from the kerb. Eleanor did not reply, although she wondered what kept Jace in the city so that he couldn't share the journey to the airport with her. Not, she told herself sternly, that it mattered. Determined to focus on business—which was what this whole trip *was*—she reached for a file folder and began jotting down preliminary ideas for the party.

This activity kept her busy all the way to the airport, mainly because she wanted it to. She didn't want or need time to think, to question just why the *hell* she'd agreed to come to Greece with Jace, on the pretext of some party. She'd told her mother it was business; she'd told Allie more of the truth—that she needed closure. Yet the nerves exploding inside her, her clammy hands and growing panic all made Eleanor realise that there might be more to it than that. A lot more.

She clamped down on the train of thought before it could go anywhere, and as they arrived at the terminal she gratefully slid out of the car as the driver opened the door.

'Hello, Eleanor.'

Nearly yelping in surprise, Eleanor looked up to see Jace smiling at her. He was dressed, as she'd nearly always seen him dressed, for business, and he looked, as he always did, magnificent. Eleanor swallowed rather dryly.

'I thought you'd be late,' she said, trying not to sound flustered. 'Since you didn't come in the limo—'

'I didn't have time to drive to your apartment in Chelsea,'

Jace explained, 'so I grabbed a cab. I hope it didn't inconvenience you?'

How could a limo to her front door inconvenience her? Eleanor wondered. Or was Jace obliquely referring to the fact that she'd been disappointed? How did he *know*? 'No, of course not,' she said briskly, and Jace touched her elbow to guide her inside.

They bypassed the endless queues at the ticket counters for a discreet security checkpoint for private airline passengers.

'We're travelling on your private jet?' Eleanor practically squeaked when she realised this. 'To your private island?'

'I like my privacy.' Jace smiled, a flash of white. 'And I confess I find it more convenient. No need to book tickets or schedule flights, or be at the mercy of an airline and its asinine whims.'

The security guard waved them through, and easily, naturally, Jace put his arm around Eleanor's shoulders as he shepherded her towards the boarding area. 'Come.'

Moments later they were boarding a small, sleek, and utterly luxurious aeroplane. Eleanor took in the leather sofas and teakwood coffee tables with a sense of disbelief. She'd experienced her fair share of first class service as an event planner, yet in those cases she was arranging the luxury for her clients; *she* was the service. Here she was the one being served, and it felt amazing.

'Stretch out,' Jace said with a smile as she sat on one of the sofas. 'Enjoy yourself.'

Eleanor smiled a bit uncertainly. She was torn between enjoying herself—which this jet cried out for her to do—and keeping things businesslike. Professional. Safe.

'There will be plenty of time to plan the party later,' Jace told her with a little smile, making Eleanor wonder yet again how he knew her so well.

Because, she reminded herself as reached for the seat buckle, he didn't know her well. At all. He hadn't known her well enough ten years ago to trust her with the truth, and he certainly didn't know her now.

Moodily she stared out of the window as the plane began to taxi down the runway. Within minutes they were lifting off, leaving the dank grey March skies for the vast blue above.

One of Jace's staff came to offer drinks, and Eleanor accepted a glass of orange juice. She took a sip and set it down, too restless and uneasy to drink more. She fidgeted with the clasp on her seat belt, crossed and recrossed her legs, and stared blindly out at the endless blue sky.

'You can undo your seat belt now if you like,' Jace said, and Eleanor jerked her head around. He sat stretched out on the sofa opposite her.

'Oh, yes,' she mumbled, flicking again at the clasp. 'All right.' She undid the belt and stretched her legs out, feeling as if she were participating in a charade. She didn't feel remotely relaxed, and she doubted she was giving a good impression of it either.

'Why are you so tense, Eleanor?' Jace asked. 'You look drawn tighter than a bow.'

'I feel tense,' Eleanor admitted. 'And why shouldn't I be?' she added with a note of challenge. 'I don't even know why I'm here.'

Something dark—a shadow of pain, or perhaps even uncertainty—flickered in Jace's eyes. 'To plan my father's birthday party.'

'I know, but—' Eleanor let out a long, exasperated breath. 'I don't understand why you chose me to plan this party. It makes no sense. Someone local, with Greek contacts, would have been—'

'I didn't want someone local,' Jace cut across her quietly. 'Even if it made sense.'

His words sounded like a confession, and they created a sudden awareness in the air; it crackled like a current between them. 'Well, you should have,' Eleanor replied robustly in a desperate bid to ignore the current that practically pulled her out of her seat towards Jace.

Could she *ever* resist him?

'I didn't want someone local,' Jace repeated softly. 'I wanted you.'

Eleanor felt as if all the breath had been robbed from her body; her mind spun emptily and her chest hurt. She stared at Jace, pulled by the magnetic silver of his eyes, the faint smile curling his mouth—how she remembered that mouth, how it felt, how it tasted—

Don't. Don't remember, don't want—

Somehow she managed to draw a breath in, and the desperate dizziness receded. She reached for her orange juice and took a much-needed sip. 'Don't, Jace.'

'And,' Jace continued, leaning forward, 'you want me.'

'What?' The word was a yelp, a squeal, and it didn't hold the disdain Eleanor wanted it to, nor even the outrage. She sounded like a kicked puppy. She drew herself up, replacing her juice on the table with a decisive clink. 'Don't do this, Jace.'

'I didn't want to,' Jace replied. His voice was low even though his smile remained wry, light. 'Why do you think you didn't hear from me for three months? I've been trying to forget you, Eleanor, and the damnable truth is I can't.'

He almost sounded annoyed, and that made Eleanor smile faintly. She knew just how he felt. Then reality came crashing in. 'Is that why you hired me, Jace? To—to—have some kind of—' She sputtered uselessly, unable to say the word. *Affair.*

Meaningless. Sordid.

What else could he possibly want?

'I'm talking about more than just physical attraction,' Jace said, his voice soft and yet steely, and Eleanor stiffened.

What could he possibly mean? And why did his words terrify her so much? She couldn't untangle the sudden fierce emotion within her: surprise, alarm, fear, *hope*.

'What do you mean?' she asked. She tried to sound

dismissive but came off as demanding instead. She *wanted* to know, yet she was still afraid to hear his answer.

Jace didn't reply for a long moment. He looked pensive, guarded, as if he were hiding his heart as much as she was. 'I'm not sure.'

Eleanor sank back against the soft leather cushions. 'Okay…'

'I don't know what can be between us,' Jace continued. His tone was matter-of-fact, almost flat, yet his words raced right to Eleanor's nerve endings and made her whole self tingle with both longing and fear. 'All I know is I haven't been able to put you from my mind these last three months.' He turned back to her, his expression hard and determined. 'I said goodbye to you in New York, Eleanor, and I meant it. I wanted to walk away. God knows it's easier.'

Eleanor couldn't speak. Her throat was too tight, so she just nodded—jerkily—instead. It *was* easier. Or at least it was supposed to be.

'But it hasn't been easier,' Jace continued, his voice roughening with emotion. 'It's been hell. And so I decided to invite you to Greece—and forget the party, frankly—because I want to figure out what this is between us, and the only way I know of doing that is seeing you. Being with you. Knowing you, this new you, and you knowing me. And whatever *this* is, maybe it will go somewhere, and maybe it won't.' He let out a short, sharp laugh that ended on a ragged sigh. 'That's quite an appealing proposition, isn't it?' He shook his head and glanced away, rubbing his jaw with one hand. 'I must be crazy.'

Eleanor blinked and swallowed, trying to ease the tightness in her throat. She'd expected Jace to offer her some kind of smooth suggestion of seduction; if she was honest, yes, she'd expected it from the beginning, no matter what she'd managed to convince herself about this trip being business.

But this? This was real. Honesty. Vulnerability. It sent her spinning into a void of unknowing, uncertainty, because she couldn't scoff or sneer or pretend. Jace had been honest, and he deserved an honest answer. 'No,' she finally managed, her voice scratchy, 'you're not.' Jace turned to look at her sharply, and Eleanor smiled weakly. 'Crazy, that is.'

A corner of his mouth quirked up, although his gaze remained intently, intensely fastened on hers, filled with a wary hope she both felt and understood. 'I'm not?'

She shook her head. She didn't trust herself to say anything; she didn't even know what she would say, or what she felt. Like Jace, she knew there was still something between them. She just didn't know what it was. A remnant of their youthful infatuation? Or something new? And if it was something new, it was far too tender and fragile to test it, to trust it.

She had no idea what to do, and the thought of spending two weeks in Jace's company—with him—frightened and exhilarated her more than anything ever had before. She'd been nervous before; now she was terrified.

Thankfully Jace must have sensed this, or maybe he was feeling it himself, for he leaned forward to touch her hand—lightly, so lightly—and, smiling, said, 'It's a long flight, and you look exhausted. You should get some rest.'

Eleanor nodded, grateful for the escape sleep would provide…if only she could will it to come.

Jace watched Eleanor out of the corner of his eye as she shifted and fidgeted on the sofa, trying to get comfortable. Her eyes were closed, clenched shut really, and she didn't look remotely relaxed.

Yet why should she be? He certainly wasn't. Jace stared down at the papers he'd spread out on his table tray, notes on the latest business meeting regarding an acquisition of a plastics company in Germany. Important information, yet he couldn't process a single detail. His mind was spinning from what he'd just told Eleanor…hell, what he'd just told himself. He'd never intended to say any of that. He'd never meant even to think it.

He still didn't know what it meant, what it could mean

for the next few weeks, or even longer than that—who knew how long? What was he thinking? Wanting? He'd known he wanted—needed, even—to see Eleanor again, to get her out of his system, or maybe back into it… He didn't know which, didn't know which he even wanted. He felt as if the course he'd set for himself, the life he'd planned on, had been shipwrecked and he were left tossed on a sea of new possibilities…possibilities that were bewildering and strange and perhaps unwelcome. Perhaps exciting. He didn't know what he wanted any more, what shape he hoped his life would take.

Annoyed with himself, Jace let out a frustrated breath and turned determinedly back to his papers. Enough wondering. Enough thinking. Eleanor was here with him, and he would be satisfied with that for now.

CHAPTER EIGHT

SHE must have dozed, for when Eleanor woke up, blinking groggily, she could tell some time had passed. How much she had no idea, but Jace was no longer sitting next to her, and her hair, when she patted it experimentally, was sticking up in several different directions.

Great. So much for her poised, polished, *professional* appearance. Yet hadn't that been a charade anyway?

I want to figure out what this is between us, and the only way I know of doing that is seeing you. Being with you.

Jace's words echoed through Eleanor's mind, still surprising her with their honesty. Her reaction, fizzing with excitement and uncertainty, surprised her too. She'd been so careful to be professional with Jace, and her ever-captive heart had betrayed her. She still wanted him. Maybe she even loved him. Yet how could you love someone you didn't even know, weren't sure you ever really knew? And if she didn't love him, then this whole thing was nothing but immature infatuation, and she needed to get it out of her system. Return to New York a freed woman. Maybe that was what Jace wanted as well. Freedom, not love.

'You're awake.'

Eleanor turned around in her seat to see Jace standing in the aisle. He'd exchanged his business suit for a casual polo shirt and khakis, and he looked wonderful. Relaxed and confident and approachable, like the old Jace. Not the harsh, hardened, businessman she'd already become accustomed to.

'Sorry to conk out like that. How long did I sleep?'

'Nearly four hours. We'll be there in another couple of hours. Do you want something to eat?'

In answer Eleanor's stomach rumbled audibly, and Jace grinned. 'I remember how loudly your stomach growls when you're hungry. I always knew it was feeding time.'

'I am hungry,' Eleanor admitted. It still made her feel uneasy—vulnerable—for Jace to recall those sweet, forbidden memories. Little things, silly things, and yet so achingly precious.

Jace raised a hand, and within seconds a staff member arrived with a tray of food. Eleanor took in the fresh fruit, the plates of salad and sandwiches, and realised she wasn't just hungry, she was starving.

'Dig in,' Jace said, and she did.

'So where exactly are we going?' Eleanor asked after she'd finished most of her sandwich and salad. She toyed with a bit of pineapple on her plate, shredding the succulent fruit with the tines of her fork.

'My island. It's near Naxos. Like I said, very small.'

Eleanor looked up, her eyes narrowing speculatively. 'How small?'

Jace waved a hand in dismissal. 'A couple of kilometers, no more.'

'And there's nothing on it but your villa?'

'A few staff houses, an airstrip.'

'Really.' She let out a reluctant laugh. 'I always knew you were rich, but I didn't know you were *Fantasy-Island*-type rich.'

Jace arched his eyebrows. 'What does that mean exactly?'

'Private jet, private island.' Eleanor shrugged. 'It's like a soap opera.'

'They are conveniences as well as luxuries. And I have worked hard to earn them, I must admit.'

'You have?' Why did this surprise her? She supposed it was because after Jace had left, she'd painted him in her mind as the spoiled son of a shipping magnate. It was easier to accept his abandonment that way. Over the years she'd embroidered that image, yet now she realised—of course—that might not be who Jace was—or ever had been—at all.

She really didn't know him.

She popped the piece of pineapple in her mouth. 'So what did you do to earn it?'

'Investments. Financial management.'

'I thought your father was in shipping.'

'He is. But I did not go into my father's business.' A new, steely note had entered Jace's voice although his posture and expression were both still easy and relaxed. 'He wanted a dynasty, and neither of us believed that to be a possibility.'

Eleanor straightened in her seat. She cleared her throat, wanting to ask the question that remained unspoken between them yet knowing there was so much more to Jace's alleged infertility than the condition itself; years of heartache and family strife seemed to accompany it. 'Did you…get tested again?' she finally asked. Jace's expression didn't change. 'For fertility?'

'Yes.' He gave a little shrug, as though the matter was of no consequence. Perhaps it wasn't. 'I have limited fertility, the doctor says.'

Eleanor's heart twisted, a little wrench she should have long become used to when the topic turned to children. 'That's pretty good, isn't it?' It was possibility, hope. More than she would ever have. Limited was better than nothing.

Jace shrugged again. 'Whether or not I can have children has not been a pressing issue for me as of late.' The news should have reassured her, especially considering her own situation, yet somehow it just made her sad. So much lost. So much gone…for both of them.

Jace gave her the ghost of a smile, no more than a shadow passing across his face. 'Apparently, after childhood mumps, limited fertility can return in later years.' He shook his head and laughed softly, although the sound held little humour. 'Amazing, a simple Internet search could have saved us both so much heartache.'

'I don't know about that,' Eleanor said, and Jace stilled, his expression becoming alert and a little wary.

'What do you mean, Eleanor?'

She shrugged. 'Even if you knew the baby was yours, Jace, would you have stayed?' The question seemed to drop into the stillness, tautening the very air between them.

Jace tensed, and Eleanor saw in the steely silver glint in his eyes, the thinning of his mouth, that he was angry. She'd made him angry with her question. 'Of course I would have. I would never walk away from my own child.'

She didn't want to have this fight. She didn't want to feel this hurt. Shrugging again, Eleanor turned to look out of the window, sunlight shimmering on the faint wisps of cloud. 'You didn't trust me enough to give me a chance to trust you,' she said quietly. 'No matter what might be between us now, Jace, there will always be that.'

'Then you can't forgive?'

'I'm not saying that. I'm just saying that we've never had a chance to trust each other.' She turned back to look at him directly, compelled to honesty even though she'd wanted to avoid this conversation. 'It's not something that ever comes easily, and it certainly won't now, with our history.' *Not,* she added silently, *when I'm scared to trust you. To love you.*

Jace was silent for a long moment, and Eleanor waited and watched. It was only when he spoke again that she realised she'd been holding her breath. 'Then I suppose we'll just have to see what happens,' he finally said, a faint smile curving his lips even though his eyes looked shadowed and sad. 'And what we allow to happen.'

They steered clear of such intense topics for the rest of the flight, chatting about the weather and films and other innocuous things, until Jace excused himself to finish his work before they landed on Naxos to transfer to a smaller plane that would take them on the short flight to his island.

Eleanor didn't bother to pretend to work; her nerves were leaping and jumping inside her too much to make sense of anything. She felt an unsettling mix of anticipation and alarm. The sun had set and the sky was a deep and endless black, the pinpoints of a million stars reflected in the sea below. As the island came into view, Eleanor saw the lights of Naxos's main village shimmer along the harbour.

The plane taxied to a stop and Eleanor reached for her things. Jace shepherded her out of the plane, and she barely had a chance to view the huddled whitewashed buildings of Naxos in the distance as she walked across the tarmac to a much smaller plane.

The flight to Jace's island took all of ten minutes, and when the plane landed there were no friendly village lights to welcome them. The island was dark, lost on a sea of night, and despite the balmy air Eleanor couldn't quite keep from shivering.

She tilted her head up to take in the endless sky, spangled with stars. 'I don't think I've ever seen so many stars.'

'I don't think you can see a single star in New York,' Jace agreed. 'Come. My staff will see to our bags.'

Eleanor followed him into an open-topped Jeep. She was conscious of so many things: the emptiness all around them of sea and sky, the deep darkness of the night, and the fact that, despite the discreet staff moving their luggage into another waiting Jeep, she felt as if they were the only two people left on earth.

Jace started the Jeep, flicking on the headlights, which barely pierced the darkness, unrelieved by the flicker of a single street lamp or house light. They were alone. On an island. In the middle of the sea.

Eleanor swallowed and glanced sideways at Jace. As she did she became conscious of yet another thing: how different he was here, in his casual clothes, navigating the rocky, rutted road that skirted the sea as it wound round an outcropping of rock. Here he wasn't the college student or the businessman; he was someone else entirely.

She wondered just who that was.

'It's after eleven o'clock at night,' Jace told her, 'but it's still early in East Coast time. Would you like something to eat?'

'Maybe,' Eleanor allowed. She felt tired and yet inexorably, impossibly alive, thrilled and alarmed and wary of all these new sights, sounds, and changes. 'Something small would be nice,' she decided, and Jace flashed her a quick smile.

'I'll have my cook prepare something. You can freshen up and change if you like. The luggage is right behind us.'

Jace drove the Jeep around another curve and the villa came into view: a huge, sprawling whitewashed structure, every window and doorframe spilling a riot of bougainvillea, lights glimmering from inside. Jace killed the engine on the Jeep and turned to Eleanor.

'Welcome.'

A smiling, red-cheeked woman with her hair caught up in a headscarf met them on the doorstep.

She spoke rapidly in Greek, and Jace nodded and smiled his approval. Then, in halting English, she spoke to Eleanor. 'Welcome, Miss Langley. We are happy to see you here.'

'Thank you,' Eleanor murmured. Jace touched her shoulder.

'This is Agathe. She takes care of just about everything for me.' He smiled again at Agathe and then Eleanor followed her upstairs.

Agathe led her to a spacious suite of rooms overlooking the gardens at the back of the villa, bathed in moonlight; Eleanor could only make out the twisted trunks of olive trees and the glint of the sea at their edge.

Her luggage arrived moments later, and she took the opportunity to change her clothes and wash her face. Even though it was now nearing midnight, she felt energised and awake and alive.

Agathe had gone to see to their dinner preparations, and, dressed in a pair of cotton capris and a loose, flowing top in pale green, Eleanor stepped out to explore the villa…and to find Jace.

The air was dry and smelled faintly of lavender and thyme; through the open windows Eleanor could hear the gentle shooshing of the waves on the sand. She walked down the tiled hallway to the front stairs, her hand skimming the wrought-iron bannister. The foyer below was empty, and once downstairs she peeked into a large, comfortable-looking living room and a dining room with a table that looked to seat at least twenty. Both were dark and empty.

She wandered towards the back of the house, drawn by the light spilling from an open doorway and the tempting aroma of lemon and garlic.

She stepped into the kitchen to see Agathe busy at the stove, and, to her surprise, Jace setting the table in the alcove that overlooked the water. He'd changed as well, and showered if the damp hair curling at his nape were anything to go by. Eleanor swallowed. He looked wonderful.

Jace glanced up as she stood in the doorway, and smiled easily. 'Come in! Agathe has made a feast, as always.'

Agathe protested even as she placed dish upon dish on the table. Eleanor took in the Greek salad bursting with plump tomatoes and cucumber, a thick wedge of feta cheese resting on top, and the freshly grilled souvlaki, still on its skewer. There was a lentil soup garnished with olives and crusty bread, and several traditional Greek dips to accompany it.

'I can never eat all this,' Eleanor produced, laughing a little.

'You must try,' Jace replied as he pulled out her chair. 'After all, food is love.'

Love. Eleanor swallowed again. That was a word they'd never talked about, not ten years ago and certainly not now. Oh, she'd thought it plenty of times; she'd certainly believed it before Jace had walked away. Yet now just the idea of love—the mere mention of it—made her palms slick and nerves flutter from her belly to her throat.

'Thank you for this, Agathe.'

Agathe made more protesting noises before discreetly disappearing into another room. A candle flickered on the table between them, and the room was silent save for the sound of the sea coming from the open window.

'This is lovely,' Eleanor said. 'Thank you.'

Jace gave a little shrug. 'I'm afraid I'm spoiled by Agathe. She was my childhood nurse growing up, and I employed her here when she had no more charges at my family home.'

'She loves you very much.' The words popped out inadvertently, even though Eleanor didn't want to mention that dreaded L-word. Jace just smiled and spooned some tzatziki onto her plate.

'She is a good woman.'

Eleanor took a spoonful of the hearty bean soup; it was delicious. 'So do you live here most of the year?'

'When I can. I have a flat in Athens for business, but this is really my home. Or at least my escape. I've had to travel so much for work, I don't know if I could call any place my home.'

'Those corporate takeovers,' Eleanor murmured. She took another sip of soup. 'What's the real story behind you taking over Atrikides Holdings?'

Jace looked up, surprised. 'The real story?'

'I don't think it was the heartless takeover you made it out to be.'

'I try not to have any takeover be heartless.'

Eleanor raised her eyebrows. 'I had no idea you were so sensitive.'

Jace only looked amused. 'Sensitive? No. It's simply good business. Unhappy workers are never very productive.' He gave her the glimmer of a smile. 'I don't like to lose money.'

'Ah.' She reached for a piece of bread. 'And Atrikides?'

Jace shrugged. 'It was a favour to Leandro. His son was embezzling from him and he didn't have the strength to deal with it himself. He's an old man, and he doesn't have much longer to live.'

'So it was a mercy mission.'

Jace just shrugged again, and Eleanor glanced down at her plate. 'There's so much I don't know about you.'

A tiny, telling hesitation. 'Then ask.'

She didn't know what questions to ask. Where to begin. She didn't even know enough for that. 'Were you always interested in finance?' she finally asked. 'Starting your own company?'

'Yes,' Jace answered, then added, 'but it became more important to me.'

'When?'

He paused. 'Ten years ago.'

Eleanor nodded slowly in acceptance. Ten years ago. Of course. The same time her work had become more important to her; it had filled the empty spaces in her heart, her womb. Jace, in his own way, had suffered a similar loss.

'Well,' Jace said when she didn't reply, 'if you won't ask questions, I will. What made you decide to become an event planner?'

'I needed to do something, and my mother suggested the internship. Premier Planning was her company before she retired.'

'So you're the boss's daughter?'

Eleanor shrugged. 'She certainly didn't give me any hand-outs. I had to apply for the internship like anyone else, and work my way up.'

'And what about your degree in restaurant management?'

Eleanor gave him a small smile even though his question—his ignorance—hurt. 'I never finished my degree.'

'You didn't? Why not?'

She shook her head, exasperated now. Jet lag must have caught up with her, for she suddenly felt unbearably weary. 'I was pregnant, and I intended to keep the baby. I dropped out.'

Jace looked startled, a streak of something like pain flashing in his eyes, and Eleanor knew he was realising how much he didn't know. Didn't understand. Just as she felt with him. They really did need to begin all over again—if they could.

'But after?' he persisted after a moment. 'Couldn't you have gone back?'

'I didn't want to,' Eleanor said flatly. 'Everything had changed.' She didn't want to talk about it with Jace, even though at least part of her acknowledged they would have to talk about it some time…if they wanted to have any hope of—anything—in the future. 'My turn for questions,' she said. 'What's your favourite colour?'

Jace looked startled again, but then his face relaxed in an easy smile and Eleanor knew he was as glad as she was for a safer topic of conversation. 'Purple.'

'No way.'

He arched an eyebrow. 'What? Not manly enough?'

Eleanor let out a reluctant laugh. 'There's no way purple is your favourite colour. I may not know you that well, but I know that.'

He sighed in mock defeat. 'All right, you win. It's blue.'

'Light blue or dark blue?'

'Dark. And you?'

'Orange.'

'Really?'

Eleanor smiled. 'Yes, but I picked it as my favourite colour in first grade because no one else liked it. I guess I wanted to be different.'

'You always were stubborn.'

'Determined, I call it.' Sometimes it had been the only thing that had kept her going. Another wave of fatigue crashed over her and she pushed her plate away. 'This was delicious, but I think the flight is finally catching up with me. I'm about to fall asleep in my chair.'

'Then we'd better get you to bed.'

His words, given with such lazy amusement, made awareness race through Eleanor's veins so she suddenly felt rather unbearably awake. She stood up awkwardly. 'Thank you for the meal—'

'Let me show you to your room.'

'I remember—'

'I'm a gentleman.'

Wordlessly Eleanor let him lead her from the kitchen. Her heart had begun thudding hard against her chest, and she wondered what might happen. What she wanted to happen.

Upstairs the hallway was dark, lit only by a wash of moonlight from the windows at its end. Jace led her to her door and she placed her hand on its knob, turning around so her back was pressed against the wood. 'Thank you...' The word ended in a whisper of breath for Jace was close. Very close. And she had a feeling he was going to kiss her.

She wanted him to kiss her.

He smiled at her and brushed a strand of hair away from her face, tucking it behind her ear so his thumb skimmed her cheek. Eleanor closed her eyes. The moment before his lips brushed hers seemed endless, agonising, because she wasn't sure he was even going to do it and she didn't want to open her eyes to find out.

Finally, *finally* his lips touched hers in a feather-light kiss that seemed to be more of a promise than a possession, because before Eleanor could part her lips or respond in any way—it was so sweet—he had stepped away.

Her eyes flew open and she stared at him. He gazed back at her with a rueful, almost sad smile. 'Goodnight, Eleanor.'

Before she could respond—or even think—he was already disappearing down the hallway, lost in the shadows.

Jace strode out of the villa, frustration and fury and even fear all warring within him. What had he done? And why had he done it?

He made his way down the track to the beach, awash in silver in the moonlight. A few metres away the waves crashed blackly onto the shore. Jace yanked his shirt over his head and kicked his trousers off and then, with one deep breath, he dived into the surf.

The water was cold—it was still early spring—and it made his head ache as he swam through the waves, breaking to the surface only when his lungs hurt and his head pounded.

He treaded water as he gazed up at the ink-black sky scattered with stars and wondered just why he'd brought Eleanor to Greece.

It had seemed like such a good idea when he'd spoken to Alecia. It had made sense when he'd flown to New York on the pretence of needing to visit Atrikides Holdings, which was managing just fine under Leandro's nephew. He'd justified it to himself because he'd needed to see her, because his body was hungry and his soul restless knowing she was there, knowing she'd never lied to him, thinking that maybe there could have been something between them all these years. Maybe there still could be.

Yet what he hadn't counted on was how risky it was. Eleanor wasn't interested in an emotionless affair. He'd *known* that, and yet he'd still brought her here as if they could have something else. Something more. As if he wanted that, which, God help him, maybe he did.

Even though he'd determined for ten years—and longer than that, *for ever*—never to lose his heart to anyone. Never to even have a heart to lose.

Jace cursed out loud, to the sky, the words lost in the rush of the waves. His body ached with fatigue and cold and, after another second of useless treading water—going nowhere—he headed back towards the shore.

Everything had changed when he'd kissed Eleanor—such a nothing little kiss, barely a brush of their lips. Yet in that fragile moment he'd realised just what he'd done by bringing Eleanor here. Not only had he opened himself up to possible pain and loss, but he'd exposed Eleanor to it as well. He could hurt her. Again.

Back on the beach Jace towelled himself off with his shirt and then sat on the cold, hard sand to dry off. He wasn't ready to go back into the villa, to a lonely bed just two doors from where Eleanor slept. Or maybe she wasn't sleeping. Maybe she was tossing restlessly just as he surely would, letting the memories wash over her like the surf over the sand.

The first time they'd kissed. He'd been determined to kiss her, and she'd been skittish and nervous, flitting around her apartment, plying him with cupcakes. He'd eaten them, laughing as he did so, because they'd both known what was better than any dessert. That first kiss had been so, so sweet; it had been innocence and longing entangled together.

The first time they'd made love, one Saturday afternoon, the room mellow with sunlight. He'd traced circles on her skin with his fingers and lips and she'd laughed and told him she was ticklish.

Ticklish! He'd been a little offended, because he'd been so breathless and aching with desire, and he'd set upon a course of making her want him as much as he wanted her.

He'd succeeded admirably.

But it hadn't been just sex. She'd opened up such a life to him, a sweet, simple life, and he'd let himself fall, had willingly entered into the dream she shared of a bakery and bookshop, let it all wash over him and pull him into a fantasy world that he'd never thought to inhabit because it was all so far from his life, from his father. With Eleanor he hadn't been a useless failure. He hadn't had his shortcomings tossed back at him again and again.

With Eleanor he'd just been himself. And yet he'd still run. Jace shook his head, the memories both hurting and humiliating him.

Even if you knew the baby was yours, Jace, would you have stayed?

The question, and the fact that Eleanor could ask it, damned him. And even now Jace was shamed by her lack of trust in him. Yet why should she trust him? He hadn't proved himself or his trustworthiness in any way. He'd only failed.

And he was afraid of failing again—failing Eleanor,

failing himself—by opening this Pandora's box of possibility between them.

Staying away would have been easier. Safer. He just wished he'd had the strength to do it.

Suppressing a shiver as a chilly wind blew off the water, Jace slung his damp shirt around his neck and headed back to the villa, now no more than a darkened hulk under the sky. Inside all was quiet, the only sound the whisper of the waves. Jace peeled off his damp clothes and fell into bed naked, clenching his eyes shut as if he could keep the doubts from assailing him, the memories from claiming him.

Yet as he finally drifted off to sleep he could see Eleanor as she once was, relaxed and laughing as she held out a chocolate cupcake, and he heard her laughter as she tempted him to taste it.

He woke up craving chocolate. Craving Eleanor.

CHAPTER NINE

ELEANOR woke up to the distant, mournful clanging of bells. She scrambled from her bed and peeked out the window; the sun was already high in the sky, glinting off the water, and on a rocky hill in the distance she saw the source of the sound: goats. The bells around their necks clanged and clanked as a boy shepherded them out of sight.

She quickly showered and dressed, slipping into a pair of tailored black trousers and a crisp white button-down shirt. Work clothes. Armour. After Jace's barely there kiss last night, she needed it. She felt entirely too fragile, too fearful.

Further armed with a pad of paper and the notes she'd taken earlier, she came downstairs to the kitchen, where Agathe was setting out breakfast.

'Dinner last night was delicious,' Eleanor said, wishing she spoke Greek. Agathe smiled widely, clearly understanding enough.

She waved towards the table. 'Eat. Eat.'

Eleanor sat down and, still smiling, Agathe poured her a cup of thick Greek coffee. Eleanor helped herself to yogurt, honey, and fresh slices of melon. 'Do you know where Jace is?' she asked hesitantly, and Agathe shrugged, spreading her hands. It took her a moment to finally find the word, but when she did, it caused double shafts of disappointment and relief to slice through Eleanor.

'Work. He work.'

'Ah. Right.' Nodding her thanks, Eleanor took a sip of the coffee. That was good, she decided. Jace was working, and so would she. That was why they were here, after all. To work.

Except yesterday, on the plane, Jace had told her to forget the party. The real reason she was here was because he wanted her to be. And *she* wanted to be, which was why she had agreed in the first place. God only knew what could happen, what they would allow to happen, as Jace had said yesterday.

Moodily Eleanor speared a slice of melon. If she were a less cautious person, she'd seize this opportunity with both hands and a lot more besides. She'd let herself enjoy Greece—enjoy *Jace*—and just see what happened. Such an easy thing to do. Just *see*.

Yet she wasn't that kind of person, although perhaps she once had been. Now she was careful and cautious and kept everything close, especially her emotions. Most definitely her heart. There was nothing easy about *just seeing* at all. It was impossibly difficult, incredibly dangerous, and she wasn't sure she could do it at all. She wasn't even sure she wanted to, despite the nameless longing that swelled up inside her, spilling out.

After breakfast, since Jace had not put in an appearance, Eleanor decided to explore the villa. She'd get a sense of what would work for the party, and present Jace with some kind of initial plan. She'd need to ask him about services too; Agathe certainly couldn't do all the cooking, and supplies would have to be either flown or ferried in.

Hugging her clipboard to her chest, Eleanor strolled through the villa's front rooms that she'd glimpsed last night. Both were spacious and comfortable, the scattered sofas and rugs giving a sense of casual elegance. They'd certainly suit for a party, but as she left them for the wraparound terrace, she decided the party should be held outside.

The air was dry and fragrant, the sun warm on her face,

the sea shimmering with its light. Terracotta pots of trailing bougainvillea and herbs lined the terrace and in the distance Eleanor could still hear the goats' bells clanging. She stood for a moment on the terrace, lifting her face to the sun, and let herself simply enjoy the day.

'There you are.'

Slowly Eleanor opened her eyes. She turned around to see Jace standing in the double doors that led to the kitchen.

'Do you have *goats* on this island?'

Surprised, he raised his eyebrows. 'As a matter of fact I do.'

'Why?'

'You don't like goats?'

Eleanor suppressed a smile. 'I don't really have an opinion of them, actually.'

'Well, I find them very calming,' Jace replied, straight-faced, 'as well as incredibly cute.'

She'd forgotten what a silly sense of humour he had, how much he'd made her laugh, helplessly, holding her sides. How *happy* he'd made her feel. Now a reluctant bubble burst through her lips and she shook her head, smiling.

'Seriously.'

'We have to be serious?' Jace's face fell comically. 'Very well. When I bought this island, it was inhabited by a single farmer. He'd lived here all his life, was ferrying his poor goats and their milk and cheese to Naxos. I let him stay and he supplies the villa more than adequately.'

'And when you aren't here?'

'He uses my motorboat. He had a leaky rowboat that looked likely to capsize in a breath of wind, and he'd put a goat in it. The poor animal was terrified.'

Eleanor shook her head, not sure if she should believe him. He looked utterly sincere, yet she saw laughter lurking in his eyes, glinting in their depths, and it made her smile again, from the heart. 'Why would he take his goat to Naxos? I thought you said he sold the milk and cheese.'

'The creature was sick.' Jace took her arm, his fingers warm on her skin. 'Terribly so. Really quite nasty. You don't want to get too close to a sick goat. They're bad-tempered creatures as it is. Now come. I have a surprise for you.'

As Jace led her from the terrace all thoughts of goats, sick or otherwise, fled from her mind. She struggled to keep her tone businesslike and brisk. 'Actually I wanted to talk about the party—'

Jace waved a hand in airy dismissal. 'Plenty of time for that. Now come into the kitchen—'

'Is Agathe—?'

'She went to Naxos right after breakfast for supplies.'

'Then what—?' Eleanor stopped in the doorway of the kitchen and stared at the pile of supplies laid out on the granite worktop. Muffin pans and parchment paper, cake tins and cookie cutters. Sacks of flour, sugar, at least three dozen eggs.

Everything needed for baking. A bakery.

Eleanor swallowed. 'You got this all for me?'

'I thought you'd have some time to do what you always wanted to do,' Jace said.

'Thank you,' she said after a moment. 'It's very thoughtful.'

'There are recipe books,' Jace continued, 'although I know you liked to make your own. I remember that coffee-bean cupcake—'

Eleanor smiled wryly. That, actually, had been one of her less successful attempts. She left Jace's side to move to the worktop, letting her fingers run over the gleaming, pristine surface of a never-used cast-iron pan.

'I got everything I thought you'd need.'

'Very thorough.' He must have spent several hundred dollars, Eleanor thought. Pennies to a millionaire like him, and yet...

'So I'll leave you to it, then?' Jace asked, clearly not expecting an answer. 'Enjoy yourself, Eleanor. Go to town.'

Town, Eleanor wondered ruefully as Jace left the kitchen. Where was that? And was she supposed to enjoy herself baking? She hadn't baked so much as a single cookie in ten years.

And that had been a *decision*. One she'd made with purposeful determination.

Sighing, she pulled a cookbook towards her and flipped through its glossy pages. It reminded her of the little leather notebook she'd kept to write her own creative concoctions in. It had been well loved, covered in splotches of batter and dollops of dough, filled with excited scribbles and dreams. She didn't even know where it was now.

As she perused the tantalising items detailed in the cookbook, each with its own coloured photo, she realised none of them appealed. Baking no longer appealed. The dream of opening her own bakery had died long ago, and she had no desire to resurrect it now. She had no desire to be the woman she once was: carefree, naive, *stupid*.

Eleanor pushed the cookbook away, and then, finding herself annoyed, angry and unable to articulate why, she left the kitchen with all of its ingredients and utensils and walked back outside.

The terrace was deserted and she took the stairs down to the path that led to the beach. She kicked off her sandals—the sexy little kitten heels were ridiculous beachwear—and walked towards the water. The sand was silky-soft under her feet, the salty breeze blowing her hair into tangles as she let the waves lap her feet, the water as warm and salty as tears.

She wasn't sure how long she stood there, her hair blowing around her face, the bottoms of her dryclean-only trousers getting wet and ruined, but she knew the exact moment that Jace came onto the beach.

She didn't have to turn to know he was there, to *feel* him. She also felt his confusion, his uncertainty, perhaps even his sorrow. Sighing, she sat down hard on the sand and drew her knees up to her chest.

'Eleanor?' Jace came closer, standing a few feet away. Eleanor could see his bare, sandy feet in her peripheral vision; he'd rolled his trousers up so his ankles were bare as well. 'Is everything—?'

'I didn't feel like baking,' she said rather flatly. 'To tell you the truth, I haven't felt like baking in—in a long time.'

Jace was silent. He sat down next to her, resting his forearms on his knees. 'For about ten years?' he guessed quietly and Eleanor let out a little laugh that sounded far too bitter.

'I told you I was a different person.'

Jace nodded slowly. 'Why did you stop baking?'

'I'm not sure,' Eleanor answered. She gazed out at the waves, glittering in the sunlight. 'I haven't really stopped to analyse it, but I suppose I wanted to separate myself from the person I was because—' she let out her breath slowly '—that person didn't work.'

Next to her she felt Jace stiffen. 'What do you mean?'

Eleanor shrugged. Every conversation kept leading to this, to what had happened between them, and all the things Jace still didn't know. She wasn't ready to talk about it. She didn't want to tell Jace just how desperate, how destroyed she'd truly been after his departure. She didn't want to feel so vulnerable. Couldn't.

'After—everything,' she began hesitantly, choosing her words with care, 'I decided to change myself. Be—someone new. It just felt like something I needed to do. And like I said, I didn't feel like baking.' Baking had reminded her of Jace. Even chocolate, supposedly a woman's dearest comfort, had reminded her of Jace. She didn't eat it even now. She turned to face him. 'I know you meant well, Jace, but—but doesn't this just show how different we are? How little we know each other any more, if we ever did?' Her voice had turned ragged, edged with desperation, and she realised she didn't know what she wanted him to say. Agree or disagree? Either would bring both disappointment and relief. Both had the capacity for heartache.

'Only if baking defined you,' Jace said slowly. 'Was it who you were, or simply something you enjoyed doing?'

Eleanor scooped up a handful of sand and let it trickle through her fingers. 'Both, in a way. And neither. I think the bakery idea was a reaction to the way I grew up. I wanted to create a place that was like home, or at least the home I'd always wanted.' She gave a little laugh. 'I think I was trying to be like the mother I'd always wanted, but I'm not sure that's really who I ever was.' She turned to look at him. 'You said I've become the person I never wanted to be, Jace, and perhaps that's true. But maybe that's the person I really *am*.'

She didn't add what she was really thinking: that that was a person Jace could never want or love. She understood why she was angry now, why she was afraid. Jace might have loved the woman she once was, but he didn't love her now. Everything he'd done was to try to turn her back into that young woman—girl—and Eleanor knew she could never be her again. She didn't even want to.

'I think you're overestimating how much you've changed,' Jace said carefully. Eleanor shook her head.

'Don't, Jace—'

'I'm not talking about opening a bakery or having a high-flying career,' Jace cut her off. 'Your job isn't who you are. I'm talking about something deeper. And I think I've come to know you enough to see that hasn't changed—not as much as you think. I don't want to change you, Eleanor. I want to know you.' Jace stood up before she could reply—she didn't even know what she would say—and held out his hand. 'Come on. I can see I made a mistake buying you all those ridiculous pans. Let's do something different.'

'Okay,' Eleanor said after a moment, and, accepting his hand, she came to her feet. She glanced down at her damp, sandy trousers with a grimace. 'Whatever it is, I should probably change—'

'Definitely.' Jace scooped up one of her sandals and dangled it by a finger. 'These may do in New York, or maybe even Mykonos, but not where we're going.'

To her surprise, Eleanor felt she was smiling. She'd been dreading that conversation, yet it hadn't been as hard as she'd thought. She knew there was still more to say, but now was not the time, and she felt relieved. 'Where are we going?'

'Hiking.' Jace pulled on her hand, a smile tugging the corner of his mouth. 'It's an adventure. You must have something suitable.'

'Maybe,' Eleanor allowed, and followed him back into the house.

Ten minutes later she'd exchanged her uniform—her armour—for more casual jeans, sneakers—she had no boots—and a plain tee shirt she'd intended only to wear to bed. She hadn't dressed like this in years; in New York she'd always had to look tailored and turned out, even when off duty. Her image was part of her profession.

Now she felt both a little self-conscious and refreshingly relaxed, the sun warm on her face, her hair curling in the heat. She had not blow-dried it that morning into her usual sleek, glossy bob.

'So where are we going?' she asked Jace as he struck out down the dirt track that led in the opposite direction they'd come the night before. 'Where *is* there to go on this island?'

'I thought I'd show you the sights,' Jace replied easily. 'As few of them as they are.'

They walked in companionable silence for a quarter of an hour, the only sound the rustle of wind in the olive trees that lined the track and the shoosh of the surf on the rocks below them. Then they rounded a curve and came face to face with a goat.

Eleanor skidded to a halt, an uneasy alarm creeping over her that was a step or two down from pure panic. Jace, who had kept walking, stopped when he realised she hadn't kept up. He glanced behind him, his eyebrows arching as he saw her frozen stance.

'Eleanor…you're not scared of a *goat*?'

'Not scared precisely,' she corrected him stiffly. 'I'm a city kid, Jace. Most animals I see are safely behind cages.'

'These goats are harmless,' Jace assured her. 'I promise.' As if to contradict him, the goat bleated loudly. Eleanor jumped. She'd never thought a bleat could sound so menacing. 'Just walk past her,' Jace assured her. 'She won't even care.'

'How do you know it's a she?'

'Her name is on the bell.' He pointed to the tarnished bell hanging around the goat's scruffy neck. 'See? Tisiphone.'

'Tisiphone? Isn't that one of the Furies?'

'Spiro likes Greek mythology,' Jace said quickly. He sounded earnest, but Eleanor could see he was trying not to smile. 'Honestly, it's no more than that.'

'And not the fact that these goats might be bad-tempered?' Eleanor countered. 'Like you told me this morning?'

'Only when on boats.'

Eleanor laughed, the sound rising from within her, freeing her somehow, loosening all those tightly held parts of herself. She wasn't *really* afraid. Well, maybe only a little. But with Jace standing just a few feet away, smiling, relaxed, his eyes warm and steady on her, she felt as if she could do anything. She could certainly walk past a goat.

Taking a deep breath, Eleanor marched rather quickly past the animal, her head held high. She let out her breath in a long shaky shudder as Jace put his arm around her shoulder.

'See? Not so bad.'

'Not so cute, either,' she muttered, and he gave out a shout of laughter, pulling her close to his side.

The contact, the intimacy, both physical and emotional, stole the breath from her lungs. She had missed this so much. This closeness, this connection. This was what being known was all about: letting another person see all the silly and stupid and sick parts of yourself, as well as all the wonderful and beautiful things. All of it, everything, out there, exposed, accepted. She craved it, and yet still it scared her.

'We need to climb now,' Jace told her, sparing her sneakers a single, dubious glance before he led her off the dirt road and straight into the scrubby hills dotted with lavender bushes and the twisted, gnarled trunks of olive trees. 'Careful. You can sprain your ankle on one of these loose rocks.'

Nodding, Eleanor picked her way carefully across the tumbled boulders. She stumbled once, and Jace was there in an instant, his hand holding hers with firm tenderness. Even when she'd righted herself he didn't let go.

They walked through the hills for another quarter of an hour before Jace stopped in what appeared to be nothing more than a rock-strewn meadow and nodded in approval. 'Here we are.'

'What—?'

'Look,' he said softly. 'Do you see?'

Eleanor looked around, taking in the scrubby bushes and twisted trees, the rocks lying in neat rows…and then she saw. Out of the wilderness there was order, the crumbling foundations of a house—many houses—hidden among the scrub.

'It was a village,' Jace said quietly. 'Two thousand years ago.' He walked over to a low wall and touched one of the ancient stones. 'I've done a little amateur archaeology, and found a few bits. Clay pots, a broken pipe. Fascinating stuff.'

Eleanor walked between two rows of walls, realising after a moment she was actually walking down a street. It was beautiful, eerie, and a little sad. 'What happened?' she asked as she stepped in the gap between two walls: a doorway. 'Why did it all fall to ruin?'

Jace shrugged. 'A flood, a famine, plague or pirates? Who knows? Something happened that forced them to flee—but I did a little research to find out where they all went.'

Eleanor turned around. 'They went somewhere?'

He nodded, smiling. 'Yes, there's an archaeological dig on Naxos that shows some of the same pieces of pottery and sculpture that were here. Historians think it's likely that they took a boat over there and started again.'

'Just like the goat.'

'Exactly.'

They lapsed into silence and Eleanor gazed at all the ruined houses, now no more than lines of stone in the dirt. She could make out an entire village now, a whole society, and she felt a strange pang of sorrow. 'And they never came back?' she asked, hearing a wistful note in her voice.

Jace glanced around at the ruins, bemused. 'So it would appear.'

'I suppose they learned you can never go back,' Eleanor said. Her words sounded heavy, too heavy, and she wondered what she was really talking about.

Jace glanced at her sharply, clearly aware of the double entendre. 'No, you can't,' he agreed. 'But you can always go forward. Like they did.' He reached for her hand, lacing his fingers through hers. Eleanor let him, let him lead her back down the hillside. 'And forward is better,' he continued lightly. 'You should see the ruins at Naxos. Now those are amazing.'

Eleanor laughed, glad the moment had been defused. She didn't want to feel sad or worried or afraid. She just wanted to enjoy being with Jace.

And she *was*. That was the wonderful thing, she thought as they walked back down the dusty road. Somehow Jace had managed to dispel her fears and her worries, and she felt carefree and relaxed as she let the wind blow her tangled hair away from her face, her hand still held in Jace's.

By the time they reached the villa, Eleanor was hot and sweaty, and when Jace suggested a swim she accepted with alacrity.

Yet as she slipped into the relatively modest one-piece she'd brought she found herself conscious of all the bare skin she was showing…all the bare skin *Jace* would be showing, and her temperature soared higher.

He was already at the beach when she arrived, a towel

wrapped firmly around her waist. Eleanor couldn't tear her gaze away from him; his chest gleamed bronze and he walked with a loose-limbed elegance, every muscle rippling with easy power. He looked wonderful, amazing, and her body kicked into gear, her heart thudding and a lazy warmth spiralling upwards inside her. He turned and smiled at her, his warm gaze sweeping over her with obvious appreciation. Eleanor's whole body tingled.

Jace stretched out his hand. 'Come on in. The water's fine this time of year.'

Despite the warmth of the sun, Eleanor thought the churning waves looked decidedly chilly. 'It's quite early to swim, isn't it?' she asked, chewing her lower lip. 'It's still only March.'

'End of March,' Jace replied and dived neatly into the water.

Emboldened, Eleanor followed suit. Seconds later she felt as if her entire body had been encased in ice. 'Aargh!' She came up gasping and choking on a mouthful of salt water. Finding her footing on the sandy bottom, she glared at Jace. 'It's freezing!'

'Bracing, we call it,' Jace replied with a grin. 'And didn't you grow up spending your summers on Long Island? You should be used to this!'

'We never swam in March,' Eleanor grumbled, but she was laughing inside, and she couldn't contain her grin as she struck out through the water to be near Jace.

They swam for nearly an hour, laughing and playing in the water, until Jace informed Eleanor that her lips were blue. Before she could form a protest, he'd scooped her up in his arms, holding her against his chest as he strode from the sea. Eleanor's laughter died in her throat as she pressed her cheek against Jace's bare, dripping chest—she just couldn't help herself—and let him take her into the villa.

He carried her all the way upstairs, to her bedroom door, and there he set her down, her body sliding sinuously against his before he steadied her on her feet. Their faces were inches apart and Eleanor didn't speak, couldn't speak. All she could do was wait, breathless, for Jace to kiss her.

He didn't. Smiling, he touched her cheek with his cold fingers and said, 'I'll see you at dinner. Seven o'clock. And don't wear another black business suit. I want it to be special.' Pressing one finger against her lips—which parted instinctively—he left.

Shivering, aching with desire, Eleanor sagged against her door. What did Jace mean by special? And why hadn't he kissed her again? It must have been glaringly obvious that she wanted him to, that she'd been waiting for him to.

Sighing, Eleanor turned inside to her bedroom. Dinner seemed ages away.

Jace strode from the villa, whistling. He felt good, relaxed, *happy*. It made him aware of how long it had been since he'd felt that way, how Eleanor made him feel that way. He'd come to Boston all those years ago looking for a new beginning, a new life away from his father and his disappointment. He'd thought he'd found it with Eleanor. And maybe he hadn't then—but maybe he could now.

This afternoon had surprised him with its simple pleasures. He'd loved being with Eleanor, loved seeing her relaxed and happy as he had been. And, he realised, he'd loved being with *this* Eleanor, the one who had grown and changed yet still had glimmers of the woman she'd once been, the one he'd known. The youthful naiveté might be gone, but it had been replaced with something better and deeper: strength, as well as courage. He admired Eleanor for both what she'd endured and achieved. And more than admired, Jace acknowledged, which made him think of a dusty trophy or distant celebrity

Yet what did he feel for Eleanor? What was he doing here? What were *they* doing?

The tuneless whistle died on his lips as he considered the question. He'd loved spending time with Eleanor, but did he love her? Was he taking her heart in his hands, only to be poised to break it?

To hurt her—destroy her, even? Again.

Or as he'd said before, could they go forward, which was so much better than going back, and build something new? Something amazing?

Jace closed his eyes. He hated that he was afraid. He wanted her so much—he'd nearly accepted her silent invitation back at her bedroom door—but he didn't want to hurt her. Yet hurt and love came hand in hand, because when someone trusted you—cared for you—you were bound, at some point, to let them down.

Or was *he* the one afraid of getting hurt?

Jace opened his eyes. He knew there were no answers. He wouldn't let his own questions—his own doubts—stop him from what was surely the sweetest time of his life. These days with Eleanor were precious, and he wouldn't waste them. He would treasure and savour them.

He hadn't kissed Eleanor this afternoon because he'd wanted to wait, he wanted to be sure she was ready in both her heart and her body.

As his own body made the insistent ache of its unsatisfied desire known Jace hoped Eleanor would be ready tonight.

He certainly was.

The sun was just starting to sink below the sea, causing its placid surface to shimmer with golden light, as Eleanor slipped on the cocktail dress she'd brought. She glanced at her reflection, lips pursed as she wondered if she was trying too hard.

The dress was sexy, probably the sexiest thing she owned. The stretchy material crossed in front, the plunging neckline accentuating the curve of her breasts. She wore a sparkly snowflake pendant she'd found at a market stall in Greenwich Village, and it nestled snugly between her breasts. The dress's skirt ended above her knees and swirled out as she walked, the silky material caressing her bare legs. She left her hair loose and her face free of make-up; the dress, she decided, was enough.

Slipping on a pair of high-heeled black sandals, she headed downstairs to meet Jace. From the top of the stairway she saw a spill of light coming from the living room, and her heart began to beat so fiercely she was sure Jace would be able to see it through the thin fabric of her dress.

Taking a deep breath, she entered the room. Jace turned as soon as he heard her, a smile lightening and softening his features. He wore a crisp white shirt and a pair of dark trousers, both exquisitely tailored and speaking of casual elegance. His admiring gaze swept her from head to toe, a grin tugging at the corner of his mouth.

'I thought I said no black.'

Eleanor pretended to pout. 'This is hardly a business suit.'

'No, indeed it is not.' Wicked humour glinted in his eyes and Eleanor's heart picked up its pace so it felt as if it were struggling right out of her throat. She felt so nervous, and yet so alive, so happy. It was scary, feeling this much. Feeling this happy.

'I thought we'd eat on the terrace. It's a warm night.'

'Sounds good.'

'May I get you a drink beforehand?' Jace gestured to the array of drinks displayed on an antique table.

'Um, no. Just wine with dinner.' She smiled, resisting the urge to wipe her palms down the sides of her dress. Her voice sounded strained, shaky, and, seeing that Jace noticed, she let out a little laugh. 'It's strange, but I feel nervous.'

He arched an eyebrow. 'Why?'

'I don't know,' Eleanor admitted. 'I suppose…because… this all feels so new. Like we're starting over.'

'We are.' His smile warmed her straight through, and she felt her body tingle with awareness and longing and something deeper…hope. Faith. Maybe it would be all right. Maybe this could work. Maybe they *could* start over. She smiled back.

Jace reached for her hand. 'Come. Let's go out to the terrace.'

She let him lead her just as she had that afternoon. Hazily Eleanor thought she'd probably like Jace to hold her hand for ever. She loved how easily his fingers laced through hers, how protected and cherished she felt from such a small and simple gesture.

Outside a candlelit table had been elegantly laid for two; Agathe was nowhere in sight. Jace pulled out her chair and laid the heavy damask napkin in her lap, then poured her a glass of wine, the rich red liquid glinting in the candlelight. After filling his own glass, he raised it, and Eleanor did likewise. '*Opa*,' he said, and Eleanor murmured it back before they both drank.

'So what does *opa* mean?' she asked once she'd set her wine glass back down.

'I don't know if there is a direct translation, but something close to cheers or—what is it you say in English?' He pursed his lips. 'Hooray.' Jace grinned. 'But if we were going to be truly traditional, we'd throw our plates on the ground.'

Eleanor widened her eyes in mock horror. 'And waste good food?' She speared a plump olive resting on top of her Greek salad. 'I don't think so.'

'My sentiments exactly.'

The meal passed quickly as Agathe slipped in and out with dish after delectable dish, and Jace kept her wine glass amply filled. Eleanor's nerves seemed to have evaporated in the warmth of his smile, the heat of his gaze. By dessert, rich, honey-soaked baklava, Eleanor felt entirely at ease and utterly relaxed.

She propped her chin on her hands and gazed at Jace speculatively, enjoying the way the candlelight glinted on his hair and caught the silvery depths of his eyes. He lounged back in his chair, a smile curving the mouth Eleanor had spent a good part of the evening gazing at, remembering how it felt on hers.

'What are you thinking?' Jace asked, and Eleanor gave a little shrug.

'Lots of things.'

'Such as?'

She wasn't quite relaxed enough to admit the true direction of her thoughts. 'That I like olives. I never did as a child.'

'They're an acquired taste. And?'

'And what?' She was teasing, flirting, and loving it. She hadn't acted this way for so long, hadn't been this relaxed since—for ever.

'And what other things are you thinking?' Jace asked softly.

'What you're thinking,' Eleanor returned, and Jace smiled.

'I'm thinking how lovely you look tonight,' he said. 'And how jealous I am of that necklace.'

Eleanor touched the snowflake pendant that nestled between her breasts and blushed.

'So tell me what you've been doing these last ten years besides work,' Jace said, dispelling the sudden tautening moment, and, a little disappointed, Eleanor picked up her fork.

'Not much, really,' she said, spearing her last bite of baklava. 'Work has been my life, more or less.'

'And are you happy like that?' Jace asked quietly.

'Are you?' Eleanor returned. 'Because, based on your private jet and island and who knows what else, I'm guessing that work has pretty much been your life too.'

She heard the challenge in her voice, felt it in her soul, and yet it rushed out of her when Jace replied softly, 'No. I don't think I am.'

'Oh.' Eleanor sat back in her chair. 'Well, neither am I, I suppose,' she admitted. It was the first time she'd ever said it aloud. It was the first time she'd even let herself *think* it.

'So what would you like to do, if you could do anything?' Jace asked as he took a sip of wine. 'Not open a bakery, I guess.'

'Well...' Eleanor glanced down at her plate, suddenly shy. She hadn't expected Jace to ask so many questions; she hadn't expected to tell him so much. Yet somehow, strangely, it was easy. 'I had this dream—a daydream, really—about opening a non-profit foundation. I do love planning parties, and I've—dreamed—about doing it for charity. For sick kids or poor kids who can't afford or arrange a party of their own.' She looked up, smiling wryly. 'I don't know if it's even possible, but I like the thought of providing something fun—frivolous, even—for children who can never experience that.' And then, even though it had been easy to tell him, Eleanor suddenly found her throat becoming tight and her vision blurred. She looked back down at her plate and swallowed hard. She couldn't tell Jace more than that, or just why that dream was so precious. She'd told him enough already.

She felt the warmth of Jace's hand as he covered her own. 'That sounds like a very worthwhile dream.'

'Thanks.' She cleared her throat and risked looking up. 'What about you? What would you like to do with your life, if you could do anything?'

Jace sat back in his chair; Eleanor missed the warmth and security of his touch. 'I don't know. I've been so focused on building my business—making money—that I've never thought of doing anything else.'

'And it's not as if money is a concern,' Eleanor said lightly. 'You could do anything you wanted to, Jace.'

His lips twitched and from the warm gleam in his eyes Eleanor was suddenly quite sure he wasn't thinking about business. And neither was she. 'Mmm. That's an intriguing thought.'

'It is, isn't it?' she agreed shakily. Jace's gaze didn't leave hers as he drew his napkin from his lap and tossed it on the table. 'I think we're done with dinner.'

'Yes...' Eleanor whispered. Waiting.

Slowly, silently, Jace took her hand and drew her up from the table. Still without speaking he led her back into the villa, now washed in moonlight. Eleanor's heart hammered and her throat turned dry but still she followed him without a protest. Without a word.

When she saw he was leading her to his bedroom—not hers—she gave an involuntary little gasp, no more than a breath of sound, but Jace turned around to look at her, his face a question. 'Eleanor?' he asked, and she simply nodded.

Yes.

CHAPTER TEN

JACE opened the door. His bedroom was cloaked in darkness, but in the glimmer of moonlight Eleanor made out the huge shape of a king-sized bed, the sheen of a satin duvet. Jace turned to face her, and her breath caught. He looked so intent, so intense, so…reverent. And so beautiful.

She realised then just how much she wanted this. Had been waiting for this. Even so, a flutter of fear forced her to admit, 'It's been a long time…for me.'

'Me too, actually,' Jace replied, and Eleanor heard the smile in his voice.

'Really?' She couldn't keep the disbelief from her own voice. Somehow she'd imagined that Jace had been enjoying countless easy and meaningless love affairs in the last ten years while she'd had only a handful of failed relationships.

'Really,' he confirmed, one eyebrow lifting in irony. 'And just why would you think otherwise?'

She shrugged, unable to admit that when he'd left her she'd painted him as a womaniser, a user. It had made her own loss more bearable. She was still holding onto what she'd once believed—assumed—about him, rather than what she really knew. What she was beginning to believe.

'I don't know,' she admitted softly. 'Maybe it's because I can't imagine any woman resisting you.'

'I only care about one woman,' Jace replied, his voice as soft as hers, 'and she's been quite accomplished at resisting me.' His voice caught, and Eleanor heard the vulnerability. 'I only hope she doesn't resist me now.'

'She won't,' she whispered, and Jace drew her to him, cupping her face in his hands as he kissed her with a sweetness that left Eleanor fulfilled and aching at the same time.

He pulled away, and she saw the glimmer of his smile, the flash of his teeth in the darkness, as he led her to the bed. Nerves fluttered through her once more. She was ten years older and probably ten pounds heavier than the last time they'd been together. She might look killer in a business suit, but naked? She had *stretch marks*.

And Jace looked just amazing. That belief was confirmed as he shrugged out of his shirt, his chest gleaming in the moonlight. He reached for the zip of her dress, and in one simple, sensual tug he pulled it all the way down to her waist. Eleanor shrugged, instinctively, and the dress slithered to the floor. She caught her breath, waiting as Jace gazed at her; she wore only her bra and underwear.

'You are beautiful,' he whispered. 'And I've waited a long time for this.'

'So have I,' Eleanor whispered back, a laugh lurking in her voice. Smiling, Jace slipped her bra straps from her shoulders. Within seconds she was naked, struggling between self-consciousness and a confidence she wasn't sure she really felt. Yet when Jace reached out one hand and with his fingertips gently traced a path down her body from her collarbone to her hip she felt as if he were memorising the map of her body, as if he were treasuring it. And she relaxed.

Even better, Jace shrugged out of the rest of his own clothes so he stood there, magnificent and naked, before leading her to the bed. The satin duvet was slippery on her skin until Jace peeled it back, stretching out beside her so their bodies just barely touched. The only sound was their breathing. Carefully, cautiously, Eleanor laid a hand on Jace's chest. His skin was warm. God help her, she was so nervous. So afraid. And yet still so happy. It was a strange, unsettling mix of emotions.

'Don't be afraid,' Jace whispered. He brushed a strand of hair away from her face, dipping his head so his lips were inches from her. 'We don't have to do this.'

Eleanor felt the plunging sensation of deep disappointment. 'Oh yes, we do. You're not running away now.'

'I'm not moving,' Jace assured her. His lips grazed her ear, her jaw, and Eleanor shuddered. 'I'm not going anywhere,' he promised.

Eleanor closed her eyes as his lips moved from her jaw to her neck to her breast, and she added silently, *Not ever*.

Conversation became improbable after that, and then impossible. The exquisite sensation of being, not only cherished, but also possessed forbade all speech or even thought. Jace moved over her, teasing, treasuring as Eleanor's slick fists bunched on his back, her nails digging into his skin as he kissed his way up and down her body, taking his time in the most sensitive places.

Then, when Eleanor thought she could bear it no more, he rolled over so she was on top of him, his erection pressing insistently against her stomach as he looked up at her and smiled. 'Your turn.'

'My—turn?' Now she was shy. Now she had control. Slowly Eleanor lowered her head and kissed his chest. She remembered this, remembered how good it had once been between them. It had been so long, but she remembered. She moved lower, gaining confidence as she heard Jace's moan of pleasure.

Then, before she could move to the very heat and heart of him, he flipped her over and with a low growl said, 'All right. Now it's *both* of our turns.'

He entered her in one sweet, smooth stroke, and Eleanor closed her eyes, felt the surprising sting of tears behind her lids. This was so good. So right. To know and be known. To be as one.

One. One *person*.

That was how it felt in this moment of sweet union, the connection between them more intense and powerful than it had ever been, wiping away ten years of history, ten years of memories and sorrow and pain. This was more. This was better.

This really was starting over. Something new, something new and good and pure.

Afterwards they lay silently, Eleanor in the circle of Jace's arm, her head on his shoulder. She drifted her hand across the taut skin of his abdomen, half amazed at how comfortable she already was with his body.

'You know,' Jace said quietly, 'we didn't use protection.' Instinctively Eleanor stiffened, and Jace felt it, his arms tightening around her. 'I've never thought I had to ask this before, but is there any chance you could become pregnant?'

Such a simple question. So honest, so blunt, so basic. Eleanor swallowed. 'No,' she said quietly, her throat tight, 'there isn't. It's—taken care of. I'm on the pill.'

Jace nodded, saying nothing, and Eleanor was too afraid to ask. Did he *want* a baby, now he thought it might be a possibility? He'd implied before that his fertility wasn't a concern, yet how could it not be? How could it not be a consuming desire?

Her throat was tight, too tight, and the sleepy, sated feeling that had been stealing through her now seemed to evaporate completely, leaving her tense and wide awake. She should say something, start explaining, yet she couldn't. She was too afraid to ruin this moment, to ruin everything.

She closed her eyes, her throat still tight, the emotion too near the surface, seeping through.

'Eleanor?' Jace queried softly. She knew he could sense her sorrow. She just shook her head, unwilling to speak. In response Jace pulled away a little, but it was still too much. Her eyes were still closed, but she knew he was looking at her. Examining her. Then, with one gentle finger, he traced the silvery line of one of the stretch marks that ran along the inside of her hip. His voice, when it came, was no more than a husky murmur. 'Tell me about our daughter.'

Eleanor let out a choked sob of surprise. *'Jace—'*

He bent his head and kissed that silver streak of skin, the badge of her motherhood that never was. 'Tell me,' he whispered, but Eleanor knew it was a command. She knew he deserved to know. And, surprisingly, amazingly, she realised she wanted to tell him.

In actuality it was easy. She'd been dreading this conversation for days, weeks, *years*, but now that it was here, that Jace had asked, the words spilled from her lips. No one else knew. No one else had been there.

'She was beautiful,' she whispered. *'Beautiful.'* Jace didn't speak, but she felt the welling of his own emotional response, the swell of sorrow he must now feel that she had been living with for ever. 'Perfect,' she added. 'And I don't just mean the usual ten fingers, ten toes. Her face was like a little rosebud. A folded up, unfurled rosebud.' Eleanor could still see the closed eyes, the pursed lips. God, it hurt.

Jace's hand found hers. He squeezed her fingers tight, hard, almost hurting, and Eleanor welcomed the touch. *Touch me,* she silently commanded. *Hold me. Don't ever let me go. Not now, especially not now.*

'What happened?' he finally whispered. Eleanor shook her head, her eyes still clenched shut.

'It was her heart. It had a defect and it just—stopped. Like a clock winding down. Nothing else was wrong. She was perfect in every way. But when I went for my six-month check-up, there was no heartbeat.' She drew in a ragged breath. 'They said it happens sometimes with the Dopplers, they can't find the heartbeat. They told me not to worry—yet.' Jace squeezed her hand harder, and Eleanor squeezed back, holding on, needing him now as her anchor. 'So I had an ultrasound. I saw her there on the screen, all curled up, unmoving. Silence.' The room had echoed with it. She drew in another breath, the sound a desperate gasp. 'So I had to be induced. Like labour. Like birth—only, it wasn't. It was the hardest, loneliest thing I've ever done.'

'Was your mother there? Or a friend?'

'No. My mother was in California on a business trip and couldn't get back. And my friends were in college. This was totally out of their realm.'

'So you went through it alone? Eleanor, I'm sorry.' His voice was rough, his hand still clenched over hers.

'The thing that kept me going was knowing I would at least see her. Hold her in my arms. That would have to be enough.' She turned to him, her hand slipping from his to rest on his chest in an act of supplication. 'And I did, and she was beautiful, Jace, oh, God, she *was*—' And then the tears she'd been holding back for far too long finally fell, streaming down her cheeks in hot, healing rivers as Jace held her and rocked her silently.

Finally, after an eternity, she drew in a gulping breath and tried, if not to smile, at least to seem calm. And she did feel calm, now. 'I've never told anyone that before.'

'No one?'

She shook her head. 'It was easier not to. But you—you deserve to know.'

'Do I?' Eleanor heard the bitter note of recrimination in his voice. 'What a bastard I was. You never—never should have had to go through that on your own.'

'It's okay—'

'No,' Jace said savagely, 'it's not okay. I'll never accept that it was.' He clasped her hands, still resting on his chest, in his, and gazed at her with tear-bright eyes. 'Forgive me, Eleanor, for what I did. For what I assumed. And most of all for how I failed you…in so many ways. I don't ever want to fail you again.'

Eleanor nodded jerkily. 'I forgive you,' she whispered, and this time she meant it and believed in it with all of her heart. When he'd asked in the park it had been too soon. She hadn't been able to let go, and Jace hadn't known enough. Now it was real. Now it was true.

Now it was good.

She rested her head against his chest, exhausted, emotionally drained, yet still sated and, surprisingly, happy. She knew there was more to say, and she felt then she had the strength to say it. Just not now. Not yet.

Jace gathered her in his arms, resting his chin on top of her head, and Eleanor felt as if she could happily stay like that all night or, even better, for ever.

He'd had no idea. No true idea of all the pain and heartache and grief he'd caused. Still holding Eleanor in his arms, Jace closed his eyes in bitter and desperate regret. He'd known he'd hurt her, but he'd had no idea of how much. No wonder she couldn't trust him.

Except now he thought she did, and the realisation terrified him. He wasn't ready for that kind of trust. He didn't know what to do with it.

He was afraid of failing.

What good are you? What use?

Jace closed his eyes. Gently he stroked Eleanor's tear-dampened hair, awed by the courage she'd shown in so many amazing and unbearable ways. She still had the sweetness of the woman he'd known ten years ago, but now with it she possessed a strength that humbled him.

Jace's heart contracted and he felt a tightness in his throat as Eleanor curled her body into his in an act more intimate than what they'd just done. She rested her head on his shoulder, her hair tickling his nose, and with a satisfied little sigh she slept.

When Eleanor awoke Jace was gone. She stretched sleepily before feeling the empty space next to her in the bed, feeling it in her heart. Her whole body went rigid. Where had he gone? Did he regret last night? She thought of all the things she'd done—*said*—and closed her eyes. She couldn't bear it if he regretted it.

'Good morning.'

She bolted upright, the sheet falling from her naked body. Jace sat in a chair across from the bed, his laptop opened on the coffee table next to him. He wore only a pair of jeans and his hair was a little mussed.

'Good morning,' Eleanor answered. She slipped back down under the sheet.

'I didn't want to disturb your sleep,' Jace told her, giving her that wonderful crooked smile, 'but I couldn't leave you either.'

'You couldn't?'

'No.' The word was a confession, and it was enough. Eleanor didn't want to test or examine anything; she just wanted to trust. Finally. She smiled, shyly, and Jace stood up, stretching out one hand towards her.

'Let's get some breakfast. I'm starving.'

'So am I,' she admitted and slipped from the bed.

The morning was touched by magic. When they came into the kitchen breakfast had already been laid and the aroma of fresh coffee filled the room, although Agathe was nowhere in sight. She had, it seemed, anticipated their every need and then tiptoed quietly away.

After a lazy hour or two of eating and talking—Eleanor couldn't believe how relaxed she felt—she decided she needed to do a little work at least.

She stretched and regretfully pushed away from the table. 'I should start planning this party.'

'We have time.'

'Jace, your father's party is in ten days. It takes time to order things, food—'

He shrugged, reaching for her hand. 'We still have time—'

'I need to think of a theme,' she insisted even as she let him slide his fingers along hers, his thumb finding her palm and brushing against it in a way that made her whole body faint with longing. 'I was wondering,' she continued, still determined to do some work, 'if you have any photos or things from your childhood. We could put them around—'

Jace's fingers tightened on hers for a tiny second. 'Why? This isn't my party.'

'No, but we're celebrating your father's life. Memories are important—'

'Are they?' he asked with a strange little smile and withdrew his hand.

Eleanor frowned. She knew Jace's relationship with his father must have been difficult at times; he'd indicated as much, especially in regards to his alleged infertility. Yet this was his *father*, and he was throwing a party for him. Would a photo or two really be unwanted? Resented, even?

Jace's face had gone strangely still, even blank, and Eleanor was left with the feeling that he was wearing a mask, just as she'd felt when he'd danced with her at the party. Except this was a different mask, a colder, crueller one, and she had no idea what emotion—what person—hid underneath. Even after last night and everything she had shared, she suddenly wondered if she still knew Jace…at all.

She pushed the thought away, not liking it. 'Do you have any better ideas?' she asked, lightly, and Jace shrugged.

'There is a box of old photographs up in one of the spare bedrooms. My sister Alecia had them and she didn't have room in her new flat, so she brought them here one visit. You can take a look through them, if you like.' He rose from the table, his face still ominously blank. 'If you're going to do some work, so should I. I'll see you at lunch?' Although it was a question, Jace didn't give her time to answer. Eleanor watched him stride from the room without a backward glance, and she felt his withdrawal—emotional and physical—like a coldness creeping into her bones and stealing over her soul.

She sat in the kitchen for a few minutes, listening as a door in the distance clicked firmly shut. She thought of all the things she'd said last night. What had Jace said? What had *he* shared?

Uncomfortably, painfully, she became aware of how one-sided last night had really been…how one-sided everything had been. It seemed *she* was the only one starting over.

Sighing, trying to push away her growing sense of

discouragement, she decided to find the photographs. She was used to immersing herself in work to stop the hurt. The fear. She could do it again, even if she was tired of it. Even if she didn't want to.

Upstairs she walked along the silent corridor, poking her head in empty bedrooms, peering in darkened cupboards until she finally came across a wardrobe filled with cardboard boxes. Hesitantly she pulled one out; a faded photograph fluttered to the ground and Eleanor stooped to get it. She studied the picture: five darling, dark-eyed girls, and a laughing little boy who had the same crooked smile she knew—and loved.

Loved. The word caught her by surprise. Did she love Jace? Did she know enough about him to love him? Eleanor tried to study the question from an objective, analytical standpoint, and failed. How could you be objective about love? She knew her heart raced when she saw him. She knew how treasured and cherished she felt in his arms. She knew how happy he made her feel, and how he always could make her laugh, even when she didn't want to.

Was that love? Was it real? Could it be enough?

There were so many things she didn't know about him. His secrets. His hopes. His fears. His favorite colour.

Purple.

Her lips twitched and a smile bloomed on her face, stirred in her heart. Perhaps she did know him enough. Perhaps you didn't need to know someone's whole history to love him. And, Eleanor thought as she opened the box she pulled out, perhaps she could find out some of the things she didn't know. Yet.

She spent the rest of the morning and a good part of the afternoon gazing at a lifetime of photos. Birthday parties, Christmas dinners, lazy summer days on the beach, from round-cheeked babies to curly-haired toddlers, the scraped knees of early childhood to the gangly insecurity of adolescence. She saw Jace's early life documented in snapshots, from a laughing little boy to a solemn-eyed youth whose expression looked…haunted. Gazing at those photos, Eleanor guessed Jace must have been about fifteen. He would have already had mumps. He would have learned of his own infertility. She could see the struggle and the sorrow in every taut line of his adolescent face.

And yet the man she'd known in Boston, the student she'd fallen in love with, had been young and laughing and seemingly carefree. Had that been a façade, just as it had been the night of the party? A pretence, to cover the pain? She knew all about that.

'I see you've found them.'

Eleanor's head jerked up and she saw Jace lounging in the doorway. From the long shadows slanting across the floor, she figured she must have been in this room for hours. 'Yes,' she said. She glanced down at the photo of Jace she was still holding: a snap of him as a teen, his father standing behind him, his hand heavy on Jace's shoulder. Neither were smiling. 'Yes, I did.'

Jace ambled into the room. 'Let me see,' he drawled, reaching for the photograph. Eleanor gave it to him wordlessly. As Jace took it his face tightened, his eyes narrowing, and Eleanor's heart ached. She thought of how much that photo revealed, and yet how much it didn't say. How much she still didn't understand. 'Ah, yes,' he said as his gaze flicked over the photo before he handed it back to Eleanor. 'You might not want to put that one on display.'

Eleanor put it back in the box. 'Jace…tell me about it.'

'It?' he repeated, the single word not inviting questions.

Still Eleanor persevered. 'Your family. Your past. Your father.'

Jace hesitated, and Eleanor held her breath. *Tell me,* she implored silently. *Open up to me like I opened up to you.* That was what love was. To know and be known. Then he gave her a cool little smile and turned back to the door. 'There's nothing really to tell. Agathe's made dinner. You haven't eaten all day. You must be hungry.'

And leaving her with more questions—and more disappointment—than ever before, he left the room.

Jace walked quickly from the bedroom, from Eleanor. He felt restless, edgy, even angry. He didn't like the thought of her thumbing through those photos; he didn't like what they revealed. He didn't like Eleanor asking questions, wanting answers. What answers could he give? How could he tell her the truth? He didn't want her to know about his father's disappointment, how *he* had been such a disappointment.

He didn't want to be a disappointment to Eleanor.

Sighing, Jace raked a hand through his hair. Everything had been going so well. They'd both been so relaxed, so happy. Why did a few meaningless snaps have to ruin it? Why did these old feelings of fear and inadequacy have to swamp him, rushing through him in an unrelenting river as he looked through those photos, as he remembered every tiny sigh and little remark his father made, each one wounding the boy he'd been so deeply?

He wasn't that boy any more. He wasn't even infertile any more. Yet here he was, still mired by feelings of fear and inadequacy. It came to him then in a startling flash of insight that he wasn't just afraid of hurting Eleanor; he was afraid of being hurt himself.

That was what caring—love—did to you. It opened you up, it left you open and exposed, raw and wounded.

And yet it was—it could be—the best thing to ever happen to him…if he let it.

He just didn't know if he could.

As he retreated to his office, burying his thoughts and his fears with paperwork and business deals, he wondered if perhaps the past couldn't truly be forgotten. Perhaps you could never escape the old memories, fears, failures. Perhaps you couldn't start over after all.

By the time Eleanor had cleaned herself up and arrived downstairs for dinner, any remnant of the darkness and anger she'd felt from Jace upstairs had vanished. Instead he was his usual relaxed, carefree self, smiling readily, chatting easily, pouring her wine—yet Eleanor didn't trust any of it.

Now her mind seethed with questions, and they made her heart hungry and restless. Why was Jace holding back now, when she'd given him nearly everything? Was he regretting the night they'd shared, the secrets *she'd* shared? She still felt painfully conscious that he hadn't shared anything, that he was keeping himself distant and remote and *safe*, and it scared her.

Yet after dinner, when Jace led her upstairs, she didn't have the strength or even the desire to protest. Eleanor's heart bumped against her ribs and her fingers tingled where he'd laced them through his, pulling her along gently.

'Jace—'

'Is something wrong?' he murmured, lifting his free hand to brush it against her cheek. Eleanor leaned her face into the cup of his palm as a matter of instinct, a decision of need. She didn't just want him any more; she needed him. She couldn't fight this, and she didn't even want to, not for something so nebulous as a few haunted memories. Didn't she have those too?

You told them to Jace. He's keeping them from you.

She pushed the thoughts—and the fears—away and, smiling softly, followed him into the bedroom.

CHAPTER ELEVEN

THE next week followed the same pattern. When they weren't working—Jace on his business and Eleanor on the party— they were enjoying each other's company, in bed as well as out of it, but Jace still seemed distant to Eleanor, withdrawing more each day. His heart felt hidden, and she didn't know how to find the true him, the man she thought she loved.

Every question she asked that would make him talk about himself he deflected with a joke or a question back at her, and Eleanor realised how, in all the time she'd known him, he'd never really talked about himself. He'd never been vulnerable, or emotional, or even real, the way she had.

The inequality of it made her feel even more exposed, and terribly uncertain. Perhaps, when these two weeks were over, she would go back to New York and Jace would return to Athens. Perhaps these two weeks were all they were ever meant to have. What had Jace said? *And whatever* this *is, maybe it will go somewhere, and maybe it won't.* It was so little, Eleanor thought now. So very little, and yet she'd accepted it, fallen into his hand with the ease of a ripe peach. And that was what she felt like: something to be plucked, enjoyed, and then discarded.

With the party only a week away, Eleanor was forced to push aside her own personal concerns for the far more pressing one of the upcoming event. She'd made preliminary orders for food, and booked a band from Naxos, but she still felt she lacked the key idea that would bring this party together, that would give it both a theme and a heart.

And Jace wasn't helping at all.

'Does your father have any favourite foods?' she asked one afternoon. She'd sought Jace out in his office, and now he barely looked up from his laptop as she waited for his answer. Last night they'd made love—at least it had felt like love—but now Eleanor thought they seemed like strangers.

'I really don't know.'

Eleanor sighed impatiently. 'What about music? Games? Activities? Help me out here, Jace. This is your father's party.'

Jace looked up, his lips pressed together, his eyes flashing. 'And, as you can probably see for yourself, I never knew my father very well. We've barely talked in fifteen years.'

Eleanor's mouth dropped open as shock raced icily through her. She'd guessed their relationship was strained, but this? Utterly estranged?

'Why, Jace? And why on earth are you having the party here if that's—'

He shrugged, the gesture one of dismissal. 'If you need details, you can ring my sister Alecia. The party was her idea—she can tell you what you need to know.'

Eleanor bit back the retort that he might have volunteered this information several days ago; she didn't want to argue. And even though they hadn't had an argument, precisely, she left the room feeling disgruntled and unhappy and heartsore.

Up in her room she reached for the phone and dialled the number Jace had given her. After a few rings a bright, cheerful voice answered.

'*Kalomesimeri.*'

Eleanor scrambled for the basic Greek phrases she'd learned in the last week. Fortunately, most people she'd dealt with had spoken English. She hoped Jace's sister was the same. '*Kalomesimeri... Mi la te Anglika?*'

'Yes, I certainly do,' Alecia replied, her voice warm with laughter. 'And you sound American.'

'Yes. My name is Eleanor Langley, and I'm planning your father's birthday party.'

'An American planning the party! How original of Jace. And I suppose he's not being helpful at all, and sent you to me?'

'That's it exactly,' Eleanor said in relief, and Alecia gave a gurgle of laughter.

'Typical Jace. So busy with his precious work. He wasn't always like this, you know.'

'No,' Eleanor agreed, then realised Alecia would have no idea she had a history with Jace. She didn't particularly want to share that information, either. 'No?' she said again, this time a question.

'No, he was quite fun in his youth,' Alecia replied dryly. 'But I suppose everyone must grow up. What is it you want to know?'

'I'd love some details about his—your—father. I found some photographs, but—'

'Oh, yes, I dropped those off ages ago.'

'Well, what is your father like?' Eleanor asked. 'And what kind of party would he like? I've been trying and—'

'Oh, you don't need anything fancy,' Alecia assured her. 'My father grew up on the docks of Piraeus. He was a street rat, and he worked his way up to what he is now. He can't stand anything ostentatious or ornate…he likes things plain. And he speaks plainly too. He can be a grumpy old bear sometimes, to tell the truth, but I know he loves us all.'

Silently Eleanor wondered if Jace knew that as well. From everything she'd witnessed so far, she doubted it. 'All right,' she said slowly, still wondering just what kind of party she could put together.

'He loves old rembetika music,' Alecia told her. 'You know the street music with guitars? He grew up on it, and he's not ashamed of his past.'

'Rembetika,' Eleanor repeated. She reached for her notebook.

'But, you know, the main reason for the party is for us to be all together as a family,' Alecia continued, her voice turning serious. 'We haven't been together properly in years—one of my sisters is usually off having a baby, or Jace can't make it because of work. Having everyone together will be the most important thing about the party—that's what really matters.'

'I see,' Eleanor said. She wondered how Alecia could speak about her father in such a warm, loving way when Jace's experience was obviously so different.

'Of course, you must have tarama salata—fish-roe salad—and loukomia, a kind of jellied sweet. They are his favourites.'

'Tarama, loukomia,' Eleanor repeated, scribbling madly. 'Thank you.'

Armed with this new information, she set about arranging orders, finding a provider of the aforementioned food, and ringing up the band in Naxos to ask if they played rembetika. She still felt utterly out of her depth, and, combined with the sudden alienation she felt from Jace, it made her feel more like a lonely stranger than ever.

'How's it going?' Jace asked that evening as Eleanor pored over her notes spread across the kitchen table. Jace had skipped dinner, claiming work, and Eleanor had eaten with Agathe. She'd barely seen him all day, and now the moon was high in the sky, casting its lambent light across the smooth surface of the sea.

'Fine,' Eleanor replied a bit shortly. 'Your sister had some good information.'

'Good.' They both fell silent, the tension tautening between them. Eleanor turned back to her notes. 'Come to bed,' Jace said finally, his voice a lazy murmur.

She looked up, saw Jace's sleepy smile, and knew he wanted to solve everything with sex. And it would be so easy to say yes; God only knew, her body wanted to. She felt longing uncoil sinuously within her as Jace stretched out his hand.

'No, Jace.' He stilled, wary, and Eleanor shook her head. 'I…I need to work for a little while longer. The party is in just a few days.'

'Fine.' He dropped his hand, and Eleanor saw a new coolness creep into his eyes, harden the planes and angles of his face. Without another word he turned and left the room.

An hour later she came to her own bed, not Jace's, and crept into it alone. Half of her wanted to find Jace, or have him find her, yet she knew neither would solve what was—and wasn't—between them. She needed more than what they found together in bed, good as that was. She needed honesty, yet she was too much of a coward to ask for it.

The next morning when Eleanor came into the kitchen Jace was already there. In a business suit. His briefcase rested against the leg of his chair. Eleanor's stomach plunged icily, right down to her toes. Jace looked up from the newspaper he'd been scanning.

'Good morning.'

'Are you leaving?' Eleanor blurted, hating how afraid she sounded.

'I need to go to Athens for a short business trip,' Jace replied smoothly. 'I'll be back for the party.'

'For the *party*? You're leaving me here until the party?' She hadn't expected *that*. She hadn't expected Jace to run away again.

'I'll be back before the party,' Jace explained, and Eleanor heard a bite of impatience in his voice. 'Surely you don't need me to help plan it? I wasn't being much help, as far as I could tell.'

'No, you weren't,' Eleanor agreed, sitting opposite him. She reached for the coffee pot, then pulled her hand back. Her fingers were trembling, and she didn't trust herself to hold it. She didn't trust herself at all. 'But I didn't expect you to *leave*—' Her voice caught, and she swallowed. 'What's going on, Jace?'

He didn't answer for a moment. Eleanor looked up at him, saw his expression was guarded, wary. 'Nothing,' he finally said. 'I told you, I have some business to attend to. I'll try to wrap it up as quickly as I can.' He turned back to his newspaper, conversation clearly over.

Frustration, disappointment, and fear all warred within her, bubbling up. 'And when you come back?' Eleanor asked evenly. 'What's going to happen then, Jace? Just what is between us?'

He looked up from his paper. 'I know there are things that need explaining between us,' he said slowly. 'We're both still figuring out what's going on—and what we want.'

Eleanor nodded jerkily. It all sounded so nebulous, so nothing. 'And?'

'And I think we can have that conversation when I return,' Jace finished. 'When the party is over, and we're both more relaxed.' He glanced at his watch. 'I have an eleven o'clock meeting this morning. I should go.' He rose from the table, and Eleanor just watched him numbly. She could hardly believe he was going, that he was leaving her here alone.

'Eleanor,' Jace said quietly. He reached out and gently— so gently—touched her cheek. 'This isn't the end.' Before Eleanor could respond or even process that statement, he'd picked up his briefcase and was gone.

As she heard the front door open and then click softly but firmly shut she realised she didn't believe what Jace had said. This certainly *felt* like the end.

There had been no real reason to go to Athens. Jace knew that, and the knowledge ate at him as he flew across the Aegean Sea, azure blue flooding his senses from both above and below. He was running away…again.

Yet he couldn't stay with Eleanor, couldn't bring himself

to give her what she needed—honesty, trust, *love*—until he had figured out what he was going to do. If anything was possible.

If *they* were possible.

Yet if he'd thought he might clear his head away from the island and Eleanor, he was completely mistaken. The doubts and fear seethed through his mind, tormenting him here just as they had at the villa.

I'll disappoint her. I won't be enough. She'll hurt me.

Wasn't that what he was afraid of? Hurt? Opening himself up to the pain and beauty of love? He was a coward, a frightened little boy. *Life* was pain. Life was hope.

And, burying himself in work, he'd avoided truly living for far too long.

His intercom buzzed, startling him from his thoughts.

'Alecia is here,' his assistant said, and Jace sighed wearily.

'Send her up.'

'I heard you were in Athens,' Alecia said as she breezed into the room, airily trailing shopping bags. Jace stifled a groan. He loved his sister, but he didn't particularly feel like seeing her now. Alecia was far too astute.

'How did you hear that?'

'I rang that American party planner of yours and she told me,' Alecia said as she sprawled in the chair across from Jace's desk. 'She sounded terribly gloomy, Jace. Are you sure she can pull off this party?'

'Absolutely.'

Alecia's eyes narrowed and she leaned forward. 'You have quite a lot of faith in her, don't you? Where did you meet this paragon?'

'She planned a party for me in New York,' Jace replied, shuffling some papers on his desk. He could feel his cheeks warm, damn it.

'New York…' Alecia repeated thoughtfully. 'And I *did* say you've been so grumpy since you came back from there…'

'Whatever it is you're thinking, Alecia—'

'It is a woman, isn't it? It's this—Eleanor. Another American.' She shook her head, even though she was smiling gleefully. 'Well, I hope she treats you better than—'

'Don't.'

'Oh, Jace.' Alecia leaned forward. 'You know we're the last holdouts for marriage and babies and all that. I'd love to find Mr Right, of course I would, but sometimes I think I'd rather you found your Princess Charming.'

Jace's mouth twitched. 'I didn't know there was such a person.'

'You know what I mean. It's not good to be alone. And I'd love to see you settled with a wife and babies—a little girl with your eyes—'

Pain pierced Jace's shell, the armour he'd been building around his heart. He'd had a daughter. Maybe she'd had his eyes. He'd never know. 'I don't know if that's in store for me, Alecia,' he said quietly. Even if it was possible.

'Why not? Why shouldn't you have a family of your own, a family to love?'

A family. The word caught Jace by surprise, on the raw. He felt his thoughts tumble and slide, for ever shift. A family. Not a child, an heir, a dynasty. Not a thing to be obtained, a possession, a means to an end, the way his father had seen a son, a grandson.

A *family*.

In that moment he could picture it so clearly, so beautifully. He saw himself, he saw a baby, he saw *Eleanor*, and all the fear fell away.

This was what he wanted. What he needed.

He loved Eleanor. It was suddenly so obvious, so overwhelming. It wasn't a possibility or a fear or a hope. It was *real*. His love. His family.

'Yes,' he said slowly, starting to smile. 'A family.'

For the next few days Eleanor immersed herself in work. She was good at that, good at using it to push her thoughts and fears away. Yet overseeing food deliveries and arranging catering still left her with far too much time to remember how good it had been between her and Jace, and wonder whether it really was over. He didn't call, and although she had his mobile number she wasn't quite desperate enough—yet—to ring him, when he obviously had no interest in speaking with her.

The afternoon before the party Eleanor was in the kitchen, going over sleeping arrangements of all the guests with Agathe, when her mobile phone finally trilled tinnily. Eleanor reached for it with a sense of relief; she'd been waiting for Jace to call all this time, even if she'd pretended—to herself—that she wasn't.

'Jace?'

'Hello, Eleanor.' His voice sounded warm, and even happy, and Eleanor felt it reverberate all through her body. She closed her eyes in relief. It was going to be okay. She hoped. 'How's the party planning going?'

'Good, I think. The party is tomorrow, you know,' she added, trying to sound light but not quite able to keep the edge from her voice. 'Your family is arriving all throughout the day. When are you coming home?' Home. She should have said *back*. Maybe this wasn't home; maybe *she* wasn't home.

'I'll be back tonight. I'm sorry I was delayed. I was waiting on something.'

'Waiting on something?' Eleanor repeated, wishing she had just a little bit more information, a little bit more insight into Jace's mind.

'I'll tell you everything tomorrow,' Jace said. 'I promise.'

Yet as Eleanor hung up the phone she knew she had no idea what *everything* was. What he'd been doing for the last few days, or the secrets of his heart that he'd been keeping from her.

Disconsolately she turned back to the to-do list she'd left on the table.

* * *

Jace hung up the phone, smiling. He knew Eleanor felt uncertain and confused and perhaps even afraid, but if she could hold on for one more day—if he could—then he knew everything would work out. Everything would be perfect.

Amazing, how his doubts and fears had fallen away in light of that one word, that one great truth: family.

For years he'd simply seen his infertility as his inability to sire a child, to please his own father. He hadn't considered—hadn't let himself consider—what it really meant. What he'd really been missing. And now that it could be a reality, now that the floodgates of his heart had finally opened, he knew exactly what he wanted. A family, with the woman he loved. Eleanor.

Love had been such a scary word, a terrifying idea. Love meant you let people in, and once you did they held the power to hurt you. Hurt him the way his father had, the way Eleanor had—or he'd thought she had. He hadn't ever wanted to experience that again, and so for ten years he hadn't let anyone in. He hadn't let anyone even close.

Yet now he was ready; he was more than ready. He was eager, excited, as giddy as a child. Tomorrow he would tell Eleanor he loved her. He would ask her to marry him and they would start their future together. He could see it all perfectly bright, shining and pure.

The day of the party dawned bright, hot, and clear. Eleanor gazed out at the flat, endless blue sky, devoid of a wisp of cloud, or the telltale streak of a jet. She hadn't heard Jace come back last night, even though she'd stayed up past midnight. She wondered if he'd returned at all.

Resolutely Eleanor turned away from the window. She still had a lot to do.

Yet when she came down into the kitchen, Jace sat at the table, drinking coffee and scanning the newspaper, looking wonderful. Eleanor's heart seemed to clamber right up into her throat.

'Jace—' she managed. She felt a smile spread across her face.

'Good morning.' He turned, his eyes warm as his gaze swept over her. 'I came in so late last night, I didn't want to disturb you.'

She nodded, swallowing. 'I'm just glad you're here.'

'As am I.' He paused, and Eleanor suddenly had the feeling that he was going to say something important, maybe even something wonderful, and her heart began to beat with a fast, unsteady rhythm. Then he smiled and said, 'I just heard that my sister Parthenope will be arriving with her brood in just a few minutes. But…we need to talk. There are things I want to tell you.'

Eleanor nodded mechanically. 'Okay.' What things? she wanted to ask. Demand. Good things? Jace rose from the table and came towards her. He brushed an unruly strand of hair from her face and then bent to kiss her. His lips were cool and soft.

'I have so much to say to you,' he said, and it felt like a promise. Eleanor made herself believe it was.

Jace's family arrived throughout the day, throngs of children and five glamorous sisters who possessed the same ink-black hair and grey eyes that he did. Eleanor greeted them all, trying to keep their names straight, smiling politely and nodding her head, all too aware that to them—to anyone—she was nothing but a stranger to fade into the background. The party planner. As far as they were concerned, she had no importance or relationship with Jace at all. And Jace was kept busy with the demands of his family so that Eleanor wondered if that was indeed all she had become. The very fact that she didn't know, that she might have handed Jace Zervas her heart again only for him to break it, was more than aggravating. It was agonising.

By mid-afternoon the party was in full swing, although Jace's parents hadn't arrived. Children played on the beach and climbed on the deckchairs while their parents lounged around, talking and laughing. Eleanor went from room to room, making sure there was enough food and drink, that everyone was happy. Jace was surrounded by his sisters, although Eleanor saw him beckon her over several times. She ignored it out of some perverse sense of duty, and also because she wasn't sure she wanted to hear how Jace introduced her.

This is my indispensable party planner...

'You've done such a wonderful job.' Alecia found her in the foyer, straightening the collection of photos she'd retrieved from upstairs and arranged in a display that highlighted what looked like the happiest moments of the Zervas family. Eleanor turned from the photos. 'Thank you.'

'My father will be so pleased, when he arrives.'

'Do you know when that will be?'

Alecia gave a little laugh. 'Who knows? Soon, I hope. He's like Jace, works all the time. Those two are really far too alike.'

'Are they?' Eleanor murmured, and Alecia cocked her head.

'How did Jace hire you?' she asked, and Eleanor heard suspicion. 'An American is really an unusual choice.'

'We're—acquaintances,' Eleanor prevaricated, and a feline smile curled Alecia's mouth.

'Acquaintances? Because I was quite sure when I saw Jace a few weeks ago that he'd met a woman. And when I suggested he hire someone to plan this party, he brightened considerably.' She pursed her lips, gazing at Eleanor with open speculation. 'I wonder if you know anything about that?'

Eleanor flushed. She was not about to reveal the intimacies of her relationship with Jace, not when she still had no idea what the future could possibly hold. 'I'm not sure,' she hedged.

The front doors of the villa were suddenly flung open, freeing her from a more detailed reply.

Aristo Zervas stood in the doorway, tall and imposing, the same steely eyes as Jace's sweeping over the room—and his family—with a cold assessment. His wife, Kalandra, her dark hair streaked with grey and her face wreathed in a welcoming smile, held onto his arm.

'Papa!' Alecia hurried towards her father, enveloping him in a hug, which he returned stiffly. Two of Jace's other sisters, Parthenope and Elana, followed suit. Jace, having entered the hallway upon his father's arrival, didn't move. Eleanor could feel the tension thrumming through him; she felt it in herself. It was as if they were waiting for a storm to break.

'Jace.'

Jace inclined his head. 'Father.' He drew himself up. 'There's someone I want you to meet.'

It felt unreal when Jace reached for her, a dream, as his arm curved around her waist. 'Father, this is Eleanor Langley.'

Aristo moved towards them. His silver gaze turned on Eleanor, took her in from her toes to the top of her head in one arctic sweep. Jace's arm tightened around her protectively. 'She is very important to me, Father.'

'Is she?' The corner of Aristo's mouth twitched up in what could be a smile or a sneer. Still spinning in shock, Eleanor managed to find her voice.

'It's nice to meet you, sir.'

Aristo nodded gruffly, then turned back to his son. 'So you were able to come to my party. Not working for once.' He paused, meaningfully. 'I don't know why you work so hard. Who are you going to pass it all on to?'

Eleanor flinched, the barb hurting her as well as Jace, although his face remained expressionless. He'd lived for years with remarks like that, she supposed. She felt nerves dance low in her stomach, a reminder that she hadn't told him everything. Yet when could she confess? What if it changed things? How could she *still* be such a coward, even now with Jace's arm around her, when he'd told his own father how he felt?

She is very important to me.

'The work is its own reward, Father,' Jace replied evenly. 'Now I'm sure you want to greet everyone else.' With a stiff nod, he drew Eleanor away from Aristo and everyone else crowding the foyer. Eleanor was barely aware of where he was going until they were on the terrace, and Jace tugged her towards the beach.

'Jace—the party—'

'They can do without us for a while. I've been trying to talk to you all day. I'd almost think you were avoiding me.'

'No—' Eleanor protested, half-heartedly, for she knew she had been avoiding him. Even now she was afraid, and it wasn't just because of what Jace might say, but what she *hadn't* said.

The sky was lavender, darkening to violet, the first stars visible on the horizon. Despite the lingering warmth of the sun, the wind that blew off the water was chilly. Eleanor kicked off her sandals as Jace led her across the beach; the sand under her feet was silky and cool.

'I'm sorry I didn't speak to you sooner.'

'It's all right.'

Jace turned back to her. The wind ruffled his hair and in the growing darkness Eleanor couldn't quite make out his expression. 'I'm sorry about my father as well. As you can see, we don't have a very close relationship.'

'Has it always been that way?' Eleanor asked.

'Ever since the mumps made me infertile.'

'Why would that affect your relationship so much?' Eleanor burst out. 'It wasn't your fault—you're still his son—'

He sighed and raked a hand through his hair. 'After five girls, my father's every hope was realised when I was born. I was the apple of his eye for the first fifteen years of my life—I still have those memories to hold onto.' He paused, and Eleanor thought he might stop, he might distance himself again as he'd done in the past. Then he continued more quietly, 'And my father's every hope dashed when I contracted mumps, and the doctor told him I would be infertile. All his life he'd worked hard building up an empire to pass onto his son, his son's sons. The Zervas dynasty.' He gave a short, humourless laugh. 'His dreams of a legacy—a dynasty—were destroyed that day. I was as good as useless. And he never let me forget it. And the damnable thing is, the doctor was *wrong.*'

Eleanor swallowed, her throat tight. 'Oh, Jace—'

'It doesn't matter any more.'

'But it does, of course it does—'

'No,' Jace corrected softly, 'it doesn't. I don't care what my father thinks of me, Eleanor. I'm not living my life to gain his approval, although perhaps I was doing that subconsciously by working so hard. Who knows?' He spread his hands wide. 'But when I went to Athens I realised what I wanted out of life.'

Her breath dried in her throat. 'What do you want?'

'You. I love you.'

Eleanor blinked back tears. She hadn't expected this; even now, when everything seemed so good, she hadn't expected so much. Honesty and love. Everything. 'I love you too,' she whispered.

'I went to Athens because I was scared,' Jace said. 'Everything was happening so fast, and I didn't know if I could handle it. I told myself I was afraid of hurting you, but I think I was really afraid of being hurt myself.'

'I know what that feels like,' Eleanor whispered.

'Ever since my father learned I was infertile, I felt like a failure to him, and in a way to everyone. I wasn't good enough on my own, just as a person. So I had ways of keeping people out. To keep from letting them in.' He gave her a crooked smile. 'I'd play the clown or just act like I didn't care. If you act like you don't care, perhaps you really won't.' Eleanor nodded, understanding, recognising those self-protective tendencies in herself, and Jace continued, his voice roughening with emotion, 'But that changed when I met you all those years ago. I let *you* in. With your kindness and your laughter and even your chocolate cupcakes. I couldn't help myself. And when I thought you'd lied to me—it hurt. So much. I was wrong, and yet I let that hurt fester inside me for years.' He shook his head in sorrowful acknowledgement of the years they'd lost. 'Then I found myself letting you in again, here on the island, and it scared me. I didn't want to be scared, but I was, and that's why I went to Athens. I needed to sort things out in my own mind—'

'And you did?' Eleanor broke in. 'You seem different now. More…sure.'

'I am.' Jace drew her to him, his hands smoothing the hair away from her face. 'I'm so sure, Eleanor. It was hell without you, even for just a few days, and it made me realise— actually my sister made me realise—'

He paused, laughing a little, and Eleanor prompted, 'Your sister?'

'Funny, the power of just one word. Family.' Eleanor shook her head, not understanding, and Jace reached for her hands. 'She told me she'd always wanted me to have a family, and I'd never thought of children that way before. I haven't thought of children at all for so long—I've even avoided my own nieces and nephews. But when I thought of my own inability to have children, it was simply as a failure. A disappointment to my father, to myself to provide an heir. To continue the dynasty. I never thought of it—of them—as a *family*.'

Jace was smiling, yet each word was a hammer blow to Eleanor's heart. Her throat was too tight to speak, so she just shook her head. She should have told him. Of course she should have told him. Why hadn't she? How could she have allowed it to come to this?

'But in that moment,' Jace continued, squeezing her hands, 'I realised what I wanted. What I've wanted all along, even though I've been fighting it. Love is scary, Eleanor. You know it as well as I do. Hope is dangerous.'

Oh, God help her, Eleanor thought numbly. So scary. *So* dangerous. She just shook her head, helplessly, as a tear slid down her cheek. In the darkness she didn't think Jace saw it.

'I want us to be a family, Eleanor,' Jace said softly. 'More than anything. And more than just that—I want us to spend the rest of our lives loving each other. I want to see you hold my son—or daughter, I don't care which. I never thought I could have it, I didn't even dare dream—but now I know it can be, and I want it all with you.' The moon slid from behind the clouds and in its silver rays Eleanor saw the tender, triumphant smile on Jace's face. She felt him slip his hands from hers as he dropped to his knee and fumbled in his pocket for what could only be a jewellery box.

'This is what delayed me an extra day in Athens. I wanted it to be perfect. It was my grandmother's, but I had the stone reset.' With a growing sense of unreality Eleanor watched as Jace stretched out his hand, flicking open the box. The moonlight glinted off the most amazing, enormous antique diamond she'd ever seen. 'Eleanor Langley, will you marry me?'

CHAPTER TWELVE

ELEANOR gazed at the ring, gazed at Jace and all the love shining in his eyes, and shook her head helplessly. 'Oh, Jace.'

'Is that a yes?'

'I never expected this,' she began, helplessly, for her mind was seething with disappointments and fears. She really *hadn't* expected this. She'd been living in the moment, enjoying Jace, loving him, yet her stupid, stubborn mind had pushed away any real thoughts of the future. Conveniently ignored the realities—the truths Jace had given her tonight. She'd wanted his honesty, yet now that she had it she realised it changed everything. For the worse.

'Eleanor?' Jace asked softly. 'What's wrong?' He stood up, reaching out to brush her damp cheek with one thumb. 'You're crying.'

'I'm overwhelmed.'

'That's okay.'

She nodded, jerkily, because it wasn't okay. It wasn't remotely okay. Of course Jace wanted children. A family. She'd been a blind fool, a willingly blind fool, not to see it—think it—before now. She hadn't wanted to think it. Hadn't wanted to be completely honest with Jace. She'd lacked—still lacked—the courage.

Jace wanted children—a family—and there was no way she could fit into that happy picture. Just as there was no way she could take that dream away from him now.

'Jace!' One of his sisters—Eleanor thought it was Parthenope—called from the terrace. She didn't understand the Greek, but the gist was all too apparent. They needed Jace back at the party.

'Photographs,' he explained tersely. 'I don't—'

'No. Go.' She shook her head, wiping her wet cheeks, and tried to smile. 'This is a party, Jace. We can talk—later.'

'Come with me. You should be in the photos—'

'No, no one even knows me yet. Besides, I need to check on the food. I'll see you later.' Already Eleanor was walking away from him, reaching for her sandals, not looking back.

'Eleanor,' Jace called, and she heard the frustration and confusion in his voice, sharpening her name. 'Whatever this is, it can be solved.'

Two more tears slid down her cheeks. Jace knew her, understood her so well. But he didn't know the most important thing, the thing she'd kept hidden. Shame roiled through her. All this time she'd been berating Jace for hiding his heart from her, yet now he'd been as honest and vulnerable as he could be, and she was the one who was still hiding. Who had been hiding all along, and who was still afraid. And some things couldn't be solved.

Jace smiled for photo after photo, his cheeks aching, as his gaze swept through the foyer. Where was Eleanor? She'd disappeared from the beach after his proposal—and that hadn't gone nearly as well as he'd expected.

In the moment when he'd shared that precious dream, Eleanor had looked devastated. And Jace had no idea why.

Frustration gnawed at him and as the photographer readied for yet another snap he broke away from the gathered crowd of his family.

'Jace,' Alecia protested, but he just shrugged as he strode away.

'I need to find Eleanor.' A feeling of foreboding stole over him as he walked through the empty rooms of the villa. He shouldn't have waited for so long.

* * *

Halfway to the kitchen the answer had presented itself, so apparent, so appalling. She needed to leave. She needed to leave *now*. If she stayed, she'd tell Jace the truth; he'd wrestle or coax it from her, and she didn't have the strength to resist. Then she would have to face the unbearable pain of his rejection, or, perhaps worse, the stoic acceptance of her own inadequacy. She couldn't do that to herself. She couldn't do it to Jace.

Yet she was on an island, and the only way off was Jace's private jet. Where could she hide? How could she escape? The questions pounded inside Eleanor's mind; she forced all other, more rational thoughts away.

Then Eleanor saw the lights of a farmhouse glimmering in the distance, heard the clank of a bell, and the answer came to her. *Of course.*

Hurrying upstairs to change into more serviceable clothes, she grabbed her purse and her passport—leaving everything else—and desperate, despairing, headed out into the night.

The track winding through the hills was lit only by a pale wash of moonlight, and Eleanor stumbled on the rocks and twisted tree roots. Even as she ran she knew she was being foolish. Yet she also knew she couldn't stay and watch Jace's dream be destroyed—or hers. She couldn't face him. She couldn't face the truth because it hurt too much.

Love hurt. Why had she risked it again after all these years? Why had she risked it with *Jace*?

After a quarter of an hour she found the farmhouse, huddled among the hills, and knocked on the door. Behind her somewhere a goat bleated.

The man who answered the door was grey-haired and a bit scruffy, a mug of coffee held in one hand. He stared at her blankly.

'Yassas...parikalo...' Every Greek word evaporated from her frazzled mind as she gazed at him helplessly.

'I speak English,' he told her, the words flat and a bit rough.

'Oh, thank God. I need to go to Naxos—on your boat—'

'At this hour?' He looked appalled.

'It's important—*please*.'

Something must have convinced him—the wildness in her eyes, or perhaps the ragged edge fraying her voice, or the wad of crumpled twenties she thrust at him. In any case, he shrugged, nodded, and said, 'I get my boots. It take twenty minute in the boat.'

Eleanor sagged against the doorway in relief.

A few minutes later they were on the beach, the sea no more than a sound in the darkness, the waves crashing onto the shore. The wind whipped Eleanor's hair into tangles, and she stared at the forlorn little rowboat dubiously. It really was small.

Good Lord, what was she *doing*?

'Is this the only boat?'

The farmer shrugged. 'The motorboat, it belong to Zervas.' He gazed at her speculatively, and Eleanor wondered how much he knew. How much he'd seen over the last few weeks.

For a moment—a second—she hesitated, wondering if she could go back to the villa and explain everything to Jace. Maybe he would understand. Maybe it would be okay. *Maybe.* She couldn't trust a maybe, she couldn't act on it. The fear that had taken root in her heart was too pervasive, twining its poisonous tendrils around every thought, every dashed hope.

She couldn't go back. She couldn't tell Jace the truth. She couldn't bear to see him disappointed, the dream he'd shared with her dashed, destroyed—

I want to see you hold my son—or daughter, I don't care which. I never thought I could have it, I didn't even dare dream—but now I know it can be, and I want it all with you.

Eleanor closed her eyes, a tiny sob escaping her. Her shoulders shook.

'You get in the boat?' The farmer held onto the edge of the boat with one work-roughened hand as the waves churned around him. Eleanor could hardly believe what she was doing, yet she was too afraid to face the other choices.

Coward. You're more of a coward than Jace ever was.

'Miss?'

'What the *hell* do you think you're doing?'

Eleanor froze. She felt a hand clamp down hard on her shoulder and whirl her around. Her purse slipped onto the sand. 'Jace—' She was glad to see him, even now, after everything. Glad and relieved, even though Jace looked livid. His angry gaze travelled from her to the man waiting with the boat. He spoke a few terse phrases of Greek and numbly Eleanor watched the man give a philosophical shrug before hauling his boat back onto the beach. Within seconds he was gone, swallowed up by the darkness.

Jace's gaze snapped back to her; his eyes were the colour of cold iron. 'So what is this?' he growled, his voice low and savage. 'Some kind of *revenge*?'

'Revenge?' Eleanor repeated blankly. Then her eyes widened and her heart squeezed painfully, robbing her of the ability to talk or even think—

'So I can see how it feels,' he sneered. 'Is that what this was all about, Eleanor? Coming to Greece, being with me, everything—' His voice tore and he pressed his lips together, his eyes flashing furiously.

He was *hurt*. She'd hurt him with her disappearance, of course she had. She'd hurt him more than the truth ever could.

She really was a coward.

'It's nothing like that, Jace,' she whispered, but he didn't look as if he'd even heard her. 'I swear to you, this wasn't revenge!' Her voice rose in a yelp as he pulled her along the beach, driven by his own fury and pain. 'Where are we—?' She stopped talking when she realised Jace was not in a mood to listen.

He led her away from the beach, back towards the villa, its

lights twinkling in the distance. Eleanor thought of facing all his family there and closed her eyes. She couldn't. 'Please,' she managed. 'Can't we just talk—alone?'

'Oh, yes,' Jace growled back at her. 'We are most certainly going to talk.'

Yet he didn't speak again until they'd reached the villa; he stalked past it, with Eleanor having no choice but to follow, her arm still in his strong grip.

'Where are we—?'

'Where do you think?' he snarled. 'Where you want to go.'

Eleanor didn't understand what he meant until she saw the dull gleam of his private jet under the moonlight.

'Jace—'

'Now.' He let go of her and she stumbled at the sudden release. The jet loomed in front of her, large and silent. 'I rang the pilot—he lives on Naxos. He should be here in a few minutes.'

Eleanor gazed at him, his face hard and implacable, his eyes two narrowed slits. 'Why—?'

'He can take you wherever you want to go. Back to New York, I presume.' He drew a breath, and it hitched. 'You didn't have to take a leaky rowboat in the middle of the night if you wanted to leave me, Eleanor. All you had to do was say.'

The look of naked pain on his face was too much for Eleanor to bear. She wrapped her arms around herself even though the wind wasn't that cold. What a mess everything was. What a mess *she'd* made. 'I don't want to leave you, Jace,' she whispered.

'Considering I found you trying to board a boat to Naxos without a single word of explanation, I find that hard to believe.'

'It's true.'

'So did it feel good? To leave me hanging, just as I did you? No word, no warning? Had you been waiting for this?' Each question was a laceration on her soul.

'*Stop.* I wasn't—I didn't mean—'

'Excuses!' Jace slashed a hand through the air. 'Well, get on the plane, Eleanor. Nothing is stopping you now.'

Anger made her straighten her shoulders and cross the tarmac to poke a finger in the hard wall of his chest. 'I'm not getting on that plane, Jace. Not yet, anyway. Yes, I ran away. But I didn't mean to leave you—it wasn't some kind of revenge—' Her voice broke on that horrible word, but she forced herself to go on. To confess the truth. 'It was fear. I was *scared*, Jace. I still am.' She dropped her hand and bowed her head, felt the sting of tears in her eyes.

Jace was silent for a long moment. 'What are you afraid of, Eleanor?' He didn't sound angry any more. He didn't sound particularly forgiving, either. Eleanor looked up. This was the hard part. This was why she'd run away in the first place.

'Afraid of disappointing you. Of you leaving me or staying with me for the wrong reasons—I'm not sure which would be worse.'

Jace's expression didn't change, didn't soften. 'Now it sounds like *you* don't trust *me*. Why would you disappoint me? Why would you think you could?'

She drew a breath and met his gaze directly. It hurt. 'Children, Jace,' she said rawly. 'I should have told you before. I meant to tell you—when we—that first night—' She swallowed, her throat so very tight. 'But I couldn't. I was too scared. And then everything was going so well, and I just stopped thinking about it because I wanted to be happy—for a little while—and you said you didn't even think about children very much—' She let out a hiccuppy sob, knowing she wasn't making sense yet unable to speak the bald, bare truth.

Jace's face darkened, his mouth thinning. 'What are you saying?'

'I can't have children.' She saw the shock slice across his features, his mouth dropping open before he snapped it shut.

'What—how—?'

'It's not a fertility issue. I mean, I can *have* children, but—'
She closed her eyes. In her mind she saw the ominous, silent
screen of the ultrasound. Saw her baby's heart stilled for
ever. 'Our daughter had a heart defect. She was never going
to develop properly, never going to live. After—afterwards
I had some testing done.' She opened her eyes. 'It's genetic,
Jace. A genetic defect. A fluke, inexplicable, but there it is.
And the doctors said it's seventy-five per cent likely that
the same thing will happen again—with any pregnancy of
mine.' She swallowed past the aching tightness in her throat.
She couldn't bear to look at Jace now, so she gazed into the
distance, in the darkness. 'I can't live with those odds. I
can't—I can't go through it again. Not ever.'

Jace was silent for a long moment. Too long. Eleanor had
no idea what he was thinking, feeling. She didn't think she
could bear to know. She stared down at her feet, her vision
blurring. Somewhere she found her voice. 'I should have told
you, I know. I felt like you weren't being honest with me, but
I was the one who was hiding something. I'm sorry.' Jace
still didn't say anything, and it was the second time in her
life that silence had been such an endless agony. She drew a
long, shuddering breath and turned towards the plane. 'I…I
guess I'll go now.'

'*Eleanor.*' Before she could even move, Eleanor found
herself surrounded by Jace, his arms around her, pulling her
towards his chest. She was enveloped so her cheek rested
against the warmth of his neck, her body tucked wonderfully
into his. 'I'm sorry,' he whispered. 'I'm so sorry that you had
to go through that.'

'I'm sorry I can't—'

'I'm sorry too,' Jace whispered against her hair. 'I won't
pretend that I'm not, or that it doesn't hurt.' Eleanor swallowed a sob, and she felt Jace's fingers brush at the tears that
were sliding coldly down her cheeks. 'But, Eleanor, *Ellie*,
when I told you I wanted us to be a family… I wasn't—it's
more to me than just having a biological child. Yes, I expected

that, because I didn't know it was any different for you. But do I want a biological child—an *heir*—more than I want you? No. Never.' His arms tightened around her, drawing her closer to himself. 'God knows, my father drilled into me the utter importance of an heir, and it wrecked a good part of my life. Do you think I want to make that mistake again?'

Stunned, Eleanor couldn't answer. Couldn't think. She only hoped. Jace brushed the tangled curls away and cupped her face in his hands in a gesture so tender and achingly sweet that she couldn't keep the tears from slipping down her cheeks. He brushed at them with his thumbs.

'I was telling you I love you, Eleanor. *You*. All of you. Neither of us is perfect or even whole. We have scars. Memories. Regrets. But that's what love is. What it *does*. It takes everything—good and bad—and lives with it. Accepts it. Do you accept me with all *my* failings and mistakes?' He smiled crookedly, and Eleanor let out a sound that was half-laugh, half-sob.

'Yes.'

'And I accept you. I'm not walking away because of this. I'm not walking away at all.' He brushed his lips softly across hers. 'Not this time, and not ever.'

'But I don't want you to be disappointed,' Eleanor whispered, her throat still so very tight.

'Disappointed?' Jace's face seemed to crumple for a moment. He shook his head. 'I always felt my father was disappointed in me for not giving him what he wanted, the ability to continue our precious bloodline. I lived with that shame for years, and I don't think I ever escaped it until I met you. You made me feel whole. Happy. Like the man I was supposed to be, the man I wanted to be.'

'But if you want—'

'I want *you*. And I could never make any person—and especially you—feel that way. And I could never be disappointed in *you*. Yes, I'm disappointed that we won't have a child that is part of both of us, but that's something we can

deal with together. I love you, Eleanor. I love your strength
and your courage and your humour and your smile—everything. I love that you have drawn out the best in me, made me
the man I want to be. No matter what, you couldn't disappoint
me.'

Eleanor could hardly believe what he was saying. She
wanted to trust it—with all her heart, she wanted to trust
it—yet even so she still felt the lingering traces of fear.

'You told me—you wanted children. That's a big thing,
Jace.'

'I want a family. Our family. And there are more ways
than one to have children. We could adopt—do you want
children, Eleanor?'

'I never—' She swallowed, nodded. 'Yes.'

'Then we'll work it out. We'll face it together. And whatever disappointments come our way, we'll face *them* together.'
He drew her to his chest once more. 'That's what I want more
than anything. No more running away, for either of us.'

Eleanor slipped her arms around Jace's waist, felt the
warmth and strength of him and knew she had it—him—
to lean on for now, for ever. The thought was amazing.
Humbling too. 'No running away,' she repeated softly. She
leaned back so she could look up at Jace and see the love and
tenderness turn his eyes to soft grey. 'I love you, Jace. I'm
sorry I panicked. I shouldn't have run away. I just couldn't
think—'

'I know how that feels. But from now on we think. We
talk. And we do it together.'

She nodded, unbelievably happy, incredibly grateful.

Jace turned back to the track that led to the villa. 'I'll
have to ring the pilot and tell him the flight is cancelled.'
He nodded to the house, glimmering with lights ahead. 'I'm
afraid we have a good deal of explaining to do. My sisters
are going to be seething with questions.'

'That's okay.'

There was a lot ahead, Eleanor knew. A lot to figure out.

Work, children, family—even what continent they were going to live on. Yet as Jace led her back to his home she realised she wasn't afraid any more. She was excited. Whatever lay ahead, they would face it—together.

WHAT THE GREEK WANTS MOST

MAYA BLAKE

To my editor, Suzanne Clarke, for your
unfailingly brilliant insight and support!

CHAPTER ONE

THEO PANTELIDES ACCELERATED his black Aston Martin up the slight incline and screeched to a halt underneath the portico of the Grand Rio Hotel.

He was fifteen minutes late for the black tie fund-raiser, thanks to another probing phone call from his brother, Ari.

He stepped out into the sultry Rio de Janeiro evening and tossed the keys to an eager valet who jumped behind the wheel of the sports car with all the enthusiasm Theo had once felt for driving. For life.

The smile that had teased his lips was slowly extinguished as he entered the plush interior of the five-star hotel. Highly polished marble gleamed beneath his feet. Artistically positioned lighting illuminated the well-heeled and threw the award-winning hotel's design into stunning relief.

The hotel was by far the best of the best, and Theo knew the venue had been chosen simply because his hosts had wanted to show off, to project a false image to fool him. He'd decided to play along for now.

The right time to end this game would present itself. Soon.

A sleek designer-clad blonde dripping in diamonds clocked him and glided forward on sky-high stilettos, her strawberry-tinted mouth widening in a smile that spelled out a very feminine welcome. And more.

'Good evening, Mr Pantelides. We are so very honoured you could make it.'

The well-practised smile he'd learnt to flash on and off since he was eighteen slid into place. It had got him out of trouble more times than he could count and also helped him hide what he did not want the world to see.

'Of course. As the guest of honour, it would've been crass not to show up, no?'

She gave a little laugh. 'No, er, I mean yes. Most of the guests are already here and taking pre-dinner drinks in the ballroom. If there's anything you need, anything at all, my name is Carolina.' She sent him a look from beneath heavily mascaraed eyelashes that hinted that she would be willing to go above and beyond her hostess duties to accommodate him.

He flashed another smile. '*Obrigado*,' he replied in perfect Portuguese. He'd spent a lot of time studying the nuances of the language.

Just as he'd spent a lot of time setting up the events set to culminate in the very near future. For what he planned, there could be no room for misunderstanding. Or failure.

About to head towards the double doors that led to the ballroom, he paused. 'You said most of the guests are here. Benedicto da Costa and his family. Are they here?' he asked sharply.

The blonde's smile slipped a little. Theo didn't need to guess why. The da Costa family had a certain reputation. Benedicto especially had one that struck fear into the hearts of common men.

It was a good thing Theo wasn't a common man.

The blonde nodded. 'Yes, the whole family arrived half an hour ago.'

He smiled at her, effectively hiding the emotions bubbling beneath his skin. 'You've been very helpful.'

Her seductive smile slid back into place. Before she could grow bolder and attempt to ingratiate herself further, he turned and walked away.

Anticipation thrummed through his veins, as it had ever

since he'd received concrete evidence that Benedicto da Costa was the man he sought. The road to discovery had been long and hard, fraught with pitfalls and the danger of letting his emotions override his clear thinking.

But Theo was nothing if not meticulous in his planning. It was the reason he was chief troubleshooter and risk-assessor for his family's global conglomerate, Pantelides Inc.

He didn't believe in fate but even he couldn't dismiss the soul-deep certainty that his chosen profession had led him to Rio, and to the man who'd shattered what had remained of his tattered childhood twelve years ago.

Every instinct in his body yearned to take this to the ultimate level. To rip away the veneer of sophistication and urbanity he'd been forced to operate behind.

To claim his revenge. Here. Now.

Soon...

He grimaced as he thought of his phone call with his brother.

Ari was beginning to suspect Theo's motives for remaining in Rio.

But, despite the pressure from his family, neither Ari nor Sakis, his older brothers, would dare to stop him. He was very much his own man, in complete control of his destiny.

But that didn't mean Ari wouldn't try to dissuade him from his objective if he'd known what was going on. His oldest brother took his role as the family patriarch extremely seriously. After all, he'd had to step up after the secure family unit he'd known for his formative years had suddenly and viciously detonated from the inside out. After his father had betrayed them in the worst possible way.

Theo only thanked God that Ari's radar had been momentarily dulled by his newfound happiness with his fiancé, Perla, and the anticipated arrival of their first child.

No, he wouldn't be able to stop him. But Ari...was Ari.

Theo shrugged off thoughts of his family as he neared

the ballroom doors. He deliberately relaxed his tense shoulders and breathed out.

She was the first thing he saw when he walked in. His lips started to curl at his clichéd thought but then he realised she'd done it deliberately.

The dress code for this event had been strictly black and white.

She wore red. And not just any red. Her gown was blood-red, provocatively cut, and it lovingly melded to her figure in a way that made red-blooded males stop and stare.

Inez da Costa.

Youngest child of Benedicto. Twenty-four, socialite… seductress.

Against his will, Theo's breath caught as his gaze followed the supple curve of a breast, a trim waist and the flare of her hips.

He knew each and every last detail of the da Costas. For his plan to succeed, he'd had to do what he did best. Dig deep and extract every last ounce of information until he could recite every line in the six-inch dossier in his sleep.

Inez da Costa was no better than her father and brother. But where they used brute force, blackmail and thuggery, she used her body.

He wasn't surprised lesser men fell for her Marilyn Monroe figure. A true hourglass shape was rare to find these days. But Inez da Costa owned her voluptuousness and confidently wielded it to her advantage. Theo's gaze lingered on her hips until she moved again, dropping into conversation with the consummate ease of a practised socialite. She had guests eating out of her hands, leaning in close to catch her words, following her avidly when she moved away.

As he advanced further into the room, she turned to speak to another male guest. The curve of her bottom swung into Theo's eye line, and he cursed under his breath as heat raced up through his groin.

Hell, no.

His fists curled, willing his body's unwanted reaction away. It had been a while since he'd indulged in a mindless, no-holds-barred liaison. But this was most definitely not the time for a physical reminder, and the instigator of that reminder was most definitely not the woman he would choose to end his short dry spell with.

He exhaled in a slow, even stream, letting the roiling in his gut abate and his equilibrium return.

As he made his way down the stairs to join the guests, the deep-seated certainty that he was meant to be here—in the right place at the right time—flared high.

If Pietro da Costa's love of excess hadn't led him down the path of biting off more than he could chew, this time in the form of commissioning a top-of-the-line Pantelides super-yacht he could ill afford, Theo wouldn't have flown down to Rio to look into the da Costas' finances three years ago.

He wouldn't have become privy to the carefully hidden financial paper trail that had led right back to Athens and to his own father's shady dealings almost a decade and a half ago.

He wouldn't have dug deeper and discovered the consequences of those dealings for his family. And for him personally.

Memory stirred the unwanted threads of anxiety until it threatened to push its way under his control like Japanese knotweed. Gritting his jaw, he smashed down on the poisonous emotion that had taken too much from him already. He was no longer that frightened boy unable to stem his fears or chase away the screaming nightmares that plagued him.

He'd learned to accept them as part of his life, had woven them into the fabric of his existence and in doing so had triumphed over them. Which wasn't to say he wasn't determined to make those who'd temporarily taken power from him pay dearly for that error. No, that mission he was very much looking forward to.

Focusing his gaze across the room to where Benedicto and his son held court among Rio's movers and shakers, he strategised how best to approach his quarry.

Despite the suave exterior he tried to portray with his tailor-made suit and carefully cropped hair, Benedicto could never mask his lizard-like character for very long. His sharp, angular face and reptilian eyes held a cruelty that was instinctively felt by those around him. And Theo knew that he honed that characteristic to superb effect when needed. He bullied when charm failed, resulting in the fact that half of the people in this room had attended the fund-raiser tonight just to stay on Benedicto's good side.

Five years ago, Benedicto had made his political aspirations very clear, and since then he'd been paving the way for his rise to power through mostly unsavoury means.

The same unsavoury means Theo's own father had used to bring shame and devastation to his family.

Grabbing a glass of champagne, Theo sipped it as he slowly worked his way deeper into the room, exchanging pleasantries with ministers and dignitaries who were eager to find favour with the Pantelides name.

He noticed the moment Benedicto and Pietro zeroed in on his presence. Bow ties were surreptitiously straightened. Smiles grew wider and spines straighter.

He suppressed a smile, deliberately turned his back on the father and son and made a beeline for where the daughter was smiling up at Alfonso Delgado, the Brazilian millionaire philanthropist, who was her latest prey.

'If you want me to host a gala for you, Alfonso, all you have to do is say the word. My mother used to be able to throw events like these together in her sleep and I've been told that I've inherited her talent. Or do you doubt my talents?' Her head tilted in a coquettish move that most definitely would've made Theo snort, had his eyes not been drawn to the sleek line of her smooth neck.

Alfonso smiled, his expression beginning to closely resemble adoration.

Forcing himself not to openly grimace, Theo took another sip of champagne and brushed off an acquaintance who tried to catch his eye.

'No one in their right mind would doubt your talent. Perhaps we can discuss it over dinner one night this week?'

The smile that started to curve her full, glossy lips forced another punch of heat through him. 'Of course, I would love to. We can also discuss that pledge you made to support my father's campaign…?'

Theo moved closer, deliberately encroaching on the space between the two people in the centre of the room.

Alfonso's attention jerked towards him and his smile changed from playboy-charming to friendly welcome.

'*Amigo*, I wasn't aware that you had returned to my beloved country. It seems we cannot keep you away.'

'For what I need to achieve in Rio, wild horses couldn't keep me away,' he replied, deliberately keeping himself from glancing at the woman who stood next to Alfonso. He breathed in and caught her scent—expensive but subtle, a seductive whisper of flowers and warm sunshine.

His friend's eyes gleamed. 'Speaking of horses—'

Theo shook his head. 'No, Alfonso, your racehorses don't interest me. Speedboat racing, on the other hand… Just say the word and I'll kick your ass from one end of the Copacabana to the other.'

Alfonso laughed. 'No can do, my friend. Everyone knows underneath that tuxedo you're part shark. I prefer to take my chances on land.'

A delicate clearing of a throat made Alfonso turn, a smile of apology appearing on his face as he slipped back into playboy mode. For the ten years that Theo had known him, Alfonso had had a weakness for curvy brunettes.

Inez da Costa had curves that required their own danger

signs. His friend risked being easy prey for whatever the da Costas had in mind for him.

'Apologies, *querida*. Please allow me to introduce you to—'

Theo stopped him with a firm hand on his shoulder. 'I'm perfectly capable of making my own introductions. Right now, I think you're needed elsewhere.'

Alfonso's eyes widened in confusion. 'Elsewhere?'

Theo leaned and whispered in his friend's ear. Shock and anger registered on Alfonso's face before his jaw clenched and he reined his emotions back in. His gaze slid to the woman next to him and returned to Theo's.

Taking in a deep breath, he held out his hand. 'I guess I owe you one, my friend.'

Theo took the proffered hand. 'You owe me several, but who's counting?'

'And I shall repay you. *Até a próxima.*'

'Until next time,' Theo repeated. He heard the disbelieving gasp from Inez da Costa as Alfonso walked away without another glance in her direction.

A thread of satisfaction oozed through him as he tracked his friend to the ballroom doors. Scanning the room, he saw Pietro da Costa's thunderous look in his sister's direction.

Theo lifted his glass to his lips and took a lazy sip then turned his attention to Inez da Costa.

Her large brown eyes were filled with anger as she glared at him.

'Who the devil are you and what did you say to Alfonso?'

CHAPTER TWO

THEO DIDN'T LIKE the idea that he'd been less than one hundred per cent thorough in covering every angle in his investigations.

His surveillance of Inez da Costa had been from afar simply because until recently he'd deemed her involvement in his investigation peripheral at best.

The extent of her role in her father's organisation had only come to light a few days ago. But even then he should've recognised her power.

Now, at the first proper sight of what was turning out to be the jewel in Benedicto da Costa's crown, the essential cog in the sinister wheel that his enemy was intent on using to his full advantage, he experienced a pulse of heat so strong, so powerful, he sucked in a quick breath.

Up close, Inez da Costa's heart-shaped face was flawless…breathtaking, her skin a silky, vibrant complexion even the best cosmetics couldn't hope to produce.

Not that she hadn't attempted to enhance her beauty even further. Her make-up was impeccable, her lids smoky in a way that drew attention to her wide, doe-like stare.

Long-lashed eyes that bored into him with unwavering demand and a healthy dose of suspicion. Her nose flared with pure Latin ire and her full lips parted as she released another agitated breath.

The pictures in his dossier did her no justice at all. Flesh and blood wrapped in red silk from cleavage to toe, she made his senses ignite in a way he hadn't felt in a long time. The earlier pull deep in his groin returned. Harder.

'I asked you a question.' Her voice held a hint of dark sultriness that reminded him of a warm Santorini evening spent drinking ouzo on a deserted beach. And the mouth that framed her words, painted a deep matt red, reminded him of what happened on the beach after the ouzo had been consumed and inhibitions were at their loosest.

She glanced over his shoulder and Theo's jaw clenched at the thought that she was more concerned with the departing Alfonso than she was with him.

'Why is one of my guests walking out the door right this moment?'

'I told him that if he didn't want a noose slipped around his neck before he was ready to be hog-tied, he needed to stay away from you.'

Her parted mouth gaped wider, showing a row of perfect white teeth. *'Excuse me—?'*

'You're excused.'

Eyes the colour of dark caramel flashed. 'How dare you refer to me as such—?'

'Careful, *anjo*, you're causing a scene. *Pai* would not be happy to see his event ruined by a tantrum now, would he?'

Her eyes didn't stray from his, her stare direct and cutting in a way that made it difficult for him to look away. Or maybe it was because, despite the boldly challenging stare, he spied a quickly hidden vulnerability that tweaked his radar?

'I don't know who you think you are but perhaps you need to be educated in the etiquette of social gatherings. You don't deliberately set out to insult your host or—'

'My intention was quite simple. I wanted to get rid of the competition.'

'The *competition?*'

The doors to the larger ballroom where the dinner fund-raiser was to be held were thrown open. Theo turned to her. 'Yes. And now Alfonso's gone, I have you all to myself. And, as to who I am, I'm Theo Pantelides, your VIP guest of honour. Maybe you should add another bullet point to your rules of etiquette. That the hostess should know who her most important guests are?'

Her mouth started to drop open but she caught her reaction and pursed her lips.

'You're Theo Pantelides?' she muttered.

'Yes, so I suggest you make nice with me to stop me from leaving. One high net worth guest departing before dinner may be excusable. Barely. Two will certainly not go down well with your crowd. Now, smile and take my arm.'

Inez reeled under the steely punch packed behind the suave, sophisticated exterior and charming smile.

Theo Pantelides.

This was the man her father and Pietro had talked about. The one who would be taking over majority shares in Da Costa Holdings until after the elections. The one her brother Pietro had referred to as an arrogant bastard.

Well, he certainly was arrogant all right. The swiftness with which he'd dispatched Alfonso and assumed he could control her confirmed that assertion. As to whether he was a true bastard...well, that was something to be determined. But so far all signs pointed in that direction.

What she hadn't been aware of was that the man spoken of with such scorn would be so...visually breathtaking.

'I thought you would be older.' The words tripped from her tongue before she could stop herself.

'As opposed to young, virile and unbelievably handsome?' he drawled.

Shock jolted though her at his unapologetic, irritatingly justified confidence. Because he undeniably was. A full head of vibrant jet-black hair was common enough among her countrymen. Even his hazel eyes, sculpted cheekbones

and square jaw were conventional in the polo-loving jet
set crowd her father and brother encouraged her to associate with.

On this man, though, the whole combination had been
elevated several hundred notches to an entirely different
level of magnetism that demanded attention and got it. There
was a quality about the way he carried himself, his broad
shoulders unyielding, that spelled a tough inner core anyone would be foolish to mess with.

And yet that danger Inez could feel rising off him was…
compelling. Alluring.

She found her gaze drifting over his face, past the tiny
dimple in his chin to the dark bronze throat as he lazily
swallowed a mouthful of champagne.

She inhaled a sharp dart of air as she watched his Adam's
apple move. Then jerked back when her fingers flexed suddenly with the urge to touch him there.

Santa Maria!

She fought to remember her anger at this stranger. As
much as she detested her role in tonight's events—the blatant begging for campaign funds disguised as a charity
event—she couldn't let opportunities slip through her fingers.

It was the deal she'd made with her father.

An education in return for serving her time. In six short
weeks she would be free to pursue her dreams. Free of her
father's influence, of the sleazy, horrifying rumours that
had been part of her childhood and what had driven her
mother to quiet despair when she thought she wasn't being
observed.

She needed to focus, not moon over how coarse this arrogant stranger's faintly stubbled jaw would feel against
her skin.

'*Make nice?* After you rudely interrupted my conversation and sent my guest for the evening running without so
much as a goodbye?'

'Think about that for a minute. Do you really want a man who would abandon you so easily on the strength of a few whispered words?'

Genuine anger replaced the momentary sensory aberration. 'That you needed to whisper those words instead of state them in my hearing makes me wonder just how confident you are of your manhood.'

Inez was used to being the butt of male jokes. Pietro and her father had mocked and dismissed her career ambitions until the day she'd picked up her suitcase and threatened to leave home for good.

But she was still shocked when the man in front of her threw back his head and laughed. Even more so when the sight of his strong white teeth and the genuine twinkling merriment in his eyes sent her pulse racing. An alien tingling started in her belly and spread outward like fractured lightning.

'Did I say something funny?'

Light hazel eyes speared hers. 'I've been challenged on a lot of things, *querida*, but never over my manhood.'

The political career her father so desperately craved produced men who could fake confidence with the best of them. She'd seen political candidates on a clear losing streak fake bravado until they were on the verge of looking totally ridiculous.

This man oozed confidence and power so very effortlessly it was like a second skin. Couple those two elements with the dangerous magnetism she could feel and Theo Pantelides was positively lethal.

Over her thundering heartbeat, she heard the master of ceremonies announce that the fund-raiser she'd so carefully orchestrated—the platform that would see her achieve her freedom—was about to begin.

Beyond one broad shoulder of the man who seemed to have sucked the air from the large ballroom, she saw her father and Pietro heading towards her.

Her father would want to know what had happened to Alfonso. The Brazilian businessman had promised to host a polo match on his large ranch where he bred the finest thoroughbreds. Securing a time and a date and a campaign donation had been her job tonight.

A much needed win this man had cost her.

Frustrated anger flared anew.

'This can be resolved very easily, Inez,' Theo Pantelides murmured in her ear. His voice was deep. Alluring. To hear him use her given name, the version her half-American mother had so lovingly bestowed on her, made her momentarily lose her bearings. A state that worsened when his hot breath washed over her neck.

Barely managing to suppress a shiver, she snapped herself back into focus. 'Don't say my name. In fact, don't speak to me. Just…just go away!'

Inez knew she was on the verge of displaying childish behaviour but she needed to regroup quickly, find a solution to a situation that had been so cut and dried fifteen minutes ago.

She watched her father and brother approach and the dart of pain that resided beneath her breastbone twisted. For a long time she'd yearned for a connection with them, especially after *Mãe* had been so cruelly ripped from their lives following a fall from a racehorse a week before Inez's eighteenth birthday. But she'd soon realised that she was alone in the pain and loneliness brought on by the loss of the mother who'd been her everything. Pietro had been given no time to grieve before their father had stepped up his grooming campaign. As for Benedicto himself, he'd barely finished burying his wife before resuming his relentless pursuit of political power.

The only other male she'd foolishly thought was honourable had turned out to be just as ruthlessly power-hungry as the men in her family.

Constantine Blanco—one lesson well and truly learned.

'I see the rumours were false after all,' the man who loomed, large and imposing, in front of her drawled in that deep voice of his, capturing her attention so effortlessly.

She pushed down the bitterness that swirled through her at the thought of what she'd allowed to happen with Constantine. How low she'd sunk in her need for love and a desire for a connection.

'What rumours?' She infused a carelessness in her voice she was far from feeling.

'The ones that said you exhibit grace and charm with each bat of your eyelids. At the moment all I can see is a hellcat intent on scoring grooves into my skin.'

'Then I suggest you stay away from me. I wouldn't want to ruin your *unbelievably handsome* face now, would I?'

She hurried away from his magnetic presence towards where the tables had been set out with highly polished sterling silver cutlery and exquisitely cut crystal. At twenty thousand dollars a plate, the event was ostensibly to raise money for the children trapped within Rio's *favelas*, a cause dear to her heart.

Shame it had to be tainted with power-hungry sharks, mild threats to secure votes and…devastatingly handsome rogues with piercing hazel eyes who made her breath catch in a frighteningly exciting way…

The direction of her thoughts made her stumble lightly. Catching herself, she smiled at a guest who slid her a concerned glance.

Each table was set for eight. Her father had insisted their table was placed in the centre, where all eyes would be on them.

With Alfonso's unexpected departure, the empty seat would stick out like the proverbial sore thumb once the Secretary of State and his wife and the other power couple had taken their places.

She had no choice but to bump someone to the high table. All she needed to figure out was who—

'Staring at the empty seat will not make your departed guest suddenly reappear, *senhorita*,' the deep voice uttered from behind her.

That hot shiver swept up her spine again.

Before she could summon an appropriately scathing retort, her chair and the one bearing Alfonso's name were pulled back.

'What are you doing?' she demanded heatedly under her breath. She continued to stare down at the place setting, unwilling to look up into those hazel eyes. Something in their light depths made her hyperaware of her body, of her increased heartbeat. As if she was prey and he was the merciless predator.

It was preposterous. She didn't like it. But it was undeniable.

'Saving your skin. Now, smile and play along.'

'I'm not a puppet. I don't smile on command.'

'Try. Unless you want to spend the rest of the evening sitting next to the equivalent of an elephant in the ballroom?'

Something in his voice made her forget her vow not to look into his eyes. Something…peculiar. Her head snapped up before she could stop herself.

Their eyes clashed. And she found herself in that hyperaware state again. She forced herself to breathe through it. 'You created the very situation you now seem intent on fixing. Why don't you save us both time and state what your agenda is?'

A look passed over his face. Too quickly for her to decipher but whatever it was made her breath catch in a totally different way from before. Warning spiked the hairs on her nape.

'I merely want to redress the situation a little. And, as talented as you seem to think you are at hiding it, I can see my actions caused you distress. Let me help make it better.'

'So you cause me grief then swoop in to save me like a knight in shining armour?'

'I'm no one's knight, *senhorita*. And I prefer Armani to armour.'

He pointedly held out her seat.

Casting a swift glance around, Inez saw that they were attracting attention. Short of causing a scene, there was nothing she could do. Willing her facial muscles to relax into a cordial smile, she slowly sat down and watched as Theo Pantelides folded himself into the seat next to her.

He reached for his champagne at the same time as she reached for her water glass. The brush of his knuckle against her wrist made her jump.

'Relax, *anjo*. I've got this,' came the smooth, deep reassurance.

A hysterical laugh bubbled up her throat, curbed at the last minute by a cough. 'Pardon me if that assurance brings me very little comfort.'

He lifted the glass she'd abandoned and held it out to her. 'Tell me, what's the worst that could happen?'

She took the glass and stared into the sparkling water. The need to moisten her dry throat had receded. 'Believe me, the worst already has happened.'

For a long time she'd hidden from the truth—that her father had his heir, and she was a useless spare part.

Pain writhed through her and her breath grew shaky as her throat clogged with anger and bitterness.

'Get yourself together. Now isn't the time to fall apart. Trust me, Delgado may be a good friend but he has a wandering eye.' The hard bite to his tone cut a path through her emotions.

Setting the glass down, she faced him. 'I have been toyed with enough to last me a century, and I know your business here tonight has nothing to do with me, so do me a favour, *senhor*, and tell me straight—what do you want?' she whispered fiercely. She noted vaguely that her heartbeat was once again on rapid acceleration to sky-high. Her fingers shook and her belly churned with emotions she couldn't have named to save her life.

'First of all, cut out the *senhor* bit. If you want to address me in any way, call me Theo.'

'I will address you how I see fit, Mr Pantelides. And I see that once again you have failed to give me a straight answer.'

'No, I've failed to jump when you say. You need to be taught a little patience, *anjo*.'

She lifted a deliberately mocking brow. 'And you propose to be the one to teach me?'

That wide, breathtaking smile appeared again. Just like that, her pulse leapt then galloped with a speed even the finest racehorse would've strained to match.

What was going on here?

'Only if you ask nicely.'

She was searching for an appropriately cutting response when her father reached the table with the rest of the guests.

He cast her a narrow-eyed glance before his gaze slid to Theo Pantelides.

'Mr Pantelides, I had hoped for a few minutes of your time before the evening started properly,' her father said as he took his seat across the table.

Inez wasn't sure whether she imagined the slight stiffening in the posture of the man beside her. Her senses were too highly strung for her to trust their accuracy. Searching his profile as he stared at her father, nothing in his face gave any indication as to his true feelings.

'I'm all for mixing business with pleasure. However, I draw the line at mixing business with the plight of the poor. Let the *favela* kids have their cause heard. *Then* we will attend to business.'

The firm put-down sent an arctic chill around the table. The Secretary's wife gave a visible gasp and her skin blanched beneath her overdone make-up. Pietro, who'd just approached the table as Theo replied, gripped the back of his chair, anger embedded in his face.

Silence reigned for several fraught seconds. Her father flicked a glance at Pietro, who yanked back his seat and sat down. The hands her brother placed on the table were curled into fists and for a moment Inez wondered if his famous temper was about to be let loose on their guests.

Benedicto smiled at Theo. 'Of course. This cause is extremely dear to my heart. My own mother was brought up in the *favelas*.'

'As indeed you were, no?' Theo queried silkily.

Again, the Secretary's wife gasped. She reached for her wine glass and took a quick gulp. When she went to take another, her husband surreptitiously stayed her hand and sent her a stern disapproving look.

Her father nodded to the waiter, who stood poised with a bottle of the finest red wine. He took his time to savour his first sip before he answered.

'You are quite mistaken, Mr Pantelides. My mother managed to escape the fate most of her lot failed to and bettered her life long before she bore me. But I inherited her fighting spirit and her determination to do what I can for the bleak place she once called home.'

Theo's eyebrow quirked. 'Right. I may have been misinformed, then,' he said, although his dry tone suggested otherwise.

'I assure you misinformation is rife when it comes to the ploys of political opponents. And I have been told more than once that only a foolish man believes everything he reads in the papers.'

Theo slashed a smile that had a definite edge to it across the table. 'Trust me, I know a thing or two about what lengths newspapers will go to achieve a headline.'

'We seem to have lost Alfonso. Would you care to explain his absence, Inez?' Pietro's voice slid through the conversation.

Anger still rippled off him and Inez was acutely aware that he hadn't directly addressed Theo Pantelides.

Before she could speak, the man in question turned to her brother. 'He was called away suddenly. Emergency business elsewhere. Couldn't be helped. Since I was there when he took his leave, your sister offered me his seat and I graciously accepted, didn't you, *anjo*?'

She saw Pietro's eyes visibly widen at the blatant endearment. Just as swiftly, they narrowed and she could almost see the wheels spinning in a different direction as his gaze swung between her and Theo Pantelides.

No! Never! Her fingers curled into fists and she glared at him until he looked away.

'Well, perhaps Delgado's loss is our gain, *sim*?' her father prompted.

Again Theo smiled. Again her heart thudded hard at the sheer magnetism of his smile, even though it sorely lacked any humour.

The man was an enigma. He'd inveigled his way onto the top table, then proceeded to insult his host, just as he'd insulted her.

Inez had little doubt her father would unleash his anger at the slight later.

But right now she was more puzzled by the man next to her. What was his game plan? If he was in a position to acquire a controlling share of their company then clearly he was a man of considerable means. But he wasn't Brazilian. That much she knew. So why was he interested in her father's political ambitions?

She realised she was staring when that proud head turned and gold-flecked hazel eyes captured hers, one eyebrow quirked in amusement.

Hastily averting her gaze, she picked up her glass and took another sip.

Thankfully, the master of ceremonies chose that moment to climb onto the podium to announce the first course and the first speaker.

Inez barely tasted the salmon mousse and the wine that

accompanied it. Nor did she absorb the speech given by the health minister about what was being done to help the poor.

Her hyperawareness of the man beside her interfered with her ability to think straight. The last time she'd felt anything remotely like this, she'd wandered down a path she'd hated herself for ever since. She'd almost given herself to a man who had no use for her besides using her as a pawn.

Never again!

Six more weeks. She needed to focus on that. Once her father was on his campaign trail, she could start her new life.

She'd heard the rumours about her father's ruthless beginnings when she was growing up; a couple of her school friends had whispered about unsavoury dealings her father had been involved in. Inez had never found concrete proof. The one time she'd asked her mother, she'd been quickly admonished not to believe lies about her family.

At the time, she'd assured herself that they weren't true. But the passage of time had whittled away that assurance. Now, with each day that passed, she suspected differently.

'You look as if the world is coming to an end, *anjo*,' the man she was desperately trying to ignore murmured. Again the endearment rolled off his tongue in a deep, seductive murmur that sent shivery awareness cascading over her skin.

'I hope you're not going to ask me to smile again, because—' She gasped as he took her hand and lifted it to his mouth.

Firm, warm lips brushed her skin and Inez's stomach dipped in sensual free fall that took her breath away. Desperately, she tried to snatch her hand back.

'What the hell do you think you're doing?' she snapped.

'Helping you. Relax. If you continue to look at me like you want to claw my eyes out, this won't work.'

'What exactly *is* this? And why on earth should I play along?'

'Your brother and father are still wondering why Delgado

left so abruptly. Do you want to suffer the third degree later or will you let me help you make it all go away?'

She eyed him suspiciously. The notion that there was something going on behind that smooth, charismatic façade didn't dissipate. In fact, it escalated as he stared down at her, his features enigmatic save for that smile that lingered on his wide, sexy mouth.

'Why do you want to help me?' Again she tried to take back her hand but he held on, one thumb smoothing over her inner wrist. Blood surged through her veins at his touch, her pulse racing at the spot that he so expertly explored.

'Because I'm hoping it would persuade you to have lunch with me tomorrow,' he replied.

His gaze flicked across the table. Although his expression didn't change, she again sensed the tension that hovered on the edge of his civility. This man didn't like her family. Which begged the question: what was he doing here investing in their company?

He swung that intense stare back to her and she lost her train of thought. Grabbing it back, she shook her head.

'I'll have to refuse the lunch offer, I'm afraid. I have other plans.'

'Dinner, then?'

'I have plans then, too. Besides, don't you have business with my father tomorrow?'

'Our business won't take longer than me signing on a dotted line.'

'A dotted line that gives you a permanent controlling share in my family's company?'

His eyes gleamed. 'Not permanent. Only until I have what I want.'

CHAPTER THREE

'AND WHAT IS it you want?'

'For now? Lunch. Tomorrow. With you.' Another pass of his thumb over her pulse.

Another roll of sensation deep in her belly. The temptation to say yes suddenly overcame her, despite the warning bells shrieking at the back of her mind.

She forced herself to heed those warning bells. Her painfully short foray into a relationship had taught her that good looks and charm often hid an agenda that would most likely not benefit her or her heart. And Theo Pantelides had metaphorical skull and crossbones stamped all over him.

'The answer is still no,' she replied, a lot sharper than she'd intended.

His lips compressed but he shrugged. As if her answer hadn't fazed him.

And it probably hadn't. He was one of those men who drew women like bees to pollen. He could probably secure a lunch date with half of the women in this room and tempt the other married half into sin should he choose to.

With his dark, exquisite looks and deep sexy voice, he could have any woman he chose to display even the mildest interest in.

The thought that he would do just such a thing punched so fierce a reaction in her belly that she suppressed a shocked gasp.

What on earth is wrong with me? She needed to get herself back under control before she did something foolish—like discard her plans for tomorrow in favour of spending more time with this infuriatingly self-assured, visually stunning man.

Giving herself a fierce pep talk, she pulled her hand from his grasp.

She folded her hand in her lap and wrapped her other hand over her wrist. But suddenly her own touch felt…inadequate.

She was saved from exploring the peculiar feeling when the lights dimmed and the projector started reeling pictures of miles and miles of rusted shingle roofs that formed the world famous Rio *favelas*.

Her father climbed onto the podium to begin his speech.

The tale of despair-driven prostitution, violence, gang warfare and kidnapping of innocents, and the need to do whatever was needed to help was one she'd heard at many fund-raisers and charity dinners.

She clenched her fist. Knowing that half the people in here, dripping in diamonds and tuxedos worth several thousand dollars, would've forgotten the plight of the *favela* residents by the time dessert was served made her silently scream in frustration.

The need to get up, to walk out almost overwhelmed her but she stayed put.

There would be no running. No walking away from the work she'd committed herself to, nor walking away from the formative minds that were depending on her.

Fierce pride tightened her chest at the part she was playing in the young lives under her charge. And the fact that she'd managed to change that part of her own life without her father or brother's interference.

She refocused as her father finished his speech to rousing applause. The projector was shut off and the lights grew brighter.

She reached forward for her glass of wine and noticed that she was once again the focus of Theo's gaze.

'Should I be offended that I'm being so comprehensively ignored?' he asked.

'It's not a state you're used to, I expect?' With her surroundings once more in focus, she noticed the looks he was getting from women on other tables. She didn't delude herself that any of them were interested in his views on politics or world peace. No, each and every one of them would vie for much more personal, much more physical contact with the lean, broad-shouldered man next to her, whose hands casually caressed his wine glass stem in a way that made her think indecent thoughts.

She noticed the young famous actress on the next table where Theo should have been sitting gazing over at him, and again felt the sharp edge of an unknown emotion pierce her insides.

His smile grew hard. 'You'd be surprised.'

Curiosity brought her gaze back to his. 'Would I? How?'

'That question makes me think you've formed an opinion of me.'

'And that answer convinces me that you're very good at deflecting. You may fool others, but you do not fool me.'

He stared at her for a moment before one corner of his mouth lifted. Abruptly, he stood and held out his hand. 'Dance with me, *anjo*, and enlighten me further as to what you think you know about me.'

The demand was silky and yet implacable. In full view of the other guests, her refusal would be extremely discourteous.

Her heart hammered as she slowly slid her hand into his and let him draw her to her feet.

Emotions she was trying and failing to suppress flared up at the warmth and firmness of his grip. Fervently, she prayed for time to speed up, for the evening to end so she could be free of this man. Her reaction to him was puzzling in the extreme and the notion that she was being toyed with unsettled her more with each passing second.

As they skirted the table to head for the dance floor, her gaze met her father's. Expecting approval for accommodating the man whose business he was so obviously keen to garner, she was taken aback when she saw his icy disapproval.

Through the elite Rio grapevine she knew Alfonso Delgado's net worth and knew he couldn't afford to acquire a controlling share of Da Costa Holdings. So why did her father disapprove of a man who was clearly superior in monetary worth to Alfonso?

'You really have to do better with your social skills than this. Or I'll have to do something drastic to retain your attention.' The hard bite to Theo's voice slashed through her thoughts. 'Or were you really that into Delgado?'

'No, I wasn't.'

Her immediate denial seemed to pacify him. 'Then tell me what's on your mind.'

Inez found herself speaking before she could snap at him not to issue orders. 'Have you ever found yourself in a position where everything you do turns out wrong, no matter how hard you try?'

'There have been a few instances.' He pulled her close and slid an arm around her back. Heat transmitted to her skin via the soft material of her dress and flooded through her body. This close, his scent washed over her. Strong but not overpowering, masculine and heady in a way that made her want to draw even closer, touch her mouth to the bronze skin just above his collar.

Deus!

'You think this is one of those occasions for you?'

'I don't think; I know.'

'Why?'

Her laugh grated its way up her throat. 'Because I have a perfectly functioning brain.'

'You're worried because your father and brother are displeased with you?'

'Everything else this evening has gone according to plan
except…'

'Delgado. You're worried that your father offered you
up on a silver platter because he seems to think you're a
prize worth winning and now he'll demand to know what
you did wrong.'

Her eyes snapped to his, the insult surprisingly painful.
'What do you mean by *seems to think*? What do you know
about my father? Or about me, for that matter?'

Theo forced himself not to tense at the question. Or let
the fact that her body seemed to fit so perfectly in his arms
impact on his thinking abilities. 'Enough.'

'Do you always go around making unfounded remarks
about someone you've just met?'

He let a small smile play over his mouth. 'Enlighten me,
then. Are you a prize worth winning?'

'There's no point enlightening you because it will serve
no useful purpose. After tonight you and I will never meet
again.'

She took a firm step back. Attempted to prise herself out
of his arms. He held her easily, willing back the thrum of
anger and bitterness that rose like bile in his throat.

'Never say never, *anjo*.'

Her fiery brown eyes glared at him. 'Don't.'

He feigned innocence. 'Don't what?'

'Don't keep calling me that.'

'You don't like it?'

'You have no right to slap a pet name on someone you
just met.'

The hand holding hers tightened. 'Calm down—'

'No, I won't calm down. I'm not an angel. I'm certainly
not *your* angel.'

'Inez.' A warning, subtle but effective.

Inez's pulse stalled, then thundered wildly through her veins.

'Don't,' she whispered again. Only this time she wasn't sure what she pleaded for.

He leaned closer until his mouth was an inch from her ear. When he breathed out, warmth teased her earlobe. 'Don't use your given name? It's either that or *anjo*. All the other words are only appropriate for the bedroom.'

Heat flamed through her belly as indecent thoughts of rumpled sheets, sweaty bodies and incandescent pleasure reeled through her mind.

She shook her head to dispel the images and heard his low laugh.

When she stared up at him, his eyes blazed down at her with a hunger that smashed through her body. Her nipples slowly hardened and the fire raged higher as his lips parted on another heart-stopping smile. Unable to help herself, her eyes dropped to the sensual curve of his mouth.

'I think it's my turn to say *don't*. Not if you don't want to be thrown over my shoulder and raced to the nearest cave.'

She forced a laugh despite the sensations rushing through her. 'This is the twenty-first century, *senhor*.'

'But what I'm feeling right now isn't. It's very basic. Primeval, in fact.'

He swerved her out of the path of another couple and used the move to draw her even closer. At the fierce evidence of his arousal against her stomach, Inez swallowed hard.

Her confusion escalated.

Constantine had been charismatic and breathtaking in his own right. But he'd never made her feel like *this*, not even in the beginning…before everything had gone disastrously wrong.

Thinking of the man who'd broken her heart and betrayed her so cruelly threw much needed ice over her heated senses. She'd made a fool of herself over one man. Foolishly believed he was the answer to her prayers. She was wise enough now to know Theo Pantelides wasn't the answer to any prayer, unless it was the crash and burn type.

'I believe I've fulfilled my obligatory dance duty to you. Perhaps you'd like to find a more unwitting female to club over the head and drag to your cave?' She injected as much indifference into her voice as possible.

'That won't be necessary. I've already found what I'm looking for.'

Theo watched several emotions chase over her features before Inez da Costa regained her impeccable hostess persona.

Although he silently cursed himself for his physical reaction, he was thankful she realised her effect on him.

Let her think she held the power. Allow her to believe that he could be manipulated to her advantage. Or, rather, her father's advantage.

Her reaction to Delgado's departure had shown him that fulfilling her role as her father's Venus flytrap was most important to Inez da Costa. Or was it something else? Did she hope to bag *herself* a millionaire while serving her father's purpose? She came from a family ruthless in its pursuit of wealth and power. Was that her underlying agenda?

That knowledge demanded that he rethink his strategy. The conclusion he'd arrived at was surprising but easily adaptable.

He had an opportunity to kill a few more birds with one stone. With any luck, he would conclude his business in Rio in a far shorter time than he'd already anticipated if he played his cards right.

Inez tried to wrench herself from his grasp once more. The primitive feelings he'd mentioned so casually a moment ago resurfaced. When she tugged harder, he forced himself to release her. Her soft hand slid from his, leaving a trail of sensation that made his groin pound and his blood heat.

The plan he'd hatched solidified as he gazed down into

her heart-shaped face, saw her fighting to stop her clear agitation from messing with her breathing.

Theo hid a smile.

Either she was offended at his primitive declaration or she was turned on by it. Since she wasn't slapping his face, he concluded that it was the latter.

His gaze dropped lower, and the sight of her tightly beaded nipples against her gown made his own breathing stall in his chest. Lower still, her tiny waist gave way to those tempting hips that his palms ached to explore.

Even as he talked himself into believing his reaction would ultimately serve his purpose, a part of Theo was forced to acknowledge that he hadn't reacted this strongly to a woman in a very long time. Everything about her brought his senses to roaring life in a way only the thought of re-venge had for the past decade.

Revenge...retribution over the person who had created such chaos in his life.

He gritted his teeth as the sound of tinkling laughter and animated conversation refocused his mind to his task and purpose.

'Good evening, Mr Pantelides. I hope you enjoy the rest of your evening,' Inez said stiltedly.

She turned and walked off the dance floor before he could reply. Not that he felt like replying. Although he'd mostly kept on track throughout the evening, a large part of him had become far too consumed by her seductive pres-ence.

Inez da Costa was only one part of the game. To keep on track he needed to keep his head in the *whole* game.

He headed for the bar and sensed the moment Benedicto and his son halted their conversation and moved pincer-like towards him.

Dreaded anxiety washed over his senses but he forced himself to breathe through it.

I am no longer in that dark, cold place. I am in light. I am free…

He tersely repeated the short statement under his breath as he tossed back the shot of vodka and set it down with cold, precise care.

He was no longer weak. No longer helpless.

And he most certainly would never be put in a position to beg for his life. Ever again.

By the time they reached him, he'd regained control of his body.

'Senhor Pantelides—'

'We're about to become business partners—' his gaze slid over Pietro's head to where Inez was holding court in a group of guests; the sleek line of her neck and the curve of her body sent another punch of heat straight to his groin '—and hopefully a little bit more than that. Call me Theo.'

The younger man looked a little taken aback, but he rallied quickly, nodded and held out his hand. 'Theo…we wanted to hammer down a time to discuss finalising our agreement.'

He took Pietro's hand in a firm grip. Benedicto started to offer his hand. Theo deliberately turned away. Catching the bartender's eye, he held up his fingers for three more drinks. By the time he faced them again, Benedicto had lowered his hand.

Theo breathed through the deep anger that churned through his belly and smiled.

'Tomorrow. Ten o'clock. My office. I'll have the documents ready for us to sign.'

This time it was Benedicto who looked taken aback. 'I was under the impression that you wanted to iron out a few more details.'

Theo's gaze flicked back to Inez. 'I had a few concerns but they no longer matter. Your campaign funds will be ready in the next twenty-four hours.'

Father and son exchanged triumphant looks. 'We are pleased to hear it,' Benedicto said.

'Good, then I hope the three of you will join me for dinner tomorrow evening to celebrate our new deal.'

Benedicto frowned. 'The three of us?'

'Of course. I expect that, since this is a family company, your daughter would wish to be included in the celebrations? After all, the company was her mother's family's business before it became yours, Senhor da Costa, was it not?' he queried silkily.

The older man's eyes narrowed and something unpleasant slid across his face. 'I bought my father-in-law out over a decade ago but yes, it's a family business.'

Bought out using money he'd obtained by inflicting pain and merciless torment.

The bartender slid their shots across the polished counter.

Theo picked up the nearest shot glass and raised it. 'In that case, I look forward to welcoming you all as my guests tomorrow evening. *Saúde.*'

'*Saúde,*' Benedicto and his son responded.

Theo threw back the drink and this time didn't hold back from slamming it down.

Again he saw father and son exchange looks. He didn't care.

All he cared about was making it out of the ballroom in one piece before he buried his fist in Benedicto da Costa's bony face. The urge to tear apart the man who'd caused his family, caused *him*, so much anguish reared through him.

The sound of his phone vibrating in his jacket pocket brought a welcome distraction from his murderous thoughts.

'Excuse me, gentlemen.' He walked away without a backward glance, gaining the double doors leading out to the wide terrace before activating his phone.

'Heads up, you're about to get into serious trouble with Ari if you don't fess up as to why you're really in Rio,' Sakis, his brother, said in greeting.

'Too late. I've already had the hairdryer treatment earlier this evening.'

'Yeah, but do you know he's thinking of flying down there for a face-to-face?'

Theo cursed. 'Doesn't he have enough on his hands being all loved up and taking care of his pregnant fiancé?' He wasn't concerned about a confrontation with Ari. But he was concerned that Ari's presence might alert Benedicto to Theo's true intentions.

So far, Benedicto da Costa was oblivious as to the connections Theo had made to what had happened twelve years ago. The older man had been very careful to erase every connection with the incident and sever ties with anyone who could bear witness to the crime he'd committed. He hadn't been careful enough. But he didn't know that.

Having another Pantelides in Rio could set off alarm bells.

'You need to stall him.'

'He's concerned,' Sakis murmured. Theo heard the same concern reflected in his brother's voice. 'So am I.'

'It needs to be done,' he replied simply.

'I get that. But you don't need to do it alone. He's dangerous. The moment he guesses what your true intentions are—'

'He won't; I've made sure of it.'

'How can you be absolutely certain? Theo, don't be stubborn. I can help—'

'No. I need to see this through myself.'

Sakis sighed. 'Are you sure?'

Theo turned slowly and surveyed the ballroom. Rio's finest drank and laughed without a care in the world. In the centre of that crowd stood Benedicto da Costa, the reason why Theo couldn't sleep through a single night without waking to hellish nightmares; the reason anxiety hovered just underneath his skin, ready to infest his control should he loosen his grip for one careless second.

Inexorably, his eyes were drawn to the female member of the diabolical family. Inez was dancing with a man whose blatant interest and barely disguised lust made Theo's fist curl over the cold stone bannister.

His stomach churned and adrenaline poured through his system the same way a boxer experienced a heady rush in the seconds before a fight. This fight had been long coming. He would see it through. He had to. Otherwise he feared his demons would never be exorcised.

He'd lived with them for far too long, and they needed to be silenced. He needed to regain complete, unshakeable hold of his life once more.

His other hand tightened around his mobile phone, his heart thundering enough to drown out the music. He spoke succinctly so his brother would be in no doubt that he meant every word.

'Am I sure that I need to bring down the man who kidnapped and tortured me for over two weeks until Ari negotiated a two million ransom for my release? *Hell, yes.* I'm going to make him feel ten million times worse than what he did to me and to our family and I don't intend to rest until I bring all of them down.'

CHAPTER FOUR

'A DOUBLE-SHOT AMERICANO, *por favor*.' Inez smiled absently at the barista while she tried to juggle her sketchpad and fish out enough change from her purse to pay for the coffee.

It was barely nine o'clock and yet the heat was already oppressive, even more than usual for a Thursday morning in February. Normally, she would've opted for a cool caffeine drink but her energy levels needed an extra boost this morning.

She'd slept badly after the fund-raiser last night. And what little sleep she'd managed had been interspersed with images of a man she had no business thinking, never mind dreaming, about.

And yet Theo Pantelides's face had haunted her slumber…still haunted her, if truth be told.

The last time she'd seen him he'd been leaning against the terrace bannister outside the ballroom, his eyes fixed firmly on her. Inez wasn't sure why her attention had been drawn outside. All she knew was that something had compelled her to look that way as she danced with a guest.

Even from that distance the tension whipping through his frame had been unmistakable, as had the blatant dark promise in his eyes as his gaze raked her from head to toe.

More than anything she'd wished she could lip-read when she'd watched his lips move to answer whoever was at the other end of his phone conversation.

That last look plagued her. It'd held hunger, anger and another emotion that she couldn't quite decipher. Brushing it off, she smiled, accepted her coffee and headed outside. She was a little early for her class with the inner city kids but she hadn't wanted to spend another moment at the tension-fraught breakfast table with her father and brother this morning.

In contrast to Pietro's third degree as to what exactly had happened with Alfonso Delgado, her father had been cold and strangely preoccupied. The moment he'd stood abruptly and left the table, she'd made her excuses and walked away.

Even Pietro's reminder that they had a dinner engagement she couldn't recall making hadn't been worth stopping to query. All she'd wanted was to get out of the mansion that felt more and more as if it was closing in on her.

'*Bom dia, anjo.*' The deep murmured greeting brought her thoughts and footsteps to a crashing halt.

Theo leaned casually against a gleaming black sports car, a pair of dark sunglasses hiding his eyes from her. But her full body tingle announced that she was the full, unwavering focus of his gaze. Her breath stalled, her heart accelerating wildly as her pulse went into overdrive.

'What the hell are you doing here?' she blurted before she could stop her strong reaction.

Aside from the devastation his tall, lean suited frame caused to her insides, the thought that he could discover where she was headed or what she did with her Tuesday and Thursday mornings made her palms grow clammy. By lunchtime today, if Pietro were to be believed, Theo would be firmly entrenched as a business partner in her family's company. Which meant constant contact with her family. Which meant he could disclose parts of her life she wasn't yet ready to disclose to her family.

'Are you following me?' she accused hotly as she approached him, her senses jumping with the possibilities and consequences of her discovery.

'Not today. My trench coat and fedora are at the laundry.'

'Keep them there. In this heat, you'd boil to death.'

A smile broke across his face. 'Do I detect a little un-ladylike relish in your voice, *anjo*?'

'What you detect is high scepticism that you're here by accident and not following me,' she snapped.

'You give me too much credit, *agape mou*. I asked for the best coffee shop in the city and I was directed here. That you're here too merely confirms that assertion. Unless you go out of your way to sample bad coffee?'

Before she could respond, he straightened and reached for the hand wrapped around her coffee. Curling his hand over hers, he brought his lips to the small opening on her coffee lid and tilted the cup towards him.

He savoured the drink in his mouth for a few seconds before he swallowed.

Inez fought to breathe as she watched his strong throat move. The slow swirl of his tongue over his lower lip caused darts of sharp need to arrow straight between her legs.

'Delicious. And surprising. I would've pegged you for a latte girl.'

'Which goes to show you know next to nothing about me,' she retorted.

He slowly raised his sunglasses and speared her with his mesmerising eyes. Although a smile hovered over his sensual lips, some unnameable tension hovered in the air between them. A charged friction that warned her all was not as it seemed.

Hell, she knew that. Theo Pantelides spelled danger. Whether smiling or serious, dallying with him was akin to playing with electricity. Depending on his mood, you could either receive a mild static frizzle or a full-blown electro-cution. And she had no intention of testing him for either.

'*Sim*, I don't know enough about you. But I intend to remedy that situation in the near future.'

She shrugged. 'It is your time to waste.'

He merely smiled and turned towards his car.

'I thought you came to get coffee?' she probed, then bit her lip for prolonging a meeting she wanted over and done with. Last night she'd told herself to be thankful that she would never see this man again. And yet, here she was, feeling mildly bereft at the notion that he was leaving.

He paused and his gaze slid over her. Immediately, she became supremely conscious of the white shorts and blue tank top she'd hurriedly thrown on this morning. Her hair was caught up in a ponytail because it helped keep it out of the way during her class. Her face was devoid of make-up except for the light sunscreen and the gloss she'd passed over her lips. All in all, she projected a much different image this morning than the sophisticated hostess she'd been last night.

Catching herself wondering whether he found her wanting now, she mentally slammed the thought down. She didn't care what Theo thought of her.

'I have the kick I need to keep me going. See you tonight.'

'Tonight? Why would you be seeing me tonight?' she demanded.

His smile slowly disappeared as his gaze slid over her again. This time, his hot gaze held an element of possessiveness that made her fight to keep from fidgeting under his keen scrutiny.

Stepping back, he activated a button on his car key and the door slid smoothly upward. She watched, completely captivated, as he lowered his tall masculine frame inside the small space. A touch of a slim finger on a button and the engine roared to life.

'Because I want to see you. And I always get what I want, Inez,' he said cryptically, his tone suddenly hard and biting. 'Remember that.'

I always get what I want.

Another shiver of apprehension coursed down her spine. All through the two art and graphic design classes she taught from ten till midday, the infernal words throbbed through her head as if someone had set them on repeat.

She managed to keep her focus, barely, as she demonstrated the differences between charcoal and pencil strokes to a group of ten-year-olds. Once or twice she had to repeat herself because she lost her train of thought, much to the amusement of her pupils, but the satisfying feeling of imparting knowledge to children who would otherwise have been left wandering the streets momentarily swamped the roiling emotions that Theo had stirred with his unexpected appearance this morning.

The suspicion that he had been following her didn't go away all through her hurriedly taken lunch and the meeting she'd scheduled with the volunteer coordinator at the centre.

Her decision to forge her own path by seeking a permanent position at the centre had solidified as she'd tossed and turned through the night.

Seeking her independence meant finding a paying job. To do that she needed more experience, which she hoped her longer hours spent volunteering would give her.

Thanks to her father's interference, all she had was one semester at university. It wasn't great but, until such time as she could further her education, it was better than nothing. That plus her volunteering was a starting point.

A starting point that was greatly enhanced when the coordinator agreed to increase her hours to three full days.

She was smiling as she activated her phone on the way to her car after leaving the centre.

The first text was from Pietro, reminding her that they were dining out that evening. With Theo Pantelides.

The unladylike curse she uttered won her a severe look of disapproval from an elderly lady walking past. The urge to text back a refusal was immediate and visceral.

After last night and this morning, exposing herself to the raw emotions Theo provoked was the last thing she needed. And even more than her suspicions this morning, she had a feeling he'd engineered this dinner. Hell, he'd as much as taunted her with it with his last words to her this morning.

As much as she tried to think positive and hope that the dinner would be quick and painless, a premonition gripped her insides as she slid behind the wheel and headed home.

'*Filho da puta.*' Her brother's habitual crude cursing wasn't a surprise to her. That it had seemingly come out of nowhere was.

'What's wrong?' She eyed him as they stepped out of the car at the marina of the exclusive Rio Yacht Club just before seven p.m.

She pulled down her box-pleated hem and wished she'd worn something a little longer than the form-fitting mid-thigh-length royal-blue sleeveless dress. The traffic had been horrendous and she'd arrived home much later than planned. The dress had been the nearest thing to hand. Now she stared down at the four-inch black platform heels she'd teamed with it and grimaced at the amount of thigh and legs on show.

The light breeze lifted a few strands of her loose hair as she turned to her brother and saw him jerk his chin towards the largest yacht moored at the far end of the pier. 'Trust Pantelides to rub my nose in it,' he said acerbically.

She looked from the sleek black, gold-trimmed vessel back to her brother. 'Rub your nose…what are you talking about?'

With a sullen look, he strode off down the jetty. 'That's my boat.'

'*Yours*? When did you buy a boat?'

'I didn't. I couldn't. Not after the mess up with *Pai*'s last campaign. That boat was supposed to be mine!' Dark anger clouded his face.

Her heart jumped into her throat. 'Pietro, a boat like that costs millions of dollars. Besides that very unsubtle hint that

I in any way stood in the way of your acquiring it—which is preposterous, by the way—there's no way you could ever have afforded a boat like that, so—'

'Forget it. Let's go and get this over with. It's bad enough *Pai* pulled out of coming tonight. Now I have to schmooze for both of us. You have to play your part, too. It's clear Pantelides's got a thing for you.'

Disgust and anger rose in her and she snatched her hand away from Pietro when he tried to lead her down the gang-plank.

'I won't participate in another of your soulless schemes. So you may as well forget it right now.'

'Inez—'

'No!' Feelings she'd bottled up for much longer than she cared to think about rose to the surface. 'You keep asking me to throw myself at prospective investors so you can fund *Pai*'s campaign. You're his campaign manager and yet you can't seem to function without my help. Why is that?'

Pietro's eyes darkened. 'Watch your mouth, sister.'

'Show me some respect and I'll consider it,' she challenged.

'What the hell has got into you?'

'Nothing that hasn't always been there, Pietro. But you need me to point it out to you so I will. I'm done. If you want me to accompany you as your *sister* to Theo Pantelides's dinner, then I will. If you have another scheme up your sleeve, then you might as well forget it because I am not interested.'

Her brother's lips pursed but she saw a hint of shame in his eyes before his gaze slid away. 'I don't have time to argue with you right now. All I ask, if it's not too much, of course, is that you help me secure this deal with Pantelides, because if we lose his backing then we might as well pack up and head back up to the ranch in the mountains.' He set off down the jetty.

She hurried to keep up, picking her way carefully over

wooden slats. 'But I thought everything was done and dusted this morning?' she asked when she caught up with him.

Anxiety slid over Pietro's face. 'Pantelides cancelled the meeting. Something came up, he said. Except I know it was a lie. I have it on good authority he was parked outside a coffee shop chatting up some girl when he was supposed to be meeting us to finalise the agreement.'

Inez stumbled, barely catching herself from toppling headlong into the water a few feet away.

'*You're having him watched?*' How she managed to keep her voice even, she didn't know.

Petulance joined anxiety. 'Of course I am. And I'd bet my Rolex that he's doing the same to us.'

The thought of being the subject of anyone's surveillance made her skin crawl, even though a part of her had reluctantly accepted the truth: that her father's business dealings weren't always legitimate. But hearing her brother admit it made her stomach turn.

And if that was the way Theo Pantelides conducted his business as well…

She pressed her lips together and looked up as Pietro strode past the potted palm lined entrance to the Yacht Club.

'Aren't we dining in there?'

He shook his head. 'No. We're dining on my…on *his* boat,' he tossed out bitterly.

Inez glanced at the yacht they were approaching.

This close, the vessel was even more magnificent. Its sleek lines and exquisite craftsmanship made her fingers itch for her sketching pad. She was so busy admiring the boat and yearning to capture its beauty on paper that she didn't see its owner until she was right in front of him.

Then everything else ceased to register.

He wore a black shirt with black trousers, his dark hair raked back from his face. Under the soft golden lights spilling from the second deck his sculpted cheekbones and strong jaw jutted out in heart-stopping relief.

At the back of her mind, Inez experienced a bout of irritation at the fact that he captured attention so exclusively. So effortlessly.

Even as he shook hands with Pietro and welcomed him on board the *Pantelides 9*, his eyes remained on her. And God help her, but she couldn't look away.

On unsteady feet, which she firmly blamed on the swaying vessel, she climbed the steps to where he waited. When his eyes released hers to travel over her body, she grappled with controlling her breath. She reached him and reluctantly held out her hand in greeting.

'Thank you for the dinner invitation, Mr Pantelides.'

With a mocking smile, he took her hand and used the grip to pull her close. Despite her heels, he was almost a foot taller than her, easily six foot four. Which meant he had to lean down quite a bit to whisper in her ear, 'So formal, *anjo*. I look forward to loosening your inhibitions enough to dissolve that starchy demeanour.'

Her pulse, which had begun racing when his palm slid against hers, thundered even harder at his words. 'I can see how not having a woman fall at your feet the moment you crook your finger can present a challenge, *senhor*. But you really should learn the difference between playing hard to get and being plainly uninterested.'

His eyebrow quirked. 'You fall into the latter category, of course?' he mocked.

'*Sim*, that is exactly so.'

He looked towards where Pietro had accepted a glass of champagne from a waiter and was admiring the luxuriously decorated deck, at the end of which a multi-coloured lit jet pool swirled and shimmered.

When his gaze re-fixed on hers, there was a steely determination in his eyes that sent a shiver down her spine. All the earlier alarm bells where Theo was concerned clanged loudly in her brain.

'Then I will have to get a little more inventive,' he murmured silkily before dropping her hand.

Inez clenched her fist and fought the urge to rub the tingling in her palm. She didn't want him getting inventive where she was concerned because she had a nasty feeling she wouldn't emerge unscathed from the encounter.

But she kept her mouth shut and followed him onto the deck. The cream and gold décor was the last word in luxury and opulence. Plump gold seats offered comfort and a superior view onto the well-lit marina and the open sea to their right. To their left, the lights of Rio gleamed, with the backdrop of the huge mountain, on top of which resided the world-famous Cristo Redentor.

A sultry breeze wafted through the deck as a waiter served more flutes of champagne. She took a glass as Pietro rejoined them. His glass was already half empty and she watched him take another greedy gulp before he pointed a finger at Theo.

'I wish you'd given me the chance to make you another offer for this boat before you pulled the plug on our sale agreement, Pantelides.'

Theo's jaw tightened before he answered. 'You had several opportunities to make good but you failed to close the deal. So I cut my losses.' He shrugged. 'Business is business.'

Pietro bristled. 'And cancelling our meeting today? Was that for business too, or pleasure?'

Theo's eyes caught and held hers. Inez held her breath, wondering if he was about to give her up. His eyes gleamed with a mixture of danger and amusement. Somehow he'd sensed that he held her in his power. And he relished that power. Her hand trembled slightly as she waited for the axe to fall.

'I'm not in the habit of discussing my other business interests, or my pleasurable ones, for that matter. But, suffice it to say, what kept me away from our meeting was very much worth my time.' His gaze swept down, lingering over her breasts and hips in a blatant appraisal that made her breathing grow shallow. When his eyes returned to hers, Inez was sure all the oxygen had been sucked out of the atmosphere.

'Our business together should be equally worth your time,' Pietro countered.

Theo finally set her free from his captivating gaze. Narrow-eyed, he glanced at Pietro.

'Which is why I rescheduled for this evening. Of course, your father chose not to grace us with his presence. So the song and dance continues, I guess.' The hard edge was definitely in his tone again, prompting those alarm bells to ring louder.

Pietro muttered something under his breath that she was sure wasn't complimentary. He snapped his fingers at the waiter and swapped his empty glass for a full one.

'Well, we'll be there at the appointed time tomorrow. We can only hope that you will not be delayed...elsewhere.'

The upward movement of Theo's mouth could in no way be termed a smile. His eyes flicked back to her. 'Don't worry, da Costa, I intend to hammer out the final points of our agreement tonight. When I turn up to sign tomorrow, it will be with the knowledge that all my stipulations have been satisfied.'

The firm belief that his statement was connected to her wouldn't dissipate all through dinner. As a host, Theo was effortlessly entertaining. He even managed to draw a chuckle from Pietro once or twice.

But Inez couldn't shake the feeling that they were being toyed with. And once or twice she caught the faintest hint of fury and repulsion on his face, especially when her father's name came up.

She shook herself out of her unsettling thoughts when the most mouth-watering dessert was set down before her.

Whatever Theo was up to, it was nothing to do with her. Her father had managed their family business with enough savvy not to be drawn into a scam.

With that comforting thought in mind, she picked up her spoon and scooped up a mouthful of chocolate truffle-topped cheesecake.

Her tiny groan of delight drew intense eyes back to hers. Suddenly, the thought of dishing out a little of the mockery he'd doled out to her tingled through her. Keeping her gaze on his, she slowly drew the spoon out from between her lips, then licked the remnants of chocolate with a slow flick of her tongue.

His nostrils flared immediately, hunger darkening his eyes to a leaf-green that was mesmerising to witness. With another swirl of her tongue, she lowered the spoon and scooped up another mouthful.

His large fist tightened around the after-dinner espresso he'd opted for and she momentarily expected the bone china to shatter beneath his grip. But slowly he released it and sat back in his chair, his eyes never leaving her face.

'Enjoying your dessert, *anjo*?' he asked in that low, rough tone of his.

She hated to admit that the endearment was beginning to have an effect on her. The way he mouthed it made heat bloom in her belly, made her aware of her every heartbeat… made her wonder how it would sound whispered to her at the height of passion. *No!*

'Yes. Very much.' She fake smiled to project an air of nonchalance.

He smiled at her mocking formality. 'Good. I'll make a note of it for the next time we dine together.'

Before she could tell him she intended to move heaven and earth to make sure there wouldn't be a next time, Pietro lurched to his feet. 'I never got the chance to inspect my…this boat before the opportunity to buy it was regrettably taken away. You won't mind if I take a look around, would you?' he slurred.

Theo motioned the hovering waiter over. He murmured to him and the waiter went to the deck bar and picked up a handset. 'Not at all. My skipper will give you the tour.'

A middle-aged man with greying hair climbed onto the deck a few minutes later and escorted a swaying Pietro towards the stairs.

Inez watched him go with a mixture of anxiety and sympathy.

'He's drunk.' Her appetite gone for good, she set her spoon down and pushed the plate away.

'You say that as if it's my fault,' he replied lazily.

'Did you really have to do that?' She glared at him.

He raised a brow. 'Do what, exactly?'

'This was supposed to be Pietro's boat.' No matter how unrealistic that notion had been, her brother didn't deserve to be humiliated like this.

'*Supposed* being the operative word. We had a *gentleman's* agreement.' That hard bite was back again, sending trepidation dancing along her nerve ends. 'He didn't hold out his end of the deal.'

'Regardless of that, do you have to rub his nose in it like this?' she countered.

'As I said before, I'm a businessman, *anjo*. And I currently have a yacht worth tens of millions of dollars that needs an owner. The Boat Show starts next week. I relocated aboard in order to get it in shape for prospective buyers, otherwise our dinner would have taken place at my residence in Leblon and your brother's delicate feelings would've been spared.'

She frowned. 'You're selling the boat?' The thought of the beautiful vessel going to some unknown, probably pompous new owner made her nose wrinkle in distaste. The design was exquisite, unique…sort of like its owner.

As hard as she tried to imagine it, she couldn't see anyone else owning the boat besides Theo. Not even Pietro. Its black and gold contrasts depicted darkness and light in a complementary synergy—two fascinating characteristics she'd glimpsed more than once in Theo.

'Needs must.'

She looked around the beautiful deck, imagined its graceful lines awash with sunlight, and sighed.

Theo's eyes narrowed as he stared across at her. 'You like the boat.'

'Yes, it's…beautiful.'

He watched her for a few minutes then he nodded. 'Let's make a date for Sunday afternoon. We'll take her out for a quick spin.'

She laughed. 'Unless I'm mistaken, this is a four hundred foot vessel. You don't just take her out for a *quick* spin.'

'A long spin, then. I need to make sure it runs perfectly. If you still like it when we return to shore, I'll keep it.'

Her heart lurched then sped up like a runaway freight train. 'You would do that…for me?'

'*Sim*,' he replied simply.

Genuine puzzlement, along with a heavy dose of excitement she didn't want to admit to, made her blurt, 'Why?'

He strolled lazily to where she stood. This close, she had to tilt her head to catch his gaze. *Darkness and light.* He might have been smiling but Inez could almost reach out and touch the undercurrent of emotions swirling beneath his civility. She jumped slightly when he brushed a forefinger down her cheek.

'Because I intend to keep you, *anjo*. And while you will not have a lot of choice in the matter, I'm willing to make a few adjustments to ensure your contentment.'

CHAPTER FIVE

THEO WATCHED HER grapple with what he'd just said. Unlike her brother, she wasn't inebriated—she'd barely touched her glass of the rich Barolo 2009 he'd specially chosen for their dinner.

She shook her head in confusion. 'You intend to *keep* me?'

Her skin, satin-smooth beneath his touch, begged to be caressed. He gave in to the urge and traced her from cheek to jaw. When she withdrew from him, he followed. He stroked the pulse beating in her neck and pushed back the need to step closer, touch his mouth to the spot.

He'd learnt two things last night.

The first was that Benedicto da Costa, for all his cunning and veneer of sophistication, was still a greedy, vicious snake who thought he could con millions of dollars out of an unsuspecting fool like him.

The second was that Inez da Costa could be a key player in the slow and painful revenge he intended to exact for the wrong done to him. It didn't hurt that the chemistry between them burned the very air they breathed.

In the past Theo had made several opportune decisions by switching tactics at the last minute and making the most of whatever situation he found himself him.

With the newfound information at his fingertips, he'd found a way not only to end the da Costas once and for all, but also to make a tidy profit to boot.

He barely stopped himself from smiling as he looked down into Inez's face. She really was stunningly beautiful. With a mouth that begged to be explored.

'Mr Pantelides?'

'Theo,' he murmured, anticipating her refusal to use his first name.

She blew out an exasperated breath. 'Theo. Explain yourself.'

The unexpected sound of his name on her lips sent a pulse of heat through his body. Followed swiftly by a feeling he recognised as pleasure.

With a silent curse he dropped his hand. Pleasure featured nowhere on his mission to Rio. Nor was standing around, gazing into the face that reminded him of the painting of an angel that used to hang in his father's house.

Pain. Reparation. Merciless humiliation. Those were his objectives.

'There's no hidden message in there, *anjo*. For the duration of my stay in Rio I expect you to make yourself available to me, day and night.'

Her genuine laughter echoed around the open deck. When he didn't join in, she quickly sobered. 'Oh, I'm sorry. But I believe you have me confused with a certain type of woman you must encounter on your travels.'

Theo let the insult slide. He'd told his skipper to take his time with the tour, but even his trusted employee couldn't keep Pietro away for ever. And it looked as if he needed to step up this part of his strategy in order to forward his overall objective.

'I was supposed to sign documents that guaranteed your father's campaign funds this morning but I didn't turn up. Aren't you even a little bit curious as to why?'

A touch of confusion clouded her brown eyes but she shrugged one silky-smooth shoulder that shimmered softly under the deck lights. 'Your business with my father is not my concern.'

A little of that control he kept under a tight leash threatened to slip free. 'You don't care where the money comes from as long as you're kept in the style to which you've grown accustomed, is that it?'

Her eyes widened at the acid leaching from his tone. 'You may think you know me but, I assure you, you've got things wrong—'

'Have I? From where I'm standing it's very evident you're the bait he uses to trap weak, pathetic fools into opening their wallets.'

Her ragged gasp accompanied a look of outrage so near authentic Theo would've believed her reaction had he not seen her in action with Delgado last night.

'If it is your intention to be offensive to show your *machismo*, then *bravo*, you've succeeded,' she threw at him and whirled away.

He caught her wrist before she could take a step.

'Let me go.'

'I've yet to outline my plans, *anjo*.'

'I think you've *outlined* enough. I won't stand here listening to your unfounded insults. I'm going to find Pietro. And then we're leaving.' She tried to free herself. He tightened his grip until he could feel her pulse under his fingers. Furious. Passionate.

His groin stirred and he forced himself to ignore the throb of arousal determined to make itself known. 'You're not leaving here until we have this discussion.'

'What we're having is not a discussion, *senhor*. What you're doing is holding me captive, torturing me with—'

She broke off, no doubt in reaction to his hiss of fury and the flash of icy memory that made his whole body go rigid for one long second.

Theo released her, turned away sharply and shoved his hand through his hair. He noted his fingers' faint trembling and willed himself to stop shaking.

'Th...Theo?' Her voice came from far away, filled with confusion and a touch of concern.

He willed away the effect of the trigger words and forced himself to breathe. But they pounded through his brain nonetheless—*captive, prisoner, torture, darkness...*

Fingers closed over his shoulder and he jerked around. *'Don't!'*

She jumped back, snatching back her hand. It took several more seconds for him to recall where he was. He wasn't in some deep, dark hole in a remote farm in Spain. He was in Rio. With the daughter of the man who continued to cause his recurring nightmares.

'What's...what's wrong with you?' she asked with a wary frown.

He drew in a steady breath and gritted his teeth. 'Nothing. I'll get to the point. The agreement was that I'd take control of Da Costa Holdings and keep a fifty per cent share of the profits in exchange for liquidated funds to finance your father's political campaign. However, the papers your father had drawn up contain a major loophole that I can easily exploit.'

Slowly, his panic receded and he noticed she was absently rubbing her wrist. He quickly replayed his reaction to her touch and breathed a sigh of relief when he confirmed to himself that he hadn't grabbed her in his panic.

She continued to rub her skin and slowly another earthy emotion replaced his roiling feelings. He welcomed the pulse of arousal despite the fact that he had no intention of falling prey to the easy wiles of Inez da Costa. No matter how mouth-watering her body or how angelic her face.

'Shouldn't you be telling my father this, give him a chance to fix the loophole before you sign?'

He smiled at her naiveté. 'Why should I? I stand to gain by signing the agreement as it's drawn up.'

Her brow creased. 'Then why tell me about it? What's

to keep me from telling my father about it the moment I leave here?'

'You won't.'

One expertly plucked eyebrow lifted. 'Again, I think you underestimate me.'

He strode to the extensively stocked bar and poured himself a shot of vodka. 'You won't because if you do I won't sign the agreement in any form. And the offer of financial backing vanishes.'

All trace of colour left her face. 'So this is a blackmail attempt. To what purpose?'

'The purpose needn't concern you. All I want you to know is that there is a loophole which I can choose to exploit or leave alone, depending on your cooperation.'

'But what is to stop you from going ahead with whatever you have planned after I've cooperated with…what exactly is it you want from me?'

'That's the simple part, *anjo.* I want to keep you. Until such time as I tire of you. Then you will be set free.'

When the full meaning of his words finally became clear, ice cascaded down Inez's spine. Despite the warm temperature, she shivered.

Oh, how easily he said the words. As if her answer meant nothing to him. But of course it did. He'd been planning this for a while. The meeting this morning outside the coffee shop—which she was now certain hadn't been coincidental—the dinner invitation that he'd probably known her father wouldn't be able to attend due to his long-standing monthly dinner with the oil minister, the invitation to the yacht, which was sure to cause a reaction in her brother, letting Pietro drink far more than he should've so he'd get her alone…

'You planned this,' she accused in a hushed tone because her throat was working to swallow down her rising anger.

'I plan everything, Inez,' he replied simply.

She looked into his face. The indomitable determination stamped on his harsh features sent a wave of anxiety through her.

She started to speak, to say the words that seemed unreal to her and her mouth trembled. His gaze dropped to the telling reaction and she immediately clamped her lips together. Showing weakness would only get her eaten alive.

Not that she wouldn't be anyway. A bubble of hysteria threatened. She swallowed and held his gaze.

'You want me to be your *mistress*?'

He laughed long and deeply. 'Is that what you would call yourself?'

She flushed. 'How else would you describe what you've just demanded of me? This *keeping* me? What you're suggesting is archaic enough to be described as such. Or does *plaything* more suit your pseudo-modernistic outlook?'

'No, Inez. I don't like the term plaything either. I have no intention of playing with you. No, what I foresee for us is much more grown up than that.' The sexual intent behind the statement was unmistakable.

Rather than being offended or shocked, Inez found herself growing breathless. Excited.

No!

'Yes,' he murmured as if he'd read her mind.

'Whatever term you slap on your intentions, I refuse to be a part of it. I'm going to find my brother—'

He slowly sank onto the plush seat, curved his hand along the back of the chair and levelled one ankle over his knee. 'And tell him that you've dashed his hopes of a possible high profile position in your father's administration because you couldn't take one for the team? I don't think you're in a position to refuse any demands I make, *anjo*.'

'Stop calling me that! And I won't be a pawn in whatever game you're playing with my father and brother. Pietro is well aware of that.'

'Really? Since when? Wasn't serving on your father's

campaign the reason you dropped out of university? Clearly, you play a part in your father's political ambitions or you wouldn't have been trying to fleece poor Alfonso. Why stop now when you're so close to achieving your goals? And why claim innocence when it's something you've done before?'

The hurt that scythed through her was deep and jagged. She wasn't aware she'd moved until she stood over him, glaring down at the arrogant face that wore that oh, so self-assured smile.

'I've never wanted to be this...this person you think I am. I was merely trying to help my family. I misjudged the situation and—'

'You mean you fell in love with your mark.'

She swallowed. 'I don't know what you're getting at.' But deep down she suspected.

'I mean you were set a target and you fell in love with your target. Isn't that what happened with Blanco?'

Light-headedness assailed her as he confirmed her suspicion. 'You know about Constantine?'

'I know everything I need to know about your family, *anjo*. But by all means enlighten me as to why you've been so misjudged.'

His cynicism raked her nerves raw. 'I made a mistake, one that I freely admit to.'

'What mistake do you mean, *querida*? I want to hear it.'

'I misjudged a man I thought I could trust.'

'You mean you meant to use him but found out he intended to use you too?' he mocked. 'Some would call that poetic justice.'

Recalling Constantine's public humiliation of her, the names he'd called her in the press, her stomach turned over. 'You're despicable.' She raised her chin. 'And assuming you're even close to being right, won't I be a fool to repeat that mistake again?'

'No.'

'No?'

His eyes fixed on hers. Serious and intense. 'Because this time you know exactly what you're getting. There will be no delusions of love on either of our parts. No pretence. Just a task, executed with smooth efficiency.'

'But you intend to parade me about as your...lover? What will everyone think?'

He shrugged. 'I don't care what everyone thinks. And I don't much think that bothers you either.'

She shivered. 'Of course it bothers me. What makes you think it won't?'

'You're the ultimate young Rio socialite. You have a dedicated following and young impressionable girls can't wait to grow up and be you.' His mockery was unmistakable.

Heat crept up her cheeks. 'That's just the media spinning itself out of control.'

'Carefully fuelled by you to help your father's status. You're always seen with the right offspring of the right ministers and CEOs. You're the attraction to draw the young voters, are you not?'

She couldn't deny the allegation because it was true. Nor did she want to waste time straying away from the more serious subject of the demand he was making of her.

The demand she wouldn't—*couldn't*—consent to.

But there was something about him...a reassurance... and expectation of acquiescence that made the hairs on her nape stand on end.

'What happens if I refuse this...this sleazy proposal?'

'I sign the agreement then use the company as I wish. I could dismantle it piece by piece and sell it off for a neat profit. Or I could just drive down the share price and watch the company implode from the inside out. But that's all boring business. What do you care?'

Her fists clenched. 'I care because my grandfather built that company from nothing.'

'And now your father's willing to hand it over to a complete stranger just so he can further his political career.'

She pursed her lips and fought not to react. She'd been deeply concerned when she'd first heard how her father planned to raise funds for his campaign. Concerns that had been airily brushed away with reassurances of airtight clauses.

Clauses which Theo had apparently easily loopholed.

Maybe it wasn't too late. She could tell him to go to hell and warn her father and brother about the danger their proposed business partner presented and advise them to walk away. Surely that would be better than admitting the lion into their midst and letting him wreak havoc at whim?

Light hazel eyes watched her with a predatory gleam. 'If you're thinking of warning your family, I'd think twice. Remember how easily I dispatched Delgado?'

She stiffened, recalling how a few whispered words had caused one investor in her father's campaign to walk away. 'You don't mean that,' she tried.

He slowly rose from the chair and towered over her. Every protective instinct screamed at her to step back but she stood her ground. Any show of weakness would be mercilessly pounced on.

'Do you want to test me, *anjo*?' The blade of steel that hovered over the endearment sent a shiver down her spine.

She slowly uncurled her fists and forced herself to breathe. 'What do you expect me to do?'

His smile was equally as predatory as the look in his eyes. 'You will inform your father and brother tomorrow that you and I are an item—our meeting last night sparked a chemistry so hot we couldn't *not* be together.'

A tiny sliver of relief eased her constricted chest. 'If that's all you want, I'm sure I can convince them—'

His mocking smile stopped her words.

'After you tell them that, you'll pack your bags and move in with me.'

Shock slammed her sideways. 'Are you serious?'

He gripped her chin and held her pinned under his gaze. 'I've never been more serious in my life.'

'But…why?'

'My reasons are my own. You just need to do as you're told.'

Do as you're told. Constantine had tried to blackmail her with those very words. When she'd refused he'd spread rumours about her in the newspapers.

Anger grew in her belly. But it was a helpless anger born of the knowledge that there was nothing she could do. Once again she was trapped in a hell that came from trying to do what was right for her family.

Only this time she was to truly pay with her body. In a stranger's bed. Her heart tripped before going into fierce overdrive.

She gazed at Theo's face, then his body. A body she would in the very near future become scorchingly intimate with. The horror she'd expected to feel oddly did not materialise.

'How long exactly will I be expected to *do as I'm told*?' she snapped.

'Until after the elections.'

A horrified gasp escaped her throat and she forcibly wrenched herself from his grip. 'But…that's…the elections are *three months* away!'

'*Sim*,' he replied simply.

'*Sim*? You expect me to put my life on hold for the next three months, just like that?' She clicked her fingers.

He raised an eyebrow. 'Do you want me to repeat the part about you not having a choice?'

She searched his face, trying to find meaning behind his intentions. 'What did my father do? Did he best you at a deal? Bad-mouth you to investors? Because I can't see what would make you want to go down this path of trying to get your own back.'

She watched his eyes darken, and his nostrils flare. All

traces of mockery were wiped from his face as he stared down at her. Only she was sure he wasn't really seeing her.

His usual intense focus dulled for several seconds and his jaw clenched so tight she feared it could crack. Whatever memory he was reliving caused volcanic fury to bubble beneath the harsh, ragged breath he expelled and this time she did take that step back, purely for self-preservation.

Voices sounded on the deck below. In a few minutes Pietro and the skipper would return from their tour. Inez wasn't sure whether to be grateful for the disruption or frustrated that her opportunity to find out Theo's reasons for demanding her presence in his bed had been thwarted.

His gaze sharpened, flicked towards the steps and back to her.

'It's time for your answer. Do you agree to my terms?'

She shook her head. 'Not until you tell me— *what are you doing*?' she blurted as he snapped out an arm and tugged her close.

One large bold hand gripped her waist and the other speared through her hair. Completely captured, she couldn't move as he angled her face to his. The unsettling fury was still evident in his darkened eyes and taut mouth. Despite the heat transmitted from his grip, she shivered.

'You seem to think you can talk or question your way out of this, *anjo*. You can't. But perhaps it was a mistake to expect a verbal agreement. Perhaps a physical demonstration is what's best?'

Despite his rhetorical question, she tried to answer. 'No…'

'Yes!' he muttered fiercely. Then his mouth smashed down on hers.

She'd been kissed before. By casual boyfriends in her late teens who she'd felt safe enough with.

By Constantine, in the beginning, before he'd revealed his true ruthless colours.

Nothing of what had gone before prepared her for the power and expertise behind Theo's kiss. Her world tilted beneath her feet as his tongue ruthlessly breached the seam of her lips. Hot, erotically charged and savagely determined, he invaded her mouth with searing passion. Bold and brazen, he flicked his tongue against hers, tasting her once and coming back for more.

The shocked little noise she made was a cross between surprise and her body's stunned reaction to the invasion.

The hand at her waist pressed her closer to his body. Whipcord strength, sleek muscles and his own unique scent brought different sensations that attacked her flailing senses.

Fire lashed through her belly as liquid heat pooled between her thighs. Her breasts, crushed against his chest, swelled and ached, her nipples peaking into demanding points with a swiftness that made her dizzy.

Deus!

Feeling her world career even faster out of control, she threw up her hands. Hard muscle rippled beneath her fingers. The need to explore slammed into her. Before she could question her actions, she slid her hands over his warm cotton-covered shoulders to his nape, her fingers tingling as they encountered his bare skin.

He jerked beneath her touch, pulled back with a tug on her hair. Breathing harshly, he stared into her eyes for several seconds. Hunger blazed in his, turning them a dark, mesmerising molten gold that stole what little breath she had from her lungs. Then his eyes dropped lower to her parted mouth.

A rough sound rumbled from his throat. Then he was kissing her again. Harder, more demanding, more possessively than before.

Inez pushed her fingers through his hair as arousal like she'd never experienced before bit deep. This time, when his tongue slid into her mouth, she met it with hers. Boldly, she tried to give as much as she got, although she knew she was hopelessly inadequate when it came to experience.

The hand around her waist tightened and she was lifted off her feet. Seconds later, she found herself on the bar stool, her legs splayed and Theo firmly between thighs exposed by her stance. He came at her again, the force of his sensual attack tilting the stool backwards.

She threw out her hands onto the counter to keep from toppling over. Theo growled beneath his breath, his hands moving upward from her waist to cup her breasts. He moulded her willing, aching flesh so expertly she whimpered and arched into his hold. Beneath her clothes, her tight nipples unfurled in eager anticipation when his thumbs grazed over them. The deep pleasurable shudder made him repeat the action, eliciting a soft cry of pleasure from deep inside her.

'Inez!'

The rapier-sharp call of her name doused her with ice-cold water. She wrenched herself from Theo's hold…or at least she tried to.

The hands that had dropped from her breasts to her waist at the sound of Pietro's return stayed her desperate flight.

'What the *hell* do you think you're doing?' Pietro growled, no longer looking as drunk as he'd been half an hour ago.

'If you need it explained to you, da Costa, then I'm wondering who the hell I'm getting into business with.'

Her brother flushed in anger. 'I wasn't talking to you, Pantelides. But maybe I should ask you what you're doing, pawing my sister like some mad animal.'

Inez desperately tried to pull her dress down. But Theo stood firmly between her thighs, making the task impossible. Her sound of distress drew his attention from Pietro. He stared down at her for a second before he adjusted his stance. But although he allowed her to close her legs and pull her dress down, his hands didn't drop from her waist.

If anything, they tightened, their hold so possessive she fought to breathe.

'Inez was going to tell you tomorrow. But I guess tonight's as good a time as any.'

Pietro's gaze shifted from Theo's face to hers. 'Tell me what?'

'Do you want to do the honours, *anjo*? Or shall I?' he queried softly.

Her heartbeat accelerated but not with the arousal pounding through her bloodstream. She heard the clear warning in Theo's tone. Anything short of what he'd demanded of her would see her family ruined completely.

She opened her mouth. Closed it again and swallowed hard.

A trace of fear washed over Pietro's face. Despite their strained relationship, there'd been times in the past when they'd been close. She knew how much a political career of his own some day meant to him. How much he was pinning his hopes on what her father's campaign would mean to him personally.

She tried again to speak the words Theo demanded she speak. But her vocal cords wouldn't work.

'Would someone hurry up and tell me what's going on?'

Fierce hazel eyes drifted over her face in a look that spelled possession so potent her breath caught.

Theo curled his arm over her shoulders and pulled her into the heat of his body. He drifted his mouth over her temple in an adoring move so utterly convincing she reeled at his skilful deception.

She was grappling with that, and with just how much of the kiss they'd shared had been an exercise in pure ruthless seduction on his part, when he spoke.

'Your sister and I have become…enamoured with each other. We only met last night but already I cannot bear to be without her.' His voice held none of the mockery from before, sparking another stunned realisation of his skill. He stared down at her and she caught the implacable determination in his eyes.

When his gaze reconnected with Pietro's she stared, mesmerised, at his profile then shivered at the iron-hard set to his jaw.

'Tomorrow she will be moving out of your home. And into mine.'

CHAPTER SIX

'*LIKE HELL YOU are*,' Pietro repeated for the hundredth time as their chauffeur-driven car stopped outside the opulent Ipanema mansion she'd grown up in.

She quickly threw open the door and hurried up the steps leading to the double oak front doors although she knew escape wouldn't be easy. Pietro was hard on her heels.

'Did you hear what I said?' he demanded.

'I heard you loud and clear. But you fail to realise I'm no longer a child. I'm twenty-four years old—well over the age when I can do whatever the heck I want.'

He slid a hand through his hair. 'Look, I know I may have pushed you into playing a greater part in *Pai*'s fund-raising campaign. But…I don't think getting involved with Pantelides is a good idea,' he said abruptly.

Inez's heart lurched at his concern but she couldn't reassure him because she herself didn't know what the future held. 'Thank you for your concern but like I said, I'm a grown up.'

He swivelled on his heel in the vast entrance hall of the villa. 'Are you really that into him? I know what I saw on his deck tells its own story but you only met him last night!'

'I hadn't met Alfonso Delgado before last night either and yet you expected me to charm him.'

'*Charm* him, not move in with him!'

'There's no point arguing with me. My mind is made up.'

Pietro's face darkened. 'Is this some sort of rebellion?'

Inez sighed. 'Of course not. But I'd planned to move out anyway, once you and *Pai* started on the campaign trail.'

'Move out and go where? This is your home, Inez,' he replied.

She shook her head. 'My world doesn't begin and end in this house, Pietro. I intend to rent an apartment, get a job.'

'Then don't start by ruining yourself with Pantelides.'

Her throat clogged. 'My reputation is already in shreds after Constantine. I really have nothing left to lose.'

She turned to head up the grand staircase that led to the twin wings of their villa. Behind her, she could still hear Pietro pacing the hallway.

'This doesn't make any sense, Inez. Perhaps a good night's sleep will bring you to your senses.'

She didn't answer. Because she didn't want to waste her time telling him the decision had already been made for her.

For Theo to have gone to the effort of staging that kiss and paving the way for the lies she had to perpetuate, she knew without a shadow of a doubt that his demands were real.

He'd gone to a lot of trouble to set up tonight's meeting. She would be a fool to bait him to see if he would carry out his threat.

Her heart hammered as she undressed and stepped beneath the shower. Slowly soaping her body, she found her mind drifting back to their kiss. The incandescent delirium of it was unlike anything she'd felt before.

Her fingers touched her lips, and they tingled in remembrance.

Tomorrow she was inviting herself into the lion's den to be devoured whole for the sake of her family.

A hysterical laugh became lost in the sound of the running water.

Pietro was finally showing signs of being the brother she remembered before their mother died. Shame that she'd had to sacrifice herself on the altar of their family's prosperity before he'd come round. As for her father…sadness engulfed her at the thought that even if he knew of her sacrifice, he probably wouldn't lift a finger to shield her from it.

Theo's gaze strayed to his phone for the umpteenth time in under twenty minutes and he cursed under his breath.

He'd called Inez this morning and they'd agreed a time of eleven o'clock, two hours before he was due to sign the documents at her father's office.

It was now eleven twenty-five and there was no sign of her. No big deal. She was probably stuck in traffic. Or she hadn't left her home on time, especially if she was packing for a three-month stay.

Besides, women are always late.

Even as a child he'd known this. His mother had never been on time for a single event in her life.

His mother…

Memory rained down vicious blows that had him catching his breath. His mother, the woman who'd been nowhere in sight, either before or after he was kidnapped and held for ransom by Benedicto da Costa's vicious thugs.

For weeks after he'd been rescued and returned home, broken and devastated by his ordeal, he'd asked for his mother. Ari had made several excuses for her absence. But Theo had been unable to reconcile the fact that the mother who'd once treated him as if he'd been the centre of her world suddenly couldn't even be bothered to pick up the phone and enquire about her mentally and physically traumatised child.

No. She'd been too preoccupied with wallowing in her misery following her husband's betrayal to bother with her own children.

Ari had been the one to hold them together after their family was shattered by the press uncovering their father's many shady dealings and philandering ways.

For a very long time he'd laboured under the misconception that out of the three brothers he was the most special in their father's eyes. That just because he was the miracle baby his parents had never thought they'd have, he was their favourite. His kidnapping and what he'd uncovered since had mercilessly ripped that indulgent blindfold away.

Finding out that his father had known about Benedicto da Costa's escalating threats and that he'd done nothing to warn or protect him had forced the cruellest reality on him.

And his mother's response to all that had been to abandon him, together with her other two children, and go into hiding.

Hearing of his father's eventual death had made him even angrier at being robbed of the chance to look his father in the eye and see the monster for himself.

Because, even now, a pathetic part of him clung to the hope that maybe his father hadn't known the full extent of the kidnapping threat; hadn't known that Benedicto da Costa's reaction to being thwarted out of a business deal would be to kidnap a seventeen-year-old boy, and have his torture photographed and sent to his family to pressure them into finding the millions of dollars owed to him.

His phone rang, wrenching him out of the bitter recollections. Glancing down at the number, a bolt of white-hot anger lanced through him. He forced himself to wait for a couple more rings before he answered it. 'Pantelides.'

'*Bom dia.* I've just had a very interesting conversation with my daughter.' Theo detected the throb of anger in Benedicto da Costa's voice and a grim smile curved his own lips. 'She seems determined to pursue this rather *sudden* course of action where you're concerned.'

'Your daughter strikes me as a very determined woman who knows exactly what she wants,' he replied smoothly.

'She is. All the same, I can't help think that this decision is rather precipitate.' There was clear suspicion in Benedicto's voice now.

'Trust me, it's been very well thought through on my part. Tell me, Benedicto, has she left yet?'

'*Sim*, against my wishes, she has left home,' he replied, his voice taut with displeasure.

A wave of satisfaction swept through Theo. 'Good. I'll await her arrival.'

'I hope this will not delay our meeting,' the older man enquired.

'Don't worry. The moment I welcome your daughter into my home, I'll head to your offices.'

An edgy silence greeted his answer and Theo could sense him weighing his words to perceive a possible threat. Finally, Benedicto answered, 'We should celebrate our partnership once the documents are signed.'

Theo's mouth twisted. Benedicto had already moved on from the subject of his daughter. And he noticed there had been no admonition to treat her well, *or else…*

But the knowledge that Benedicto had intensely disapproved of Inez's intentions and had called him to air that disapproval was good enough for him.

'Great idea. Unfortunately, I'll be busy for the next few nights. Perhaps some time next week Inez and I will have you and Pietro over for dinner.'

The fiery exhalation that greeted his indelicate words made Theo's grin widen.

'Of course. I'll look forward to it. *Até a próxima,*' Benedicto said tightly.

Theo ended the call without responding. He absorbed the pulse of triumph rushing through his bloodstream for a pleasurable second before he exhaled.

His plan was far from being executed. But this was a brilliant start.

He looked out of the floor to ceiling window at the sparkling pool and the beach beyond and tried to push away the images that had visited him again last night and the single hoarse scream that had woken him.

A full body shudder raked his frame and he shoved a hand through his hair. Although he'd long ago accepted the nightmares as part of his existence, he loathed their presence and the helplessness he felt in those endless moments when he was caught in their grip.

The single therapy session he'd let Ari talk him into attending had mentioned triggers and the importance of anxiety-detectors.

He laughed under his breath. Putting himself within touching distance of the man responsible for those nightmares would be termed as foolhardy by most definitions.

Theo chose to believe that exacting excruciating revenge would heal him. *An eye for an eye.*

And if he had to suffer a few side-effects during the process, then so be it.

He tensed as his security intercom buzzed. Crossing the vast sun-dappled room, he picked up the handset.

'*Senhor*, there's a Senhorita da Costa here to see you.'

A throb of a different nature invaded his bloodstream. 'Let her in,' he instructed.

Replacing the handset, he found himself striding to the front door and out onto his driveway before he realised what he was doing.

Hands on his hips, he watched her tiny green sports car appear on his long driveway. The top was down and the wind was blowing through her loose thick hair. Stylish sunglasses shielded her eyes from him but he knew she was watching him just as he was studying her.

She brought the car to a smooth stop a few feet from him and turned off the ignition. For several seconds the only sound that impinged on the late morning air was the water cascading from the stone nymph's urn into the fountain bowl. Then the sound of her seat belt retracting joined the tinkling.

'You're late,' he breathed.

She pulled out her keys and opened her door. 'It took

a while to uproot myself from the only home I've ever known,' she said waspishly.

A touch from a well-manicured finger and the boot popped open. He strolled forward, viewed its contents and his eyes narrowed.

'And yet you only packed two suitcases for a three-month stay?' he remarked darkly. 'I hope you don't think you can run back to *Pai*'s house each time you need a new toothbrush?'

She got out of the car.

From across the width of the open top, she glared at him. 'I can afford to buy my own toothbrush, thanks,' she retorted.

Theo nodded. 'Good to hear it.' Unable to stop himself, his gaze travelled down her body.

Faded jeans moulded her hips and her cream scooped-neck silk top left her arms bare. Its short-in-the-front, longer-at-the-back design exposed a delicious inch of golden, smooth midriff when she turned to shut her door and the air lifted the light material.

Heat invaded his groin, once again reminding him of their kiss last night.

The kiss that had blown him clean away and rendered him almost incoherent by the time her brother had rudely interrupted them.

Hell, she'd been so responsive, so intoxicatingly passionate, she'd gone to his head within seconds. What had set out as a hammering-a-point-home exercise to convince her he meant business had swiftly morphed into something else. Something he'd still been struggling to decipher when she'd been hustled off his boat by her suddenly protective brother.

One thing he'd been certain of was that had Pietro been a few more minutes returning to the top deck, Theo was sure he would've had his hands on her bare skin, exploring her in a more earthy way, propriety be damned.

Luckily, he'd come to his senses. And, from here on in, he intended to focus on his plan and his plan alone.

She went to the boot and bent over to lift the first case. The sight of her rounded bottom made a vein throb in his temple.

He stepped forward, grabbed the cases from her and handed them to his hovering butler. 'I'm running late for my meeting. We should have done this last night like I suggested.'

He'd tried. But she'd stood her ground and he had quickly decided that there was nothing to be gained from getting into a slanging match with Pietro da Costa. That he'd also realised that his change of timing was to do with that kiss and nothing to do with his carefully laid plans had had him sharply reassessing his priorities.

'I'm here now. Don't let me stop you from leaving if you wish to.'

He smiled at the undisguised hope in her voice. 'Now what kind of host would I be if I desert you the moment you turn up?'

'The same as the one who blackmailed me into this situation in the first place?' she replied caustically.

There was a thread of unhappiness in her voice that grated at him.

'This will go a lot easier if you accept the status quo.'

'You mean just shut up and *do as I'm told*?' she snapped bitterly as she slammed the boot shut and walked towards him.

Unease weaved through him. With restless shoulders, he shrugged it away. 'No. You can protest all you want. I just want you to be aware of the futility of it.'

She snorted under her breath, a sound that made his smile widen. She had spirit, and wasn't afraid to bare her claws when cornered. Which made him wonder why she withstood the unreasonable control from her father. Were material benefits so important to her?

The heavy glass front door slid shut behind them and he watched her reaction to his house. It was an architectural masterpiece, and had featured in several top magazines before he'd bought it a year ago and ceased all publicity of the award-winning design.

'Wow,' she breathed. 'This place must have cost you a bomb.'

Theo had his answer. Disappointment scythed through him as he watched her move to the bronze sculpture he'd acquired several weeks back.

'I saw the exhibition on this two months ago. This piece is worth a cool half million,' she gasped in wonder. 'And that one—' she pointed to another smaller sculpture he'd commissioned by his favourite New York artist '—is an exclusive piece, worth over two million dollars.'

His lips twisted. 'Should I be worried that you know the monetary value of every piece of art in my house?'

She whirled to face him. 'Excuse me?'

'I hope we can engage in more meaningful dialogue than how much everything is worth. I find the subject of avarice…distasteful.'

Her gasp sounded genuinely hurt-filled. 'I wasn't…I'm just…that's a horrible thing to say, Mr Pantelides.'

His eyebrow lifted. 'I thought I kissed all the formality out of you last night?'

She flushed a delicate pink that made her skin glow. Her expressive brown eyes slid from his and she turned back to examine the room.

It was then that he noticed the faint bruises on her left arm. He was striding to her and lifting her arm to examine the marks before his brain had connected with his body.

'Who did this to you?' he demanded.

Her surprised gaze snapped from his to her arm. Her flush deepened as she swiftly shook her head. 'I…it doesn't matter; it's nothing—'

He swallowed hard. 'Like hell it is.' The idea that his demands on her might have caused this to happen to her made a thread of revulsion rise in his belly. He forced it down and concentrated on her face. 'Tell me who it was.'

She swallowed. 'My father.'

Pure fury blurred his vision for several seconds. 'Your *father* did this to you?'

She gave a jerky nod.

Why the hell was he surprised? 'Has he done anything like this before?' he bit out.

She pressed her lips together in a vain attempt not to answer. A firm grip of her chin, tilting it to his gaze, convinced her otherwise. 'Once. Maybe twice.'

His vicious curse made her shiver. Theo examined the marks, which would grow yellowish by nightfall, and pushed down the mounting fury. 'That son of a bitch will never touch you again.'

Shock made her gasp. 'That *son of a bitch* is my *father*. And I've given you what you wanted, so I expect you to hold up your end of the bargain.'

He frowned with genuine puzzlement. 'Why do you tolerate this, Inez?' He glanced from the bruises to her face. 'You're more than old enough to live on your own. Hell, if money and a rich lifestyle are what you crave, you're sufficiently resourceful to find some wealthy guy who would—'

She snatched her arm from his grasp. It was then that he realised he'd been caressing her soft skin with his thumb. He missed the connection almost immediately.

'I certainly hope you're not about to suggest what I think you are?'

Keen frustration rocked him into movement. 'I'm curious, that's all.'

'I'm not here to satisfy your curiosity. And perhaps you've been lucky enough to be granted a perfect family but not everyone has been afforded the same luxury. We made do with what we… Did I say something funny?' she snapped.

He cut off the mirthless laughter that had bubbled up at

her words. 'Yes. *You're damned hilarious.* You obviously don't know what you're talking about.'

She stared at him with confusion and a little trepidation. 'No. But how can I? We only met two nights ago. And now I'm here, your possession for the foreseeable future.'

The simple statement twisted like live electricity between them. The look in her eyes said she was daring him to react to it. But the off-kilter emotions swirling through his chest made him back away from it. He shouldn't have dealt with her so soon after speaking to Benedicto. He should've left Teresa, his housekeeper, to see to her needs.

He turned and headed for the door. 'I'll show you upstairs. And then I need to go.'

Striding into the hallway, he started up the grand central stairs that led to the upper two floors of his house. After a few steps, he noticed she wasn't behind him.

Turning, he found her paused on the second step, her gaze once again wide and wondrous as she stared around her.

'What?'

'There are no concrete walls.' She looked up at the all-encompassing glass around her. 'Or ceilings.'

He resumed climbing the stairs. 'I don't like walls. And I don't like ceilings,' he threw over his shoulder.

She hurried after him and caught up with him as they neared the first suite of rooms. She regarded him for a few seconds then bit her lip.

He paused with a hand on the doorknob. 'What?' he asked again, trying and not succeeding in prising his gaze from her plump lips.

'I'm not sure whether to take that as a metaphor or not.'

'*Anjo*, there's no hidden meaning behind my words. I literally do not like concrete walls or ceilings.'

She frowned in puzzlement. 'I don't understand.'

'It's very simple. I don't like being closed in.'

'You're…*claustrophobic*?' She whispered the word as if she wasn't sure how to apply it to him.

He shrugged and hurriedly threw open the door, a part of him reeling at what he'd just admitted. 'We all have our flaws,' he retorted.

'Were you born with it?'

His jaw clenched once. 'No. It was a condition thrust upon me quite against my will.'

'But…you seem…'

'Invincible?' he mocked.

Her lips pursed. 'I was going to say self-assured.'

'Appearances can be deceptive, *querida*. After you.' He indicated the door he'd just opened.

She stopped dead in the middle of the room. From where he stood, Theo could see what she was seeing. With the glass walls and white carpet and furnishings and nothing but the view of the blue sky and sea beyond, the vista was breathtaking.

'*Deus*, I feel as if I'm floating on a cloud,' she murmured with an awe-filled voice.

'That is the primary aim of the property. Light, air, no constrictions.'

He'd learned to his cost that constrictions triggered his anxiety and fuelled his nightmares. Which was why every single property he owned was filled with light.

'It's beautiful.'

The strong pulse of pleasure that washed through him had him stepping back. Things were getting out of hand. He needed to walk away, go to his meeting with Benedicto and remind himself why he was in Rio. This need to bask in Inez's presence, touch her skin, indulge in the urge to taste her sensual lips once more needed to killed. He had to stick to his game plan.

'Make yourself at home. I'll be back later. We're going out this evening. Dinner at Cabana de Ouro, then probably clubbing. Wear something short and sexy.'

Her eyes widened at his curt tone but he was already turning away. He didn't stop until he reached the landing.

On a completely unstoppable urge, he looked over his shoulder. Through the glass walls, he saw her frozen in the middle of her suite, her eyes fixed on him.

She looked lost. And confused. And a little relieved.

With grim determination he turned and headed down the stairs. And he hated himself for needing the reminder that Benedicto da Costa had damaged not just him, but his whole family.

The payback should be equal to the crime committed.

The black satin boy shorts she chose to wear were plenty stylish and sexy. They also moulded her behind much more than she was strictly comfortable with but everything else she'd hastily packed was too formal for dinner at Cabana de Ouro, the trendy restaurant and bar in Ipanema. Coupled with the dark gold silk top, with her hair piled on top of her head and gold hoops in her ears and bangles on her wrist, she looked good enough for whatever club Theo intended to take her to after dinner.

Clubbing wasn't strictly her entertainment of choice. But since, for the next twelve weeks, Theo expected her to obey his every command, the least she could do was learn to pick her battles. And she'd already endured one battle this morning in the form of confrontation with Theo. And found out he was claustrophobic.

He'd been right; she'd secretly imagined him to be invincible. The way he carried himself, the innate authority and self-assurance that seemed part of his genetic make up, she'd had no trouble seeing him best each situation he found himself him.

Hearing him admit to a deep flaw that most grown men would be ashamed of had floored her. Coupled with his concern when he'd seen the marks her father had inflicted when she'd announced she was moving in with Theo, she'd been seriously floundering in a sea of uncertainty by the time he'd left her bedroom.

She examined the marks on her arm now and released a shaky breath to see that they were fading. She was shrugging on the shoulder-padded waist-length leather jacket that went with the outfit when she heard Theo's Aston Martin roar into the driveway.

Her fingers trembled as she fastened the long-chained gold medallion necklace at her nape.

He'd left her so abruptly this morning she hadn't had the time to question him about sleeping arrangements. A closer examination of her suite after he'd left had revealed no presence of another occupant, and after talking to Teresa, his housekeeper, she'd found out that the *senhor*'s suite was directly above hers, taking up the whole glass-roofed top floor of the house.

The fact that she wouldn't be expected to share his bed immediately should've pleased her. Instead she was more on edge than ever. Or maybe that was what he wanted? That she should be kept guessing, kept on a knife-edge of uncertainty like some sort of game?

Deus!

She'd barely spent one day under his glass roof and already she was being driven mad. His response to her admiring his sculptures had been too infuriating for her to explain how she'd come to acquire such knowledge of sculptures— her late mother's talent. If he wanted to believe Inez appreciated beautiful art purely with dollar signs in her eyes, that was his problem.

Her breath caught as she heard distinct footsteps in the hallway. Teresa had shown her how to shroud the bedroom glass for privacy and she'd activated it before she'd gone in to take a shower. It was still shrouded now although she could make out a faint outline of the towering man who knocked a few seconds later.

'Come in.' She cringed at the husky breathlessness of her voice.

The heavy glass swung back and Theo stood framed in the doorway.

Light hazel eyes locked on her with the force of a laser beam for several seconds before they travelled slowly down her body.

Before meeting him, Inez would've found it hard to believe she could physically react so strongly to a look from a man. Constantine, with all his misleading smiles and false charm, had never affected her like this, not even when she'd believed herself in love with him.

With Theo the evidence was irrefutable—in the accelerated beat of her heart, the tightening and heaviness of her breasts and the stinging heat that spread outward from her belly like a flash fire.

She watched his mouth drop open as his gaze reached her shorts and her own mouth dried at the look that settled on his face.

'What the hell are you wearing?'

'What? I'm wearing clothes, Mr Pantelides,' she snapped, once she was able to get her brain working again.

He stepped into the room and the door slid shut behind him. All at once, she became aware of the sheer size of him, of the restriction in her breathing and the fact that her eyes were devouring his magnificent form.

'Let's get one thing straight. From now on you'll address me as Theo. No more *senhor* and no more Mr Pantelides, understand?'

'Is that an order?' She tilted her chin to see his face as he stopped before her.

'It's a friendly warning that there will be consequences if you don't comply.'

'What consequences?' she huffed.

'How about every time you call me *senhor* I kiss that sassy mouth of yours?'

CHAPTER SEVEN

'EXCUSE ME?' HER voice was a little more breathless. With excitement. *Deus*, what was wrong with her? This man was threatening her family, was effectively turning her life upside down for the sake of some unknown grudge. And all she could think of was him kissing her again.

'No, you're not excused. Use my first name or I'll kiss it into you. Your choice. Now tell me what the hell you're wearing.' His gaze dropped back to her shorts, his eyes glazing with hunger so acute, her heart hammered.

'These are shorts. You said "short and sexy".'

His mouth worked for a few seconds before he nodded. 'I said short, but I don't think I meant that short, *anjo*.'

Heat raced up her neck and she barely managed to stop her hand from connecting with his face. 'They are not that bad.'

His rasping laugh made her face flame. 'Trust me, from where I'm standing, they're lethal.'

'I have nothing else to change into. Everything else is too formal for a club.'

Dark eyes rose, almost reluctantly, to clash with hers. 'I find that very hard to believe.'

'It's true. I didn't have enough time to pack properly. Besides, I didn't take you for…'

His eyes narrowed. 'Didn't take me for what?'

She shrugged. 'You don't strike me as the clubbing type.'

One corner of his mouth lifted. 'Have you been forming impressions about me, *anjo*?'

She kicked herself for that revelatory remark. 'Not really.'

He looked down at her shorts one more time and he turned abruptly for the door. 'I'll be ready to go in fifteen minutes. You can tell me what other impressions you've formed about me at dinner.'

Inez exhaled and realised she hadn't taken a full breath since he'd walked into her presence. Her whole body quivered as she shoved her feet into three-inch platforms and made sure her cell phone and lipstick were in the black and gold clutch.

She caught sight of herself in the hallway mirror as she made her way down and cringed at the feverish look in her eyes.

Reassuring herself firmly that it was anger at Theo for his overbearing treatment of her, she made her way to the living room.

Floodlights illuminated the pool and gardens in a stunning display of shimmering light and shrubbery. Like every single aspect of the building, the sight was so breathtaking her fingers itched with the need to draw.

Setting her clutch down, she went to the large duffel bag she'd brought down this afternoon and took out her sketchpad and pencil.

She was so lost in capturing the vista before her, she didn't sense Theo enter the room until his unique scent wrapped itself around her.

She jerked around to see him standing close behind her, his eyes on her picture.

'You draw?' he asked in surprise.

Unable to answer for the loud hammering of her heart, she nodded.

He reached forward and plucked the pad from her nerveless fingers. Slowly, he thumbed through the pages. 'You're very talented,' he finally said.

Expecting a derogatory remark to follow, like his comment on his art this morning, her eyes widened when she realised he meant it. 'You really think so?' she asked.

He closed the pad and handed it back to her, his eyes speculative as they rested on her face. 'I wouldn't say it otherwise, *anjo*.'

Pleasure fizzed through her. 'Thank you.' She smiled as she stood. Crossing over to her duffel bag, she bent to place the pad back into it.

'*Thee mou!*'

She dropped the pad and hastily straightened. 'What?'

'You bend over like that while we're out and I will not be responsible for my actions, understood?' he growled.

Her mouth dropped open at the dark promise in his voice. A shudder ran through her body as hunger further darkened his eyes. She licked her lip nervously as the atmosphere thickened with sensual charges that crackled and snapped along her nerves.

'We…we don't have to go out if what I'm wearing offends you…Theo,' she ventured hesitantly, sensing that he held himself on the very edge of control.

He inhaled deeply, his chest expanding underneath the dark green shirt and black leather jacket he wore with black trousers. 'That's where you're wrong. What you're offering doesn't offend me in the least. But I'm a red-blooded, possessive male who is finding it difficult not to roar out his primitive reaction to the idea of other men looking at you.' He said it so matter-of-factly she couldn't form a decent response. 'But I'll try to be a *gentleman*. Come.' He held out his arm.

With seriously indecent thoughts of Theo fighting to the death for her flitting through her mind, she crossed the room to his side.

He led them out and held the passenger door of his car open. The first few minutes of the ride to Ipanema was conducted in silence. Every now and then, he raked a hand through his hair and slid a glance at her naked thighs. Each time, he exhaled noisily.

A wild part of her wanted to flaunt herself for him, revel in his very physical reaction to her attire. Another part of her wanted to run and hide from the volatile emotions swirling through the enclosed space of the luxurious sports car.

By the time they drew up in the car park of the exclusive restaurant her pulse was jumping with anxiety. She forced the feeling down and followed him into the restaurant. Finding out they were dining in the even more exclusive upper floor led to all sorts of renewed anxiety as she preceded him up the steps.

The moment they were seated, he leaned forward. 'The moment we return home, I'm burning those shorts.'

She glared at him. 'No, you are not, *senhor!* They're my favourite pair.'

'Then frame them and mount them on a wall. But you most definitely will not be wearing them out again.'

That wild streak widened. 'I thought you would be man enough to handle a little…challenge. Are you saying you're not?'

His eyes narrowed. 'Don't bait a hungry lion, *querida*, unless you're prepared to be devoured,' he grated out.

'Did you tell your last girlfriend how she should dress too?' she challenged.

His mouth compressed. 'My last girlfriend was under the misconception that the more frequently she walked around naked the more interested I would be in her. She lasted ten days.'

Inez's curiosity spiked, along with an emotion she was very loath to name. 'How long did your longest relationship last?'

'Three weeks.'

Her breath caught. 'So why three *months* with me?' she asked.

He looked startled for a moment then he shrugged. 'Because you're not my girlfriend. You're so very much more.'

Inez was struck dumb by his reply. A small foolish part of her even felt giddy, until she reminded herself that she was intended to be nothing but his *mistress*. Again unfathomable emotions wrapped themselves around her heart. She cleared her throat and fought to keep her voice even. 'Why *misconception*?'

'Very few women manage to catch and keep my interest for very long, *anjo*.'

'Because you get bored easily?' she dared.

His lashes swept down for a few seconds before they rose again to capture hers. 'Because my demons always win when pitted against the rigours of normal relationships.'

'*Demons?*'

'*Sim, anjo*. Demons. I have a lot of them. And they're very possessive.' A wave of anguish rolled over his face, then it was gone the next instant. He nodded to the hovering *sommelier* and ordered their wine. Another pulse of surprise went through her when she noticed it was the same wine she'd served at the fund-raiser and her favourite.

'The burning is now off the table. Hell, you can even keep the damn shorts. But, for the sake of my sanity, can we agree that you don't wear them outside?' he asked with one quirked eyebrow.

She pretended to consider it. 'What is your sanity worth to me?'

'You think you're in a position to bargain with me, Inez?' he asked, his voice deceptively soft.

'I never pass up an opportunity to bargain.'

He regarded her silently for several minutes. Then he shrugged. 'As long as I achieve my goals in the end, I see no reason why the road to success shouldn't be littered with minor obstacles. Tell me what you desire.'

'Is that what I am, a minor obstacle?'

'Don't miss your opportunity with meaningless questions.'

The need for clarity finally forced her to speak. 'I wish to know exactly what you want of me.'

'Sorry, I cannot answer that.'

She frowned. 'Why not?'

'Because my needs are…fluid.' The peculiar smile accompanying his answer sent a tingle of alarm down her spine.

'So I am to live in uncertainty for the next three months?'

'The unknown can be challenging. It can also be exciting.'

'Is that why you came to Rio? To seek challenge and excitement?'

For several seconds he stared at her. Then he slowly shook his head. 'No, my reason for being in Rio is specific and a well-planned event.'

Inez shivered at the succinct response. 'I can't help but be frightened by your answer.'

Her candid admission seemed to surprise him. 'Why is that?'

'Because I have a feeling it has something to do with my family. Pietro has his flaws but he's never done anything without my father's express approval. Besides, you're much older than him, which makes it unlikely that he's the one you came here for. You're here because of my father, aren't you?'

It took an astonishing amount of control not to react to her simple but accurate summation of the single subject that had consumed him for over a decade.

Thinking back, he realised he'd given her several clues to enable her to reach this conclusion. Somehow, in the mere forty-eight hours that he'd known her, Inez had managed to slip under his guard and was threatening to uncover his true purpose for being in Rio.

He also realised that he'd given her much more leeway than he'd ever intended to when he'd formulated his plan. Inviting her to compromise? Inviting her to state her desires with the knowledge that he was seriously considering granting them?

After his hasty departure this morning he'd realised that he'd let those marks on her arms sway him into going easy on her. *Because he hadn't wanted her to think he was a monster like her father?*

The man who hadn't so much as asked after his daughter when Theo had attended his office to sign the agreement papers?

The man whose eyes had shone with greed and triumph even before the ink had dried on the documents?

No, he was nothing like Benedicto da Costa. He wasn't about to lose any already precious sleep wondering about that little statement.

What he had to be careful of was that his enemy's daughter didn't guess his intentions. He was so very close to having Benedicto right where he wanted him. He couldn't afford to be swayed by a heart-shaped face or the most sinfully sexy pair of shorts he'd ever seen in his life, no matter how acute the ache in his groin.

'Will you please tell me why you're after my father?' she implored softly. The concern on her face appeared genuine and he suddenly realised that, despite Benedicto's treatment of her, Inez cared for her father.

His nostrils flared as bitterness rocked through him. He'd once been in that same position, foolishly believing that the father he'd idolised and loved beyond reason cared just as deeply for him. That he wasn't the fraudster and philanderer the press were making him out to be.

Now, he wanted to rip the blindfold from her eyes, make her see the true monster in the man she called *Pai*. Make her see that her love was nothing but a manipulative tool that would be used against her eventually.

Except he had a strong feeling she already knew, and chose to overlook it. Which made his blood boil even more.

'Why, do you plan to sacrifice yourself to save him?' he taunted.

She gasped, dropping the sterling silver fork she'd been nervously toying with. 'So, it *is* my father!'

He cursed under his breath. 'If you so much as breathe a word in his direction about your suspicions, I'll make sure you regret it for the rest of your life.'

She paled. 'You really expect me to sit back and watch you destroy him?'

'I expect you to hold up your end of the bargain we struck. Live under my roof in exchange for me leaving the loophole in the contract alone. Are you prepared to do that or do I need to plot another plan of action?' he asked, not bothering to hide the threat in his voice.

She stared back at him apprehensively. Her chin rose and her brown eyes burned holes in him but she nodded. 'I'll stick to our agreement.'

When their wine was served, he watched her take a big gulp and curbed the desire to follow suit. He was driving and needed to restrict his drinking. Nevertheless, a sip of the Chilean red went a way to restoring a little order to his floundering thoughts.

Thee mou, he hadn't even fired the first salvo and things were getting out of hand. Why on earth had he shared the presence of his demons with her? And that comment about her being so much more than a girlfriend? He silently shook his head and sucked in a control-affirming breath.

Their dinner progressed in near silence. Theo reminded himself that his main reason for bringing her out hadn't been for conversation. When she refused dessert, he settled the bill quickly and rose to help her out of her seat.

Fire shot through his groin, hard and fierce, as he was once again confronted with the risqué shorts. While they'd been seated, he'd managed to tamp down the effect of those shorts on his raging libido.

Now, as she walked in front of him, he was treated to a mouth-watering sight of her deliciously rounded bottom and stunning legs. With each sway of her hips, he grew harder until he wondered if he had any blood left in his upper extremities that hadn't migrated south.

He was reconsidering his decision not to burn the shorts at the earliest opportunity when he caught a male diner staring in blatant appreciation at her legs.

His growl was low but unmistakable. The man hastily averted his gaze but Theo was still simmering in primitive emotions when they reached the car park.

He followed her to the passenger side but, instead of opening the door for her, he braced his hand on either side of her and leaned in close. With her front pressed against the door, her bottom was moulded into his groin in such a way that she couldn't fail to notice his state of arousal.

Her breathing quickened, but she stayed put. 'What are you doing?'

'Delivering the punishment I promised.'

'Sorry?'

'You called me *senhor* when we were in the restaurant.'

She tried to turn around but he pressed her more firmly against the car. 'I...don't remember.'

'Of course you do. You also thought I wouldn't act on my promise in full view of other diners, didn't you?'

'No, I wasn't—'

'Maybe you were right. Or maybe we both knew I'd want to do more than just kiss you.'

'You're wrong...'

'Am I?'

'Yes...'

'So you'd prefer I let this one slide?' He rocked his hips against her bottom and her breath hitched. 'You won't think me weak?'

Her shocked laugh heated the air around them. 'Only someone foolish would think you weak.'

'I'm not sure whether there's a compliment in there. Is there?'

Her head fell forward, exposing the seductive line of her neck. 'Am I to pander to your ego too, Theo?'

He laughed. 'How can you appear submissive and yet taunt me at the same time?'

She lifted her head and turned to stare at him. Whatever she saw in his face made her squirm harder. Provocatively. Her gaze dropped to his mouth and Theo could no more resist the temptation than he could breathe.

Fingers sliding beneath her knotted hair to hold her still, he caught her mouth in a fierce kiss. Every emotion he'd experienced since waking that morning was delivered in that kiss—passion, arousal, confusion, anxiety and anger. He pinned her against the car so she couldn't move, couldn't put those seductive hands on his body.

Although he missed her touch, a part of him was thankful because, had she had access, he would've lost even more of his mind than he suspected he was losing.

He registered the brief flashes behind his closed eyelids but didn't break the kiss. He suspected Inez had no idea what had just happened. And even if she had, she wouldn't have suspected the true reason behind the paparazzi shots because she was used to being the darling of the press.

Well, she was in for a rude awakening…

She started to open her mouth wider, to return his demanding kiss.

He slowly lifted his head. When she made a tiny sound of protest and tried to recapture his mouth, he forced himself to step away. He'd achieved one part of what he'd set out to do. The second part was a short drive away.

Curving his arm around her waist, he peeled her away from the door, opened it and deposited her inside, all the time trying not to stare down at her legs and imagine how they would feel wrapped around his waist.

He swallowed hard as he rounded the hood and slid behind the wheel.

'Time to head to the club before I give in to the urge to deliver more punishment.'

Her eyes dropped to his mouth and he barely suppressed a groan as she licked her lips.

'For your mercy, I will teach you how to samba like a true Brazilian,' she replied huskily.

Inez lay among the white sheets the next morning, trying hard not to relive the events of the night before but it was as futile as trying to stop a tidal wave.

They'd eventually emerged from the nightclub at two in the morning. She'd been flushed and sweaty from being plastered to Theo's superb body for three straight hours. But the wild racing of her heart had nothing to do with her exertions on the dance floor and everything to do with the man who'd focused on her as if she was the only woman in the whole club.

And *Deus*, had he danced like a dream? Far from tutoring him on the correct steps of her native dance, she'd found herself following his lead as he'd moved expertly on the dance floor.

When he'd caught her to him, her back to his front and re-played the scene in the car park, but this time to music, she'd seriously feared her heart would beat itself to expiration.

In that moment, she'd forgotten that there was a sinister purpose to Theo's plan; that he'd all but admitted she was being used as a pawn in some deadly game he was playing with her father. When he'd laid his stubbled jaw against her cheek and hummed the sultry samba music in her ear, she'd closed her eyes and imagined what it would be like to belong—truly belong—to a man like Theo.

Turning over in bed, she groaned in disbelief at how

susceptible she'd been to his hard body and magnetic charisma. *Santa Maria*, she'd been all but putty in his hands.

Luckily, the fresh air and the long drive back had hammered some sense into her. The moment they'd returned, she'd bidden him a curt *boa noite*, left him standing in the hallway and retreated as fast as her sore feet would carry her.

And she intended to carry on like that. She might not know what his end game was, but she refused to be a willing participant in his campaign.

The last thing she wanted to do was to fall for another manipulator like Constantine.

She was here only because she had no choice but she didn't intend to idle away her time in this house. Theo expected her to stay here for three months, which meant whatever he had planned was not to be executed immediately. Perhaps she could convince him to change his mind in that time.

Yeah, and fairy tales really did come true...

Or she could find out exactly what his intentions were.

She'd seen the look in his eyes when he spoke about her father. Whatever vendetta he'd planned, he intended to see it through.

Helplessly, she rolled over in bed and her eyes lit on the bedside clock. She jerked upright and threw the sheet aside. She might not have anywhere to be on this Saturday morning but lazing about in bed past ten o'clock wasn't her style.

She jumped into the shower, shampooed her hair and washed her body with quick, regimented movement ingrained in her from her time at the Swiss boarding school her father had sent her to just to impress his friends.

Leaving her damp hair to dry naturally, she pulled on an aqua-coloured sundress and slipped her feet into low-heeled thongs. Smoothing her favourite sunscreen moisturiser over her face and arms, she left her room and headed downstairs.

Teresa was crossing the hallway carrying a *cafetière* of freshly made coffee and indicated for Inez to follow her.

She led her out to the terrace that overlooked the immense square infinity pool. Light danced off the water but her attention was caught and held by the man seated at the cast iron oval breakfast table.

His white short-sleeved polo shirt did amazing things to his eyes and olive-toned skin. And loose green shorts exposed solid thighs and lightly hair-sprinkled legs that made her mouth dry before flooding with moisture that threatened to choke her.

'*Bom dia, anjo.* Are you going to stand there all morning?' he mocked.

She forced her legs to move and took the chair he indicated to his right.

'Coffee?' he asked, his voice deep and low.

'Yes, please.' Her voice had grown husky and emerged barely above a whisper.

He nodded to Teresa who smiled, filled her cup then made herself scarce.

Inez sipped the hot brew just as a delaying tactic so she didn't have to look at him.

So far she'd seen Theo in formal evening wear and smart casual and each look had threatened to knock her sideways. But seeing him now, with so much of his vibrant olive skin on show, threatened to topple her completely. She took another hasty sip and choked as the liquid scalded her mouth.

Grabbing the napkin to stop herself from dribbling like an idiot, she looked up and caught his mocking smile. 'You'd rather blister yourself than converse with me?'

She swallowed and fought to present a passable smile. 'Of course not. I was just enjoying the…view.' She indicated beyond his shoulder, where the garden extended beyond the pool and sloped down to the sandy white beach and sparkling ocean.

With a disbelieving smile, he picked up the paper next to his plate and shook it out. 'If you say so—'

Her horrified gasp made him lower the newspaper. 'Something wrong?'

'Is that a picture of *us*?' she demanded through a severely constricted throat. The question was redundant because the picture taking up the whole of the front page was printed in vivid Technicolor.

He'd already seen it, of course, so he didn't bother to glance where her appalled gaze was riveted. 'Yes. Fresh off the morning press.'

'*Meu deus!*' She reached out and snatched the broadsheet out of his grasp. It was even worse up close. 'It looks as if...as if—' Disbelief caught in her throat, eating the rest of her words.

'As if I'm taking you from behind?' he supplied helpfully.

Humiliating heat stained her cheeks. '*Sim*,' she muttered fiercely. 'With your jacket covering me that way it looks as if I'm wearing nothing from the waist down! It's...it's disgusting!'

He plucked the paper from her hand and studied the picture. 'Hmm, it certainly is...*something*.'

'How can you sit there and be so unconcerned about it?' The picture had been taken with a high-resolution camera but, with the low lighting in the car park, the suggestiveness in the picture could be misinterpreted a thousand ways. None of them complimentary.

'Relax. We weren't exactly having sex, were we?'

'That's not the point.' She grabbed the paper back and quickly perused the article accompanying the gratuitous picture, fearing the worst. Sure enough, her father's political campaign had been called into question, along with an even more unsavoury speculation on her private life.

If this is what they do in public we can only imagine what they do in private...

Her hands shook as she threw the offending paper down. 'I thought this was a reputable paper.'

'It is.'

'Then why would they print something so...offensive?'

'Perhaps because it's true. We were kissing in the car park. And you were pushing your delectable backside into my groin as if you couldn't wait till we got home to do me.'

She surged to her feet, knocking her chair aside. Her whole body was shaking with fury and she could barely grasp the chair to straighten it.

'We both know I was not!'

'Do we? I told you those shorts were a bad idea. Do you blame me for getting carried away?'

'Oh, you're *despicable!*'

'And you're delicious when you're angry,' he replied lazily, picked up the paper and carried on reading.

The urge to drive her fist through the paper into his face made her take another hasty step back.

She abhorred violence. Or at least she had before she'd met Theo Pantelides. Now she wasn't so sure what she was capable of...

'Aren't you going to eat, *anjo?*' he asked without taking his eyes off the page.

'No. I've lost my appetite,' she snapped.

She fled the terrace to the sound of his mocking laughter and raced up to her room, her face flaming and angry humiliation smashing through her chest.

He found her on the beach an hour later. She heard the crunch of his feet in the warm sand and studiously avoided looking up. She carried on sketching the stationary boat anchored about a mile away and ignored him when he settled himself on the flat rock next to her.

He didn't speak for a few minutes before he let out an irritated breath. 'The silent treatment doesn't work for me, Inez.'

She snapped her pad shut and turned to face him. His

lips were pinched with displeasure but his eyes were focused, gauging her reaction…almost as if her reaction mattered.

'Having my sex life sleazily speculated about in the weekend newspaper doesn't work for me either.' She blinked to dilute the intense focus and continued. 'I agree that perhaps those shorts were not the best idea. But I saw the other diners in that restaurant. There were people far more famous than I am. But still the paparazzo followed us into the car park and took our picture.'

Inez thought he tensed but perhaps it was the movement of his body as he reached behind him and produced a plate laden with food. 'It's done. Let's move on.'

She yearned to remain on her high horse, but with her exertions last night, coupled with having eaten less than a whole meal in the last twenty-four hours, it wasn't surprising when her stomach growled loudly in anticipation.

He shook out a napkin and settled the plate in her lap. 'Eat up,' he instructed and picked up her sketchpad. 'You have an hour before the stylist arrives to address the issue of your wardrobe.'

She froze in the act of reaching for the food. 'I don't need a stylist. I can easily go back home and pack up some more clothes.'

'You'll not be returning to your father's house for the next three months. Besides, if your clothes are all in the style of heavy evening gowns or tiny shorts, then you'll agree the time has come to go a different route?'

She mentally scanned her wardrobe and swiftly concluded that he was probably right. 'There really is no need,' she tried anyway.

'It's too late to change the plan, Inez.'

And, just like that, the subject was closed. He tapped the plate and, as if on cue, her stomach growled again.

Giving up the argument, she devoured the thick sliced beef sandwich and polished off the apple in greedy bites.

She was gulping down the bottled water when she saw him pause at her sketch of a boat.

'This is very good.'

'Thank you.'

He tilted the page. 'You like boats?'

'Very much. My mother used to take me sailing. It was my favourite thing to do with her.'

He closed the pad. 'Were you two close?'

'She was my best friend,' she responded in a voice that cracked with pain. 'Not a day goes by that I don't miss her.'

His fingers seemed to tighten on the rock before they relaxed again. 'Mothers have a way of affecting you that way. It makes their absence all the harder to bear.'

'Is yours…when did you lose yours?' she asked.

He turned and stared at her. A bleak look entered his eyes but dissolved in the next blink. 'My mother is very much alive.'

She gasped. 'But I thought you said…'

'Absence doesn't mean death. There are several ways for a parent to be absent from a child's life without the ultimate separation.'

'Are you talking about abandonment?'

Again he glanced at her, and this time she caught a clearer glimpse of his emotions. Pain. Devastating pain.

'Abandonment. Indifference. Selfishness. Self-absorption. There are many forms of delivering the same blow,' he elaborated in a rough voice.

'I know. But I was lucky. My mother was the best mother in the world.'

'Is that why you're trying to be the best daughter in the world for your father, despite what you know of him?'

His accusation was like sandpaper against her skin. 'I beg your pardon?'

He shook his head. 'Don't bother denying it. You know exactly what sort of person he is. And yet you've stood by him all these years. Why—because you want a pat on the head and to be told you're a good daughter?'

The truth of his words hit her square in the chest. Up until yesterday, everything she'd done, every plan of her father's she'd gone along with had been to win his approval, and in some way make up for the fact that she hadn't been born the right gender. She didn't want to curl up and hide from the truth. But the callous way he condemned her made her want to justify her actions.

'I'm not blind to my father's shortcomings.' She ignored his caustic snort. 'But neither am I going to make excuses for my actions. My loyalty to my family isn't something I'm ashamed of.'

'Even when that loyalty meant turning a blind eye to other people's suffering?' he demanded icily.

She frowned. 'Whose suffering?'

'The people he left behind in the *favelas* for a start. Do you know that less than two per cent of the funds raised at those so-called charity events you so painstakingly put together actually make it to the people who need it most?'

She felt her face redden. His condemning gaze raked over her features. 'Of course you do,' he murmured acidly.

'It happened in the past, I admit it, but I only agreed to organise the last event if everything over and above the cost of doing it went to the *favelas*.' At his disbelieving look, she added, 'I do a lot of work with charities. I know what I'm talking about.'

'And did you ensure that it was done?'

'Yes. The charity confirmed they'd received the funds yesterday.'

One eyebrow quirked in surprise before he jerked to his feet. Thrusting his hands into his pockets, he turned to face her. 'That's progress at least.'

'Thank you. I don't live in a fairy tale. Trust me, I'm trying to do my part to help the *favelas*.'

'How?'

She debated a few seconds before she answered. 'I work at an inner city charity a few times a week.'

His gaze probed hers. 'That morning outside the coffee shop, that was where you were going?'

'Yes.'

'What does your father think?'

She bit her lip. 'He doesn't know.'

His mouth twisted. 'Because it will draw attention to his lies about his upbringing? Everyone knows he was born and raised in the *favelas*.'

'It's part of the reason why I didn't tell him, yes. But he denies his *favela* upbringing because he's…ashamed.'

'And yet he doesn't mind anyone knowing about his mother?'

'He thinks it gives him a little leverage with the common man to be indirectly associated with the *favelas*.'

'So he likes to rewrite his history as he goes along?'

'Perhaps. I don't delude myself for one second that my father doesn't bend the rules and the truth at times.'

His harsh laugh made her start. 'Right. Are you talking about, oh, let's see…doing ninety on a sixty miles per hour road, or are we talking about something with a little more…teeth?'

That note she'd heard before. The one that sent a foreboding chill along her spine, that warned her that something else was going on here. Something she should be running far and fast from. 'I…I'm not sure what you're implying.'

'Then let me spell it out for you. Are we talking about harmless anecdotes or are we talking about actual deeds? You know—broken kneecaps? Ruptured spleens. *Kidnap for ransom*?'

Her hand flew to her mouth. 'What the hell are you talking about?'

'Come on, you know what your father is capable of. Do

I need to remind you of what he did to you when you displeased him?'

She followed his gaze to the marks on her arm and slowly shook her head. 'I don't excuse this but I refuse to believe he's the monster you describe.'

His mouth twisted. 'I'll let you enjoy your rosy outlook for now, *querida*. I, too, felt like that once about my own father.'

'Is that what you're going to do to my father? Make him accountable for the things he's done?'

For several heartbeats she was sure he wouldn't answer her, or would change the subject the way he'd done in the past. But finally he nodded.

'Yes. I intend to make him pay for what he took from me twelve years ago.'

Her breath froze in her lungs. 'What did he take from you?'

He turned abruptly and faced the water, his stance rigid and forbidding. But Inez found herself moving towards him anyway, a visceral need driving her. She reached out and touched his shoulder. He tensed harder and she was reminded of his reaction to her touch on his boat. 'Theo?'

'I don't like being touched when my back's turned, *anjo*.'

She frowned. 'Why not?'

'Part of my demons.'

Her gut clenched hard at the rough note in his voice. 'Did…did my father do that to you?'

'Not personally. After all, he's an upright citizen now, isn't he? A man the people should trust.' He whipped about to face her.

'But he had something to do with your claustrophobia. And this?'

'Yes.'

'Theo—'

'Enough with the questions! You're forgetting why you're here. Do you need a reminder?'

She swallowed at the arctic look in his eyes. All signs of the raw, vulnerable pain she'd glimpsed minutes ago were wiped clean. Theo Pantelides was once again a man in control, bent on revenge. Slowly, she shook her head. 'No. No, I don't.'

CHAPTER EIGHT

THEIR CONVERSATION AT the beach set a frigid benchmark for the beginning of her stay at Theo's glass mansion.

The next two weeks passed in an icy blur of hectic days and even more hectic evenings. They'd quickly fallen into a routine where Theo left after a quick cup of coffee and a brief outline of when and where they would be dining that evening.

On the second morning when she'd told him she was heading for the charity, he'd raised an eyebrow. 'What sort of work do you do there?'

'Whatever I'm needed to do.' She'd been reluctant to tell him any specifics in case he disparaged her efforts as a rich girl's means of passing the time till the next party.

He'd returned to his coffee. 'Your time is your own when I'm not around. As long you're back here when I return, I see no problem.'

That had been the end of the subject.

After repeating his warning not to mention anything to her father he'd walked away. The man who'd shown her his pain and devastation had completely retreated.

His demeanour during their time indoors was icily courteous. However, when they went out, which they did most evenings, he was the attentive host, touching her, threading his fingers through her hair and gazing adoringly at her.

It was after the fifth night out that she realised he was

pandering to the paparazzi. Without fail, a picture of them in a compromising position appeared in the newspapers the very next morning.

But while she cringed with every exposing photo, he shrugged it off. It wasn't until her third weekend with him, when the newspapers posted the first poll results of the mayoral race, that she finally had her suspicions confirmed.

He was swimming in the pool, his lean and stunning body cutting through the water like the sleekest shark. The byline explaining the reasons behind the voters' reaction had her surging to her feet and storming to the edge of the pool.

'Is this why you've been taking me out every night since I moved in? So I'd be labelled the slut daughter of a man not fit to be mayor?' She raised her voice loud enough to be heard above his powerful strokes.

He stopped mid-stroke, straightened and slicked back his wet hair. With smooth breaststrokes he swam to where she stood barefoot. Looking down at his wet, sun-kissed face, she momentarily lost her train of thought.

He soon set her straight. 'Your father isn't worthy to lead a chain gang, never mind a city,' he replied in succinct, condemning tones. 'And before I'm done with him, the whole world will know it.'

Despite seeing the evidence for herself two weeks ago at the beach, despite knowing that whatever her father had done to him had been devastating, she staggered back a step at that solid, implacable oath.

He planted his hands on the tiles and heaved himself out of the water. It took every ounce of her self-control not to devour him with hungry eyes. But not looking didn't mean not feeling. Her insides clenched with the ever-growing hunger she'd been unable to stem since the first night he'd walked into her life. And, with each passing day, she was finding it harder and harder to remain unaffected.

It seemed not even knowing why she was here, or the full extent of how Theo intended to use her to hurt her father, could cause her intense emotional reaction to his proximity to abate.

Which made her ten kinds of a fool, who needed to pull her thoughts together or risk getting hurt all over again.

'So you don't deny that you used me as bait to derail my father's campaign?'

Hazel eyes, devoid of emotion, narrowed on her face. 'That was one course of action. But you haven't been labelled a slut. I'll sue any newspaper that dares to call you that,' he rasped.

Her laughter scraped her throat. 'There are several ways to describe someone without using the actual derogatory word, Theo.'

He paused in drying his hair and looked at her. Slowly, he held out his hand. 'Show me.'

She handed the paper over. He read it tight-jawed. 'I'll have them print a retraction.'

Dismay roiled through her stomach, along with a heavy dose of rebellious anger.

'That's not the point, though, is it? The harm's already done. You know this means I'll have to stop volunteering, don't you? I can't bring this sort of attention to the charity.'

He frowned and she caught a look of unease on his face. 'I'll take care of this.'

'Forget it; it's too late. And congratulations; you've achieved your aim. But I won't be paraded about and pawed in public any more, so if you're planning on another night on the town you'll have to do it without me.'

His gaze slowly rose to hers and he resumed rubbing the towel through his hair. 'Fine. We'll do something else.' He threw the paper on the table.

She regarded him suspiciously. 'Something like what?'

'I promised you a trip on the yacht. We'll sail this evening and spend tomorrow aboard. Would you like that?'

At times like these, when he was being a courteous host,

she found it hard to believe he was the same man who was hell-bent on seeking revenge on her father for past wrongs.

She'd given in to her gnawing curiosity after his revelations on the beach and searched the Internet for a clue as to what had happened to him. All she'd come up with were scant snippets of his late father's dirty dealings before Alexandrou Pantelides had died in prison. As far as she knew, there was no connection between Theo's family and hers. The Pantelides brothers, one of whom was married and recently a parent, and the other engaged to be married, were a huge success in the oil, shipping and luxury hotel world. Theo's job as a troubleshooter extraordinaire for the billion-dollar conglomerate meant he never settled in one place for very long. An ideal job for a man whose personal relationships were fleeting at best.

And a man tormented by a horde of demons.

She looked closer at him, tried to see the man behind the wall, the man who'd bared his soul for a brief moment when he'd spoken of his mother's abandonment.

But that man was closed off.

'What does it matter what I want? Frankly, I'm surprised my father hasn't been in touch about this.'

'He has. I refused to take his calls.'

'I didn't mean you. Since I was also the subject in these photos, I'm surprised he hasn't called me to vent his anger.'

His eyelids swept down and shielded his gaze from her. Apprehension struck a jagged path through her. 'He has, hasn't he?'

'He tried. I suggested that perhaps he refrain from contacting you and concentrate on kissing babies and convincing little old ladies to cast their ballot in his favour.'

Shock rooted her to the ground. 'How dare you take control of my life like this?'

'Would you rather I gave him access so he airs his disappointment?'

'What do you care? It's a little late to protect me, don't you think?'

His jaw tightened. 'For as long as you remain under my roof, you're under my protection.'

'*Meu deus*, please don't pretend you care!'

She realised how close she was to tears and swallowed hard. Fearing she would break down in front of him, she whirled round, intent on heading for her room. She made it two steps before he stopped her.

Flinging away the towel, he cupped her cheeks with both hands. 'Stop getting yourself distressed about this.'

'Is that another command?'

His eyes narrowed. 'You're angry.'

'Damn right I am. I wish I'd never set eyes on you. In fact I wish—'

His mouth slanted over hers, hot, hungry and all consuming. Her groan of protest was less than heartfelt and devoured within a millisecond.

A part of her was furious that he'd resorted to kissing her to shut her up. But it was only a minuscule part. The rest of her body was too busy revelling in the feel of his warm bare back and the fine definition of muscles that rippled beneath her caress.

His hands speared into her hair, imprisoning her for the invasion of his tongue as he took the kiss to another level.

His first kiss over two weeks ago had been a pure threat and the two that followed a show of mastery. This kiss was different. There was hunger and passion behind it, but also a gentleness that calmed her roiling emotions and slowly replaced them with a different sensation. Need clamoured inside her; a need to be closer still to his magnificent body; a need to dig her hands into his back and feel him shudder in reaction.

His groan was smothered between their melded lips as she dug her fingers even deeper. Power surged through her when he jerked again.

One hand dropped to her bottom and yanked her lower body into his groin. His erection was unmistakable. Bold, thick and hot, it pressed against her belly with insistent power that made her heartbeat skitter out of control.

She wanted him. Above and beyond all sense, she wanted this man. Her willpower, when it came to the chemistry between them, was laughably negligible.

But she couldn't give in. *Couldn't…*

The gentleness she'd sensed in him was false, she reminded herself fiercely. The bottom line was that in a few short weeks he would walk away. Leave her and her family devastated.

'I'm losing you. Come back, *anjo*,' he murmured seductively against her mouth. He ran his tongue over her lower lip and her knees weakened.

When he cupped her bottom and squeezed, she desperately summoned all her resolve and pushed against his chest. 'No.'

He raised his head and she saw behind the wall. He was as caught in this insane chemistry as she was. A little part of her felt better.

'I can change your mind, Inez. Regardless of what I intend for your father, what is between us is undeniable.'

'Do you hear yourself? You think I should forget everything else and sleep with you just because you made me feel a certain way?'

'That's generally the reason why men and women have sex.'

'But we're not just any man and any woman, Theo, are we?'

He stiffened, and a hard look entered his eyes. 'Are you saying that you've been in love with every man you've slept with?' he queried.

She froze and prayed her humiliation wouldn't show on her face as she tried to stem the memory of Constantine's treatment of her.

His cruel rejection was still an ache beneath her breastbone.

'Inez?' Theo interjected harshly.

'My past relationships are none of your business.'

His slightly reddened mouth twisted. 'Far be it for me to request to be lumped in with your other lovers, but isn't it a touch hypocritical to apply one criteria to me that you haven't done with one of your lovers, in particular?'

'If you're referring to Constantine, let me assure you that you have no idea what you're talking about.'

His hand tightened around her waist. 'Then enlighten me. Why did he dump you?'

Inez broke free. 'We weren't compatible.'

'Or he found out the true reason you were with him and wanted nothing to do with you?'

'No. That wasn't why…' She screeched to a stop as the words stuck in her throat.

'So what was it? Did you really love him or did you convince yourself you did in order to achieve your aims?'

She bit her lip as he shone a light on the stark question. Had she blown her feelings out of proportion? Constantine had been charismatic, yes, but he'd never created the decadent chaos that Theo created in her.

When she'd imagined love, she'd always imagined passion, hunger and a keen pleasure even the slightest thought of that special someone brought. She'd believed herself in love with Constantine and yet she'd never experienced those emotions.

Well, she most definitely wasn't feeling them now.

'I believed my emotions were genuine at the time. But he didn't. He believed I was using him to further my father's campaign.'

'What did he do?' he asked. She looked into his eyes and fooled herself into thinking she saw a thawing of the hardness there.

'He made painful digs at me whenever he gave interviews. He made the tabloids call my character into question…much the same way you're doing now.'

He dropped his hand. 'It's not the same—'

'Yes, it is. Look Theo, I just want to be left alone to do my time.'

He paled. 'You're not in prison, Inez.'

She put much needed distance between them. 'Am I not? How else would you describe my presence here?'

Theo watched her walk away and curled his fists at his sides. The urge to call her back was so strong he forced himself to exhale slowly to expel the need. Her reference to her presence under his roof as a prison sentence had stung badly.

But hell, the truth was irrefutable. He'd forced her to make a choice, and no amount of dinner dates or designer shopping sprees would gloss over the fact that he'd set the tabloids on her as a way to dismantle her father's campaign.

Witnessing her clear distress just now had made his chest ache in a way that confused and irritated him.

Perhaps he needed to step up his agenda, end this dangerous game once and for all and move on with his life.

His brothers would certainly agree. He'd been avoiding their calls for the best part of a fortnight, replying only by email and with curt one-liners that he knew would only go so far before something gave.

He gritted his teeth against the prompt to deliver a swift killing blow to Benedicto da Costa.

His own ordeal hadn't been swift. It'd been long and tortuous. The punishment should fit the crime. Any hesitation on his part now merely stemmed from the afterglow of the chemistry between him and Inez. He freely admitted that theirs was a strong and potent brand, more intense than anything he'd ever experienced before.

It was messing with his mind, the same way the thought of her ex-lover had made him see red for several long seconds. But there was no way he was letting it impede his goal.

Which meant he had to come at this problem from another angle.

He swallowed the acrid taste in his mouth at the thought that Inez had put him into the same class as Constantine Blanco.

Slowly walking back indoors, he turned over the dilemma in his mind. By the time he reached his suite and changed out of his swimming trunks, a smile was curving his lips.

An hour later, he watched her descend the stairs, her duffel bag slung over her shoulder and an overnight case in her hand.

'Did Teresa tell you to pack your swimming gear?'

She regarded him warily. 'Yes. But I thought we were just taking the boat out?'

He shrugged. 'I thought you would welcome the opportunity to sunbathe away from the prying lenses of the paparazzi? There are several decks on the yacht that you can sunbathe on. Or we can swim in the sea, dine alone under the stars. Would you like that?' he asked, then felt a jolt at how much he wanted her to answer in the affirmative. In the past, he'd never taken the time to seek out what pleased his girlfriends beyond the usual gifts and fine dining. It was why he operated his relationships on a strict short-term basis with as little maintenance as possible.

Inez was far from low maintenance. And yet he found himself even more drawn to her.

She glanced pointedly over his shoulder. 'I'll think about it and let you know.'

His unsettled feelings escalated. He reminded himself that they were heading for his boat. She liked his boat. Perhaps she would relent enough to forget that she was angry with him. Forget about Blanco and forget that she was being blackmailed.

Theo was still debating why her feelings meant so much to him when he pulled up at the marina.

* * *

'You've been smiling ever since we set sail.'

Her voice was full of heavy suspicion. Theo's smile widened as he tilted his face up into the sunshine. 'Have I? It must be the weather.'

'The weather has been the same for the last month,' she replied sourly.

He slowly lowered his head and captured her gaze with his. 'Then it must be the company.'

A delicate wave of heat surged up her neck into her cheeks, making him wonder, as he had more than once these past two weeks, how she could have been involved with someone like Blanco and still blush like a schoolgirl.

Theo had looked into Constantine Blanco and had not been surprised to find that he was cut from the same cloth as Benedicto. It was perhaps why Da Costa had chosen to ally himself with the younger man politically. He'd sent his daughter to spy on Blanco and had been double-crossed in the bargain.

Theo's smile slipped as he recalled her hurt when he'd thrown her relationship with Blanco at her. He reached for the glass of wine that had accompanied their late afternoon meal and took a large gulp.

The guilt tightening in his chest since her accusation at the pool squeezed harder.

What the hell was going on with him?

'Have you decided whether you're selling the boat or not?' she asked.

In the sunlight, her black hair gleamed like polished jet, making him burn to feel its silkiness beneath his fingers.

He stared into his drink. 'Maybe. I'll have to weigh up practical usage versus the desire to hang on to something beautiful.'

'But you're a billionaire. Isn't collecting toys part and parcel of your status?'

'I wasn't always a man of means. In fact my brothers and

I worked our backsides off to achieve the level of success we enjoy now.' His smile felt tight and strained.

'Your brothers…Sakis and Arion…'

He looked up in surprise. 'You've been playing around on the Internet, I see.'

She raised her chin. 'I thought it wise to learn a little bit more about my enemy.'

The label grated. Badly. 'What else did you try to discover while you were rooting around my family tree?'

'Your brother Sakis had some trouble with a saboteur on one of his oil tankers.'

He nodded. 'We dealt with that quite satisfactorily.'

'And now your brother Ari is engaged to the widow of the man who tried to throw your company into chaos?' She frowned.

A reluctant grin tugged at his mouth. 'What can I say; we thrive on interesting challenges.'

'You also seem to make enemies with the people you do business with. So far you've led me to believe it was my father who wronged you. How do I know it's not the other way round? That you're not here because you deserved everything you got?'

The stem of the wine glass snapped with a sickening crack. Even then it took the cold wine seeping into his shirt to realise what he'd done.

The top part of the glass landed on the table, rolled off and smashed onto the deck.

Inez gasped. 'Theo, you're bleeding!' She surged to her feet and sprang towards him.

'Stop!'

'But your finger…'

'Is nothing compared to what will happen to your foot if you take another step.'

She glanced down at the broken glass an inch from her bare foot and glanced back at his bleeding forefinger. Anguish creased her pale features.

'Sit down, Inez,' he instructed tersely.

'Please, let me help,' she implored.

Gritting his teeth, he grabbed a napkin and formed a small tourniquet around the gaping wound. 'It's not deep but will need to be cleaned properly. There's a first aid kit behind the bar.'

She nodded, slipped on her sandals and dashed for the bar. Theo stood and moved from the dining table to the wraparound sofa to give the crew member who'd arrived on deck room to sweep up the broken glass. He glanced up as Inez rushed back and set the kit on the coffee table.

Her eyes were turbulent with worry as she glanced from his face to the blood-soaked napkin.

'Are you going to stand there staring at me all evening? I'm bleeding to death here.'

With a hoarse croak, she jerked into action. She carefully cleaned the wound with antiseptic and applied gauze before securing it with a plaster. All through the procedure, she darted quick, apologetic glances at him.

As he stared at her, he felt a different sort of jolt run through him. One he hadn't been aware he was missing until he felt it.

Care. Concern. Fear for him.

When was the last time anyone besides Ari and Sakis had felt like that about him? When was the last time his own mother lavished such attention on him? Inez slid him another worried glance and his breath shuddered out.

'Calm yourself, *anjo*. I'll live. I'm sure of it.'

She exhaled noisily and her agitated pulse pounded at her throat. '*Sinto muito*,' she said in a rush.

'Don't apologise. It wasn't your fault.'

'But…if I hadn't accused you of…'

'You're operating in the dark and want to find out the truth. I respect that. But I can't tell you what my business with your father is until I'm ready. You have to respect that.'

'But…this…' She glanced down at his finger and shook

her head. 'Your reaction…the claustrophobia and the touching thing…I can't help but fear the worst, Theo,' she whispered.

Against his will, his chest constricted at the anguish in her voice. He wanted to comfort her. Wanted to take that look of anticipated pain from her face. He wanted to kiss her until they both forgot why she was his prisoner and why he was beginning to dread the day he had to set her free.

He swallowed hard.

'Let's make a deal. For the next twenty-four hours, no talk of your father or the reason why I'm in Rio. Agreed?'

Her mouth wobbled and her teeth worried her bottom lip as she glanced back at his finger. Her eyes were no less turbulent when they rose to his but he saw determination flare in their depths. 'Agreed.'

Theo stood at the railing on the third floor deck and watched her swim in the pool on the second deck the next morning. She moved like a water nymph, her long black hair streaming down her back as she scissored her arms and legs underwater.

He gripped the rail until his knuckles turned white but still he couldn't take his eyes off her.

'I'm waiting for an answer, Theo,' came the weary voice at the end of the line.

Theo sighed. 'Sorry, remind me again what the question was.'

Ari grunted with annoyance. 'I asked you why I couldn't have one peaceful breakfast without opening the papers to find you wrapped around some poor girl. Seriously, my digestive system has sent me a stern memo. Either I treat it better and not subject it to such images or it goes on permanent vacation.'

Theo heard Perla, his soon-to-be sister-in-law, laughing in the background.

'The answer is simple. Don't read the papers.'

Ari sighed. 'How long is this going to go on for?'

'Everything should be signed, sealed and delivered in a week or two,' he responded, rolling his shoulders to ease the tension tightening his muscles. Another sleepless night, plagued with nightmares. He'd given up on sleep somewhere around three a.m.

'You sound very sure.'

His grip tightened around the phone. As he'd lain awake he'd briefly toyed with the idea of ending this vendetta sooner. And he'd been stunned when the idea had taken firm hold. 'I am.'

'And nothing you're doing down there will affect the wedding? Don't forget it's in two weeks. If you can prise yourself away from that piece of skirt for long enough—'

'She's not a piece of skirt,' he snarled before he could catch his response. Ari's silence made him hurry to speak. 'I'll be at your wedding.'

'Good, since you've missed most of the rehearsals, I'll send you the video of what you need to do. Make sure you get it right; we'll do a quick rehearsal when you get here. I'm not having you mess things up for Perla.'

'Sure. Fine,' he murmured.

He followed the curvy, sexy shape underneath the water and held his breath as Inez broke the surface and rose out of the pool. Dripping curves and sun-kissed skin made his body clench unbearably. He wanted to trace every single inch of her with his hands, his mouth, his tongue. 'Oh, and tell Perla I'm bringing a guest.'

His brother muttered a curse and relayed the message. Theo heard Perla's whoop of delight. 'The love of my life grudgingly agrees but suggests that perhaps, next time, you could be courteous enough to give us a heads-up sooner?'

'Next time? You mean you'll be getting married for a third time?'

He hung up to more pithy curses ringing in his ears and found himself smiling. Without taking his eyes off the figure below, he descended the spiral staircase and walked towards the bikini-clad goddess reaching for the towel on the shelf next to the pool.

Her back was turned and he slowed to a stop as the sight of her tiny waist and curvy hips made blood rush through his veins. Lust twisted through his gut, hard and demanding.

Hell, this was getting unbearable.

He threw his cell phone on the breakfast table and watched her jerk around to face him. The towel she was holding to her hair stilled.

'Hi.'

'Good morning. Enjoy your swim?'

'It was very refreshing,' she replied huskily, her eyes following him warily as he strode towards her. 'So, what's the plan for today?' she asked.

I want to haul you off to my bed and keep you underneath me until we both pass out from the pleasure overload.

He wrenched his gaze from her full breasts, lovingly cupped by damp white triangles, and concentrated on breathing. 'We're headed for Copacabana. We'll stop for something to eat then head back tonight. Or if you want we can stay on the boat and leave in the morning?'

She thought about it for a second and nodded. 'I'd love to draw the boat in the moonlight.'

'Then that's what you shall do.'

Her gaze turned puzzling, weighing.

'What's on your mind?' he asked.

She shook her head slightly and slowly folded the towel. 'Sometimes I feel as if I'm dealing with two people.'

Something hard tugged in his chest. 'Which one do you prefer?'

'Are you joking? The person you are now, of course.'

He froze as the tug tightened its hold on him. His breath came in short pants as he closed the distance between them. 'I thought we weren't going to delve into our issues today.'

'You asked me what was on my mind.'

He nodded. 'I guess I did.' He stared into the pure, make-up-free perfection of her face and something very close to regret rose in his gut.

'Now it's my turn to ask you what's on your mind, Theo,' she murmured thoughtfully.

'It's completely pointless, of course, but I'm wishing we'd met under different circumstances.'

Her mouth dropped open. 'You are?'

The urge to touch grew, and he finally gave in. He traced his thumb over her lips and felt them pucker slightly under his touch. 'As I said, it's pointless.'

'Because you would've been done with me within a week?' she ventured.

'No. I would've kept you for much longer, *anjo*. Perhaps even for ever.'

He forced himself to step away. Once again she'd slid so effortlessly under his skin, opened him up to wishes and possibilities he'd forced himself never to entertain after what their respective fathers and his mother had done to him. She was making him believe in impossible dreams, feelings he had no business experiencing.

He strode quickly towards the pool. A cold dip would wash away the fiery need and alien emotions tearing his insides to shreds. He hoped.

He emerged twenty minutes later to find her polishing off the last of her scrambled eggs and coffee. Over the past fortnight he'd noticed that she ate with a gusto that triggered his own appetite. Or *appetites*.

As he poured his coffee and helped himself to fruit, she reached for the ever-present duffel bag and pulled out her sketchpad.

'Have you thought of doing something with your talent?' he asked.

A shadow passed over her face before she tried to smile through it, but he guessed the reason behind it. Her father.

'I will once I resume my education. I put pursuing my degree on hiatus for a while.'

He didn't need to ask why. 'Until when?'

She shrugged and searched for a fresh page in her pad. 'I haven't decided yet.'

Theo tried not to let his anger show. They'd called a truce for twenty-four hours.

'What will you study when you return?'

'I love buildings and boats. I may go into architecture or boat design.'

He glanced from her face to the pad. 'Boat design, huh?' She nodded.

He picked up his coffee and regarded her over the rim. 'Why don't you design me one?'

'You want me to design a boat for you?'

'Yes. I'm sure your research showed you what sort of designs we specialise in. It has to be up to the Pantelides standard. But use your own template. Make it state-of-the-art, of course.'

'Of course,' she murmured but he could see the gleam of interest in her eyes as she stared down at her pad.

Her pencil flew across the paper as he devoured his breakfast. She didn't look up as he rose and rounded the table to where she sat. He didn't glance down at her drawing; he was too absorbed with the sheer joy on her face as she became immersed in her task.

Even when his finger drifted down her cheek to the corner of her mouth she barely glanced up at him. But her breath hitched and she jerked a tiny bit towards his touch before he withdrew his hand.

As he walked away, Theo marvelled at how light-hearted he felt.

CHAPTER NINE

THEY DROPPED ANCHOR about a mile away from Copacabana Beach and took a launch ashore.

Inez looked to where Theo stood, legs braced, at the wheel of the launch. The wind rushed through his dark hair, whipping it across his forehead. Stupid that she should be jealous of the wind but she clenched her fingers in her lap as they tingled with the need to touch him.

I would've kept you for much longer, anjo. *Perhaps even for ever.*

Try as she had for the last few hours, she couldn't get his words out of her head. They struck her straight to the heart in unguarded moments, made her breath catch in ways that made her dizzy. Every time she pushed the feeling away. But, inevitably, it returned.

She was in serious trouble here...

A shout from nearby sunbathers drew her attention to the fact that they were not alone any more.

She watched the surge of people and the noise of tourists enjoying a Sunday stroll along the beach roads and suddenly felt as if she was losing the tenuous connection she'd made with Theo last night and this morning. Which was silly. There was no connection. Just a precarious truce.

And an exciting task designing a Pantelides boat, which had made joy bubble beneath her skin all day.

He brought the launch to a smooth stop at the pier and

turned off the engine. Jumping out with lithe grace, he held out his hand to her, the smile on his face making her breath stutter in her chest as she slipped her hand into his.

'I'm in the mood for some traditional food and I know just the place for it. You happy to trust me?'

Safely on solid ground, she glanced up and found herself nodding. 'Yes.'

His eyes darkened. 'It's a bit of a walk.' He glanced at her high-heeled wedges with a cocked eyebrow.

'Don't worry about me. I was born in heels.'

'Then I pity your poor *mãe*.'

She laughed and saw his answering smile.

Gradually they fell silent and his gaze drifted over her face, resting on her mouth for a few seconds before he tugged on her hand. 'Come on, *anjo*.'

He led her along the pier and towards the streets. Ten minutes later, she stared in surprise when they stopped outside a door with a faded sign and a single light bulb above it.

'I hear they serve the best *feijoadas* in Rio,' he said, his gaze probing her every expression.

Inez forced the lump in her throat down as she stared at the sign that had been very much part of a long ago, happier childhood. 'It's true. I…how do you know about this place?'

The hand he'd captured since they alighted from the boat meshed with hers, causing her heart to flutter wildly as he brought it to his lips and kissed the back of it. 'I made it my business to find out.'

Again tears choked her and she couldn't speak for several moments. 'Thank you.'

He nodded. 'My pleasure.'

They stopped in the doorway to allow their eyes to adjust to the candlelit interior.

'*Pequena estrela!*' A matronly woman in her late forties approached, her face lit up with a smile.

After exchanging hugs, Inez turned to introduce Theo.

'Camila and my mother were best friends. I used to have supper here many times after school when I was a kid.'

Theo responded to the introduction in smooth, charming Portuguese that had the older woman blushing before she led them to a table in the middle of the room.

'You want the usual?' Camila asked after she'd brought over a basket of bread and taken their wine order.

Inez glanced at Theo. 'Will you let me choose?'

He sat back in his chair, his gaze brushing her face. 'It's your show, *anjo.*'

She rattled off the order and added a few more dishes that had Camila nodding in approval before she bustled off.

Alone with Theo, she tried to calm her giddy senses. Not read too much into why he'd brought her here of all places. But her emotions refused to be calmed.

He was making her feel things she had no business feeling, considering their circumstances. Her heart was very much in danger of being devastated. And this time the danger signs were not disguised as they'd been with Constantine. She was walking into this with her heart and eyes wide open…

'You're frowning too hard, *querida.*'

Plucking a piece of bread from the basket, she fought to focus on not ruining their truce. 'I think I may have ordered too much food.'

'You have a healthy appetite. Nothing wrong with that.'

'It's that healthy appetite that keeps me on the wrong side of chubby.'

'You're not chubby. You're perfect.'

Her hand stilled on the way to her mouth. In the ambient light, she witnessed the potent, knee-weakening look of appreciation on his face. The look slowly grew until hunger became deeply etched into his every feature.

Desire pounded through her, sending radial pulses of heat through her body to concentrate on that needy place between her legs. '*Obrigado,*' she murmured hoarsely.

He nodded slowly, leant forward and took the piece of bread from her hand. Tearing off a piece, he held it against her mouth. When she opened it, he placed it on her tongue and watched her chew.

Then he sat back and ate the remaining piece.

She eventually managed to swallow and cast around for a safe topic of conversation that didn't involve her father or the dangerous emotions arcing between them.

Whether he noticed her floundering or not, she smiled gratefully when he asked, 'Did your mother grow up around here?'

'No, both she and Camila grew up near the Serra Geral, although she spent part of her childhood in Arizona where my grandmother was from. Their fathers were ranch-owning *gauchos* and neighbours but after they both married they moved to Rio and stayed in touch. Camila is like a second mother to me...'

'Da Costa Holdings isn't a cattle business, though,' he replied, then stiffened slightly.

She smiled quickly, wanting to hold onto the animosity-free atmosphere they'd found. 'No, after my grandfather died, my mother sold the ranch and let my father expand the company instead.' She breathed in relief when Camila returned with their wine and first course.

The older woman's warm smile and effusive manner further lightened the mood. By the time she took her first sip of the bold red wine the slightly chilly interlude had passed.

Theo complimented her on the food choice and tucked into the grilled fish starter. The conversation returned to safer topics and eventually turned to his previous career as a championship-winning rower.

'Why did you stop competing?'

He shrugged. 'I tried a few partners after Ari and Sakis retired. The chemistry was lacking. In a sport like that chemistry is key.' He topped up her wine and took a sip of his own.

'You've been lucky to have had the opportunity to do something you loved,' she replied wistfully.

His smile looked a little taut around the edges. 'Luck is a luxury that normally comes along as a result of hard work.'

She glanced down into her wine. 'But sometimes, no matter how hard you try, fate has other ideas for you.'

His eyes narrowed into sharp laser-like beams. 'Yes. But the answer is to turn it to your advantage.'

'Or you can walk away. Find a different option?'

One corner of his mouth lifted. 'Walking away has never been my style.'

She slowly nodded. 'You wouldn't have won championships if you were a man who walked away.'

His expression morphed into something that resembled gratitude. She couldn't claim she understood all his motives but she was beginning to grasp what made Theo tick. As long as he could see a problem in any area of his life, he would not walk away until it was resolved. It was why he was the troubleshooter for Pantelides Inc.

She'd watched footage of him rowing. His grit and determination had held her enthralled throughout the feature and she would be lying now if she didn't admit it was a huge turn-on.

'But there's also strength in walking away. You walked away from rowing rather than risk partnering up with the wrong person.'

He stiffened. 'Inez…'

She fought the urge to back down. 'I don't want to mess up our truce but I want you to just think about it. There's no shame in forgiving. No shame in letting the past *stay* in the past.'

His eyes grew dark and haunted. 'What about my demons?'

'Do you have a cast-iron guarantee that they will be vanquished by the path you've chosen?'

He frowned for several seconds before his eyes narrowed. 'You're right. Let's not mess up the truce, shall we?'

'Theo…'

'*Anjo*. Enough. Have some more wine.' He smiled.

And, just like that, her pulse surged faster. Hell, everything he did made her pulse race. She took a sip and licked her lips as the languorous effect of the wine and the captivating man sitting opposite her took hold.

She really needed to stop drinking so much. She pulled her gaze from the rugged perfection of his face as Camila returned to offer them coffee.

Inez declined and looked over to see his eyes riveted on her.

'I think we need to get you back to the boat.'

Laughter that seemed to be coming easier around him escaped her throat. 'You make me sound as if I've been naughty,' she said after Camila collected their empty plates and left.

'Trust me, I would tell you if you'd been.'

'Well, the night is still young and I'm not ruling anything out.' She laughed again.

His mouth curved in one of those devastating smiles as he reached for his wallet and extracted several crisp notes.

'I say it's definitely time to get you back and into bed.'

Her breath caught. He didn't mean what she thought he meant. Of course he didn't. But images suddenly bombarded her brain that had her blushing.

As she said goodbye to Camila and headed outside, she prayed he wouldn't see her reaction to his words.

'Hey, slow down, you'll break your ankle rushing in those heels.' He caught up with her outside and slid a hand around her waist.

The warmth of his body was suddenly too much to bear. 'It's okay, I'm fine.' Her voice emerged a touch too forceful and he glanced sharply at her.

'What's wrong?'

She raked an exasperated hand through her hair and tried to stem the words forming at the back of her mind. They came out anyway. 'You're supposed to be my enemy. And yet you brought me to one of my favourite places in the world. You're being so kind and attentive and I can't help… I…I want you.'

The transformation that occurred sent her senses reeling. From the charming, desirous dinner companion, Theo turned into a hungry predatory beast in the space of a heartbeat.

He pulled her into a dark alley between two high-rises. Her heart hammered as he held her against the wall and leaned in close.

'You don't want to say things like that to me right now, Inez,' he grated harshly.

His mouth was so tantalising close, she shut her eyes to avoid closing the gap between them and experiencing another potent kiss. 'I don't want to be saying them either. I can't seem to stop myself because it's the truth.'

'That's just the wine talking,' he replied.

She nodded then groaned when he leaned in closer. Heat from his body burned hers and his breath washed over her face. When his stubbled jaw brushed her cheek, she bit hard on her lower lip to stop another groan from escaping.

'Open your eyes, Inez.'

She shook her head. *'Nao…por favor…'*

'What are you begging me for?' he whispered in her ear.

A deep shudder coursed down her spine. 'I don't know…' She stopped and sucked in a desperate breath. 'Kiss me,' she pleaded.

With a dark moan, he touched his mouth to the corner of hers. Fleeting. Feather-light. Barely enough.

Her hands gripped his waist and held on tight. *'Please,'* she whispered.

'Anjo, if I start I won't be able to stop. And neither of us wants to spend the night in jail for lewd behaviour.'

She finally opened her eyes. He stood, tall, dark, devastatingly good-looking and tense, with a hunger she'd never seen in a man's eyes. That it was directed at her made her pulse race that much harder.

'Theo.' Her fingers crept up to his face, dying to touch his warm olive skin. 'Let it go. Whatever my father did, revenge would only bring you fleeting satisfaction.'

His jaw tightened but he didn't look as forbidding as he'd looked before. 'It's the only thing I've dreamed about for the last twelve years.'

Her hand crept up to settle over his heart. 'Have you stopped to think that obsessing about it may just be feeding the demons?'

One large hand settled over hers and he stared fiercely down at her. 'Are you offering me another way to quiet them, *anjo*?'

'Maybe.'

He captured her hand and planted a kiss in her palm. When he glanced down at her, a feverish light burned in his molten eyes. 'He doesn't deserve to have you as a daughter.'

'I can say the same about your parents but we play the hand that is dealt us the best way we can. And when it gets really bad I try to remember a happier time. Surely you must have some happy memories with your mother? And was your father really all bad?'

His mouth tightened. Then, slowly, he shook his head. 'No. It wasn't always bad.'

'Tell me.'

He frowned slightly. 'They thought Sakis would be their last child. I came as a surprise, or so my mother tells me. She used to call me her special boy. My father…he took me everywhere with him. He had a sports car—an Aston Martin—that I loved riding in. We'd take long drives along the coast…' He stopped and his eyes glazed over.

She kept silent, letting him relive the memories, hoping that he would find a way to soften the hard ache inside him. But when his eyes refocused, she saw the raw pain reflected in them.

'I'm not a father, and I probably never will be. But even I know those things are easy to do when life's a smooth sail. The true test comes when things get rough. I find it hard to believe that my brothers and I were ever in any way special to our parents when they turned their backs on us when we needed them most. He could've saved me, Inez—' He stopped abruptly and her heart clenched with pain for him.

'How?'

'One simple phone call to warn me and I wouldn't be here…I wouldn't be afraid of going to sleep each night because of hellish nightmares…' A deep shudder raked his tall frame.

'Oh, Theo,' she murmured. He leaned into the hand she placed on his cheek for several seconds then he pulled away and tilted her chin up.

The vulnerable man was gone. 'This changes nothing. I am what I am. Do you still want me?'

She swallowed. 'Yes.'

Something resembling relief swept through his eyes. 'You have half an hour and a lot of head-clearing air before we're back on the boat. I suggest you use that time to think carefully about whether you want this to go any further. Because, once we cross the line, there won't be any going back.'

CHAPTER TEN

THEO THREW THE reins of the launch to the waiting crew member and turned to help her out. Her bare feet hit the landing pad and she swayed a little when the boat rocked.

Contrary to her thinking he would rush her back to the boat after his pronouncement, Theo had taken his time walking her back down the streets to the promenade and onto the beach that led to the pier.

Hell, he'd even taken the time to help her out of her shoes so they could walk along the shore.

But the plaguing doubt that perhaps he didn't want her as much as her screaming senses craved him evaporated the moment she looked into his eyes.

Burnt a dark gold by volcanic desire, he stared down at her for several seconds before he demanded in a hoarse voice, 'Well?'

She licked her lips and watched his agitated exhalation. 'I still want you.'

'Are you sure? There will be no room for regret in the morning, Inez. I won't allow it.'

'I'm not drunk, Theo. Besides, I wanted you this morning and I wasn't drunk then. Or last week, or the first night we met.'

His nostrils flared as he dragged her close on the deserted lower deck. 'That first night, you felt what I felt?'

An impossible attraction that had no rhyme or reason? 'Yes,' she answered simply.

He swung her up in his arms and strode into the galley and down the steps into his large, opulent suite. Somewhere along the line, her shoes fell from her useless hands. She knew they had because her fingers were buried in his hair, and her mouth was on his by the time he kicked the door shut behind them.

Their tongues slid erotically against each other as they explored one another, his forceful, hers growing bolder by the second. Because she knew he liked it, she nipped his bottom lip with her teeth.

His deep growl echoed inside her before he pulled away. Eyes on hers, he slowly lowered her body down his sleek length. Hard muscles and firm thighs registered against her heated skin and even after her feet hit the plush carpet she held onto him, fearful she'd dissolve into a pool of need the moment she let go.

'I need to undress you,' he said raggedly.

Unable to look away from him, she nodded. The dark purple knee-length dress was form-fitting and secured by a side zip. After a couple of minutes of frustrated searching, she laughed and pointed to the hidden zip beneath her arm.

With a dark curse, he lowered it and tugged the dress over her head.

He dropped the dress. He swallowed. Then he stared so hard she stopped breathing.

'*Thee mou*, you're so beautiful,' he groaned.

The feeling suffusing her was different from her reaction to the incandescent hunger in his eyes. It was pleasure that he liked what he saw, that he might well pardon her for her inexperience.

Eager to experience more of the feeling, she reached for her bra clasp.

'No,' he commanded. He grabbed her hands and placed them on his chest. 'That's my job. *You* don't move.'

He drifted his fingers up her sides, eliciting a deep shiver that brought a satisfied smile to his lips. Her bra came undone a second later and he glanced down at her heavy breasts.

'Do you know how long I've waited to taste these?' He cupped one globe in his hand, lowered his head and flicked his wet tongue repeatedly over her nipple.

Fire scorched through her veins and her head fell back as pleasure surged high.

'Theo,' she gasped as he delivered the same treatment to her other nipple. Caught in the maelstrom of sensation, she wasn't aware her nails were digging into his pecs until he hissed against her skin.

'Take my shirt off, *querida*. I want to feel those nails on my bare skin.'

Fingers trembling, she complied with his demand, pulling the shirt off his broad shoulders and down his arms before giving in to the need to caress his bronzed skin. Heated and satin-smooth, his muscles bunched beneath her touch as she explored him.

But, much too soon, he was pulling her hands away, catching her around the waist and striding to the bed.

Depositing her in the middle of the king-sized bed, he stood staring down at her, one hand on his belt. The power and girth of him knocked the breath out of her lungs and a momentary unease sliced across her pleasure.

So far, Theo hadn't commented on her inexperience but the evidence would become glaringly apparent in a few minutes. She opened her mouth to tell him but he was crawling over the bed towards her, his intense focus paralysing her to everything but the pleasure his eyes promised.

He kissed her again, deeper, more forceful than all the times before. She gave in to her need and buried her hands in his hair, scraped her nails along his scalp and won herself a deep groan of pleasure from him. His lips moved along her jaw to nip her earlobe before going lower to explore her neck and lower.

Once again, he suckled her breasts and once again she lost the ability to think straight.

'You love that, don't you?' he observed huskily when he raised his head.

'*Sim*,' she groaned.

'There are many more pleasures, *anjo*. So many more.'

His lips trailed down her midriff…he kissed his way to the top of her panties before he gripped the flimsy material in his hands. Expecting them to be ripped off—a notion that made her wildly breathless—she was surprised when he slowly and gently lowered them down her legs and drew them off.

Equally slowly, taking his time to savour her, he kissed her from ankle to inner thigh. When his mouth skated over her secret place, her hips arched off the bed in delirious anticipation.

She'd never imagined she'd want a man to go down on her but now she couldn't imagine *not* feeling Theo's mouth on her heated core.

At the touch of his mouth, she cried out, her body twisting as pleasure scythed through her. He tasted her so very thoroughly, his tongue, teeth and lips working in perfect harmony to drive her straight out her mind.

She slid ever closer to breaking point, both fearing and yearning for what lay ahead.

Theo slipped his hands beneath her bottom and pulled her even closer to his seeking mouth. With quick expert flicks of his tongue, he sent her careening over the edge.

Her scream was an alien sound, hoarse and pleasure-ravaged, her grip on the sheets tight as she was buffeted by blissful sensation.

He continued to kiss her until she calmed, then kissed his way up her body to seal her mouth with his.

The earthy taste of her surrender seemed to trigger an even more primitive reaction in him. By the time he lifted his head, his eyes were almost black with hunger.

'Did Blanco make you feel like this?' he grated.

She shook her head. 'No.'

Satisfaction gleamed in his eyes. 'By the time I finish making you mine, you will not remember anyone else who came before me.'

Knowing he would discover her inexperience in a matter of minutes, she took a sustaining breath and blurted, 'I never slept with Constantine. Theo, I'm a virgin.'

He froze in the act of reaching for a condom. Several expressions raced over his face before he spoke. 'So I'm to be your first lover?'

She gave a jerky nod. 'Yes.'

Theo absorbed the news and tried to weigh which was the greater emotion swirling through him—shock or elation. The shock was understandable. But the elation, the fact that he was *pleased* he was to be her first? It'd never crossed his mind that she would be a virgin. But suddenly a few things fell into place. Her blushes, her furtive innocent looks, her surprise at his demanding kisses.

Another feeling rose to curl itself around his chest. Possessiveness.

The fact that he was to be her first made him want to beat his chest like a wild jungle animal. He ripped the condom packet open and stared down at her.

The look of apprehension forced him to slow down. He was moving too fast, possibly scaring her. Time to turn it down a notch.

'I'll go as slow as you want, *querida*, but I won't stop,' he warned. He couldn't. He'd come too far. He wanted her too much.

I would've kept you... Perhaps even for ever.

His own words echoed in his head and yet another emotion swept over him. If they'd met in another time, would she be the one? The idea of Inez as his wife, the mother of his children if he'd been normal, washed over him. His heart raced as he stared down at her, so beautiful, so giving.

Thee mou, what the hell was he doing wishing for the impossible? He wasn't normal...

'I don't want you to stop,' she replied. Then she performed one of those actions that illuminated her inexperience. Her gaze flicked down to his groin and she bit her lip. She had no idea how hot that little gesture made him.

A groan ripped from his chest and effectively wiped away the useless yearning.

Planting his hands on either side of her, he parted her thighs with his and settled himself at her entrance.

'Hold onto me, and feel free to dig your nails into my back if it all gets too much.' He attempted a smile and felt a touch of relief when she returned it.

The seductive bow of her mouth called to him and, leaning down, he drove his tongue between her lips. Gratifyingly, she opened up to him immediately. He deepened the kiss and swallowed her groan.

Carefully, he nudged her entrance, fed himself slowly into her wet heat.

He froze as she tensed. 'Easy, *anjo.* Relax,' he murmured soothingly against her mouth.

With a rough little sound she complied. Except now the tension was channelled into him. The feel of her closing around him threatened to tear him apart. Lying in the cradle of her hips, a sense of wonderment stole over him he'd never felt before. And he wasn't afraid to admit it scared the hell out of him.

'Theo.' She said his name with a touch of imploration and frustration that ramped up his tension. Never had he wanted to make it more right for a sexual partner.

He pushed deeper and felt the resistance of her innocence. Those nails dug in. Pleasure roared through him as he pulled back and looked into her beguiling face.

A face that held a touch of apprehension and breathless anticipation.

'Please, Theo. I want you.'

Her husky entreaty was the final straw. With a hoarsely muttered apology, he breached the flimsy barrier and buried himself deep inside her.

She made a sound of pain that pierced his heart then her head was rolling back on a long moan that echoed around the room. He waited until she had adjusted to him. Then he pulled out and rocked back in.

'*Meu deus*,' she voiced her wonder.

'Inez…' he waited until her glazed eyes focused on him, then he repeated the move '…tell me how you feel.'

'*Fantastico*,' she groaned, and Theo was sure she didn't realise she spoke her native tongue.

Her fingers spiked into his hair and when he thrust into her, she met him with a bold thrust of her own. His breath hissed out.

'You're a fast learner, *querida*.' He increased the tempo and gritted his teeth for control when she immediately matched his pace.

All too soon her back arched off the bed, her chest rising and falling in agitation as she neared her climax. Hot internal muscles rippled along his length and he shut his eyes for one split second to rein in his failing grip on reality. Leaning lower, he took one tight nipple and rolled it in his mouth. Her cry of pleasure was music to his ears. He treated its twin to the same attention then lowered himself on her. Sliding his arms under her shoulders he brought her flush against him and thrust in fast, deep movements.

She screamed once before her teeth closed over the skin on his shoulder. Deep shudders rocked through her as her bliss pulled her completely under.

She bit him harder, her nails scouring his back as she rode the unending wave.

When her head fell back towards the pillow, he raised his

head and looked at her face. The expression of wonder and ecstasy sheening her eyes finally sent him over the edge.

With a roar torn from deep inside him, he gave into the shattering release.

He clamped his mouth shut as new, confusing words threatened to burst free. Praise? Gratitude? Hell, *adoration*? When had he ever felt those emotions in connection to a woman he'd just bedded?

He buried his face in her neck and let the ripples of pleasure wash him away in silence. Until he could fathom just what the hell was going on beyond the chemical level with Inez, he intended to keep his mouth shut.

Inez slowly caressed her hands down his back, not minding at all that she was pinned to the bed by his heavy, muscled weight. Right at that moment, she couldn't think of a better way to suffocate to death. The thought made her giggle.

Theo turned his head and nuzzled her cheek. 'Not the reaction I expect after a mind-blowing orgasm but at least it's a happy sound.'

Immediately her mind turned to the dozens of women he'd pleasured before her. Hot green jealousy burned through her euphoric haze and her hands stilled.

'Hey, what did I say?' His voice rumbled through her. When she didn't immediately answer, he raised his head and stared down at her. 'Inez?'

'It's nothing important,' she replied. And it wasn't.

Earlier this evening, she'd tried to make him see a different way. But he'd refused. This thing between them would last until his vendetta with her father was satisfied. She had no business thinking about what women had come before her or who would replace her once he was done with her family and with Rio.

She endured his intent gaze until he nodded and rose. The feeling of him pulling out of her created a further emptiness inside that made her heart lurch wildly.

Deus, she needed to get a grip. Her hormones were a little askew because she had experienced her first sexual act.

No need to descend into full melt-down mode.

She watched him leave the bed, his body in part shadow in the lamp-lit room. He entered the bathroom and returned a minute later with a damp towel. When she realised his intention, she surged up and tried to reach for the towel.

'No,' he murmured softly. 'Lie back.'

Her face heating up, she slowly subsided against the pillows and allowed him to wash her.

Incredibly, the hunger returned as he gently saw to her needs and when he finally glanced back at her his nostrils were flared, a sign she'd come to recognise as a control-gathering technique.

Her nipples puckered and her body began to react to the look on his face.

'You need time to recover.'

Her body refuted that but her head knew she needed to take time to regroup. When she nodded, he looked almost disappointed. He returned the towel to the bathroom but left the light on as he came back to bed. Getting into bed, he pulled the covers over their bodies and pulled her into his arms.

She settled her hand over his chest and felt his steady heartbeat beneath her fingers. They lay there in silence until another giggle broke free from her jumbled thoughts.

'I'm beginning to get a complex, *anjo.*' He brushed his lips over her forehead.

'I believe this is the part where we make small talk after sex but I can't come up with a single subject.'

She felt his smile against her temple. 'Wrong. Normally this would be the part when I either leave or do what I just did to you all over again.'

Her heart caught. 'And?'

'I'm trying to rein in my primal instincts and not flatten you on your back again.'

Feeling bolder than was wise, Inez opened her mouth to tell him that he needn't hold it back for much longer. Instead a wide yawn took her unawares.

It was his turn to laugh. 'I think the decision on small talk has been shelved in favour of sleep.' He turned her face up to his and pressed his mouth to hers. Within seconds the kiss threatened to combust into something else. He pulled back with a groan and tucked her against him. 'Sleep, Inez. Now,' he commanded gruffly.

With a secretly pleased smile, she slid her arm around his waist, already feeling the drowsy lure of sleep encroaching.

She woke to moonlight streaming through the windows. The bedside lamp glowed and she judged that she'd been asleep for a few hours.

Beside her, Theo lay on his side, tufts of sleep-ruffled hair thrown over his forehead. In the soft lighting he looked younger and peaceful but still so damn sexy her breath caught just looking at him.

She suddenly needed to commit his likeness to paper. Her pad was next door in her suite. Slowly extracting herself from the arm he'd thrown over her, she pulled on his shirt and went to retrieve it.

Returning just as quietly, she settled herself cross-legged at the foot of the bed and began to draw. Every now and then she paused and took a breath, unable to fathom the circumstances she found herself in.

She was in bed with a man who was bent on destroying her family. And yet the overwhelming guilt she expected to feel was missing. Instead she yearned to save him from the demons that she'd glimpsed in his eyes when he spoke of his nightmares.

She swallowed as a well of sadness built inside her. Despite his outward show of invincibility she'd seen his battle. A battle he believed only revenge would win for him...

She froze as Theo made a sound. It was somewhere between a moan of pain and the bark of anger. His hand jerked out and then closed into a tight fist.

His whole body tensed for a breathless second before his chest started to rise and fall in agitated pants.

She dropped the sketchpad. 'Theo?'

'*No. No! No! Thee mou, no!*' The words were hoarse pleas, soaked with naked fear.

Both hands shot out in a bracing position and his head twisted from side to side.

'Theo!' She rose to her knees, unsure of what to do.

'No. Stop! *Arghh!*' With a forceful lunge, he jolted upright with a blood-curdling cry. Sweat poured down his face and he sucked in huge gulping breaths.

'*Deus*, are you okay?' The question was hopelessly inadequate but it was all she could manage at that moment. Because her heart was turning over with pain for what she'd just witnessed him go through.

She reached out and he jerked back away from her. 'Don't touch me!'

'Theo, it's me. Inez.' Tentatively, she reached out and touched his arm.

He shuddered violently and lurched away from her, staring blankly at her for several seconds before his face grew taut and haunted.

'Inez,' he said with a dark snarl. 'I fell asleep?' There was self-loathing in the question, as if he hated himself for having lowered his guard enough to let the demons in.

Her stomach flipped and her fingers curled into her palm. 'Yes. You…you had a nightmare.'

His mouth twisted with a cruel grimace. 'No kidding. What the hell are you doing here?' he snapped, looking around the room with unfocused eyes.

She frowned. 'We…um, we fell asleep together after…' She stopped as heat rushed up her face.

He turned back to her and his gaze slowly travelled over her. He brushed the hair out of his eyes and gradually the dull green lightened into golden hazel. 'We had sex. I remember now.'

She flinched and watched him with wary eyes.

With sure, predatory moves, he lifted the tangled sheet off his body and prowled to where she was poised on her knees. He stopped a hairsbreadth from her.

'Can I…can I touch you?' she asked, unwilling to have him pull away from her, but a part of her longed to soothe the turbulent blackness in his eyes.

His mouth pinched and he took several steadying breaths before he spoke. 'You want to comfort me?'

'If you'll let me.'

Another deep shudder and he closed his eyes. His head lowered until his forehead rested between her breasts. His arms closed around her and tightened so hard she couldn't move. They stayed like that until his breathing steadied.

'Theo?'

'Hmm?'

'Tell me about your dream.'

He tensed immediately and she bit her lip. He raised his head and stared at her.

'Take my shirt off,' he commanded, his voice hardly above a tortured whisper.

Concern spiked through, despite the heat his words generated. 'Theo, you just had a nightmare—'

'One I want to forget.' His hands were on the back of her thighs, hard and demanding as they caressed up to her bottom. He cupped the globes with more roughness than before but there was no pain in the caress. 'Inez, if you want to help me, do it.'

She drew the shirt over her head and dropped it. His eyes devoured her breasts and his tongue darted out to rest against his bottom lip.

Between her legs, liquid heat dampened her folds and he groaned in dark appreciation as his seeking fingers found her core.

'So ready. So tight,' he rasped. With almost effortless ease, he picked her up, pivoted off the bed and sat on the side. Grabbing a condom, he slipped it on and positioned her legs on either side of him.

'You will *make* me forget.' The words were almost a plea but with a promise of things to come. 'Yes?'

Before she could do so much as nod, he pressed her down on top of him. She cried out as he filled her with his hot, heavy length. His hard grip on her hips controlled the rhythm, which grew more frantic with each thrust.

'Theo,' she gasped as pleasure scalded her insides and rushed her towards ecstasy.

'Shh, no talking,' he instructed.

Biting her lip, she stared into his face.

Torment, anger, pleasure and more than a dose of anxiety mingled into an oddly fascinating tableau. He was still caught up in the hell of his nightmare and her heart broke over his anguish.

She tried to catch his gaze, to transmit a different sort of comfort from the carnal that he clearly sought but he avoided her eyes. Instead he buried his face between her breasts and mercilessly teased her nipples until she whimpered at the torture.

He increased his thrusts, bouncing her on top of him with almost superhuman strength that had her reeling.

Her orgasm crashed into her, flattening her under its fierce onslaught before proceeding to completely drown her.

Through the thunderous rush in her ears, she heard his guttural roar as he achieved his own ruthless release.

Sweat slicked their skin and their breaths rushed in and out in frantic pants. This time, though, there were no pleasurable caresses and giggling was the last thing she felt like doing.

With lithe grace, he twisted around and deposited her on the bed. Without speaking, he strode into the bathroom.

Inez lay on the bed, grappling with what had just happened. In the last twenty-four hours she'd glimpsed the man tortured by his nightmares, had seen a side to Theo she was certain very few people saw. Instead of guarding her own heart, she wanted to open herself up even more to him, find a way of taking away his pain and torment.

Had she not learnt her lesson with Constantine?

No, Theo was nothing like that man who'd taken delight in humiliating her. The retraction Theo had promised had appeared in the online evening edition of the newspaper and she was sure she'd seen a look of contrition in his eyes when he'd watched her read it.

Darkness and light.

She was deeply, almost irreversibly attracted to both. Again her heart twisted and she looked towards the bathroom.

A crash came a second later, followed by a pithy curse. She was off the bed and running into the bathroom before she could think twice.

'I'm fine!' he ground out.

She hesitated in the doorway and watched him. His fingers were curled around the marble sink and his head was bent forward. 'What's wrong, Theo?'

'Dammit, woman, I'm not made of glass. And I've been grappling with my nightmares long before you came along, so leave me alone!'

Hurt shredded her inside. 'Don't push me away.'

He locked eyes with her in the mirror and sighed. 'You're too stubborn for your own good, you know that?'

'Maybe, but before you throw me out I need the bathroom,' she lied.

'Fine; it's all yours.'

He started to turn. That was when she saw his scars. '*Meu deus*, what happened to you?' she whispered raggedly.

His glance ripped from her face to where she pointed to his left hip. The marks were puckered and too evenly spaced and shaped to be an accident. But still her mind couldn't grasp the idea that someone had deliberately inflicted pain on him.

'You mean you haven't guessed already, *querida*? *Your father* happened.'

CHAPTER ELEVEN

INEZ STAGGERED BACKWARDS until her legs hit the vanity unit and she collapsed onto it. 'I don't…you're saying my *father* did this to you?' She shook her head in fierce disbelief.

Theo's mouth twisted. 'Not personally, no. He hired thugs to do it.'

She felt the blood drain from her head. Had she not been seated, she would've swayed under the unbelievable accusation.

'But…why?'

He grabbed a towel and secured it around his waist. 'You did your research on my family. You know what happened to my father.'

She nodded. 'He was indicted for fraud, bribery and embezzlement.'

'Among other things. He was also involved with some extremely shady people.'

He turned and strode from the bathroom.

She followed him, the fear she'd harboured for a long time blooming in her chest. 'And my father was one of these shady people?'

Theo turned and watched her. Shocked knowledge flared in her eyes. For a brief moment, he sympathised with what she was going through. Having the truth blown up in front of you wasn't easy.

In his deepest, darkest moments he still couldn't believe how painfully raw he felt at his father's abandonment.

'My father owed him a lot of money on some crooked scheme they were working on when he was arrested and all our assets were frozen. Your father took exception to being out of pocket. When he realised he wouldn't be paid, he decided to pursue a different route.'

Her haunted eyes dropped to the scars covered by the towel and quickly looked away.

'So I'm here to pay for my father's sins,' she whispered raggedly.

That had initially been his plan. Somewhere along the line that particular plan had become questionable. But he'd be damned before he'd admit that.

'Your father made me pay for my father's. Money and power were his bottom line, and he wanted payback. Nothing else mattered to him, not even the tortured screams of a frightened boy...'

He compressed his lips as her mouth dropped open and anguish creased her face. 'How old were you?'

He raked a hand through his hair. Even as a voice shrieked in his head to stop baring his raw wounds, he was opening his mouth.

'I was seventeen. I was returning from a night out with friends when his goons grabbed me. He had me smuggled from Athens to Spain and threw me into a hole on some abandoned farm in Madrid. Ari found me there two weeks after I was taken. After he damned near bled every single cent he could find from every relative and casual acquaintance in order to stump up the two million dollars ransom that your father demanded.'

Her hands flew to her head, her fingers spiking through the long tresses to grip them in a convulsive stranglehold. 'Please tell me when you say a *hole*...you don't mean that *literally*?' The words were a desperate plea, as if she didn't want to believe how real the monster that was her father.

His smile cracked his lips. 'Oh, yes, *anjo*. A twelve-foot-deep *literal* hole in the ground with vertical sides and no hand or footholds. No light. No heat. One meal a day with a bucket for my necessaries.'

'No…'

'*Yes!* And you know what his men did for *fun* when they were bored?'

She shook her head wildly, her eyes wide and horror-struck as he loosened the towel from around his waist and exposed his puckered skin. 'Cigar tattoos, they called them.'

Tears welled in her eyes and fell down her cheeks. Still shaking her head, she walked to the bed and sank down on it. She buried her face in her hands and a gut-wrenching sob ripped from her throat. After the first one, they came thick and fast.

His chest tightened with emotions he was very loath to name. Each sob caught him on the raw, until he couldn't bear to hear another one.

'Inez! Stop crying,' he instructed hoarsely after five minutes.

She shook her head and sniffled some more.

'Stop it or I'll throw you overboard and you can swim to shore.'

That got her attention. She brushed her hands across her cheeks and speared him with wide, imploring eyes.

'If the only people you saw were his men, how did you know it was my father?'

He couldn't fault her for trying to find a different reality to the one he'd smashed her world with. Hell, he'd done that for a long time after his father had been indicted. 'I followed the money.'

She frowned. 'What?'

'I traced the ransom my brother paid through dummy corporations and offshore accounts. It took a few years but I finally found where it ended up.'

'In my father's account?'

'Yes. And since then I've made it my business to find out how every single cent was spent.'

Her shoulders slumped and tears welled again. He could tell the ground had well and truly shifted beneath her feet.

After several seconds, she raised her head.

'Okay. I'll do whatever you want. For however long you want.'

It was his turn to feel the ground shift under his feet. Shock slammed through him as he realised just how much he wanted to take her. To hang onto her.

But not for the sake of revenge. For an altogether different reason; because he wanted her. Not for her father but *for her*.

He shook his head. 'Inez…'

'I can never buy back those two weeks that were taken from you or the horror you've had to live with. But I can try and find a way to make up for what was done to you.'

'How? By giving me your body whenever and wherever I ask for it?'

She paled a little. But the brave, spirited woman he'd come to see underneath all that false gloss raised her chin. 'If that's what you want.'

His mouth twisted. 'I don't want a damned sacrificial lamb. And I sure as hell don't want you throwing yourself on your sword for that bastard's sake!'

'Then what do you want? You have his company. His campaign is falling apart. He will be left with nothing by the time you're done with him. How much more suffering do you need before you let go of this anger? When will you feel pacified?'

Theo started to answer, then realised he had no answer. The satisfaction he'd thought he'd feel was hollowly absent, as was the deep-seated sense of triumph he'd always thought he would feel when this moment came.

Looking into her face, he saw the pain and confusion reflected there and his puzzlement increased. The ground was still tilting beneath his feet but he'd been on this path for too long to let go.

Hadn't he?

He forced his gaze to meet hers.

'I will let you know when I'm adequately appeased.'

Over the next week, she watched as he slowly dismantled her father's campaign piece by piece. Allegations of impropriety surfaced, triggering an investigation. Although nothing was found to indict Benedicto, his credibility suffered a death blow and any meaningful points he'd managed to retain in the polls dropped to nothing.

On the Monday morning after returning from their sailing trip, the calls to her cell phone started. Both her father and Pietro bombarded her with messages and texts, demanding to know what was going on.

She hadn't needed Theo to warn her not to take their calls. After his revelation, each time she saw her father's name pop up on her screen, her stomach churned with pain and disgust.

Although she'd long suspected that her father's business dealings weren't as pure as the driven snow, she'd never in her wildest dreams entertained the idea that he would condone the brutality that Theo had described. Each time she saw his scars—and she'd seen them every night since their return, when he'd moved her into his suite—a merciless vice had squeezed her heart.

And that vice had tightened every time he'd cried out in the middle of the night after another nightmare.

She'd been surprised that first night after their return when he'd pulled her close after a fiery lovemaking and instructed her to go to sleep.

When he kept her with him the following night, she'd boldly asked him why.

'I don't want to be alone,' he'd stated baldly. And each time he'd come awake he'd reached for her, wrapping his trembling body around her and holding on tight until his nightmare receded and his breathing returned to normal.

More and more, her foolish heart had begun to believe that her presence was making the nightmares, if not any less horrific, then at least tolerable.

Or she could just be living in a fantasy land where her mind and heart had no idea what language the other was speaking. Because she was beginning to believe that her heart was more involved in Theo's welfare than was wise. And yet she couldn't control it enough to make it stop wrenching in pain when he suffered another nightmare, or soar with joy when he took her to the heights of ecstasy. Even the knowledge that some time in the very near future, after his goal to destroy her father was achieved, Theo would pack up his bags and leave Rio for good, made her heart ache in a way that was almost a physical pain.

Santa Maria, she was losing her mind—

'There you are. Teresa told me you're still here. I thought you'd be at the centre by now.' She'd shared more details of her volunteer work with him during the times when he'd been *Normal Theo*, not *Revenge Theo*. And she'd been ridiculously thrilled when he hadn't been judgemental or condescending.

She looked up as he entered the living room and crossed to where she sat, applying finishing touches to the sketch she'd been working on since breakfast an hour ago. She'd thought he'd left for the day but obviously she'd been mistaken.

Glancing up at his lean, solid frame and gorgeous face, her heart performed that painfully giddy flip again and she glanced away. 'I took a day off. I'm…I'm still thinking of resigning.'

He stilled then dropped to his haunches in front of her. 'Why?'

She struggled to breathe as his scent surrounded her, making her yearn to lean in closer. 'This whole thing with my father has brought unwanted attention to people who are already struggling with life's difficulties. I don't think it's fair on the children.'

A look resembling regret passed through his eyes before he blinked it away. After a full minute, he murmured, 'No, it's not. But you won't resign.'

Her heart caught. 'Why not?'

'Because I won't allow you to give up something you love doing. The publicity about your father will go away. I'll make sure of it.'

She met mesmerising hazel eyes. 'Why are you doing this?'

He shrugged. 'Perhaps I'm beginning to realise that I was mistaken about how much collateral damage I was prepared to accept.'

Collateral damage. She was grappling with that when he spoke again.

'I have something for you.'

She glanced warily at him. 'Beware of Greeks bearing gifts. I'm sure I've read that warning somewhere.'

His smile held a certain chill but was heart-stopping nonetheless. 'For the most part, I'd urge you to heed that warning. But this one is completely harmless.' He pulled something from his back pocket and presented it to her. The look in his eyes made her stomach flip as she glanced from his face to the box.

'What is it?' she asked.

'Open it and see.'

She opened the velvet case and gaped at the platinum-linked, three-tiered diamond choker nestling between the two catches.

'Are you trying to make some sort of *macho* statement?'

He shook his head in confusion. 'Sorry, *anjo,* you've lost me.'

'This is a *choker.* You want everyone to see that you own me?'

He frowned. 'What the hell are you talking about?'

'Why a choker? Why not a simple diamond pendant?'

'I asked my jeweller to send a few pieces. I liked the look of that one. So I chose it. No big deal, no mind games. I thought you'd like it,' he finished tersely.

She bit her lip and wondered if she was reading too much into it. Much like she was reading far too much into her feelings for Theo and what would happen when things ended.

'It's a beautiful piece of jewellery. But frankly it's a bit ostentatious for my taste.' She snapped the box shut and held it out to him. 'Besides, since my role as paparazzi bait is over, I don't see where I would wear something like that.'

His jaw tightened and he pushed the box back at her. 'I was just coming to that. Ari is getting married next weekend. You're coming with me as my plus one.'

She couldn't stop her mouth from gaping open any more than she could stop breathing. 'You want me to drop everything and fly to Greece with you?'

'I'm sure you can work something out with the charity. I'm happy to make a donation to cover your absence if you like.'

'I…'

'And we're not going to Greece. Ari and Perla are getting married at their resort in Bermuda.'

'Different continent, same response.'

His eyes narrowed. 'Do I need to remind you that we're only three weeks into our agreement?'

Her fingers trembled and she threw the box down on the sofa. 'No, you don't need to remind me. Call me foolish, but I thought we were getting beyond that.'

'I'm trying to, Inez.'

'Then ask me nicely. For all you know, I may be busy next weekend and would need to rearrange my plans for you.'

He raised an eyebrow. 'Busy doing what?'

'Splitting the atom. Shaving my legs. Rehearsing to join a

circus troupe. What does it matter? You didn't bother to ask. You only brought me trinkets and ordered me to be ready to fly off to Bermuda.' Her mouth trembled and she firmed it.

'You're angry.'

'You're very observant.'

'Tell me why.'

She laughed. Even to her ears it sounded as if it could've easily cut glass. His eyes narrowed as she shook her head. 'What would be the point?'

'The point would be that I would listen.'

She placed her feet on the carpet and tried to stand. He caught her hips and kept her seated in front of him.

This close she could see the hypnotic gold flecks in his eyes. She wanted to drown in them. Wanted to drown in him. She tried to calm her racing pulse.

His gaze dropped to her mouth, then down to her chest and a different sort of fever took hold of her.

'That necklace—'

'Is just a necklace. I thought I'd give it to you now so you could get an outfit to match for the wedding.'

'And the trip?'

'I need a plus one. I need *you*. And you can hate me if you want but I'm not prepared to leave you here so Benedicto can hound you.'

'I can take care of myself.'

His eyes narrowed. 'I don't doubt that. But can you tell me that he won't view your refusal to take his calls this last week as a betrayal?'

Her heart skittered. 'And you think he'll harm me in some way?'

He glanced meaningfully at her arm, then back to her face. 'Sorry, *anjo*, I'm not prepared to take that chance.'

Darkness and light. Tenderness and ruthlessness. It was what kept her emotions on a knife-edge where this man was concerned.

'Will you come to Bermuda with me? Please?'

She glanced at the velvet box. 'I will. But I'm not wearing that necklace.'

'Fine. We'll find you something else.'

'I don't need anything—' Her argument died on her lips when he picked up her sketchpad. She grabbed at it but he held it out of her reach. 'Theo, hand it over.' She breathed a secret sigh of relief when her panic didn't bleed through her voice.

'You're supposed to be designing me a boat.'

'I'm still working on it. I'll show it to you when it's done.'

His gaze brushed her face and settled on her mouth. The intensity of it made her insides contract. After a minute he handed the pad over and rose. 'I look forward to it. We're dining in tonight. I'm in the mood for an early night.'

He left the room just as silently as he'd entered. She realised her fingers were clamped white around her sketchpad and slowly relaxed them.

She flipped through the pages until she came to the one she'd been drawing. It was one of many featuring Theo asleep. She stared at it, seeing the vulnerability and gentleness in his face that he covered up so efficiently when he was awake. When he was asleep he was all light, no darkness. There was a boyishness about him that she only caught rare glimpses of during the day.

Darkness and light. Unfortunately, her heart refused to be picky about which it preferred because, awake or asleep, Theo had captured her emotions so efficiently she was beginning to fear she was falling in love with him.

The nightmare started the way it always did. A glow of light signalled the men's arrival. Followed by the rope ladder and the heavy descent of thick boots, tree trunk thighs and towering thugs.

Each time he'd fought back. A few times he'd landed blows of his own. But each time they'd eventually overpowered him. The tallest, toughest one, the one who favoured those smelly cigars, always laughed. It was the laughter not the pain that triggered his screams. It was a never-ending grating sound that churned through his gut and tripped his heart rate into overdrive.

He felt the scream build in his throat and readied himself for the roar.

Gentle but firm hands shook him awake.

'Theo...*querido!*'

He kept his eyes shut and reached for her, holding on tight as the images receded. The irony of it wasn't lost on him, the thought of how much he now needed the daughter of the man who was responsible for reducing him to a helpless wreck night after night for the last twelve years.

As he held on to her the thought that had plagued him for several days now took hold. He no longer wanted to pursue this vendetta. Yesterday, he'd found himself requesting that the board vote a different way to what he'd originally planned. They'd been stunned. He'd been twice as stunned.

He'd mentally shrugged and told himself there was no reason to turn his back on a healthy profit but he'd known he'd changed his mind for a different reason.

Benedicto was all but finished.

But ending it now would mean Inez would be free to walk away from him. And the very thought of that made him break out in a cold sweat.

He'd managed to buy himself a little more time by persuading her to come with him to Ari's wedding.

After that...

His insides churned as he lay in the darkness and felt her soft hands soothe him.

He pushed away thoughts he wasn't brave enough yet to truly examine.

'*Querido*, are you awake?' she breathed softly.

His heart flipped and his arms tightened convulsively around her soft, warm body. 'I'm awake, *anjo.*'

'I'm not an angel, Theo.'

'You are.'

'If I were an angel, I'd have the power to banish your nightmares,' she replied in a voice fraught with pain.

It took several seconds to realise she ached for him.

Pulling back, he stared into her face.

'You didn't do this to me, Inez.'

Her eyes clouded. 'I know. But that doesn't mean I don't wish you healed.'

His smile felt skewed. 'There's no cure for me, sweetheart,' he said, although he was beginning to doubt that. Just as he was beginning to think that the answer lay right there in his arms. If only there was a way...

'Are you sure? There's therapy—'

'Tried it. Didn't work,' he replied. When he heard the curtness in his voice he soothed an apologetic hand down her back.

She relaxed against him and he buried his face in her hair and breathed her in.

'What happened?'

'What, with the therapy?'

She nodded.

He slowly opened his eyes and stared into the middle distance. 'They spoke about triggers, breathing techniques and anxiety-detectors. There was mention of electro-shock therapy or good old-fashioned pills. I never went back for a second session.'

Her head snapped up. 'You mean all that was at your first session?'

He smiled and kissed her gaping mouth. 'I believed what was wrong with me couldn't be fixed by therapy.'

'Believed?'

He realised what he'd said and his breath caught. Was he grasping at straws where there were none?

'I'm beginning to think things aren't as hopeless for me, anjo.'

She paled a little but continued to hold his gaze. Slowly,

she nodded. Her luxuriant hair spilled over her shoulder onto his chest as she stared into his eyes. 'I really hope you find closure one day, Theo.'

Simple, frank words, said from the heart. But they froze his insides as surely and as swiftly as an arctic wind froze water.

Because he was seriously doubting that he would ever find peace without this woman in his arms.

CHAPTER TWELVE

THEY BOARDED THEO'S private jet late the next Friday. The moment they stepped on board, Inez sensed something was wrong.

Theo paced up and down, his agitation growing the closer they got to take-off.

When the pilot came through, Theo sent a piercing glance at him and the man hurried into the cockpit.

'Theo, sit down. You're making your pilot nervous.'

He barked out a short laugh and threw himself into the long sofa opposite her chair. His fingers drummed repeatedly on the armrest. 'Don't worry; he's used to it.'

'Used to what?'

'My aversion to enclosed spaces,' he answered tersely.

'Your claustrophobia.' Her heart squeezed as she watched his fingers grip the armrest and the skin around his mouth pale.

Unbuckling her seat belt, she crossed to the sofa and sat down next to him. A sheen of sweat coated his forehead and when his eyes sought hers she read the anxiety in them. Reaching around him, she secured his seat belt then took care of her own as the plane taxied onto the runway.

Taking the arm closest to hers, she pulled it over her shoulder and settled herself against him. He tugged her close immediately, his breathing harsh and uneven.

She hugged him harder, and when he tilted her face up to his she went willingly.

He kissed her with a desperation that tore through her soul. For long, anxiety-filled minutes, he took what she offered, until the need for air drove them apart.

'You get that we cannot kiss all the way to Bermuda, don't you?' she said, laughing.

'Is that a challenge? Because I bet I can,' he threw back with a heart-stopping smile.

Inez noticed that his breathing was no longer agitated and breathed a sigh of relief.

'No, it's not a challenge.' She rested her head on his shoulder and caressed his hard jaw. 'How do you normally get through flying?'

His jaw tightened for a second before he relaxed. 'Mild sleeping pills before take-off normally does the trick.'

'Why not today?'

'You're here,' he said simply. After a minute, he asked, 'Why are you helping me?'

'I cannot forget that my father did this to you. And no, I'm not offering myself as a sacrificial lamb. But I don't want to see you suffer either. I want to help any way I can.'

The reminder that her father loomed large between them grated more than he wanted to admit. 'For how long?' Theo demanded more harshly than he'd intended.

She stiffened. 'Sorry?'

'Are you counting the days until I set you free?' he pressed.

Her eyelids swooped down, concealing her expression. 'I…we have an agreement—'

'Damn the agreement. If you had a choice now, today, would you stay or would you leave?'

'Theo—'

'Answer the question, Inez.'

'I'd choose to stay…'

The bubble of joy that started to grow inside him burst when he registered her flat tone. 'But?'

'But… this could never go anywhere.'

A sense of helplessness blanketed him. 'Why not? Because I blackmailed you?'

She shook her head. 'No. Because a relationship between us would be impossible.

Theo's vision blurred at her words. He'd pushed her too far. Hung onto his vendetta for too long. His mouth soured with ashen hopelessness. 'I guess we both know where we stand.'

When she moved away, he fought not to pull her back. She stayed close—out of pity? His mouth curled. He told himself he didn't care but the voice in his head mocked him.

He cared, much more than he'd bargained for when he'd forced her to make that stupid choice. The idea of her walking away from him made his insides knot with a pain far greater than he'd ever known.

The plane hit a pocket of turbulence, throwing her against him. When she stayed close, he let her. Forcefully, he reminded himself of one thing.

He'd never meant to keep her for ever.

The Pantelides Bermuda resort was a breathtaking jewel set amid swaying palm trees and sugar-white sand. The sun beat down on them as Theo drove the open-top Jeep towards their villa.

Stunning buildings connected by dark wooden bridges under which the most spectacular water features had been constructed made for a visual masterpiece. All round them bold colour burst free in a heady mix of blues, greens and yellows that begged to be touched.

Their sprawling whitewashed villa featured high ceilings, cool tiled floors and a four-poster bed that dominated the master bedroom.

A tense Theo who hadn't said more than a dozen words

to her since they landed, instructed the porter to place their cases in the master bedroom and tipped the man before walking outside onto the large wooden deck.

'There's a barbecue later this afternoon. Perla thought we might want to rest before then. You can go ahead and rest if you want to. I'll go and catch up with Sakis and Ari.'

He walked away from her and headed out of the door.

The clear indication that she wasn't welcome stung, although why she was surprised was beyond her.

He'd held ajar the possibility of continuing this thing between them and she'd slammed the door shut.

A small part of her was proud she hadn't grasped the suggestion with both hands, while the larger part, the part that had fallen head over heels in love with Theo in spite of all the chaos surrounding them, reeled with heart-wrenching pain at what the future held.

But, as she'd told herself over and over again on the plane as he'd shut his eyes and surprisingly dozed off, she was taking the right steps now to prevent even more heartache later.

Because there was no way Theo would ever reconcile himself to having her as a constant reminder. Certainly not enough to love her.

The reality was that they'd fallen into bed as a result of some crazy chemistry. Chemistry fizzled out. Eventually, the constant reminder that a part of her was responsible for his inner demons and outer scars would grate and rip at whatever remained after the chemistry was gone.

He was better off without her.

Her heart protested loudly at that decision. Ignoring it, she went into the bedroom and lifted her case onto the bed. The cream sheath she'd bought for the wedding needed to be hung out before it creased beyond repair.

Unzipping her case, she opened it and froze. A red velvet box, similar to the black one Theo had presented her with a few days ago lay on top of her clothes.

With shaky hands she picked it up and opened it. The stunning necklace sparkling in the sunlight made her gasp.

The platinum chain had a small loop at one end, with a large teardrop diamond at the other that slipped easily through the hoop. The design was simple and elegant. And so utterly gorgeous she couldn't stop herself from caressing the flawless stone.

Swallowing a lump in her throat at the thoughtfulness behind the necklace, she jumped when a knock came at the door. Thinking it was Theo who'd forgotten to take a key, she opened the door with a smile.

Only to stop when confronted by two stunningly beautiful women, one of whom was heavily pregnant, while the other carried a small baby in her arms.

'Sorry to descend on you like this, only Theo was a bit vague about whether you were actually resting or if you were up for a visit.' The women exchanged glances. 'I've never seen him so scatty, have you?' the pregnant redhead asked the blue-eyed blonde.

'Nope, normally he's quick off the mark with those hopeless one-liners. Today, not so much. Anyway, we thought we'd come on the off-chance that you were *not* resting and say hello...oh, my God, that necklace is gorgeous!' The redhead reached out and traced a manicured forefinger over the diamond.

Then she looked up, noticed Inez's open-mouthed gaze and laughed. 'Sorry, I'm Perla soon-to-be Pantelides. This is Brianna Pantelides, Sakis's wife. And this little heartbreaker is Dimitri.'

'I'm Inez da Costa. I'm a...' she paused, for the first time holding up her relationship with Theo to the harsh light of day and coming up short on explanations '...business associate of Theo's.'

The two women exchanged another glance and she rushed to cover the awkward silence. 'Please, come in.'

Brianna paused. 'Are you sure?'

'*Sim*…yes, I'm sure. I was just unpacking…' she started and noticed Perla's frown.

'Why are you doing that yourself? We have two butlers and three villa staff attached to each residence.'

'I think Theo sent them away,' she said, then bit her lip as Perla's eyebrows shot upward.

'Did he? Ari did that once too, when we first arrived here four months ago. Then we proceeded to have an almighty row.' She smiled at the memory and placed her hand lovingly over her swollen belly.

Brianna laughed and walked to the sofa. Settling herself down, she opened her shirt and adjusted her son for a feed.

Perla sat on the sofa too and they both stared back at her. Their open curiosity made her nape tingle.

'We won't keep you long. I just wanted to run the itinerary by you because, frankly, I don't trust the men with the information. We have a casual dinner tonight, followed by a quick rehearsal. Most of the guests arrive in the morning and the wedding is at three o'clock, okay?'

'Okay.' She ventured a smile and Brianna's eyes widened.

'Gosh, you're stunning! How did you meet Theo again?'

'Brianna!' Perla admonished with a laugh.

'What?'

Inez fiddled with the clasp of the velvet box and pushed down the well of sadness that surged from nowhere. These two women were not only almost family, they were friends too. Whereas her family was in utter chaos and she had no friends to speak of.

She forced another smile. 'He had some business in Rio. I was…am helping him out with it.'

'Right. Okay.' Perla struggled upright and nudged Brianna. 'We'll leave you alone. I think the guys are rowing in about an hour. It's an experience you don't want to miss if you've never seen it before.'

Brianna gently dislodged her drowsy baby from her

breast and laid him on her shoulder, gently patting his back as she stood.

The door opened as they neared it and Theo's large frame filled the doorway.

His gaze zeroed in on her, then dropped to the box still clutched in her hand before coming back up. Her throat dried at the sight of him and the ever present tingle that struck her deep within flared heat outward.

'Um, Theo?' Perla ventured.

'What?' he snapped without taking his eyes from Inez.

'You need to move from the doorway so we can leave.'

He snorted under his breath and entered the villa. He turned with his hand on the door, causing Brianna to roll her eyes. 'We've given Inez the schedule so you have no excuse to be late.'

'I'm never late.'

'Yeah, right. You were almost two hours late for Perla's engagement party and an hour late for Dimitri's christening.'

'Which therefore means I'll only be half an hour late for this wedding. Now, please go and pester your other halves and leave me alone.'

The women grumbled as they left. He turned from the door with a smile on his face but it slowly dimmed as his gaze connected with hers.

'Did they harass you?' he asked, a touch of wary concern in his eyes.

She shook her head. 'No. They were lovely.'

'I don't know about lovely but I tolerate them.' Contrary to his words, his voice held a fondness that made her chest tighten.

Theo understood family. Enough that he'd been devastated when his had been broken. And yet he'd wanted to rip hers apart.

Despite understanding the reason behind his motives, the thought still hurt deeply.

'Inez?'

She turned sharply and headed back to the bedroom. He followed and grabbed her wrist as she reached out to set the box down.

'What's wrong?'

Her throat clogged. 'What *isn't* wrong?'

His eyes narrowed. 'If Brianna or Perla said something to upset you—'

'No, I told you they were wonderful! They were kind and funny and…and incredible.' Tears threatened and she swallowed hard.

'You only met them for twenty minutes.'

'It was enough.'

'Enough for what?'

'Enough to know that I want what they have. And that I'll probably never have it. So far my record has been beyond appalling.'

He frowned. 'You don't have a record.'

'Constantine used me to get dirt on my father and—'

'I don't want you to say his name in my presence,' he interrupted harshly.

'And what about you? You make me hope for things I have no right to hope for, Theo. What sort of fool does that make me?'

'No, you're not a fool. You're one of the bravest, most loyal people I know.' He said the words gravely. 'It is I who is the fool.'

Theo's words echoed through her mind as she watched the brothers row in perfect harmony across the almost still resort water a short while later.

He took the middle position with Sakis in front and Ari at the back. She watched, spellbound, as his shoulders rippled with smooth grace and utmost efficiency.

'Aren't they something to watch?' Perla sighed wistfully.

'*Sim*,' she agreed huskily.

'I think they do that just to get us girls all hot and bothered,' Brianna complained but Inez noticed that she didn't take her eyes off her husband for one second.

When the men eventually returned to shore, the two women joined them and were immediately enfolded into the group.

Theo glanced her way, a touch of irritation in his eyes. Seconds later, he broke away from the group and came towards her.

'I didn't expect you to be down here. You should be resting.'

'I was invited. I hope I'm not intruding.'

'If you were invited then you're not intruding. Come and join us.' He grabbed her hand and led her to where Ari and Sakis were turning over the boat to dry the underside.

The two brothers gave her cursory glances but barely spoke to her. When Ari abruptly asked Theo to accompany him to the boat shed, her stomach fell.

Perla organised a Jeep to take her back to their villa and when Theo returned half an hour later, his jaw was tight and his movements jerky as he swept her off her feet and strode into the bedroom.

He made love to her with a fierce, silent passion that robbed her of speech and breath before he clamped her to his side and slid into sleep.

Her eyes filled with tears and she hurriedly brushed them away. It was no use daydreaming that things would ever magically turn rosy between her and Theo.

As much as she wanted to wish otherwise, they were on a countdown to being over for good.

The wedding was beautiful and quietly elegant in a way only an events organiser extraordinaire like Perla could achieve despite being seven months pregnant. Inez watched the bride and groom dance across the polished floor of the casino, transformed into a spectacular masterpiece that stood directly on the water, and fought the feelings rampaging through her.

Theo would never be hers. She would never have a wedding like this or have him gazing at her the way Ari was gazing at his new wife.

She would never feel the weight of his baby in her belly or have it suckle at her breast.

Despair slowly built inside her, despite knowing deep down that Theo had done her a favour by bringing her here. He didn't need her to save him from whatever nightmares plagued him. He had a family that clearly adored him, who would be there for him when he chose to let them in.

She needed to stop moping and get on with her life.

Her time in Theo's house and his bed was over. In retrospect, she was thankful she'd let him talk her into keeping her volunteer position. It was a lifeline she was grateful for in a world skidding out of control. The things she couldn't control she would learn to live without.

A tall figure danced into her view and her eyes connected with the man who occupied an astonishingly large percentage of her mind. In his arms was an elegantly dressed woman with greying brown hair and a sad expression. She said something to him and he glanced down at her. His smile was gentle but wary and Inez saw her sadness deepen.

Inez heard the soft gurgle of a baby over the music and turned to see Brianna next to her. 'That's their mother.' She nodded to Theo's dance partner. 'Their relationship has been fraught but I think they're all finding their way back to each other.' She glanced at Inez with a smile. 'I hope that you two find your way too.'

Inez shook her head. 'I'm afraid that's impossible.'

Brianna laughed. 'Believe me, I've seen the impossible happen in this family. I've learned not to rule anything out.' She smiled down at her child and danced away with him towards her husband.

Tears stung her eyes as she watched Sakis enfold his wife and son in his arms.

'What's wrong now?' Theo's deep voice sounded in her ear.

She blinked rapidly and pasted a smile on her face. 'Nothing. Weddings…they make me emotional. That's all.'

His eyes narrowed speculatively on her face before he took hold of her elbow. 'Dance with me.'

He led her to the dance floor and pulled her close.

'You have a big family,' she said, more for something to fill the silence.

'They can be a pain in the rear sometimes.'

'Regardless, you all seem to watch out for each other.'

He shrugged. 'Force of habit.'

'No, it's not. Does Ari know who I am?'

His mouth tightened. 'He suspects. I didn't enlighten or deny because it's none of his business. He's welcome to draw his own conclusions. Why do you ask?'

'Because he's been watching me like a hawk since we got here and he hasn't spoken more than two words to me. That's what I mean. What you have with your brothers isn't habit. It's love.'

His mouth twisted in a way that evidenced his dark pain.

'*Love* hasn't conquered the nightmares that have plagued me for all these years, Inez.' The raw pain in his voice made her throat clog. She forced a swallow.

'Because you haven't allowed it to. You resisted any attempt at help because you thought you had to face this demon alone, do things your way.'

The honest barb struck home. He was silent for the rest of the song. Then abruptly he spoke. 'I didn't want to appear weak. I hated myself every time I couldn't walk into a dark room or down an unlit street. I haven't been able to cope with the smell of cigars without breaking out in a cold sweat. Do you know what that feels like?' he asked in a harsh undertone.

She shook her head. 'No, but I know it will never go away if you keep it buried.'

Her warmth, her strength hit him hard and he wanted to reach for her with all he had. Suddenly, everything he'd ever craved, ever wished for seemed coalesced in the woman before him.

'It's no longer buried. A month ago I was still the messed-up boy Ari dug up from that hole twelve years ago. But you did something about that.'

'No, I'm not responsible for that.'

His hand cupped her nape and he whispered fiercely in her ear. 'You are. You've seen me, Inez. I can't sleep with the lights off. I used to panic whenever someone shut a door behind me. That's why I surrounded myself with glass. With you by my side I flew here with no need for sleeping pills.'

'Even though you refused to speak to me for hours.'

He exhaled. 'Things are upside down and inside out right now. Let's just…we'll get through this wedding and head back to Rio. And we will damn well fix this thing between us. Because I'm not prepared to let you go yet.'

CHAPTER THIRTEEN

'I TOLD YOU, you're so much better than a damn sleeping pill.'

Inez laughed as Theo tugged her dress down and lifted her out of it. Leaving it on the floor of the master cabin bedroom, he waited for her to kick her shoes off before he crossed over to the bed. The diamond pendant he'd looked incredibly pleased that she'd worn lay nestled between her breasts.

'Keep that on,' he instructed, just as the plane jerked through turbulence and they fell onto the bed together, a tangle of hard and soft limbs and hot, needy kisses.

'I'm glad I have my uses,' she said, laughing, when he let her up for air.

His face grew serious as he stared down at her. 'You've attained the ultimate purpose in my life, *querida*. Now more than ever you're my saviour: *my* angel.' He cradled her head as he kissed her.

Inez closed her eyes and imagined that she could feel his soul through his reverent kiss. She studiously ignored the voice that mocked that she was deluding herself.

When he finished undressing her with gentle hands, she tried to stem her tears as he made love to her with a greedy passion that touched her very soul.

Afterwards she held him in her arms as he fell asleep. Unable to sleep, her mind drifted back to the wedding.

Theo had introduced her to his mother and again she'd witnessed the sadness in her eyes. When he'd hugged her at the end of the evening and murmured gently into her ear, his mother had burst into tears. Inez had watched as the brothers closed around her and soothed her tears.

She was still watching them when Ari had glanced her way. His measured smile and thoughtful nod in her direction had made her swallow. It hadn't been acceptance but it hadn't been the chilly reception he'd given her either.

As they'd packed to leave, Inez had asked Theo about what had happened with his mother.

'She fell apart completely after my father was arrested. She left Athens and locked herself away at our house in Santorini,' he'd replied in an offhand manner, but Inez had seen his anguish.

Recalling his words about abandonment, she'd gasped, 'She wasn't there when you were kidnapped, was she?'

Heart-shredding pain washed over his face, but a moment later it was replaced by a look even more soul-shaking. Forgiveness. 'No. She wasn't. But I had Ari and Sakis. They were strong for me. And they were that way because of her. I told her that tonight because I think we both needed to hear it.'

His words had resonated deep inside her. But most of all it had been his statement on the dance floor that continued to flash across her mind. *I'm not prepared to let you go yet.*

Her heart lurched. He meant to keep her in his bed for a while yet. Like a trophy he wasn't prepared to relinquish. And her foolish heart performed a giddy little samba at the thought of having a few more moments with him.

She woke to kisses on her forehead and her cheek and opened her eyes to bright sunshine.

'Good, you're awake. We just landed.'

She yawned widely. 'Already? I feel as if I just fell asleep.'

He laughed. 'It's three o'clock in the afternoon. And we have much to do before tonight.'

She stared at his wide grin and her heart lifted with happiness. 'You seem in very good spirits, *querido*,' she commented.

He gathered her close in his arms and gazed down at her. 'There is a reason for that.'

'Tell me,' she murmured softly.

His face turned serious, his eyes fierce as he watched her. 'For the first time in twelve years, I slept through the night without a nightmare,' he muttered hoarsely.

Theo watched her face light up with shocked pleasure before she reached up to clasp his face. Her kiss was gentle and sweet. 'Oh, Theo. I'm so happy for you.'

'I'm happy for *us*,' he replied. With another kiss, he got up and started dressing. 'Get a move on, sweetheart, unless you wish to give the customs guy an eyeful when he boards.'

With a yelp she got up and pulled her clothes on.

Theo's phone started ringing the moment they stepped off the plane. And it wasn't until they were back home that she remembered what he'd said on the plane.

'What did you mean—"we have much to do before tonight"? We're not going out, are we?' She groaned.

He took the phone from his pocket and checked it as another text message came through. She waited impatiently for him to finish.

'No, we're not going out. But we have a guest coming.'

'A guest? Who?'

'I've invited your father to dinner.'

Inez staggered as if a bucket of ice had been poured over her.

'My father is coming here?'

'Yes.'

'And you didn't think to inform me of this? What makes you think I want to see him?'

'We have to. It's time to get this thing over and done with, once and for all.'

'And you don't care how I feel about it?'

'I thought we agreed to fix things when we return to Rio?' he asked with a frown.

'Yes, but when you said *we*, I thought you meant us, you and me. More fool me. Because there is not me without my father, is there?'

'What are you talking about? Of course there is.'

'Then why would you go behind my back to arrange this?'

A tic started in his temple. 'Because it's my fault you're in the middle of all this.' He sighed and clawed a hand through his hair. 'I got a chance to fix things with my mother in Bermuda. We may never get back what we had but I'll take that over nothing. Whatever relationship you choose to have with your own father from here on in is up to you. But this is a hardship I caused in your life and one I have a duty to fix.'

The fight fizzed out of her but the fear that something had gone seriously wrong between the airport and home wouldn't go away.

At seven on the dot, the doorbell rang. She passed her hand over her black jumpsuit and tucked a lock of hair nervously behind her ear as she stood by Theo's side.

The butler entered the living room, followed by her father.

Benedicto da Costa drew to a halt. His narrowed gaze slid from Theo to her, his face a mask of dark anger and cold malice she'd forced herself to overlook in the past.

Now she saw him for who he really was. Images of Theo's scars flashed through her mind and her hands fisted at her side.

'I won't shake your hand because this isn't a social visit,' he rasped icily to Theo. 'And I won't be dining with you, either.'

'Perfectly fine by me. Frankly, the quicker we get this over with the better. But let me remind you that you're here only because of Inez. She may be your daughter but she's under my protection now. I suggest you don't lose sight of that fact. What business you and I have will be finished by week's end.'

Her father's gaze swung back to her. 'Are you just going to stand there and let him speak to your father that way? You disappoint me.'

'That's no surprise. I've been a disappointment from the moment I was born a girl, *Pai*.'

'Your mother will be rolling in her grave at your behaviour.'

She raised her chin. 'No, actually. *Mãe* told me every day she was proud of me. She also encouraged me to follow my dreams. She wanted to be a sculptor. Did you know that?'

'What's your point?'

'She was talented, *Pai*. But she gave it up for you. It was her, not you, who taught me what loyalty and family meant. You were only focused on exploiting that loyalty for your own selfish needs.'

His face tightened and his eyes flickered to Theo, who'd been standing by her with his arms folded, a half smile on his face.

'Is this what I came here for? To be lectured by an ungrateful child?'

Theo shrugged. 'I'm finding it quite entertaining.'

Benedicto growled and shot to his feet. 'If there is a point, *son*, I suggest you get to it.'

Theo grew marble-still, his smile disappearing in the blink of an eye. Pure rage vibrated off his body and Inez watched his nostrils flare as he sucked in a control-sustaining breath.

'*I am not your son*. And you are not worthy to be a father. It's a shame you didn't learn how to be a better parent from the mother who gave birth to you in that *favela* you deny you grew up in. And don't bother denying it again. I know everything there is to know about you, da Costa.'

For the first time since he'd walked in, Benedicto grew

wary. He strolled to the drinks cabinet and took his time examining all the expensive spirits and liqueurs displayed.

Without asking, he poured a measure of single malt whisky and took a bold sip. 'So I bent the truth a little. So what? You've already discredited my campaign. What do you want? My company? Is that your end game? You want to pick up the shares for Da Costa Holdings for peanuts? Well, over my dead body.'

Theo's laugh was menacing enough to cause her skin to tingle in alarm. 'Trust me, a few weeks ago it would've been my pleasure to grant you your wish. But you're wrong on that score. Your company is of no interest to me.'

His wariness increased. 'What's changed?'

Theo's eyes flicked to her and her heart thudded. 'Your daughter.'

'Really?'

Inez shook her head in astonishment. 'Do you really not know who he is, *Pai*?' she asked.

Theo's mouth curved in a mirthless smile. 'Oh, he knows who I am. He's just hoping that *I* don't know what he did twelve years ago.'

Benedicto swallowed, his gaunt face growing pale until he looked ashen. 'I have no idea what you're talking—'

She rushed towards him, anger, pain and disappointment coiling like poisonous snakes inside her. 'Don't you dare deny it. *Don't you dare!*' Her voice cracked and a sob broke through her chest. 'You had a boy kidnapped and tortured! For money. How could you?'

Eyes she'd once thought were like her own turned black with sinister rage. 'How could I? I did it for you. The fancy clothes you strut about in and that fancy car you drive? Where do you think the money came from? I needed it to save the company. Anyway, it was my money. Why did I have to go back to farming just because Pantelides couldn't keep it in his pants or stop his bit on the side from blowing the whistle on him?'

Inez's hand flew to her mouth, her insides icing over. '*Santa Maria*, you truly are a monster.'

Her father's jaw tightened and he addressed Theo. 'Is this the point where you hand whatever file you've gathered on me over to the authorities?'

Theo's mouth twisted. 'So you can bribe your way out of jail? No.'

Benedicto frowned. 'Then what the hell do you want?'

Theo glanced over at her and a look of almost relief washed over his face, as if a weight had been lifted off his shoulders. 'That's up to Inez. And only her. I'm done with you.'

Inez raised her suddenly heavy head and looked from one man to the other.

One stood tall, proud and breathtaking. A man she'd been so determined not to let in. But whose tortured vulnerability had drawn her to him, made her see beneath his skin to the frightened child who was desperately seeking answers.

Choking tears filling her eyes, she turned to the monster who was her father. 'I have nothing else to say to you. I don't want to see you ever again. Goodbye.'

Turning sharply from both men, she rushed out of the room and fled up the stairs.

Theo wasted no time in throwing Benedicto out once Inez left the room. He'd meant what he said—he was done with seeking retribution...had been done almost from the moment he'd met Inez.

Perhaps unwisely, he'd thought the meeting with Benedicto would be swift and cathartic. Instead, he'd brought Inez even more anguish.

He slashed his fingers through his hair as he vaulted up the stairs that led to his third floor suite. Perhaps she'd been right. He'd ambushed her in his rush to get this situation sorted between them.

But he would make it right for her. They would get

through this. They had to. The feelings he'd tried hard to smother had blown up in his face when he'd woken on the plane this afternoon. With the absence of anxiety and fear, the purest reason why he wanted to wake up each morning with Inez had shone through.

The feelings had been so intense he'd almost blurted it out. But he'd decided to wait until she'd confronted her father.

Now he wished he hadn't. He was wishing he'd provided her with that additional support of knowing how much she meant to him before he'd let her father loose on her.

Pursing his mouth in determination, he pushed the bedroom door open. 'Inez, I'm sorry for—'

The sight that confronted him silenced his words and turned his feet to clay. She stared at him, eyes red-rimmed with freshly shed tears.

Because of him. But even that pulse of deep regret couldn't erase the sight before him.

'What are you doing?' he asked, although the part of his brain that hadn't frozen along with his feet could work it out.

Two suitcases were open on the bed, one filled with her clothes. *She was packing...*

The silk top in her hand trembled before she turned and threw it in her case. Then her fingers curled around the edge of the lid.

When she looked at him again, more tears filled her eyes.

'Thank you for opening my eyes to what he truly is,' she murmured huskily.

'Shelve the thanks and tell me what you're doing,' he replied tersely.

One hand swiped at her cheek. 'I'm leaving, Theo.'

'You're what?' His voice rang with disbelief. 'You're going back to your father's house?'

She shuddered from head to toe. 'No. I could never live there again.'

He frowned. 'Then where are you going?'

She gave a tiny shrug. 'I'll stay with Camila.'

He finally got his feet to work and paced to where she stood. When she grabbed her shorts, he ripped them from her hand and threw them on the bed. 'I seem to be missing a link somewhere, sweetheart. Why don't you take a beat and fill me in?'

'I can't stay here.'

A merciless vice squeezed his chest. 'Why not?'

Her face creased in fresh anguish. 'Because he is right. The food he put on our table; the clothes on my back; our fancy education. They *all* came from your suffering.'

'For God's sake—'

She carried on raggedly. 'I never stopped to think about it but I remember the day he came home twelve years ago and told my mother our troubles were over. We weren't exactly poor before then, but after he pressured my mother into selling the ranch he made some bad investments and the company suffered for it. They argued a lot and I used to go to bed every night praying for a miracle just so they'd stop arguing. Can you imagine how I felt when my prayers were answered? And now, all these years later, I find out that what I'd prayed for came at the cost of your—' She choked to a stop, then frantically threw more clothes into the case.

Theo couldn't find an answer as desperately as he tried. He was watching her torture herself and he could do nothing to stop it. '*Anjo*—'

'No. I'm *not* an angel, Theo. I'm a child of the monster, a heartless devil who tortures children and doesn't feel an ounce of regret for it. How can you even bear to look at me?'

'Because you're *not* him!' he interjected fiercely. He took her hands and forced her to face him. 'You're not responsible for his actions. Stay, Inez. We said we would talk about us once we were done with him.'

'But there is no us, is there? We...we just fell into bed because of the circumstances that brought us together. If it hadn't been for my father you'd never have set foot in Brazil.'

'So you're walking away because you think we were never meant to be?' He watched her, forced himself to think how he would feel if she walked away from him. The realisation of what was happening washed over him and ashen despair filled his chest.

'I'm walking away because you need to put everything and everyone associated with your ordeal behind you. Otherwise you will never heal properly.'

He dropped her hand and stared down at her. The ice that had started to build inside him since he'd walked into the room hardened. It crept around his heart and Theo swore he heard it crack. His eyes scoured her beautiful tearstained face, looking for a tiny chink. A tiny ray of hope that would offer deliverance from the quicksand of devastation he could feel himself sinking into.

'So that's it? That's your final decision. You're doing this for my sake but I have no say in the matter?' He couldn't stop the bitterness from lacing his voice.

Her answer was to step back and gather up the last of her clothes. With trembling fingers, she zipped up the cases and lifted them off the bed.

'Inez, answer me!'

She stilled at the door. '*Adeus*, Theo.'

'Go to hell!' he snarled back.

'Table Four need a second helping of *feijoadas*. And a bottle of Rioja.' Camila bustled into the kitchen, checked on the bubbling pot Inez was stirring and nodded in approval. '*Fantastico*. I'll be back in a minute for that order.' She sailed back out on a giddy whirlwind.

Inez wiped her sweating brow and looked over her shoulder. 'Pietro, you grab the bottle; I'll serve up the *feijoadas*.'

Her brother rolled his eyes. 'Who made you queen of the kitchen?'

'I did, when I won the coin toss earlier.'

Her grin came easier today—much easier than it had for far longer than she wanted to dwell on. She still couldn't go for more than ten seconds without thinking of Theo but if she could joke with her brother, that was a good sign that this hollow, half-dead devastation she carried inside her would eventually ease. Right?

'I still think you cheated,' Pietro grumbled.

She lifted one shoulder. 'I'll let you explain to Camila, then, why the Rioja isn't here when she returns, *sim*?'

'Tomorrow, I'm tossing the coin.' He sauntered down the stairs into the basement that served as the restaurant's larder and wine cellar. The smell of the cheese Camila kept in the small space could be overpowering and she smiled again as Pietro made gagging noises.

If there was a bright side to be seen, it was that, amid all the chaos and heartache, somehow she and her brother had grown closer than she'd ever dreamed possible.

They both were yet to decide what they wanted to do with their lives after choosing to walk away from their father and the company, but Camila had encouraged them to take their time. To heal. To reconnect.

When her mother's childhood friend had offered them a job in her restaurant they'd both jumped at it. She'd worked it around her volunteer work and, between the two jobs, it kept her plenty busy.

Keeping herself occupied stopped the tight knot of pain inside her from mushrooming into unbearable agony. In the dark of the night when she lay wide awake and aching was time enough to suffer through the hell of wondering if she was doomed to heartache for ever.

Of wondering if Theo had left Rio in the three weeks since their final bitter encounter. Of wondering if his nightmares were gone for good or if her brief presence in his life had made them worse.

Her hand trembled and she immediately curled it into a fist. Theo was strong. He would survive…

Yes, but he called you his saviour. His angel. And you walked away from him.

'No,' she breathed through the pain ripping through her. She'd done the right thing—

'No what? If you tell me I've got the wrong wine, you'll have to go and get it yourself.'

She shook her head blindly and turned gratefully to the door as Camila walked in. Her quick but assessing glance at her made Inez frown.

'We have a new booking. Table One. And an order of *feijoadas* for one.'

'Wow, you're on fire tonight, sis.'

She ignored Pietro. 'Okay, I'll serve it up and—'

'No, I didn't take a drink order. And I think they want an appetiser first too. Can you go take care of it?'

Inez's eyebrow shot up. 'Me? But I'm not dressed to serve.'

'Pfft. This isn't the Four Seasons, *meu querida*. Besides, it's time you took a break from that hot stove. Tidy your hair a bit and go and take the order.'

Inez looked down at her black skirt and grey T-shirt. It wasn't standard waitress attire but, as Camila had said, this wasn't the Four Seasons. She tucked a strand of hair behind her ear and caught the worried look in the older woman's eyes. It was an expression she'd spied a few times and she reached out and shook her head before the concern could be voiced.

'I'm fine.'

Camila's mouth pursed. 'Good. Then go and attend to Table One.'

With a weary sigh, she washed and dried her hands on her apron. Unfastening it, she hung it on the hook and avoided her image in the small mirror by the door. Her red face from manning the stove for the last three hours would depress her even more.

Plucking a pencil, notebook and menu from the kitchen stand, she nudged the swinging doors with her hip and turned towards Table One.

'You...' she choked out.

Through the drumming in her ears she heard the items in her hand clatter to the floor. A couple of diners glanced her way. Someone picked up the scattered items and placed them in her numb hands. She opened her mouth to thank them but no words emerged.

Every atom in her body was paralysed at the sight of Theo Pantelides.

She heard movement behind her. 'You can't stand here all night, *pequena*. Life will pass you by that way,' Camila said solemnly.

She exhaled shakily and forced herself to move.

Those light hazel eyes never left her as she approached his table. He looked as powerful and as magnificent as ever, even if his cheekbones seemed to stand out a little more than she remembered. His hair had grown a little longer and looked a little dishevelled.

'Sit,' he rasped.

Her heart lurched at the sound of his voice. Licking her dry lips, she shook her head. 'I can't. I'm working.'

'I've received special dispensation from Camila. Sit,' he commanded again.

She sat. He stared at her for a full minute, his eyes raking over her face as if he had been starved of her... Or he was committing her face to memory one last time?

White-hot pain ripped through her. 'Why are you here, Theo?' she blurted.

His eyes rose from her mouth to connect with hers. The breath he took was deep and long. 'I was clearing out the house and I found something you left behind.' He reached down near his feet and laid her sketchpad on the table.

She stared at it, drowning beneath the weight of her despair. 'Oh, thank you.' She paused a second before the words were torn out of her. 'So you're leaving Rio?'

He shrugged. 'There's nothing left for me here.'

Tears burned her eyes as her heart shredded into a million useless pieces. 'I…I wish you well.'

He made a rough sound under his breath. 'Do you?' he asked sarcastically. She glanced up sharply but he wasn't done. 'Problem is, I'd believe those blithe words from the woman sitting across from me. But the woman who drew these…' he flicked over the pages of the sketchpad a few times before he stopped and pointed '…this woman has guts. She was brave enough to draw what was in her heart; what cried out from her soul. Look at her.'

She kept her eyes on his face, her whole body trembling wildly as she gave a jerky shake of her head.

'Look at her, dammit!'

She sucked in a breath. And looked down. The first sketch was the one she'd made of him after they'd made love that first time on the boat. The ones that followed were variations of that first sketch. She'd captured Theo in various poses, each one progressively more lovingly detailed until the final one of him with his brothers, laughing together at the wedding. She'd drawn that from memory on their final night in Bermuda. Staring at the finished picture had cemented her feelings for him.

He turned the page and the image of Brianna and Sakis's baby stared back at her. Dimitri already bore the strong, captivating mark of the Pantelides family. It was that template that she'd used in the following sketches, when capturing her own secret yearning of what her and Theo's baby would look like on paper had been too strong to resist.

'You must think I'm some sort of crazy stalker.'

'There is no stalking involved when the subject is just as crazy about the stalker,' he rasped in a raw undertone.

Her heart flipped into her belly and her whole body trembled. 'You can't be. Theo, I'll ruin your life.'

'I thought my life was ruined before I met you. I was consumed by rage and a thirst for revenge. I let the need for revenge swallow me whole, blinding me to what was important. Family. Love. I thought there was nothing else worth fighting for. But I was wrong. There was you. My life *will* be ruined. But only if you're not in it.'

The tears she'd tried to hold back brimmed and fell down her cheeks. Theo cursed and looked around. 'What's through there?' he asked.

'It's a room, for private parties.'

'Is there a party tonight?'

Before she'd finished shaking her head he was standing and tugging her after him. He kicked the door shut and turned to her.

'Listen to me. You told me I would never see you as anything but the child of a monster. But you forget you're also the child of a loving mother who celebrated every day the special person you are. How do you think she would feel to see you buried here, punishing yourself for what your father did?'

She shut her eyes but the tears squeezed through anyway.

'Open your eyes, Inez.'

She sniffed and complied, staring up at him with blurred vision. 'Now, truly open your eyes and see the wonderful person you are. See the person I see. The brave, talented person who drew those pictures.'

'Oh, Theo,' she cried.

'You have a dream. A dream I want to be a part of.' His hands shook as they traced her face.

'I want that dream to become reality so badly.'

'Then please forgive me for blackmailing me and give us that chance.'

She pulled back. 'Forgive you? There is nothing to forgive. If anything, I should be thanking you for shaking me out of my bleak existence. Even before I truly knew you, you empowered me to fight for what I wanted.'

'So will you fight for us? Will you give me the chance to prove to you that I'm worthy of your love and let me show you how much you mean to me?'

She touched his face and inhaled shakily when he turned to kiss her palm. '*Meu querido,* I fell in love with you so ridiculously soon after meeting you, I swear I'll never confess to you when it happened.'

His stunned laugh brought a wide smile to her face. '*Anjo…*' When her smile dimmed, he shook his head. 'Don't bother to argue with me. I love you with every breath I take. You're my angel and I'll keep repeating it until you believe it.'

'We're not going to have a very smooth-sailing future, are we?'

'No,' he concurred with a laugh then kissed her until her head swam with delirious pleasure. 'But that will be part of our story. And, speaking of smooth sailing…'

'*Sim?*'

'I sent a couple of your sketches to our design guys in Greece. They're interested in talking to you about them. If you're up for it?'

Her mouth dropped open. She waited until he'd kissed it shut before she tried again. '*Really?*'

'Really. And I should bring you good news more often. That happy wriggle does incredible things to my—'

She clamped her hand over his mouth and glanced, alarmed, over his shoulder, just as two text messages beeped in quick succession. He groaned and was about to activate them when a knock sounded on the door.

'*Hell*, I knew I should've found a quieter place for this.'

The door opened and Pietro entered with a bottle of champagne and two glasses.

Theo's expression grew serious as he watched him approach.

Pietro set the bottle and glasses down and stared back at Theo. 'You took care of my sister when I was too much of a *burro* to do so. I'll be for ever in your debt.' He held out his hand.

After several seconds, Theo shook it. 'Don't mention it. Any man who's not afraid to call himself an ass is all right in my book.'

With a self-conscious laugh, Pietro turned to leave.

'Thanks for the drinks,' Theo said. 'But how did you know?'

Inez suppressed a giggle. Pietro rolled his eyes and nodded to the far wall. 'There's a partition to the kitchen. Camila's been spying on you since you came in.'

Theo glanced behind him as the partition widened and Camila beamed at them. Her gaze rested on Inez. 'Your *feijoadas* are good enough, but I always believed your destiny lies elsewhere.' She blew a kiss and shut the partition.

Pietro left and Theo stared down at her. 'Are you ready to start our adventure, *agape mou*?'

'What does that mean?'

'It means *my love*.' His smile dimmed. 'I learnt to speak Portuguese for the wrong reasons. I will teach you Greek for the right ones.'

Her grip tightened on his shirt. 'Were you really planning to leave Rio?'

'Yes. After I persuaded Benedicto to sign over the company into your and Pietro's names, I was done with that soulless vendetta. The thought that I'd lost you in the process nearly killed me.'

'I…what? You got him to sign over the company to us? Theo, we don't want it!'

'It was your grandfather's, then your mother's. It's right that it should be yours and Pietro's. If you don't really want it, I'm sure you'll find a beneficial way to dispose of it.'

She nodded. 'It would go a long way to help the inner city centre and the *favela* kids.'

'Great, we'll make it happen.'

Her heart contracted as she stared into his warm eyes. 'I love you, Theo. Thank you for coming back for me.'

'I couldn't not return, *anjo*, because without you I'm lost.'

She lifted her face to his and he slanted his mouth over hers in a deep, poignant kiss that brought fresh tears to her eyes.

'We need to talk about these tears,' he said drily, then huffed in irritation as his phone beeped again.

'Your brothers?' she guessed.

'And their wives. Ari wants to know if I'm still alive. Sakis wants to know if he can hire you to design his next oil tanker.'

She laughed. 'And their wives?'

He glanced down at the screen and back at her. 'They want to know if they can start planning our wedding.'

She took the phone, flicked the off switch and slipped it into his back pocket. Gripping his waist, she raised herself on tiptoe and leaned close to his ear.

'We will reply to each one of them in the morning. Right now, I want you to take me back to the boat and make love to me, make me yours again. Is that okay?'

'It's more than okay, my angel. It's what I plan to do for the rest of our lives.'

The look of love and adoration in his eyes as he took her hand and walked her out of the room was forever branded on her heart.

* * * * *

THE BILLIONAIRE'S
SECRET PRINCESS

CAITLIN CREWS

To all the secret princesses cruelly stuck working in horrible offices: as long as you know the truth, that's what matters.

CHAPTER ONE

ACHILLES CASILIERIS REQUIRED PERFECTION.

In himself, certainly. He prided himself on it, knowing all too well how easy it was to fall far, far short. And in his employees, absolutely—or they would quickly find themselves on the other side of their noncompete agreements with indelible black marks against their names.

He did not play around. He had built everything he had from nothing, step by painstaking step, and he hadn't succeeded the way he had—building the recession-proof Casilieris Company and making his first million by the age of twenty-five, then expanding both his business and his personal fortune into the billions—by accepting anything less than 100 percent perfection in all things. Always.

Achilles was tough, tyrannical when necessary, and refused to accept what one short-lived personal assistant had foolishly called "human limitations" to his face.

He was a man who knew the monster in himself. He'd seen its face in his own mirror. He did not allow for "human limitations."

Natalie Monette was his current executive assistant and had held the position for a record five years because she had never once asserted that she was human as some kind of excuse. In point of fact, Achilles thought of her as a remarkably efficient robot—the highest praise he could think to bestow on anyone, as it removed the possibility of human error from the equation.

Achilles had no patience for human error.

Which was why his assistant's behavior on this flight today was so alarming.

The day had started out normally enough. When Achilles had risen at his usual early hour, it had been to find Natalie already hard at work in the study of his Belgravia town house. She'd set up a few calls to his associates in France, outlined his schedule for the day and his upcoming meetings in New York. They'd swung by his corporate offices in the City, where Achilles had handled a fire he thought she should have put out before he'd learned of it, but then she'd accompanied him in his car to the private airfield he preferred without appearing the least bit bothered that he'd dressed her down for her failure. And why should she be bothered? She knew he expected perfection and had failed to deliver it. Besides, Natalie was never bothered. She'd acquitted herself with her usual cool competence and attitude-free demeanor, the way she always did or she never would have lasted five minutes with him. Much less five years.

And then she'd gone into the bathroom at the airfield, stayed in there long enough that he'd had to go find her himself, and come out changed.

Achilles couldn't put his finger on *how* she'd changed, only that she had.

She still looked the part of the closest assistant to a man as feared and lauded as Achilles had been for years now. She looked like his public face the way she always did. He appreciated that and always had. It wasn't enough that she was capable of handling the complications of his personal and company business without breaking a sweat, that she never seemed to sleep, that she could protect him from the intrusive paparazzi and hold off his equally demanding board members in the same breath—it was necessary that she also look like the sort of woman who belonged in his exalted orbit for the rare occasions when he needed to escort someone to this or that function and couldn't trouble himself to expend the modicum of charm necessary to squire one of his mistresses. Today she wore one of her usual outfits, a pencil skirt and soft blouse and a feminine sort of sweater that wrapped around her torso and was no different from any other outfit she'd worn a million times before.

Natalie dressed to disappear in plain sight. But for some reason, she caught his eye this odd afternoon. He couldn't quite figure it out. It was as if he had never seen her before. It was as if she'd gone into the bathroom in the airport lounge and come out a completely different person.

Achilles sat back in his remarkably comfortable leather chair on the jet and watched her as she took her seat opposite him. Did he imagine that she hesitated? Was he making up the strange look he'd seen in her eyes before she sat down? Almost as if she was looking for clues instead of taking her seat as she always did?

"What took you so long in that bathroom?" he asked, not bothering to keep his tone particularly polite. "I should not have to chase down my own assistant, surely."

Natalie blinked. He didn't know why the green of her eyes behind the glasses he knew she didn't need for sight seemed…too bright, somehow. Or brighter, anyway, than they'd been before. In fact, now that he thought about it, everything about her was brighter. And he couldn't understand how anyone could walk into a regular lavatory and come out…gleaming.

"I apologize," she said quietly. Simply. And there was something about her voice then. It was almost...musical.

It occurred to Achilles that he had certainly never thought of Natalie's voice as anything approaching *musical* before. It had always been a voice, pure and simple. And she had certainly never *gleamed*.

And that, he thought with impatience, was one of the reasons that he had prized Natalie so much for all these years. Because he had never, ever noticed her as anything but his executive assistant, who was reasonably attractive because it was good business to give his Neanderthal cronies something worth gazing at while they were trying to ignore Achilles's dominance. But there was a difference between noting that a woman was attractive and *being attracted to* that woman. Achilles would not have hired Natalie if he'd been attracted to her. He never had been. Not ever.

But to his utter astonishment that was what seemed to be happening. Right here. Right now. His body was sending him unambiguous signals. He wasn't simply *attracted* to his assistant. What he felt roll in him as she crossed her legs at the ankle and smiled at him was far more than *attraction*.

It was need.

Blinding and impossible and incredibly, astonishingly inconvenient.

Achilles Casilieris did not do inconvenience, and he was violently opposed to *need*. It had been beaten into him as an unwanted child that it was the height of foolishness to want something he couldn't have. That meant he'd dedicated his adult life to never allowing himself to need anything at all when he could buy whatever took his fancy, and he hadn't.

And yet there was no denying that dark thread that wound in him, pulling tight and succeeding in surprising him—something else that happened very, very rarely.

Achilles knew the shadows that lived in him. He had no intention of revisiting them. Ever.

Whatever his assistant was doing, she needed to stop. Now.

"That is all you wish to say?" He sounded edgy. Dangerous. He didn't like that, either.

But Natalie hardly seemed to notice. "If you would like me to expand on my apology, Mr. Casilieris, you need only tell me how."

He thought there was a subtle rebuke in that, no matter how softly she'd said it, and that, too, was new. And unacceptable no matter how prettily she'd voiced it.

Her copper-colored hair gleamed. Her skin glowed as she moved her hands in her lap, which struck him as odd, because Natalie never sat there with her hands folded in her lap like some kind of diffident Catholic schoolgirl. She was always in motion, because she was always working. But tonight, Natalie appeared to be sitting there like some kind of regal Madonna, hands folded in her lap, long, silky legs crossed at the ankles, and an inappropriately serene smile on her face.

If it wasn't impossible, he would have thought that she really was someone else entirely. Because she looked exactly the same save for all that gold that seemed to wrap itself around her and him, too, making him unduly fascinated with the pulse he could see beating at her throat— except he'd never, ever noticed her that way before.

Achilles did not have time for this, whatever it was. There was entirely too much going on with his businesses at the moment, like the hotel deal he'd been trying to put together for the better part of the last year that was by no means assured. He hadn't become one of the most feared and fearsome billionaires in the world because he took time off from running his businesses to pretend to care about the personal lives of his employees.

But Natalie wasn't just any employee. She was the one he'd actually come to rely on. The only person he relied on in the world, to be specific.

"Is there anything you need to tell me?" he asked.

He watched her, perhaps too carefully. It was impossible not to notice the way she flushed slightly at that. That was strange, too. He couldn't remember a single instance Natalie had ever flushed in response to anything he'd done. And the truth was he'd done a lot. He didn't hide his flashes of irritation or spend too much time worrying about anyone else's feelings. Why should he? The Casilieris Company was about profit—and it was about Achilles. Who else's feelings should matter? One of the things he'd long prized about his assistant was that she never, ever reacted to anything that he did or said or shouted. She just did her job.

But today Natalie had spots of red, high on her elegant cheekbones, and she'd been sitting across from him for whole minutes now without doing a single thing that could be construed as her job.

Elegant? demanded an incredulous voice inside him. *Cheekbones?*

Since when had Achilles ever noticed anything of the kind? He didn't pay that much attention to the mistresses he took to his bed—which he deigned to do in the first place only after they passed through all the levels of his application process and signed strict confidentiality agreements. And the women who made it through were in no doubt as to why they were there. It was to please him, not render him disoriented enough to be focusing on their bloody *cheekbones*.

"Like what, for example?" She asked the question and then she smiled at him, that curve of her mouth that was suddenly wired to the hardest part of him, and echoed inside him like heat. Heat he didn't want. "I'll be happy to tell you anything you wish to hear, Mr. Casilieris. That is, after all, my job."

"Is that your job?" He smiled, and he doubted it echoed much of anywhere. Or was anything but edgy and a little but harsh. "I had started to doubt that you remembered you had one."

"Because I kept you waiting? That was unusual, it's true."

"You've never done so before. You've never dared." He tilted his head slightly as he gazed at her, not understanding why everything was different when nothing was. He could see that she was exactly the same as she always was, down to that single freckle centered on her left cheekbone that he wasn't even aware he'd noticed before now. "Again, has some tragedy befallen you? Were you hit over the head?" He did nothing to hide the warning or the menace in his voice. "You do not appear to be yourself."

But if he thought he'd managed to discomfit her, he saw in the next moment that was not to be. The flush faded from her porcelain cheeks, and all she did was smile at him again. With that maddeningly enigmatic curve of her lips.

Lips, he noticed with entirely too much of his body, that were remarkably lush.

This was insupportable.

"I am desolated to disappoint you," she murmured as the plane began to move, bumping gently along the tarmac. "But there was no tragedy." Something glinted in her green gaze, though her smile never dimmed. "Though I must confess in the spirit of full disclosure that I was thinking of quitting."

Achilles only watched her idly, as if she hadn't just said that. Because she couldn't possibly have just said that.

"I beg your pardon," he said after a moment passed and there was still that spike of something dark and furious in his chest. "I must have misheard you. You do not mean that you plan to quit this job. That you wish to leave *me*."

It was not lost on him that he'd phrased that in a way that should have horrified him. Maybe it would at some point. But today what slapped at him was that his assistant spoke of quitting without a single hint of anything like uncertainty on her face.

And he found he couldn't tolerate that.

"I'm considering it," she said. Still smiling. Unaware of her own danger or the dark thing rolling in him, reminding him of how easy it was to wake that monster that slept in him. How disastrously easy.

But Achilles laughed then, understanding finally catching up with him. "If this is an attempt to wrangle more money out of me, Miss Monette, I cannot say that I admire the strategy. You're perfectly well compensated as is. Overcompensated, one might say."

"Might one? Perhaps." She looked unmoved. "Then again, perhaps your rivals have noticed exactly how much you rely on me. Perhaps I've decided that I want more than being at the beck and call of a billionaire. Much less standing in as your favorite bit of target practice."

"It cannot possibly have bothered you that I lost my temper earlier."

Her smile was bland. "If you say it cannot, then I'm sure you must be right."

"I lose my temper all the time. It's never bothered you before. It's part of your job to not be bothered, in point of fact."

"I'm certain that's it." Her enigmatic smile seemed to deepen. "I must be the one who isn't any good at her job."

He had the most insane notion then. It was something about the cool challenge in her gaze, as if they were equals. As if she had every right to call him on whatever she pleased. He had no idea why he wanted to reach across the little space between their chairs and put his hands on her. Test her skin to see if it was as soft as it looked. Taste that lush mouth—

What the hell was happening to him?

Achilles shook his head, as much to clear it as anything else. "If this is your version of a negotiation, you should rethink your approach. You know perfectly well that there's entirely too much going on right now."

"Some might think that this is the perfect time, then, to talk about things like compensation and temper tantrums," Natalie replied, her voice as even and unbothered as ever. There was no reason that should make him grit his teeth. "After all, when one is expected to work twenty-two hours a day and is shouted at for her trouble, one's thoughts automatically turn to what one lacks. It's human nature."

"You lack nothing. You have no time to spend the money I pay you because you're too busy traveling the world—which I also pay for."

"If only I had more than two hours a day to enjoy these piles of money."

"People would kill for the opportunity to spend even five minutes in my presence," he reminded her. "Or have you forgotten who I am?"

"Come now." She shook her head at him, and he had the astonishing sense that she was trying to chastise him. *Him.* "It would not kill you to be more polite, would it?"

Polite.

His own assistant had just lectured him on his manners.

To say that he was reeling hardly began to scratch the surface of Achilles's reaction.

But then she smiled, and that reaction got more complicated. "I got on the plane anyway. I decided not to quit today." Achilles could not possibly have missed her emphasis on that final word. "You're welcome."

And something began to build inside him at that. Something huge, dark, almost overwhelming. He was very much afraid it was rage.

But that, he refused. No matter what. Achilles left his demons behind him a long time ago, and he wasn't going back. He refused.

"If you would like to leave, Miss Monette, I will not stop you," he assured her coldly. "I cannot begin to imagine what has led you to imagine I would try. I do not beg. I could fill your position with a snap of my fingers. I might yet, simply because this conversation is intolerable."

The assistant he'd thought he knew would have swallowed hard at that, then looked away. She would have smoothed her hands over her skirt and apologized as she did it. She had riled him only a few times over the years, and she'd talked her way out of it in exactly that way. He gazed at her expectantly.

But today, Natalie only sat there with distractingly perfect posture and gazed back at him with a certain serene confidence that made him want to…mess her up. Get his hands in that unremarkable ponytail and feel the texture of all that gleaming copper. Or beneath her snowy-white blouse. Or better yet, up beneath that skirt of hers.

He was so furious he wasn't nearly as appalled at himself as he should have been.

"I think we both know perfectly well that while you could snap your fingers and summon crowds of candidates for my position, you'd have a very hard time filling it to your satisfaction," she said with a certainty that…gnawed at him. "Perhaps we could dispense with the threats. You need me."

He would sooner have her leap forward and plunge a knife into his chest.

"I need no one," he rasped out. "And nothing."

His suddenly mysterious assistant only inclined her

head, which he realized was no response at all. As if she was merely patronizing him—a notion that made every muscle in his body clench tight.

"You should worry less about your replacement and more about your job," Achilles gritted out. "I have no idea what makes you think you can speak to me with such disrespect."

"It is not disrespectful to speak frankly, surely," she said. Her expression didn't change, but her green gaze was grave—very much, he thought with dawning incredulity, as if she'd expected better of him.

Achilles could only stare back at her in arrogant astonishment. Was he now to suffer the indignity of being judged by his own assistant? And why was it she seemed wholly uncowed by his amazement?

"Unless you plan to utilize a parachute, it would appear you are stuck right here in your distasteful position for the next few hours," Achilles growled at her when he thought he could speak without shouting. Shouting was too easy. And obscured his actual feelings. "I'd suggest you use the time to rethink your current attitude."

He didn't care for the brilliant smile she aimed at him then, as if she was attempting to encourage him with it. *Him*. He particularly didn't like the way it seemed too bright, as if it was lighting him up from the inside out.

"What a kind offer, Mr. Casilieris," she said in that self-possessed voice of hers that was driving him mad. "I will keep it in mind."

The plane took off then, somersaulting into the London sky. Achilles let gravity press him back against the seat and considered the evidence before him. He had worked with this woman for five years, and she had never spoken to him like that before. Ever. He hardly knew what to make of it.

But then, there was a great deal he didn't know what

to do with, suddenly. The way his heart pounded against his ribs as if he was in a real temper, when he was not the sort of man who lost control. Of his temper or anything else. He expected nothing less than perfection from himself, first and foremost. And temper made him think of those long-ago days of his youth, and his stepfather's hovel of a house, victim to every stray whim and temper and fist until he'd given himself over to all that rage and fury inside him and become little better than an animal himself—

Why was he allowing himself to think of such things? His youth was off-limits, even in his own head. What the hell was *happening*?

Achilles didn't like that Natalie affected him. But what made him suspicious was that she'd never affected him before. He'd approved when she started to wear those glasses and put her hair up, to make herself less of a target for the less scrupulous men he dealt with who thought they could get to him through expressing their interest in her. But he hadn't needed her to downplay her looks because *he* was entranced by her. He hadn't been.

So what had changed today?

What had emboldened her and, worse, allowed her to get under his skin?

He kept circling back to that bathroom in the airport and the fact she'd walked out of it a different person from the one who'd walked in.

Of course, she wasn't a *different person*. Did he imagine the real Natalie had suffered a body snatching? Did he imagine there was some elaborate hoax afoot?

The idea was absurd. But he couldn't seem to get past it. The plane hit its cruising altitude, and he moved from his chair to the leather couch that took pride of place in the center of the cabin that was set up like one of his high-end hotel rooms. He sat back with his laptop and pretended to be looking through his email when he was watching Natalie instead. Looking for clues.

She wasn't moving around the plane with her usual focus and energy. He thought she seemed tentative. Uncertain—and this despite the fact she seemed to walk taller than before. As if she'd changed her very posture in that bathroom. But who did something like that?

A different person would have different posture.

It was crazy. He knew that. And Achilles knew further that he always went a little too intense when he was closing a deal, so it shouldn't have surprised him that he was willing to consider the insane option today. Part of being the sort of unexpected, out-of-the-box thinker he'd always been was allowing his mad little flights of fancy. He never knew where they might lead.

He indulged himself as Natalie sat and started to look through her own bag as if she'd never seen it before. He pulled up the picture of her he kept in his files for security purposes and did an image search on it, because why not.

Achilles was prepared to discover a few photos of random celebrities she resembled, maybe. And then he'd have to face the fact that his favorite assistant might have gone off the deep end. She was right that replacing her would be hard—but it wouldn't be impossible. He hadn't overestimated his appeal—and that of his wildly successful company—to pretty much anyone and everyone. He was swamped with applicants daily, and he didn't even have an open position.

But then none of that mattered because his image search hit gold.

There were pages and pages of pictures. All of his assistant—except it wasn't her. He knew it from the exquisitely bespoke gowns she wore. He knew it from the jewels that flowed around her neck and covered her hands, drawing attention to things like the perfect manicure she had today—when the Natalie he knew almost never had time to care for her nails like that. And every picture he clicked on identified the woman in them not as Natalie Monette, assistant to Achilles Casilieris, but Her Royal Highness, Princess Valentina of Murin.

Achilles didn't have much use for royals, or really anyone with inherited wealth, when he'd had to go to so much trouble to amass his own. He'd never been to the tiny Mediterranean kingdom of Murin, mostly because he didn't have a yacht to dock there during a sparkling summer of endless lounging and, further, didn't need to take advantage of the country's famously friendly approach to taxes. But he recognized King Geoffrey of Murin on sight, and he certainly recognized the Murinese royal family's coat of arms.

It had been splashed all over the private jet he'd seen on the same tarmac as his back in London.

There was madness, Achilles thought then, and then there was a con job that no one would ever suspect—because who could imagine that the person standing in front of them, looking like someone they already knew, was actually someone else?

If he wasn't mistaken—and he knew he wasn't, because there were too many things about his assistant today that didn't make sense, and Achilles was no great believer in coincidence—Princess Valentina of Murin was trying to run a con.

On him.

Which meant a great many things. First, that his actual assistant was very likely pretending to be the princess somewhere, leaving him and her job in the hands of someone she had to know would fail to live up to Achilles's high standards. That suggested that second, she really wasn't all that happy in her position, as this princess had dared to throw in his face in a way he doubted Natalie ever would have. But it also suggested that third, Natalie had effectively given her notice.

Achilles didn't like any of that. At all. But the fourth thing that occurred to him was that clearly, neither this princess nor his missing assistant expected their little switch to be noticed. Natalie, who should have known better, must honestly have believed that he wouldn't notice an imposter in her place. Or she hadn't cared much if he did.

That was enraging, on some level. Insulting.

But Achilles smiled as Valentina settled herself across the coffee table from him, with a certain inbred grace that whispered of palaces and comportment classes and a lifetime of genteel manners.

Because she thought she was tricking him.

Which meant he could trick her instead. A prospect his body responded to with great enthusiasm as he studied her, this woman who looked like an underling whom a man in his position could never have touched out of ethical considerations—but wasn't.

She wasn't his employee. He didn't pay her salary, and she wasn't bound to obey him in anything if she didn't feel like it.

But she had no idea that he knew that.

Achilles almost felt sorry for her. Almost.

"Let's get started," he murmured, as if they'd exchanged no harsh words. He watched confusion move over her face in a blink, then disappear, because she was a royal princess and she was used to concealing her reactions. He planned to have fun with that. The possibilities were endless, and seemed to roll through him like heat. "We have so much work to do, Miss Monette. I hardly know where to begin."

CHAPTER TWO

BY THE TIME they landed in New York, Princess Valentina of Murin was second-guessing her spontaneous, impulsive decision to switch places with the perfect stranger she'd found wearing her face in the airport lounge.

Achilles Casilieris could make anyone second-guess anything, she suspected.

"You do not appear to be paying attention," he said silkily from beside her, as if he knew exactly what she was thinking. And who she was. And every dream she'd ever had since she was a girl—that was how disconcerting this man was, even lounging there beside her in the back of a luxury car doing nothing more alarming than *sitting*.

"I am hanging on your every word," she assured him as calmly as she could, and then she repeated his last three sentences back to him.

But she had no idea what he was talking about. Repeating conversations she wasn't really listening to was a skill she'd learned in the palace a long, long time ago. It came in handy at many a royal gathering. And in many longwinded lectures from her father and his staff.

You have thrown yourself into deep, deep water, she told herself now, as if that wasn't entirely too apparent already. As if it hadn't already occurred to her that she'd better learn how to swim, and fast.

Achilles Casilieris was a problem.

Valentina knew powerful men. Men who ruled countries. Men who came from centuries upon centuries of power and consequence and wielded it with the offhanded superiority of those who had never imagined *not* ruling all they surveyed.

But Achilles was in an entirely different league.

He took over the whole of the backseat of the car that had waited for them on the tarmac in the bright and sunny afternoon, looking roomy and spacious from the outside. He'd insisted she sit next to him on the plush backseat that should have been more than able to fit two people with room to spare. And yet Valentina felt crowded, as if he was pressing up against her when he wasn't. Achilles wasn't touching her, but still, she was entirely too *aware* of him.

He took up all the air. He'd done it on his plane, too.

She had the hectic notion, connected to that knot beneath her breastbone that was preventing her from taking anything like a deep breath, that it wasn't the enclosed space that was the issue. That he would have this same effect anywhere. All that brooding ruthlessness he didn't bother to contain—or maybe he couldn't contain even if he'd wanted to—seemed to hum around him like a kind of force field that both repelled and compelled at once.

If she was honest, the little glimpse she'd had of him in the airport had been the same—she'd just ignored it.

Valentina had been too busy racing into the lounge so she could have a few precious seconds alone. No staff. No guards. No cameras. Just her perched on the top of a closed toilet seat, shut away from the world, breathing. Letting her face do what it liked. Thinking of absolutely nothing. Not her duty. Not her father's expectations.

Certainly not her bloodless engagement to Prince Rodolfo of Tissely, a man she'd tuned out within moments of their first meeting. Or their impending wedding in two months' time, which she could feel bearing down on her like a thick hand around her throat every time she let herself think about it. It wasn't that she didn't *want* to do her duty and marry the Crown Prince of Tissely. She'd been promised in marriage to her father's allies since the day she was born. It was that she'd never given a great deal of thought to what it was she wanted, because *want* had never been an option available to her.

And it had suddenly occurred to her at her latest wedding dress fitting there in London that she was running out of time.

Soon she would be married to a man in what was really more of a corporate merger of two great European brands, the houses of Tissely and Murin. She'd be expected to produce the necessary heirs to continue the line. She would take her place in the great sweep of her family's storied history, unite two ancient kingdoms, and in so doing fulfill her purpose in life. The end.

The end, she'd thought in that bathroom stall, high-end and luxurious but still, a bathroom stall. *My life fulfilled at twenty-seven.*

Valentina was a woman who'd been given everything, including a healthy understanding of how lucky she was. She didn't often indulge herself with thoughts of what was and wasn't fair when there was no doubt she was among the most fortunate people alive.

But the thing was, it still didn't seem fair. No matter how hard she tried not to think about it that way.

She would do what she had to do, of course. She always had and always would, but for that single moment, locked away in a bathroom stall where no one could see her and no one would ever know, she basked in the sheer, dizzying unfairness of it all.

Then she'd pulled herself together, stepped out and had been prepared to march onto her plane and head back to the life that had been plotted out for her since the day she arrived on the planet.

Only to find her twin standing at the sinks.

Her identical twin—though that was, of course, impossible.

"What is this?" the other woman had asked when they'd faced each other, looking something close to scared. Or unnerved, anyway. "How…?"

Valentina had been fascinated. She'd been unable to keep herself from studying this woman who appeared to be wearing her body as well as her face. She was dressed in a sleek pencil skirt and low heels, which showed legs that Valentina recognized all too well, having last seen them in her own mirror. "I'm Valentina."

"Natalie."

She'd repeated that name in her head like it was a magic spell. She didn't know why she felt as if it was.

But then, running into her double in a London bathroom seemed something close enough to magic to count. Right then when she'd been indulging her self-pity about the unchangeable course of her own life, the universe had presented her with a glimpse of what else could be. If she was someone else.

An identical someone else.

They had the same face. The same legs, as she'd already noted. The same coppery hair that her double wore up in a serviceable ponytail and the same nose Valentina could trace directly to her maternal grandmother. What were the chances, she'd wondered then, that they *weren't* related?

And didn't that raise all kinds of interesting questions?

"You're that princess," Natalie had said, a bit haltingly.

But if Valentina was a princess, and if they were related as they surely had to be…

"I suspect you might be, too," she'd said gently.

"We can't possibly be related. I'm a glorified secretary who never really had a home. You're a royal princess. Presumably your lineage dates back to the Roman Conquest."

"Give or take a few centuries." Valentina tried to imagine having a job like that. Or any job. A secretary, glorified or otherwise, who reported to work for someone else and actually *did things* with her time that weren't directly related to being a symbol. She couldn't really wrap her head around it, or being effectively without a home, either, having been a part of Murin since her birth. As much Murin as its beaches and hills, its monuments and its palace. She might as well have been a park. "Depending which branch of the family you mean, of course."

"I was under the impression that people with lineages that could lead to thrones and crown jewels tended to keep better track of their members," Natalie had said, her tone just dry enough to make Valentina decide that given the right circumstances—meaning anywhere that wasn't a toilet—she'd rather like her doppelganger.

And she knew what the other woman had been asking.

"Conspiracy theorists claim my mother was killed and her death hushed up. Senior palace officials have assured me my whole life that no, she merely left to preserve her mental health, and is rumored to be in residence in a hospital devoted to such things somewhere. All I know is that I haven't seen her since shortly after I was born. According to my father, she preferred anonymity to the joys of motherhood."

And she waited for Natalie to give her an explanation in turn. To laugh, perhaps, and then tell her that she'd been raised by two perfectly normal parents in a happily normal somewhere else, filled with golden retrievers and school buses and pumpkin-spiced coffee drinks and whatever else normal people took for granted that Valentina only read about.

But instead, this woman wearing Valentina's face had looked stricken. "I've never met my father," she'd whispered. "My mother's always told me she has no idea who he was. And she bounces from one affair to the next pretty quickly, so I came to terms with the fact it was possible she really, truly didn't know."

And Valentina had laughed, because what else could she do? She'd spent her whole life wishing she'd had more of a family than her chilly father. Oh, she loved him, she did, but he was so excruciatingly proper. So worried about appearances. His version of a hug was a well-meaning critique on her latest public appearance. Love to her father was maintaining and bolstering the family's reputation across the ages. She'd always wanted a sister to share in the bolstering. A brother. A mother. *Someone.*

But she hadn't had anyone. And now she had a stranger who looked just like her.

"My father is many things," she'd told Natalie. It was too soon to say *our father.* And who knew? Maybe they were cousins. Or maybe this was a fluke. No matter that little jolt of recognition inside her, as if she'd been meant to know this woman. As if this was a reunion. "Including His Royal Majesty, King Geoffrey of Murin. What he is not now, nor has ever been, I imagine, is forgettable."

Natalie had shaken her head. "You underestimate my mother's commitment to amnesia. She's made it a life choice instead of a malady. On some level I admire it."

"My mother was the noblewoman Frederica de Burgh, from a very old Murinese family." Valentina watched Natalie closely as she spoke, looking for any hint of…anything, really, in her gaze. "Promised to my father at birth, raised by nuns and kept deliberately sheltered, and then widely held to be unequal to the task of becoming queen. Mentally. But that's the story they would tell, isn't it, to explain why she disappeared? What's your mother's name?"

Natalie sighed and swung her shoulder bag onto the counter. Valentina had the impression that she'd really, truly wanted not to answer. But she had. "She calls herself Erica."

And there it was. Valentina supposed it could be a coincidence that *Erica* was a shortened form of *Frederica*. But how many coincidences were likely when they resulted in two women who'd never met—who never should have met—who happened to be mirror images?

If there was something in her that turned over at the notion that her mother had, in fact, had a maternal impulse after all—just not for Valentina—well, this wasn't the time to think about that. It might never be the time to think about that. She'd spent twenty-seven years trying her best not to think about that.

She changed the subject before she lost her composure completely and started asking questions she knew she shouldn't.

"I saw Achilles Casilieris, out there in the lounge," she'd said instead. The notorious billionaire had been there on her way in, brooding in a corner of the lounge and scowling at the paper he'd been reading. "He looks even more fearsome in person. You can almost *see* all that brash command and dizzying wealth ooze from his pores, can't you?"

"He's my boss," Natalie had said, sounding amused—if rather darkly. "If he was really oozing anything, anywhere, it would be my job to provide first aid until actual medical personnel could come handle it. At which point he would bite my head off for wasting his precious time by not curing him instantly."

Valentina had been flooded with a rash of follow-up questions. Was the biting off of heads normal? Was it fun to work for a man who sounded half-feral? Most important, did Natalie like her life or merely suffer through it?

But then her mobile started buzzing in her clutch. She'd forgotten about ferocious billionaires and thought about things she knew too much about, like the daredevil prince she was bound to marry soon, instead, because their fathers had agreed regardless of whether either one of them liked it. She'd checked the mobile's display to be sure, but wasn't surprised to find she'd guessed correctly. Lucky her, she'd had another meeting with her husband-to-be in Murin that very afternoon. She'd expected it to go the way all their meetings so far had gone. Prince Rodolfo, beloved the world over for his good looks and devil-may-care attitude, would talk. She would listen without really listening. She'd long since concluded that foretold a very happy royal marriage.

"My fiancé," she'd explained, meeting Natalie's gaze again. "Or his chief of staff, to be more precise."

"Congratulations," Natalie murmured.

"Thank you, I'm very lucky." Valentina's mouth curved, though her tone was far more dry than Natalie's had been. "Everyone says so. Prince Rodolfo is objectively attractive. Not all princes can make that claim, but the tabloids have exulted over his abs since he was a teenager. Just as they have salivated over his impressive dating history, which has involved a selection of models and actresses from at least four continents and did not cease in any noticeable way upon our engagement last fall."

"Your Prince Charming sounds…charming," Natalie had said.

Valentina raised one shoulder, then dropped it. "His theory is that he remains free until our marriage, and then will be free once again following the necessary birth of his heir. More discreetly, I can only hope. Meanwhile, I am beside myself with joy that I must take my place at his side in two short months. Of course."

Natalie had laughed, and the sound had made Valentina's stomach flip. Because it sounded like her. It sounded exactly like her.

"It's going to be a terrific couple of months all around, then," her mirror image was saying. "Mr. Casilieris is in rare form. He's putting together a particularly dramatic deal and it's not going his way and he…isn't used to that. So that's me working twenty-two-hour days instead of my usual twenty for the foreseeable future, which is even more fun when he's cranky and snarling."

"It can't possibly be worse than having to smile politely while your future husband lectures you about the absurd expectation of fidelity in what is essentially an arranged marriage for hours on end. The absurdity is that *he* might be expected to curb his impulses for a year or so, in case you wondered. The expectations for *me* apparently involve quietly and chastely finding fulfillment in philanthropic works, like his sainted absentee mother, who everyone knows manufactured a supposed health crisis so she could live out her days in peaceful seclusion. It's easy to be philanthropically fulfilled while living in isolation in Bavaria."

Natalie had smiled. "Try biting your tongue while your famously short-tempered boss rages at you for no reason, for the hundredth time in an hour, because he pays you to stand there and take it without wilting or crying or selling whingeing stories about him to the press."

Valentina had returned that smile. "Or the hours and hours of grim palace-vetted prewedding press interviews in the company of a pack of advisers who will censor everything I say and inevitably make me sound like a bit of animated treacle, as out of touch with reality as the average overly sweet dessert."

"Speaking of treats, I also have to deal with the board of directors Mr. Casilieris treats like irritating schoolchildren, his packs of furious ex-lovers each with her own vendetta, all his terrified employees who need to be coached through meetings with him and treated for PTSD after, and every last member of his staff in every one of his households, who like me to be the one to ask him the questions they know will set him off on one of his scorch-the-earth rages." Natalie had moved closer then, and lowered her voice. "I was thinking of quitting, to be honest. Today."

"I can't quit, I'm afraid," Valentina had said. Regretfully.

But she'd wished she could. She'd wished she could just…walk away and not have to live up to anyone's expectations. And not have to marry a man whom she barely knew. And not have to resign herself to a version of the same life so many of her ancestors had lived. Maybe that was where the idea had come from. Blood was blood, after all. And this woman clearly shared her blood. What if…?

"I have a better idea," she'd said, and then she'd tossed it out there before she could think better of it. "Let's switch places. For a month, say. Six weeks at the most. Just for a little break."

"That's crazy," Natalie said at once, and she was right. Of course she was right.

"Insane," Valentina had agreed. "But you might find royal protocol exciting! And I've always wanted to do the things everyone else in the world does. Like go to a real job."

"People can't *switch places*." Natalie had frowned. "And certainly not with a princess."

"You could think about whether or not you really want to quit," Valentina pointed out, trying to sweeten the deal. "It would be a lovely holiday for you. Where will Achilles Casilieris be in six weeks' time?"

"He's never gone from London for too long," Natalie had said, as if she was considering it.

Valentina had smiled. "Then in six weeks we'll meet in London. We'll text in the meantime with all the necessary details about our lives, and on the appointed day we'll just meet up and switch back and no one will ever be the wiser. Doesn't that sound like *fun*?"

"It would never work," Natalie had replied. Which wasn't exactly a *no*. "No one will ever believe I'm you."

Valentina waved a hand, encompassing the pair of them. "How would anyone know the difference? I can barely tell myself."

"People will take one look at me and know I'm not you. *You* look like a *princess*."

"You, too, can look like a princess," Valentina assured her. Then smiled. "This princess, anyway. You already do."

"You're elegant. Poised. You've had years of training, presumably. How to be a diplomat. How to be polite in every possible situation. Which fork to use at dinner, for God's sake."

"Achilles Casilieris is one of the wealthiest men alive," Valentina had pointed out. "He dines with as many kings as I do. I suspect that as his personal assistant, Natalie, you have, too. And have likely learned how to navigate the cutlery."

"No one will believe it," Natalie had insisted. But she'd sounded a bit as if she was wavering.

Valentina tugged off the ring on her left hand and placed it down on the counter between them. It made an audible *clink* against the marble surface, as well it should, given it was one of the crown jewels of the kingdom of Tissely.

"Try it on. I dare you. It's an heirloom from Prince Rodolfo's extensive treasury of such items, dating back to the dawn of time, more or less." She smiled. "If it doesn't fit we'll never speak of switching places again."

But the ring had fit her double as if it had been made especially for her.

And after that, switching clothes was easy. Valentina found herself in front of the bathroom mirror, dressed like a billionaire's assistant, when Natalie walked out of the stall behind her in her own shift dress and the heels her favorite shoe designer had made just for her. It was like looking in a mirror, but one that walked and looked unsteady on her feet and was wearing her hair differently.

Valentina couldn't tell if she was disconcerted or excited. Both, maybe.

She'd eyed Natalie. "Will your glasses give me a headache, do you suppose?"

But Natalie had pulled them from her face and handed them over. "They're clear glass. I was getting a little too much attention from some of the men Mr. Casilieris works with, and it annoyed him. I didn't want to lose my job, so I started wearing my hair up and these glasses. It worked like a charm."

"I refuse to believe men are so idiotic."

Natalie had grinned as Valentina took the glasses and slid them onto her nose. "The men we're talking about weren't exactly paying me attention because they found me enthralling. It was a diversionary tactic during negotiations, and yes, you'd be surprised how many men fail to see a woman who looks smart."

She'd freed her hair from its utilitarian ponytail and shook it out, then handed the stretchy elastic to Valentina. It took Valentina a moment to re-create the ponytail on her own head, and then it was done.

And it really was like magic.

"This is crazy," Natalie had whispered.

"We have to switch places now," Valentina said softly, hearing the rough patch in her own voice. "I've always wanted to be…someone else. Someone normal. Just for a little while."

And she'd gotten exactly what she'd wanted, hadn't she?

"I am distressed, Miss Monette, that I cannot manage to secure your attention for more than a moment or two," Achilles said then, slamming Valentina back into this car he dominated so easily when all he was doing was sitting there.

Sitting there, filling up the world without even trying.

He was *devastating*. There was no other possible word that could describe him. His black hair was close-cropped to his head, which only served to highlight his strong, intensely masculine features. She'd had hours on the plane to study him as she'd repeatedly failed to do the things he'd expected of her, and she still couldn't really get her head around why it was that he was so…affecting. He shouldn't have been. Dark hair. Dark eyes that tended toward gold when his temper washed over him, which he'd so far made no attempt to hide. A strong nose that reminded her of ancient statues she'd seen in famous museums. That lean, hard body of his that wasn't made of marble or bronze but seemed to suggest both as he used it so effortlessly. A predator packed into a dark suit that seemed molded to him, whispering suggestions of a lethal warrior when all he was doing was taking phone calls with a five-hundred-thousand-dollar watch on one wrist that he didn't flash about, because he was Achilles Casilieris. He didn't need flash.

Achilles was something else.

It was the power that seemed to emanate from him, even when he was doing nothing but sitting quietly. It was the fierce hit of his intelligence, that brooding, unmistakable cleverness that seemed to wrap around him like a cloud. It was something in the way he looked at her, as if he saw too much and too deeply and no matter that Valentina's unreadable game face was the envy of Europe. Besides all that, there was something untamed about him. Fierce.

Something about him left her breathless. Entirely too close to reeling.

"Do you require a gold star every time you make a statement?" she asked, careful not to look at him. It was too hard to look away. She'd discovered that on the plane ride from London—and he was a lot closer now. So close she was sure she could feel the heat of his body from where she sat. "I'll be certain to make a note to celebrate you more often. Sir."

Valentina didn't know what she was doing. In Natalie's job, certainly, but also with this man in general. She'd learned one thing about powerful people—particularly men—and it was that they did not enjoy being challenged. Under any circumstances. What made her think Achilles would go against type and magically handle this well?

But she couldn't seem to stop herself.

And the fact that she had never been one to challenge much of anything before hardly signified. Or maybe that was why she felt so unfettered, she thought. Because this wasn't her life. This wasn't her remote father and his endless expectations for the behavior of his only child. This was a strange little bit of role-playing that allowed her to be someone other than Princess Valentina for a moment. A few weeks, that was all. Why not challenge Achilles while she was at it? *Especially* if no one else ever did?

She could feel his gaze on the side of her face, that brooding dark gold, and she braced herself. Then made sure her expression was nothing but serene as she turned to face him.

It didn't matter. There was no minimizing this man.

She could feel the hit of him—like a fist—deep in her belly. And then lower.

"Are you certain you were not hit in the head?" Achilles asked, his dark voice faintly rough with the hint of his native Greek. "Perhaps in the bathroom at the airport? I fear that such places can often suffer from slippery floors. Deadly traps for the unwary."

"It was only a bathroom," she replied airily. "It wasn't slippery or otherwise notable in any way."

"Are you sure?" And something in his voice and his hard gaze prickled into her then. Making her chest feel tighter.

Valentina did not want to talk about the bathroom, much less anything that had happened there. And there was something in his gaze that worried her—but that was insane. He couldn't have any idea that she'd run into her own twin. How could he? Valentina had been unaware that there was the faintest possibility she might have a twin until today.

Which made her think about her father and his many, many lectures about his only child in a new, unfortunate light. But Valentina thrust that aside. That was something to worry about when she was a princess again. That was a problem she could take up when she was back in Murin Castle.

Here, now, she was a secretary. An executive assistant, no more and no less.

"I beg your pardon, Mr. Casilieris." She let her smile deepen and ignored the little hum of...something deep inside her when his gaze seemed to catch fire. "Are you trying to tell me that you need a bathroom? Should I ask the driver to stop the car right here in the middle of the George Washington Bridge?"

She expected him to get angry again. Surely that was what had been going on before, back in London before the plane had taken off. She'd seen temper all over that fierce, hard face of his and gleaming hot in his gaze. More than that, she'd felt it inside her. As if the things he felt echoed within her, winding her into knots. She felt something a whole lot like a chill inch its way down her spine at that notion.

But Achilles only smiled. And that was far more dangerous than merely devastating.

"Miss Monette," he said and shook his head, as if she amused him, when she could see that the thing that moved over that ruthless face of his was far too intense to be simple *amusement*. "I had no idea that beneath your officious exterior you've been hiding a comedienne all this time. For five years you've worked at my side and never let so much as a hint of this whimsical side of your personality out into the open. Whatever could have changed?"

He knows. The little voice inside her was certain—and terrified.

But it was impossible. Valentina knew it was impossible, so she made herself smile and relax against the leather seat as if she'd never in her life been so at her ease. Very much as if she was not within scant inches of a very large, very powerful, very intense male who was eyeing her the way gigantic lions and tigers and jaguars eyed their food. When they were playing with it.

She'd watched enough documentaries and made enough state visits to African countries to know firsthand.

"Perhaps I've always been this amusing," she suggested, managing to tamp down her hysteria about oversize felines, none of which was particularly helpful at the moment. "Perhaps you've only recently allowed yourself to truly listen to me."

"I greatly enjoy listening to you," Achilles replied. There was a laziness in the way he sat there, sprawled out in the backseat of his car, that dark gold gaze on hers.

A certain laziness, yes—but Valentina didn't believe it for a second. "I particularly enjoy listening to you when you are doing your job perfectly. Because you know how much I admire perfection. I insist on it, in fact. Which is why I cannot understand why you failed to provide it today."

"I don't know what you mean."

But she knew what he meant. She'd been on the plane and she'd been the one to fail repeatedly to do what was clearly her job. She'd hung up on one conference call and failed entirely to connect another. She'd expected him to explode—if she was honest, there was a part of her that wanted him to explode, in the way that anyone might want to poke and poke and poke at some kind of blister to see if it would pop. But he hadn't popped. He hadn't lost his temper at all, despite the fact that it had been very clear to Valentina very quickly that she was a complete and utter disaster at doing whatever it was that Natalie did.

When Achilles had stared at her in amazement, however, she hadn't made any excuses. She'd only gazed right back, serenely, as if she'd meant to do whatever utterly incorrect thing it was. As if it was all some kind of strategy.

She could admit that she hadn't really thought the job part through. She been so busy fantasizing herself into some kind of normal life that it had never occurred to her that, normal or not, a life was still *a whole life*. She had no idea how to live any way but the way she'd been living for almost thirty years. How remarkably condescending, she'd thought up there on Achilles Casilieris's jet, that she'd imagined she could simply step into a job—especially one as demanding as this appeared to be—and do it merely because she'd decided it was her chance at something "normal."

Valentina had found the entire experience humbling, if she was honest, and it had been only a few hours since she'd switched places with Natalie in London. Who knew what else awaited her?

But Achilles was still sprawled there beside her, that unnerving look of his making her skin feel too small for her bones.

"Natalie, Natalie," he murmured, and Valentina told herself it was a good thing he'd used that name. It wasn't her name, and she needed the reminder. This wasn't about her. It wasn't her job to advocate for Natalie when the other woman might not wish for her to do anything like that. She was on a fast track to losing Natalie her job, and then what? Valentina didn't have to worry about her employment prospects, but she had no idea what the market was like for billionaire's assistants.

But maybe there was a part of her that already knew that there was no way Natalie Monette was a stranger to her. Certainly not on the genetic level. And that had implications she wasn't prepared to examine just yet, but she did know that the woman who was in all likelihood her long-lost identical twin did not have to work for Achilles Casilieris unless she wanted to.

How arrogant of you, a voice inside her said quietly. *Her Royal Highness, making unilateral decisions for others' lives without their input.*

The voice sounded a little too much like her father's.

"That is my name," Valentina said to Achilles, in case there had been any doubt. Perhaps with a little too much force.

But she had the strangest notion that he was...*tasting* the name as he said it. As if he'd never said it before. Did he call Natalie by her first name? Valentina rather thought not, given that he'd called her *Miss Monette* when she'd met him—but that was neither here nor there, she told herself. And no matter that she was a woman who happened to know the power of titles. She had many of her own. And her life was marked by those who used the different versions of her titles, not to mention the few who actually called her by her first name.

"I cannot tolerate this behavior," he said, but it wasn't in that same infuriated tone he'd used earlier. If anything, he sounded almost…indulgent. But surely that was impossible. "It borders on open rebellion, and I cannot have that. This is not a democracy, I'm afraid. This is a dictatorship. If I want your opinion, I'll tell you what it is."

There was no reason her heart should have been kicking at her like that, her pulse so loud in her ears she was sure he must be able to hear it himself.

"What an interesting way to foster employee loyalty," she murmured. "Really more of a scorch-the-earth approach. Do you find it gets you the results you want?"

"I do not need to breed employee loyalty," Achilles told her, sounding even lazier than before, those dark eyes of his on hers. "People are loyal to me or they are fired. You seem to have forgotten reality today, Natalie. Allow me to remind you that I pay you so much money that I own your loyalty, just as I own everything else."

"Perhaps," and her voice was a little too rough then. A little too shaky, when what could this possibly have to do with her? She was a visitor. Natalie's loyalty was no concern of hers. "I have no wish to be owned. Does anyone? I think you'll find that they do not."

Achilles shrugged. "Whether you wish it or do not, that is how it is."

"That is why I was considering quitting," she heard herself say. And she was no longer looking at him. That was still far too dangerous, too disconcerting. She found herself staring down at her hands, folded in her lap. She could feel that she was frowning, when she learned a long, long time ago never to show her feelings in public. "It's all very well and good for you, of course. I imagine it's quite pleasant to have minions. But for me, there's more to life than blind loyalty. There's more to life than work." She blinked back a strange heat. "I may not have experienced it myself, but I know there must be."

"And what do you think is out there?" He shifted in the seat beside her, but Valentina still refused to look back at him, no matter how she seemed almost physically compelled to do just that. "What do you think you're missing? Is it worth what you are throwing away here today, with this aggressive attitude and the childish pretense that you don't know your own job?"

"It's only those who are bored of the world, or jaded, who are so certain no one else could possibly wish to see it."

"No one is keeping you from roaming about the planet at will," he told her in a low voice. Too low. So low it danced along her skin and seemed to insinuate itself beneath her flesh. "But you seem to wish to burn down the world you know in order to see the one you don't. That is not what I would call wise. Would you?"

Valentina didn't understand why his words seemed to beat beneath her own skin. But she couldn't seem to catch her breath. And her eyes seemed entirely too full, almost scratchy, with an emotion she couldn't begin to name.

She was aware of too many things. Of the car as it slid through the Manhattan streets. Of Achilles himself, too big and too masculine in the seat beside her, and much too close besides. And most of all, that oddly weighted thing within her, rolling around and around until she couldn't tell the difference between sensation and reaction.

And him right there in the middle of it, confusing her all the more.

CHAPTER THREE

ACHILLES DIDN'T SAY another word, and that was worse. It left Valentina to sit there with her own thoughts in a whirl and nothing to temper them. It left no barrier between that compelling, intent look in his curiously dark eyes and her.

Valentina had no experience with men. Her father had insisted that she grow up as sheltered as possible from public life, so that she could enjoy what little privacy was afforded to a European princess before she turned eighteen. She'd attended carefully selected boarding schools run strictly and deliberately, but that hadn't prevented her classmates from involving themselves in all kinds of dramatic situations. Even then, Valentina had kept herself apart.

Your mother's defection was a stain on the throne, her father always told her. *It is upon us to render it clean and whole again.*

Valentina had been far too terrified of staining Murin any further to risk a scandal. She'd concentrated on her studies and her friends and left the teenage rebellions to others. And once out of school, she'd been thrust unceremoniously into the spotlight. She'd been an ambassador for her kingdom wherever she went, and more than that, she'd always known that she was promised to the Crown

Prince of Tissely. Any scandals she embroiled herself in would haunt two kingdoms.

She'd never seen the point.

And along the way she'd started to take a certain pride in the fact that she was saving herself for her predetermined marriage. It was the one thing that was hers to give on her wedding night that had nothing to do with her father or her kingdom.

Is it pride that's kept you chaste—or is it control? a little voice inside her asked then, and the way it kicked in her, Valentina suspected she wouldn't care for the answer. She ignored it.

But the point was, she had no idea how to handle men. Not on any kind of intimate level. These past few hours, in fact, were the longest she'd ever spent alone in the company of a man. It simply didn't happen when she was herself. There were always attendants and aides swarming around Princess Valentina. Always.

She told herself that was why she was having such trouble catching her breath. It was the novelty—that was all. It certainly wasn't *him*.

Still, it was almost a relief when the car pulled up in front of a quietly elegant building on the Upper West Side of Manhattan, perched there with a commanding view of Central Park, and came to a stop.

The late-afternoon breeze washed over her when she stepped from the car, smelling improbably of flowers in the urban sprawl of New York City. But Valentina decided to take it as a blessing.

Achilles remained silent as he escorted her into the building. He only raised his chin in the barest of responses to the greeting that came his way from the doormen in the shiny, obviously upscale lobby, and then he led her into a private elevator located toward the back and behind another set of security guards. It was a gleaming, shining thing that he operated with a key. And it was blessedly without any mirrors.

Valentina wasn't entirely sure whom she'd see if she looked at her own reflection just then.

There were too many things she didn't understand churning inside her, and she hadn't the slightest idea what she was doing here. What on earth she hoped to gain from this odd little lark across the planet, literally in another woman's shoes.

A break, she reminded herself sternly. A vacation. A little holiday away from all the duties and responsibilities of Princess Valentina, which was more important now than ever. She would give herself over to her single-greatest responsibility in a matter of weeks. She would marry Prince Rodolfo and make both of their fathers and all of their subjects very, very happy.

And a brief escape had sounded like bliss for that split second back there in London—and it still did, when she thought about what waited for her. The terribly appropriate royal marriage. The endlessly public yet circumspect life of a modern queen. The glare of all that attention that she and any children she bore could expect no matter where they went or what they did, yet she could never comment upon lest she seem ungrateful or entitled.

Hers was to wave and smile—that was all. She was marrying a man she hardly knew who would expect the marital version of the same. This was a little breather before the reality of all that. This was a tiny bit of space between her circumscribed life at her father's side and more of the same at her husband's.

She couldn't allow the brooding, unreadable man beside her to ruin it, no matter how unnerving his dark gold gaze was. No matter what fires it kicked up inside her that she hardly dared name.

The elevator doors slid open, delivering them straight

into the sumptuous front hall of an exquisitely decorated penthouse. Valentina followed Achilles as he strode deep inside, not bothering to spare her a glance as he moved. She was glad that he walked ahead of her, which allowed her to look around so she could get her bearings without seeming to do so. Because, of course, Natalie would already know her way around this place.

She took in the high ceilings and abundant windows all around. The sweeping stairs that led up toward at least two more floors. The mix of art deco and a deep coziness that suggested this penthouse was more than just a showcase; Achilles actually *lived* here.

Valentina told herself—sternly—that there was no earthly reason that notion should make her shiver.

She was absurdly grateful when a housekeeper appeared, clucking at Achilles in what it took Valentina longer than it should have to realize was Greek. A language she could converse in, though she would never consider herself anything like fluent. Still, it took her only a very few moments to understand that whatever the danger Achilles exuded and however ruthless the swath he cut through the entire world with a single glance, this woman thought he was wonderful.

She *beamed* at him.

It would not do to let that get to her, Valentina warned herself as something warm seemed to roll its way through her, pooling in the strangest places. She should not draw any conclusions about a man who was renowned for his fierceness in all things and yet let a housekeeper treat him like family.

The woman declared she would feed him no matter if he was hungry or not, lest he get skinny and weak, and bustled back in the direction of what Valentina assumed was the kitchen.

"You're looking around as if you are lost," Achilles

murmured, when Valentina didn't think she'd been looking around at all. "When you have spent more time in this penthouse over the last five years than I have."

Valentina hated the fact that she started a bit when she realized his attention was focused on her again. And that he was speaking in English, which seemed to make him sound that much more knowing.

Or possibly even mocking, unless she was very much mistaken.

"Mr. Casilieris," she said, lacing her voice with gentle reprove, "I work for you. I don't understand why you appear to be quite so interested in what you think is happening inside my head today. Especially when you are so mistaken."

"Am I?"

"Entirely." She raised her brows at him. "If I could suggest that we concentrate more on matters of business than fictional representations of what might or might not be going on inside my mind, I think we might be more productive."

"As productive as we were on the flight over?" His voice was a lazy sort of lash, as amused as it was on target.

Valentina only smiled, hoping she looked enigmatic and strategic rather than at a loss.

"Are *you* lost?" she asked him after a moment, because neither one of them had moved from the great entry that bled into the spacious living room, then soared up two stories, a quiet testament to his wealth and power.

"Careful, Miss Monette," Achilles said with a certain dark precision. "As delightful as I have found today's descent into insubordination, I have a limit. It would be in your best interests not to push me there too quickly."

Valentina had made a study out of humbly accepting all kinds of news she didn't wish to hear over the years. She bent her head, let her lips curve a bit—but not enough to be called a smile, only enough to show she was feeling… something. Then she simply stood there quietly. It was amazing how many unpleasant moments she'd managed to get through that way.

So she had no earthly idea why there was a part of her that wanted nothing more than to look Achilles straight in his dark eyes and ask him, *Or what?*

Somehow, thankfully, she refrained.

Servants came in behind them with luggage—some of which Valentina assumed must be Natalie's and thus hers—but Achilles did not appear to notice them. He kept his attention trained directly on her.

A lesser woman would have been disconcerted, Valentina thought. Someone unused to being the focus of attention, for example. Someone who hadn't spent a part of every day since she turned eighteen having cameras in her face to record every flutter of her eyelashes and rip apart every facet of whatever she happened to be wearing and how she'd done her hair. Every expression that crossed her face was a headline.

What was a cranky billionaire next to that?

"There's no need to repair to our chambers after the flight, I think," he said softly, and Valentina had that odd notion again. That he could see right through her. That he knew things he couldn't possibly know. "We can get right to it."

And there was no reason that that should feel almost… dirty. As if he was suggesting—

But, of course, that was absurd, Valentina told herself staunchly. He was Achilles Casilieris. He was renowned almost as much for his prowess in the sheets as he was for his dominance in the boardroom. In some circles, more.

He tended toward the sort of well-heeled women who

were mainstays on various charity circuits. Not for him the actresses or models whom so many other men of his stature preferred. That, apparently, was not good enough for Achilles Casilieris. Valentina had found herself with some time on the plane to research it herself, after Achilles had finished the final call she'd failed entirely to set up to his liking and had sat a while, a fulminating stare fixed on her. Then he'd taken himself off to one of the jet's finely appointed staterooms, and she'd breathed a bit easier.

A bit.

She'd looked around for a good book to read, preferably a paperback romance because who didn't like hope and happiness with a bit of sex thrown in to make it spicy, but there had been nothing of the sort. Achilles apparently preferred dreary economic magazines that trumpeted out recession and doom from all quarters. Valentina had kicked off her shoes, tucked her legs beneath her on the smooth leather chair she'd claimed for the flight, and indulged herself with a descent into the tabloid and gossip sites she normally avoided. Because she knew how many lies they told about her, so why would she believe anything she read about anyone else?

Still, they were a great way to get a sense of the kind of coverage a man like Achilles suffered, which would surely tell her…something. But the answer was…not much. He was featured in shots from charity events where other celebrities gathered like cows at a trough, but was otherwise not really a tabloid staple. Possibly because he was so sullen and scowling, she thought.

His taste in bedmates, however, was clear even without being splashed across screeching front pages all over the world. Achilles tended toward women who were less celebrated for their faces and more for their actions. Which wasn't to say they weren't all beautiful, of course. That seemed to be a requirement. But they couldn't only be beautiful.

This one was a civil rights attorney of some renown. That one was a journalist who spent most of her time in terrifying war zones. This one had started a charity to benefit a specific cancer that had taken her younger sister. That one was a former Olympic athlete who had dedicated her post-competition life to running a lauded program for at-risk teenagers.

He clearly had a type. Accomplished, beautiful women who did good in the world and who also happened to be wealthy enough all on their own. The uncharitable part of her suspected that last part was because he knew a woman of independent means would not be as interested in his fortune as a woman who had nothing. No gold diggers need apply, clearly.

But the point was, she knew she was mistaken about his potentially suggestive words. Because "assistant to billionaire" was not the kind of profession that would appeal to a man like Achilles. It saved no lives. It bettered nothing.

Valentina found herself glaring at his back as he led her into a lavish office suite on the first level of his expansive penthouse. When she stood in the center of the room, awaiting further instructions, he only crooked a brow. He leaned back against the large desk that stretched across one wall and regarded her with that hot sort of focus that made everything inside her seem to shift hard to the left.

She froze. And then she could have stood there for hours, for all she knew, as surely as if he'd caught her and held her fast in his fists.

"When you are ready, Miss Monette, feel free to take your seat." His voice was razor sharp, cut through with that same rough darkness that she found crept through her limbs. Lighting her up and making her feel something

like sluggish. She didn't understand it. "Though I do love
being kept waiting."

More chastened than she wanted to admit, Valentina
moved to one of the seats set around a table to the right of
the desk, at the foot of towering bookshelves stuffed full
of serious-looking books, and settled herself in it. When
he continued to stare at her as if she was deliberately keeping him waiting, she reached into the bag—Natalie's bag,
which she'd liberated from the bathroom when she'd left
the airport with Achilles—until she found a tablet.

A few texts with her double had given her the pass-
words she needed and some advice.

Just write down everything he says. He likes to forget he
said certain things, and it's always good to have a record.
One of my jobs is to function as his memory.

Valentina had wanted to text back her thoughts on that,
but had refrained. Natalie might have wanted to quit this
job, but that was up to her, not the woman taking her place
for a few weeks.

"Anything else?" Achilles's voice had a dark edge.
"Would you like to have a snack? Perhaps a brief nap?
Tell me, is there any way that I can make you more comfortable, Miss Monette, such that you might actually take
it upon yourself to do a little work today?"

And Valentina didn't know what came over her. Because she wanted to argue. She, who had made a virtue out
of remaining quiet and cordial under any circumstances,
wanted to fight. She didn't understand it. She knew it was
Achilles. That there was something in him that made her
want to do or say anything to get some kind of reaction.
It didn't matter that it was madness. It was something
about that look in his eyes. Something about that hard,
amused mouth of his.

It was something about *him*.

But Valentina reminded herself that this was not her life.

This was not her life and this was not her job, and none of this was hers to ruin. She was the steward of Natalie's life for a little while, nothing more. She imagined that Natalie would be doing the same for her. Maybe breathing a little bit of new life into the tired old royal nonsense she'd find waiting for her at Murin Castle, but that was all. Neither one of them was out to wreck what they found.

And she'd never had any trouble whatsoever keeping to the party line. Doing her father's bidding, behaving appropriately, being exactly the princess whom everyone imagined she was. She felt that responsibility—to her people, to her bloodline, to her family's history—deeply. She'd never acted out the way so many of her friends had. She'd never fought against her own responsibilities. It wasn't that she was afraid to do any of those things, but simply that it had never occurred to her to try. Valentina had always known exactly who she was and what her life would hold, from her earliest days.

So she didn't recognize this thing in her that wanted nothing more than to cause a commotion. To stand up and throw the tablet she held at Achilles's remarkably attractive head. To kick over the chair she was sitting in and, while she was at it, that desk of his, too, all brash steel and uncompromising masculinity, just like its owner.

She wanted to do *something*. Anything. She could feel it humming through her veins, bubbling in her blood. As if something about this normal life she'd tried on for size had infected her. Changed her. When it had only been a few hours.

He's a ruthless man, something reckless inside her whispered. *He can take it*.

But this wasn't her life. She had to protect it, not destroy it, no matter what was moving in her, poking at her, tempting her to act out for the first time in her life.

So Valentina smiled up at Achilles, forced herself to remain serene the way she always did, and got to work.

It was late into the New York night when Achilles finally stopped torturing his deceitful princess.

He made her go over byzantine contracts that rendered his attorneys babbling idiots. He questioned her on clauses he only vaguely understood himself, and certainly couldn't expect her to be conversant on. He demanded she prepare memos he had no intention of sending. He questioned her about events he knew she could not possibly know anything about, and the truth was that he enjoyed himself more than he could remember enjoying anything else for quite some time.

When Demetria had bustled in with food, Achilles had waved Valentina's away.

"My assistant does not like to eat while she works," he told his housekeeper, but he'd kept his gaze on Valentina while he'd said it.

"I don't," she'd agreed merrily enough. "I consider it a weakness." She'd smiled at him. "But you go right ahead."

Point to the princess, he'd thought.

The most amazing thing was that Princess Valentina never backed down. Her ability to brazen her way through the things she didn't know, in fact, was nothing short of astounding. Impressive in the extreme. Achilles might have admired it if he hadn't been the one she was trying to fool.

"It is late," he said finally, when he thought her eyes might glaze over at last. Though he would cast himself out his own window to the Manhattan streets below before he'd admit his might, too. "And while there is always more to do, I think it is perhaps wise if we take this as a natural stopping place."

Valentina smiled at him, tucked up in that chair of hers that she had long since claimed as her own in a way he couldn't remember the real Natalie had ever done, her green eyes sparkling.

"I understand if you need a rest," she said sweetly. Too sweetly. "Sir."

Achilles had been standing at the windows, his back to the mad gleam of Manhattan. But at that, he let himself lean back, his body shifting into something…looser. More dangerous.

And much, much hotter than contracts.

"I worry my hearing has failed me. Because it sounded very much as if you were impugning my manhood."

"Only if your manhood is so fragile that you can't imagine it requires a rest," she said, and aimed a sunny smile at him as if that would take away the sting of her words. "But you are Achilles Casilieris. You have made yourself a monument to manhood, clearly. No fragility allowed."

"It is almost as if you think debating me like this is some kind of strategy," he said softly, making no attempt to ratchet back the ruthlessness in his voice. Much less do something about the fire he could feel storming through him everywhere else. "Let me warn you, again, it is only a strategy if your goal is to find yourself without a job and without a recommendation. To say nothing of the black mark I will happily put beside your name."

Valentina waved a hand in the air, airily, dismissing him. And her possible firing, black marks—all of it. Something else he very likely would have found impressive if he'd been watching her do it to someone else.

"So many threats." She shook her head. "I understand that this is how you run your business and you're very successful, but really. It's exhausting. Imagine how many more bees you could get with honey."

He didn't want to think about honey. Not when there were only the two of them here, in this office cushioned by the night outside and the rest of the penthouse. No shared walls on these floors he owned. This late, none of the staff would be up. It was only Achilles and this princess pretending to be his assistant, and the buttery light of the few lamps they'd switched on, making the night feel thick and textured everywhere the light failed to reach.

Like inside him.

"Come here."

Valentina blinked, but her green gaze was unreadable then. She only looked at him for a moment, as if she'd forgotten that she was playing this game. And that in it, she was his subordinate.

"Come here," he said again. "Do not make me repeat myself, I beg you. You will not like my response."

She stood the way she did everything else, with an easy grace. With that offhanded elegance that did things to him he preferred not to examine. And he knew she had no desire to come any closer to him. He could feel it. Her wariness hung between them like some kind of smoke, and it ignited that need inside him. And for a moment he thought she might disobey him. That she might balk—and it was in that moment he thought she'd stay where she was, across the room, that he had understood how very much he wanted her.

In a thousand ways he shouldn't, because Achilles was a man who did not *want*. He took. Wanting was a weakness that led only to darkness—though it didn't feel like a weakness tonight. It felt like the opposite.

But he'd underestimated his princess. Her shoulders straightened almost imperceptibly. And then she glided

toward him, head high like some kind of prima balle-
rina, her face set in the sort of pleasant expression he
now knew she could summon and dispatch at will. He
admired that, too.

And he'd thrown out that summons because he could.
Because he wanted to. And he was experimenting with
this new *wanting*, no matter how little he liked it.

Still, there was no denying the way his body responded
as he watched her walk toward him. There was no denying the rich, layered tension that seemed to fill the room.
And him, making his pulse a living thing as his blood
seemed to heat in his veins.

Something gleamed in that green gaze of hers, but she
kept coming. She didn't stop until she was directly beside
him, so close that if she breathed too heavily he thought
her shoulder might brush his. He shifted so that he stood
slightly behind her, and jutted his chin toward the city
laid out before them.

"What do you see when you look out the window?"

He felt more than saw the glance she darted at him.
But then she kept her eyes on the window before them.
On the ropes of light stretching out in all hectic direc-
tions possible below.

"Is that a trick question? I see Manhattan."

"I grew up in squalor." His voice was harsher than
he'd intended, but Achilles did nothing to temper it. "It
is common, I realize, for successful men to tell stories
of their humble beginnings. Americans in particular
find these stories inspiring. It allows them to fantasize
that they, too, might better themselves against any odds.
But the truth is more of a gray area, is it not? Beginnings
are never quite so humble as they sound when rich men
claim them. But me?" He felt her gaze on him then, instead of the mess of lights outside. "When I use the word
squalor, that's an upgrade."

Her swallow was audible. Or perhaps he was paying her too close attention. Either way, he didn't back away.

"I don't know why you're telling me this."

"When you look through this window you see a city. A place filled with people going about their lives, traffic and isolation." He shifted so he could look down at her. "I see hope. I see vindication. I see all the despair and all the pain and all the loss that went into creating the man you see before you tonight. Creating this." And he moved his chin to indicate the penthouse. And the Casilieris Company while he was at it. "And there is nothing that I wouldn't do to protect it."

And he didn't know what had happened to him while he was speaking. He'd been playing a game, and then suddenly it seemed as if the game had started to play him— and it wasn't finished. Something clutched at him, as if he was caught in the grip of some massive fist.

It was almost as if he wanted this princess, this woman who believed she was tricking him—deceiving him—to understand him.

This, too, was unbearable.

But he couldn't seem to stop.

"Do you think people become driven by accident, Miss Monette?" he asked, and he couldn't have said why that thing gripping him seemed to clench harder. Making him sound far more intense than he thought he should have felt. Risking the truth about himself he carried inside and shared with no one. But he still didn't stop. "Ambition, desire, focus and drive—do you think these things grow on trees? But then, perhaps I'm asking the wrong person. Have you not told me a thousand times that you are not personally ambitious?"

It was one of the reasons he'd kept Natalie with him for so long, when other assistants to men like him used positions like hers as springboards into their own glorious careers. But this woman was not Natalie. If he hadn't known it before, he'd have known it now, when it was a full-scale struggle to keep his damned hands to himself.

"Ambition, it seems to me, is for those who have the freedom to pursue it. And for those who do not—" and Valentina's eyes seemed to gleam at that, making Achilles wonder exactly what her ambitions were "—it is nothing more than dissatisfaction. Which is far less worthy and infinitely more destructive, I think we can agree."

He didn't know when he'd turned to face her fully. He didn't know when he'd stopped looking at the city and was looking only at her instead. But he was, and he compounded that error by reaching out his hand and tugging on the very end of her silky, coppery ponytail where it kissed her shoulder every time she moved her head.

Her lips parted, as if on a soundless breath, and Achilles felt that as if she'd caressed him. As if her hands were on his body the way he wished they were, instead of at her sides.

"Are you dissatisfied?" It was amazing how difficult it was not to use her real name then. How challenging it was to stay in this game he suddenly didn't particularly want to play. "Is that what this is?"

Her green eyes, which had been so unreadable, suddenly looked slick. Dark and glassy with some or other emotion. He couldn't tell what it was, and still, he could feel it in him like smoke, stealing through his chest and making it harder than it should have been to breathe.

"There's nothing wrong with dissatisfaction in and of itself," she told him after a moment, then another, that seemed too large for him to contain. Too dark and much too edgy to survive intact, and yet here they both were. "You see it as disloyalty, but it's not."

"How can it be anything else?"

"It is possible to be both loyal and open to the possibility that there is a life outside the one you've committed yourself to." Her green eyes searched his. "Surely there must be."

"I think you will find that there is no such possibility." His voice was harsh. He could feel it inside him, like a stain. Like need. "We must all decide who we are, every moment of every day. You either keep a vow or you do not. There is no between."

She stiffened at that, then tried to force her shoulders back down to an easier, less telling angle. Achilles watched her do it. He watched something like distress cross her lovely face, but she hid that, too. It was only the darkness in her gaze that told him he'd scored a direct hit, and he was a man who took great pride in the strikes he leveled against anyone who tried to move against him. Yet what he felt when he looked at Valentina was not pride. Not pride at all.

"Some vows are not your own," she said fiercely, her gaze locked to his. "Some are inherited. It's easy to say that you'll keep them because that's what's expected of you, but it's a great deal harder to actually *do* it."

He knew the vows she'd made. That pointless prince. Her upcoming royal wedding. He assumed that was the least of the vows she'd inherited from her father. And he still thought it was so much smoke and mirrors to hide the fact that she, like so many of her peers, was a spoiled and pampered creature who didn't like to be told what to do. Wasn't that the reason *poor little rich girl* was a saying in the first place?

He had no sympathy for the travails of a rich, pampered princess. But he couldn't seem to unwind that little silken bit of copper from around his finger, either. Much less step back and put the space between them that he should have left there from the start.

Achilles shook his head. "There is no gray area. Surely

you know this. You are either who you say you are or you are not."

There was something like misery in those eyes of hers then. And this was what he'd wanted. This was why he'd been goading her. And yet now that he seemed to have succeeded, he felt the strangest thing deep in his gut. It was an unpleasant and unfamiliar sensation, and at first Achilles couldn't identify it. It was a low heat, trickling through him, making him restless. Making him as close to uncertain as he'd ever been.

In someone else, he imagined, it might be shame. But shame was not something Achilles allowed in himself. Ever.

This was a night full of things he did not allow, apparently. Because he wanted her. He wanted to punctuate this oddly emotional discussion with his mouth. His hands. The whole of his too-tight, too-interested body pressed deep into hers. He wanted to taste those sweetly lush lips of hers. He wanted to take her elegant face in his hands, tip her head back and sate himself at last. It seemed to him an age or two since he'd boarded his plane and realized his assistant was not who she was supposed to be. An agony of waiting and all that *want*, and he was not a man who agonized. Or waited. Or wanted anything, it seemed, but this princess who thought she could fool him.

What was the matter with him that some part of him wanted to let her?

He did none of the things he longed to do.

Achilles made himself do the hard thing, no matter how complicated it was. Or how complicated it felt, anyway. When really it was so simple. He let her go. He let her silky hair fall from between his fingers, and he stepped back, putting inches between them.

But that did nothing to ease the temptation.

"I think what you need is a good night's sleep," he told

her, like some kind of absurd nurturer. Something he had certainly never tried to be for anyone else in the whole of his life. He would have doubted it was possible—and he refused to analyze that. "Perhaps it will clear your head and remind you of who you are. Jet lag can make that so very confusing, I know."

He thought she might have scuttled from the room at that, filled with her own shame if there was any decency in the world, but he was learning that this princess was not at all who he expected her to be. She swallowed, hard. And he could still see that darkness in her eyes. But she didn't look away from him. And she certainly didn't scuttle anywhere.

"I know exactly who I am, Mr. Casilieris," she said, very directly, and the lenses in her glasses made her eyes seem that much greener. "As I'm certain you do, too. Jet lag makes a person tired. It doesn't make them someone else entirely."

And when she turned to walk from the room then, it was with her head held high, graceful and self-contained, with no apparent second thoughts. Or anything the least bit like shame. All he could read on her as she went was that same distracting elegance that was already too far under his skin.

Achilles couldn't seem to do a thing but watch her go.

And when the sound of her footsteps had faded away, deep into the far reaches of the penthouse, he turned back to the wild gleam of Manhattan on the other side of his windows. Frenetic and frenzied. Light in all directions, as if there was nothing more to the world tonight than this utterly mad tangle of life and traffic and people and energy and it hardly mattered what he felt so high above it. It hardly mattered at all that he'd betrayed himself. That this woman who should have been nothing to him made him act like someone he barely recognized.

And her words stayed with him. *I know exactly who I am.* They echoed around and around in his head until it sounded a whole lot more like an accusation.

As if she was the one playing this game, and winning it, after all.

CHAPTER FOUR

AS THE DAYS PASSED, Valentina thought that she was getting the hang of this assistant thing—especially if she endeavored to keep a minimum distance between herself and Achilles when the night got a little too dark and close. And at all other times, for that matter.

She'd chalked up those odd, breathless moments in his office that first night to the strangeness of inhabiting someone else's life. Because it couldn't be anything else. Since then, she hadn't felt the need to say too much. She hadn't defended herself—or her version of Natalie. She'd simply tried to do the job that Natalie, apparently, did so well she was seen by other employees of the Casilieris Company as superhuman.

With every day she became more accustomed to the demands of the job. She felt less as if she really ought to have taken Achilles up on his offer of a parachute and more as if this was something she could handle. Maybe not well or like superhuman Natalie, but she could handle it all the same in her own somewhat rudimentary fashion.

What she didn't understand was why Achilles hadn't fired her already. Because it was perfectly clear to Valentina that her version of handling things in no way lived up to Achilles's standards.

And if she'd been any doubt about that, he was the first to tell her otherwise.

His corporate offices in Manhattan took up several floors at one of Midtown's most esteemed addresses. There was an office suite set aside for him, naturally enough, that sprawled across the top floor and looked out over Manhattan as if to underscore the notion that Achilles Casilieris was in every way on top of the world. Valentina was settled in the immediate outer office, guarded by two separate lines of receptionist and secretarial defense should anyone make it through security. It wasn't to protect Achilles, but to further illuminate his importance. And Natalie's, Valentina realized quickly.

Because Natalie controlled access to Achilles. She controlled his schedule. She answered his phone and his email, and was generally held to have that all-important insight into his moods.

"What kind of day is it?" the senior vice presidents would ask her as they came in for their meetings, and the fact they smiled as they said it didn't make them any less anxious to hear her answer.

Valentina quickly discovered that Natalie controlled a whole lot more than simple access. There was a steady line of people at her desk, coming to her to ask how best to approach Achilles with any number of issues, or plot how to avoid approaching him with the things they knew he'd hate. Over the course of her first week in New York City, Valentina found that almost everyone who worked for Achilles tried to run things past her first, or used her to gauge his reactions. Natalie was less the man's personal assistant, she realized, and more the hub around which his businesses revolved. More than that, she thought he knew it.

"Take that up with Natalie," he would say in the middle of a meeting, without even bothering to look over at her. Usually while cutting someone off, because even he appeared not to want to hear certain things until Natalie had assessed them first.

"Come up with those numbers and run them past Natalie," he would tell his managers, and sometimes he'd even sound irritated while he said such things.

"Why are you acting as if you have never worked a day in my company?" he'd demanded of one of his brand managers once. "I am not the audience for your uncertain first drafts, George. How can you not know this?"

Valentina had smiled at the man in the meeting, and then had been forced to sit through a brainstorming/therapy session with him afterward, all the while hoping that the noncommittal things she'd murmured were, at the very least, not the *opposite* of the sort of things Natalie might have said.

Not that she texted Natalie to find out. Because that might have led to a conversation Valentina didn't really want to have with her double about strange, tense moments in the darkness with her employer.

She didn't know what she was more afraid of. That Natalie had never had any kind of tension with Achilles and Valentina was messing up her entire life...or that she did. That *tension* was just what Achilles did.

Valentina concentrated on her first attempt at a normal life, complete with a normal job, instead. And whether Achilles was aware of it or not, Natalie had her fingers in everything.

Including his romantic life.

The first time Valentina had answered his phone to find an emotional woman on the other end, she'd been appalled.

"There's a crying woman on the phone," she'd told Achilles. It had taken her a day or so to realize that she wasn't only allowed to walk in and out of his office when necessary, but encouraged to do so. That particular afternoon Achilles had been sitting on the sofa in his office, his feet up on his coffee table as he'd scowled down at his laptop. He shifted that scowl to her instead, in a way that made Valentina imagine that whatever he was looking at had something to do with her—

But that was ridiculous. There was no *her* in this scenario. There was only Natalie, and Valentina very much doubted Achilles spent his time looking up his assistant on the internet.

"Why are you telling me this?" he'd asked her shortly. "If I wanted to know who called me, I would answer my phones myself."

"She's crying about you," Valentina had said. "I assume she's calling to share her emotions with you, the person who caused them."

"And I repeat—why are you telling me this." This time it wasn't a question, and his scowl deepened. "You are my assistant. You are responsible for fielding these calls. I'm shocked you're even mentioning another crying female. I thought you stopped bringing them to my attention years ago."

Valentina had blinked at that. "Aren't you at all interested in why this woman is upset?"

"No."

"Not at all. Not the slightest bit interested." She studied his fierce face as if he was an alien. In moments like this, she thought he must have been. "You don't even know which woman I'm referring to, do you?"

"Miss Monette." He bit out that name as if the taste of it irritated him, and Valentina couldn't have said why it put her back up when it wasn't even her name. "I have a number of mistresses, none of whom call that line to manufacture emotional upsets. You are already aware of this." And he'd set his laptop aside, as if he needed to concentrate fully on Valentina before him. It had made her spine prickle, from her neck to her bottom and back up again. "Please let me know exactly what agenda it is we are pursuing today, that you expect to interrupt me in order to have a discussion about nuisance calls. When I assure you, the subject does not interest me at all. Just as it did not interest me five years ago, when you vowed to stop bothering me about them."

There was a warning in that. Valentina had heard it, plain as day. But she hadn't been able to heed it. Much less stop herself.

"To be clear, what you're telling me is that tears do not interest you," she'd said instead of beating a retreat to her desk the way she should have. She'd kept her tone even and easy, but she doubted that had fooled either one of them.

"Tears interest me least of all." She'd been sure that there was a curve in that hard mouth of his then, however small.

And what was the matter with her that she'd clung to that as if it was some kind of lifeline? As if she needed such a thing?

As if what she really wanted was his approval, when she hadn't switched places with Natalie for him. He'd had nothing to do with it. Why couldn't she seem to remember that?

"If this is a common occurrence for you, perhaps you need to have a think about your behavior," she'd pointed out. "And your aversion to tears."

There had definitely been a curve in his mouth then, and yet somehow that hadn't made Valentina any easier.

"This conversation is over," he'd said quietly. Though not gently. "Something I suggest you tell the enterprising actress on the phone."

She'd thought him hideously cold, of course. Heartless, even. But the calls kept coming. And Valentina had quickly realized what she should perhaps have known from the start—that it would be impossible for Achilles to actually be out there causing harm to so many anonymous women when he never left the office. She knew this because she spent almost every hour of every day in his company. The man literally had no time to go out there smashing hearts left and right, the way she'd be tempted to believe he did if she paid attention only to the phone calls she received, laden with accusations.

"Tell him I'm falling apart," yet another woman on the phone said on this latest morning, her voice ragged.

"Sorry, but what's your name again?" Valentina asked, as brightly as possible. "It's only that he's been working rather hard, you see. As he tends to do. Which would, of course, make it extremely difficult for him to be tearing anyone apart in any real sense."

The woman had sputtered. But Valentina had dutifully taken her name into Achilles when he next asked for his messages.

"I somewhat doubted the veracity of her claim," Valentina murmured. "Given that you were working until well after two last night."

Something she knew very well since that had meant she'd been working even longer than that.

Achilles laughed. He was at his desk today, which meant he was framed by the vertical thrust of Manhattan behind him. And still, that look in his dark gold gaze made the city disappear. "As well you should. I have no idea who this woman is. Or any of them." He shrugged. "My attorneys are knee-deep in paternity suits, and I win every one of them."

Valentino was astonished by that. Perhaps that was naive. She'd certainly had her share of admirers in her day, strange men who claimed an acquaintance or who sent rather disturbing letters to the palace—some from distant prisons in foreign countries. But she certainly never had men call up and try to pretend they had relationships with her *to* her.

Then again, would anyone have told her if they had? That sat on her a bit uneasily, though she couldn't have said why. She only knew that his gaze was like a touch, and that, too, seemed to settle on her like a weight.

"It's amazing how many unhinged women seem to think that if they claim they're dating you, you might go along with it," she said before she could think better of it.

That dark gold gaze of his lit with a gleam she couldn't name then. And it sparked something deep inside her, making her fight to draw in a breath. Making her feel unsteady in the serviceable low heels that Natalie favored. Making her wish she'd worn something more substantial than a nice jacket over another pencil skirt. Like a suit of armor. Or her very own brick wall.

"There are always unhinged women hanging about," Achilles said in that quietly devastating way of his. "Trying to convince me that they have relationships with me that they adamantly do not. Why do you imagine that is, Miss Monette?"

She told herself he couldn't possibly know that she was one of those women, no matter how his gaze seemed to pin her where she stood. No matter the edge in his voice, or the sharp emphasis he'd put on *Miss Monette*.

Even if he suspected something was different with his assistant, he couldn't know. Because no one could know. Because Valentina herself hadn't known Natalie existed until she'd walked into that bathroom. And that meant all sorts of things, such as the fact that everything she'd been told about her childhood and her birth was a lie. Not to mention her mother.

But there was no way Achilles could know any of that.

"Perhaps it's you," she murmured in response. She smiled when his brows rose in that expression of sheer arrogance that never failed to make her feel the slightest bit dizzy. "I only mean that you're a public figure and people imagine you a certain way based on the kind of press coverage you allow. Unless you plan to actively get out there and reclaim your public narrative, I don't think there's any likelihood that it will change."

"I am not a public figure. I have never courted the public in any way."

Valentina checked a sigh. "You're a very wealthy man. Whether you like it or not, the public is fascinated by you."

Achilles studied her until she was forced to order herself not to fidget beneath the weight of that heavy, intense stare.

"I'm intrigued that you think the very existence of public fascination must create an obligation in me to cater to it," he said quietly. "It does not. In fact, it has the opposite effect. In me. But how interesting that you imagine you owe something to the faceless masses who admire you."

Valentina's lips felt numb. "No masses, faceless or otherwise, admire me, Mr. Casilieris. They have no idea I exist. I'm an assistant, nothing more."

His hard mouth didn't shift into one of those hard curves, but his dark gold eyes gleamed, and somehow that made the floor beneath her seem to tilt, then roll.

"Of course you are," he said, his voice a quiet menace that echoed in her like a warning. Like something far more dangerous than a simple warning. "My mistake."

Later that night, still feeling as off balance as if the floor really wasn't steady beneath her feet, Valentina found herself alone with Achilles long after everyone else in the office had gone home.

It had been an extraordinarily long couple of days,

something Valentina might have thought was business as usual for the Casilieris Company if so many of the other employees hadn't muttered about how grueling it was. Beneath their breath and when they thought she couldn't hear them, that was. The deal that Achilles was so determined to push through had turned out to have more tangles and turns than anyone had expected—especially, it seemed, Achilles. What that meant was long hour after long hour well into the tiny hours of the night, hunched over tables and conference rooms, arguing with fleets of attorneys and representatives from the other side over take-out food from fine New York restaurants and stale coffee.

Valentina was deep into one of the contracts Achilles had slid her way, demanding a fresh set of eyes on a clause that annoyed him, when she noticed that they were the only ones there. The Casilieris Company had a significant presence all over the planet, so there were usually people coming and going at all conceivable hours to be available to different workdays in distant places. Something Valentina had witnessed herself after spending so much time in these offices since she'd arrived in New York.

But when she looked up from the dense and confusing contract language for a moment to give her ever-impending headache a break, she could see from the long conference room table where she sat straight through the glass walls that allowed her to see all the way across the office floor. And there was no one there. No bustling secretaries, no ambitious VPs putting in ostentatiously late hours where the boss could see their vigilance and commitment. No overzealous interns making busy work for themselves in the cubicles. No late-night cleaning crews, who did their jobs in the dark so as not to bother the workers by day. There wasn't a soul. Anywhere.

Something caught in her chest as she realized that it was only the two of them. Just Valentina and the man across the table from her, whom she was trying very hard not to look at too closely.

It was an extraordinarily unimportant thing to notice, she chastised herself, frowning back down at the contract. They were always alone, really. In his car, on his plane, in his penthouse. Valentina had spent more time with this man, she thought, than with any other save her father.

Her gaze rose from the contract of its own accord. Achilles sat across from her in the quiet of the otherwise empty office, his laptop cracked open before him and a pile of contracts next to the sleek machine. He looked the way he always did at the end of these long days. *Entirely too good*, something in her whispered—though she shoved that aside as best she could. It did no good to concentrate on things like that, she'd decided during her tenure with him. The man's appearance was a fact, and it was something she needed to come to terms with, but she certainly didn't have to ogle him.

But she couldn't seem to look away. She remembered that moment in his penthouse a little too clearly, the first night they'd been in New York. She remembered how close they'd stood in that window, and the things he'd told her, that dark gold gaze of his boring into her. As if he had every intention of looking directly to her soul. More than that, she remembered him reaching out and taking hold of the end of the ponytail she'd worn, that he'd looked at as if he had no idea how it had come to be attached to her.

But she'd dreamed about it almost every time she'd slept, either way.

Tonight Achilles was lounging in a pushed-back chair, his hands on top of his head as if, had he had longer hair, he'd be raking his hands through it. His jaw was dotted with stubble after a long day in the office, and it lent him the look of some kind of pirate.

Valentina told herself—sternly—that there was no

need for such fanciful language when he already made her pulse heat inside her simply by being in the same room. She tried to sink down a bit farther behind the piles and piles of documents surrounding her, which she was viewing as the armor she wished she was wearing. The remains of the dinner she'd ordered them many hours before were scattered across the center of the table, and she took perhaps too much pride in the fact she'd completed so simple a task. Normal people, she was certain, ordered from take-out menus all the time, but Valentina never had before she'd taken over Natalie's life. Valentina was a princess. She'd discussed many a menu and sent requests to any number of kitchens, but she'd never ordered her own meal in her life, much less from stereotypical New Yorkers with accents and attitudes.

She felt as if she was in a movie.

Valentina decided she would take her victories where she found them. Even if they were as small and ultimately pointless as sending out for a takeaway meal.

"It's late," Achilles said, reminding her that they were all alone here. And there was something in his voice then. Or the way his gaze slammed into hers when she looked up again.

Or maybe it was in her—that catch. That little kick of something a little too much like excitement that wound around and around inside her. Making her feel…restless. Undone. Desperate for something she couldn't even name.

"And here I thought you planned to carry straight through until dawn," she said, as brightly as possible, hoping against hope he couldn't see anything on her face. Or hear it in her voice.

Achilles lowered his hand to the arms of his chair. But he didn't shift that gaze of his from hers. And she kept catching him looking at her like this. Exactly like this. Simmering. Dark and dangerous, and spun through with gold. In the cars they took together. Every morning when he walked out of his bedchamber and found her sitting in the office suite, already starting on the day's work as best she could. Across boardroom tables just like this one, no matter if they were filled with other people.

It was worse now. Here in the quiet of his empty office. So late at night it felt to Valentina as if the darkness was a part of her.

And Valentina didn't have any experience with men, but oh, the books she'd read. Love stories and romances and happy-ever-afters, and almost all of them started just like this. With a taut feeling in the belly and fire everywhere else.

Do not be absurd, she snapped at herself.

Because she was Princess Valentina of Murin. She was promised to another and had been since her birth. There wasn't space in her life for anything but that. Not even here, in this faraway place that had nothing at all to do with her real life. Not even with this man, whom she never should have met, and never would have had she not seized that moment in the London bathroom.

You can take a holiday from your life, apparently, she reminded herself. *But you still take you along with you wherever you go.*

She might have been playing Natalie Monette, but she was still *herself*. She was still the same person she'd always been. Dutiful. Mindful of what her seemingly inconsequential behavior might mean to her father, to the kingdom, to her future husband's kingdom, too. Whatever else she was—and she wasn't sure she knew anymore, not here in the presence of a man who made her head spin without seeming to try very hard—Valentina was a person who had always, always kept her vows.

Even when it was her father who had made them, not her.

"If you keep staring at me like that," Achilles said softly, a kind of ferociousness beneath his rough words that made her stomach knot, then seemed to kindle a different, deeper fire lower down, "I am not certain I'll be able to contain myself."

Valentina's mouth was dry. "I don't know what you mean."

"I think you do."

Achilles didn't move, she could see that he wasn't moving, and yet everything changed at that. He filled every room he entered—she was used to that by now—but this was something different. It was as if lightning flashed. It was if he was some kind of rolling thunder all his own. It was as if he'd called in a storm, then let it loose to fill all of the room. The office.

And Valentina, too.

"No," she whispered, her voice scratchy against all that light and rumble.

But she could feel the tumult inside her. It was fire and it was light and it threatened to burst free of the paltry cage of her skin. Surely she would burst. Surely no person could survive this. She felt it shake all through her, as if underlining her fear.

"I don't know what you mean, and I don't like what you're implying. I think perhaps we've been in this office too long. You seem to have mistaken me for one of your mistresses. Or worse, one of those desperate women who call in, hoping to convince you they ought to be one of them."

"On the contrary, Miss Monette."

And there was a starkness to Achilles's expression then. No curve on his stern mouth. No gleaming thing in the seductive gold of his dark eyes. But somehow, that only made it worse.

"You're the one who manages my mistresses. And

those who pretend to that title. How could I possibly confuse you for them?" He cocked his head slightly to one side, and something yawned open inside her, as if in response. "Or perhaps you're auditioning for the role?"

"No." Her voice was no less scratchy this time, but there was more power in it. *Or more fear*, something inside her whispered. "I am most certainly not auditioning for anything like that. Or anything at all. I already have a job."

"But you told me you meant to quit." She had the strangest notion then that he was enjoying himself. "Perhaps you meant you were looking to make a lateral move. From my boardroom to my bed?"

Valentina tried to summon her outrage. She tried to tell herself that she was deeply offended on Natalie's behalf, because of course this was about her, not Valentina herself… She tried to tell herself a whole lot of things.

But she couldn't quite get there. Instead, she was awash with unhelpful little visions, red hot and wild. Images of what a "lateral move" might look like. Of what his bed might feel like. Of him.

She imagined that lean, solidly muscled form stretched over hers, the way she'd read in so many books so many times. Something almost too hot to bear melted through her then, pulling deep in her belly, and making her breath go shallow before it shivered everywhere else.

As if it was already happening.

"I know that this might come as a tremendous shock," Valentina said, trying to make herself sound something like fierce—or unmoved, anyway. Anything other than thrown and yearning. "But I have no interest in your bed. Less than no interest."

"You are correct." And something gleamed bright and hot and unholy gold in that dark gaze of his. "I am in shock."

"The next time an aspiring mistress calls the office," Valentina continued coolly, and no matter that it cost her, "I'll be certain to put her through to you for a change. You can discuss lateral moves all day long."

"What if a random caller does not appeal to me?" he asked lazily, as if this was all a game to him. She told herself it was. She told herself the fact that it was a game made it safe, but she didn't believe it. Not when all the things that moved around inside her made it hard to breathe, and made her feel anything at all but *safe*. "What if it is I who wish to alter our working relationship after all these years?"

Valentina told herself that this was clearly a test. If, as this conversation seemed to suggest, Natalie's relationship with her boss had always been strictly professional, why would he want to change that now? She'd seen how distant he kept his romantic entanglements from his work. His work was his life. His women were afterthoughts. There was no way the driven, focused man she'd come to know a bit after the close proximity of these last days would want to muddy the water in his office, with the assistant who not only knew where all the bodies were buried, but oversaw the funeral rites herself.

This had to be a test.

"I don't wish to alter a thing," she told him, very distinctly, as if there was nothing in her head but thorny contract language. And certainly nothing involving that remarkably ridged torso of his. "If you do, I think we should revisit the compensation package on offer for my resignation."

Achilles smiled as if she delighted him. But in an entirely too wicked and too hot sort of way.

"There is no package, Miss Monette," he murmured. "And there will be no resignation. When will you understand? You are here to do as I wish. Nothing more and nothing less than that. And perhaps my wishes concerning your role here have changed."

He wants you to fall apart, Valentina snapped at herself. *He wants to see if this will break you. He's poking at* Natalie *about her change in performance, not at you. He doesn't know* you *exist.*

Because there could be no other explanation. And it didn't matter that the look in his eyes made her shudder, down deep inside.

"Your wishes concerning my role now involve me on my back?" It cost her to keep her voice that flat. She could feel it.

"You say that as if the very idea disgusts you." And that crook in the corner of his lethal mouth deepened, even as that look in his eyes went lethal. "Surely not."

Valentina forced herself to smile. Blandly. As if her heart wasn't trying to claw its way out of her chest.

"I'm very flattered by your offer, of course," she said.

A little too sweetly to be mistaken for sincerity.

Achilles laughed then. It was an unsettling sound, too rough and too bold. It told her too much. That he knew— everything. That he knew all the things that were moving inside her, white hot and molten and too much for her to handle or tamp down or control. There was a growing, impossible fire raging in places she hardly understood, rendering her a stranger to herself.

As if he was the one in control of her body, even sitting across the table, lounging in his seat as if none of this was a matter of any concern at all.

While she felt as if she was both losing pieces of herself—and seeing her true colors for the very first time.

"Are you letting me down easy?" Achilles asked.

There was still laughter in his voice, his gaze and, somehow, dancing in the air between them despite all that fire still licking at her. She felt it roll through her, as if those big hands of his were on her skin.

And then she was suddenly incapable of thinking about anything at all but that. His hands all over her body. Touching places only she had ever seen. She had to swallow hard. Then again. And still there was that ringing in her ears.

"Do think it will work?" he asked, laughter still making his words sound a little too much like the rough, male version of honey.

"I imagine it will work beautifully, yes." She held on to that smile of hers as if her life depended on it. She rather thought it did. It was that or tip over into all that fire, and she had no idea what would become of her if she let that happen. She had no idea what would be left. "Or, of course, I could involve Human Resources in this discussion."

Achilles laughed again, and this time it was rougher. Darker and somehow hotter at the same time. Valentina felt it slide all over her, making her breasts feel heavy and her hips restless. While deep between her legs, a slick ache bloomed.

"I admire the feigned naïveté," Achilles said, and he looked like a pirate again, all dark jaw and that gleam in his gaze. It lit her up. Everywhere. "I have obviously failed to appreciate your acting talent sufficiently. I think we both know what Human Resources will tell you. To suck it up or find another position."

"That does not sound at all like something Human Resources would say," Valentina replied crisply, rather than spending even a split second thinking about *sucking*. "It sounds as if you're laboring under the delusion that this is a cult of personality, not a business."

If she expected him to look at all abashed, his grin disabused her of it. "Do you doubt it?"

"I'm not sure that is something I would brag about, Mr. Casilieris."

His gaze was hot, and she didn't think he was talking about her job or his company any longer. Had he ever been?

"Is it bragging if it's true?" he asked.

Valentina stood then, because it was the last thing she wanted to do. She could have sat there all night. She could have rung in a new dawn, fencing words with this man and dancing closer and closer to that precipice she could feel looming between them, even if she couldn't quite see it.

She could have pretended she didn't feel every moment of this deep inside her, in places she shouldn't. And then pretend further she didn't know what it meant just because she'd never experienced any of it before outside the pages of a book.

But she did know. And this wasn't her life to ruin. And so she stood, smoothing her hands down her skirt and wishing she hadn't been quite so impetuous in that London bathroom.

If you hadn't been, you wouldn't be here, something in her replied. *Is that what you want?*

And she knew that she didn't. Valentina had a whole life left to live with a man she would call husband who would never know her, not really. She had duty to look forward to, and a lifetime of charity and good works, all of which would be vetted by committees and commented on by the press. She had public adulation and a marriage that would involve the mechanical creation of babies before petering off into a nice friendship, if she was lucky.

Maybe the making of the babies would be fun with her prince. What did she know? All she knew so far was that he didn't do...this. He didn't affect her the way Achilles did, lounging there like hard-packed danger across a conference table, his gaze too dark and the gold in it making her pulse kick at her.

She'd never felt anything like this before. She doubted she'd ever feel it again.

Valentina couldn't quite bring herself to regret it.

But she couldn't stay here tonight and blow up the rest of Natalie's life, either. That would be treating this little gift that she'd been given with nothing but contempt.

"Have I given you leave to go?" Achilles asked, with what she knew was entirely feigned astonishment. "I am clearly confused in some way. I keep thinking you work for me."

She didn't know how he could do that. How he could seem to loom over her when she was the one standing up and looking down at him.

"And because I'd like to continue working for you," Valentina forced herself to say in as measured a tone as she could manage, "I'm going to leave now. We can pick this up in the morning." She tapped the table with one finger. "Pick *this* up, I mean. These contracts and the deal. Not this descent into madness, which I think we can chalk up to exhaustion."

Achilles only watched her for a moment. Those hands that she could picture too easily against her own flesh curled over the armrests of his chair, and her curse was that she imagined she *was* that chair. His legs were thrust out before him, long and lean. His usual suit was slightly rumpled, his tie having been tugged off and tossed aside hours earlier, so she could see the olive skin at his neck and a hint of crisp, black hair. He looked simultaneously sleepy and breathlessly, impossibly lethal—with an intensity that made that hot ache between her legs seem to swallow her whole.

And the look in his eyes made everything inside her draw tight, then pulse harder.

"Do you have a problem with that?" she asked, and she meant to sound impatient. Challenging. But she thought both of them were entirely too aware that what came out instead was rather more plaintive than planned.

As if she was really asking him if he was okay with everything that had happened here tonight. She was clearly too dazed to function.

She needed to get away from him while she still had access to what little of her brain remained in all this smoke and flame.

"Do you require my permission?" Achilles lifted his chin, and his dark eyes glittered. Valentina held her breath. "So far tonight it seems you are laboring under the impression that you give the permission, not me. You make the rules, not me. It is as if I am here for no other purpose than to serve you."

And there was no reason at all that his words, spoken in that soft, if dangerous way, should make her skin prickle. But they did. As if a man like Achilles did not have to issue threats, he was the threat. Why pile a threat on top of the threat? When the look on his face would do.

"I will see you in the morning," Valentina said, resolutely. "When I'll be happy to accept your apology."

Achilles lounged farther down in his chair, and she had the strangest notion that he was holding himself back. Keeping himself in place. Goose bumps shivered to life over her shoulders and down her arms.

His gaze never left hers.

"Go," he said, and there was no pretending it wasn't an order. "But I would not lie awake tonight anticipating the contours of my apology. It will never come."

She wanted to reply to that, but her mouth was too dry and she couldn't seem to move. Not so much as a muscle.

And as if he knew it, Achilles kept going in that same intensely quiet way.

"Tonight when you can't sleep, when you toss and turn and stare up at yet another ceiling I own, I want you to think of all the other reasons you could be wide awake in the small hours of the night. All the things that I could do to you. Or have you do to me. All the thousands of ways I will be imagining us together, just like that, under the same roof."

"That is completely inappropriate, Mr. Casilieris, and I think you know it."

But she knew full well she didn't sound nearly as outraged as she should. And only partially because her voice was a mere whisper.

"Have you never wondered how we would fit? Have you not tortured herself with images of my possession?" Achilles's hard mouth curved then, a wicked crook in one corner that she knew, somehow, would haunt her. She could feel it deep inside her like its own bright fire. "Tonight, I think, you will."

And Valentina stopped pretending there was any way out of this conversation besides the precise images he'd just mentioned, acted out all over this office. She walked stiffly around the table and gave him a wide, wide berth as she passed.

When she made it to the door of the conference room, she didn't look behind her to see if he was watching. She knew he was. She could feel it.

Fire and lightning, thunder and need.

She ran.

And heard his laughter follow behind her like the leading edge of a storm she had no hope of outwitting, no matter how fast she moved.

CHAPTER FIVE

ACHILLES ORDINARILY ENJOYED his victory parties. Reveled in them, in fact. Not for him any nod toward false humility or any pretense that he didn't deeply enjoy these games of high finance with international stakes. But tonight he couldn't seem to get his head into it, and no matter that he'd been fighting to buy out this particular iconic Manhattan hotel—which he planned to make over in his own image, the blend of European elegance and Greek timelessness that was his calling card in the few hotels scattered across the globe that he'd deemed worthy of the Casilieris name—for nearly eighteen months.

He should have been jubilant. It irritated him—deeply—that he couldn't quite get there.

His group had taken over a New York steak house renowned for its high-end clientele and specialty drinks to match to celebrate the deal he'd finally put through today after all this irritating wrangling. Ordinarily he would allow himself a few drinks to blur out his edges for a change. He would even smile and pretend he was a normal man, like all the rest, made of flesh and blood instead of dollar signs and naked ambition—an improvement by far over the monster he kept locked up tight beneath. Nights like this were his opportunity to pretend to be like anyone else, and Achilles usually indulged that impulse.

He might not have been a normal man—he'd never been a normal man—but it amused him to pretend otherwise every now and again. He was renowned for his surliness as much as his high expectations, but if that was all there was to it—to him—he never would have gotten anywhere in business. It took a little charm to truly manipulate his enemies and his opponents and even his acolytes the way he liked to do. It required that he be as easy telling a joke as he was taking over a company or using his fiercest attorneys to hammer out a deal that served him, and only him, best.

But tonight he was charmless all the way through.

He stood at the bar, nursing a drink he would have much preferred to toss back and follow with a few more of the same, his attention entirely consumed by his princess as she worked the room. As ordered.

"Make yourself useful, please," he'd told her when they'd arrived. "Try to charm these men. If you can."

He'd been deliberately insulting. He'd wanted her to imagine he had some doubt that she could pull such a thing off. He'd wanted her to feel the way he did—grouchy and irritable and outside his own skin.

She made him feel like an adolescent.

But Valentina had not seemed the least bit cowed. Much less insulted—which had only made him feel that much more raw.

"As you wish," she'd murmured in that overly obsequious voice she used when, he thought, she most wanted to get her claws into him. She'd even flashed that bland smile of hers at him, which had its usual effect—making his blood seem too hot for his own veins. "Your slightest desire is my command, of course."

And the truth was, Achilles should have known better. The kind of men he liked to manipulate best, especially when it came to high-stakes deals like the one he'd closed tonight, were not the sort of men he wanted anywhere near his princess. If the real Natalie had been here, she would have disappeared. She would have dispensed her usual round of cool greetings and even cooler congratulations, none of which encouraged anyone to cozy up to her. Then she would have sat in this corner or that, her expression blank and her attention focused entirely on one of her devices. She would have done that remarkable thing she did, that he had never thought to admire as much as perhaps he should have, which was her ability to be both in the room and invisible at the same time.

Princess Valentina, by contrast, couldn't have stayed invisible if her life depended on it. She was the furthest thing from *invisible* that Achilles had ever seen. It was as if the world was cast into darkness and she was its only light, that bright and that impossibly silvery and smooth, like her own brand of moonlight.

She moved from one group to the next, all gracious smiles. And not that bland sort of smile she used entirely too pointedly and too well, which invariably worked his last nerve, but one he'd seen in too many photographs he'd looked at much too late at night. Hunched over his laptop like some kind of obsessed troll while she slept beneath the same roof, unaware, which only made him that much more infuriated.

With her, certainly. But with himself even more.

Tonight she was the consummate hostess, as if this was her victory celebration instead of his. He could hear her airy laugh from across the room, far more potent than another woman's touch. And worse, he could see her. Slender and graceful, inhabiting a pencil skirt and well-cut jacket as if they'd been crafted specifically for her. When he knew perfectly well that those were his assistant's clothes, and they certainly weren't bespoke.

But that was Valentina's power. She made everything in her orbit seem to be only hers. Crafted specifically and especially for her.

Including him, Achilles thought—and he hated it. He was not a man a woman could put on a leash. He'd never given a woman any kind of power over him in his life, and he didn't understand how this creature who was engaged in a full-scale deception—who was running a con on him *even now*—somehow seemed to have the upper hand in a battle he was terribly afraid only he knew they were fighting.

It was unconscionable. It made him want to tear down this building—hell, the whole city—with his bare hands.

Or better yet, put them on her.

All the men around her lapped it up, of course. They stood too close. They put their hands on her elbow, or her shoulder, to emphasize a point that Achilles did not have to hear to know did not require emphasis. And certainly did not require touch.

She was moonlight over this grim, focused life of his, and he had no idea how he was going to make it through a world cast in darkness without her.

If he was appalled by that sentiment—and he was, deeply and wholly—it didn't seem to matter. He couldn't seem to turn it off.

It was far easier to critique her behavior instead.

So Achilles watched. And seethed. He catalogued every single touch, every single laugh, every single time she tilted back her pretty face and let her sleek copper hair fall behind her, catching all the light in the room. He brooded over the men who surrounded her, knowing full well that each and every one of them was imagining her naked. Hell, so was he.

But he was the only person in this room who knew what he was looking at. They thought she was Natalie

Monette, his dependable assistant. He was the only one who knew who she really was.

By the time Valentina finished a full circuit of the room, Achilles was in a high, foul temper.

"Are you finished?" he asked when she came to stand by his side again, his tone a dark slap he did nothing at all to temper. "Or will you actually whore yourself out in lieu of dessert?"

He meant that to hurt. He didn't care if he was an ass. He wanted to knock her back a few steps.

But of course Valentina only shot him an arch, amused look, as if she was biting back laughter.

"That isn't very nice," she said simply.

That was all.

And yet Achilles felt that bloom of unfortunate heat inside him all over again, and this time he knew exactly what it was. He didn't like it any better than he had before, and yet there it sat, eating at him from the inside out.

It didn't matter if he told himself he didn't wish to feel shame. All Valentina had to do was look at him as if he was a misbehaving child, tell him he *wasn't being nice* when he'd built an entire life out of being the very opposite of nice and hailing that as the source of his vast power and influence—and there it was. Heavy in him, like a length of hard, cold chain.

How had he given this woman so much power over him? How had he failed to see that was what was happening while he'd imagined he was giving her the rope with which to hang herself?

This could not go on. He could not allow this to go on.

The truth was, Achilles couldn't seem to get a handle on this situation the way he'd planned to when he'd realized who she was on the plane. He'd imagined it would be an amusing sort of game to humble a high and mighty spoiled-rotten princess who had never worked a day in her life and imagined she could deceive *the* Achilles Casilieris so boldly. He'd imagined it would be entertaining—and over swiftly. He supposed he'd imagined he'd be shipping her back to her palace and her princessy life and her proper royal fiancé by the end of the first day.

But Valentina wasn't at all who he'd thought she'd be. If she was spoiled—and she had to be spoiled, by definition, he was certain of it—she hid it. No matter what he threw at her, no matter what he demanded, she simply did it. Not always well, but she did it. She didn't complain. She didn't try to weasel out of any tasks she didn't like. She didn't even make faces or let out those long-suffering sighs that so many of his support staff did when they thought he couldn't hear them.

In fact, Valentina was significantly more cheerful than any other assistant he'd ever had—including Natalie.

She was nothing like perfect, but that made it worse. If she was perfect, maybe he could have dismissed her or ignored her, despite the game she was playing. But he couldn't seem to get her out of his head.

It was that part he couldn't accept. Achilles lived a highly compartmentalized life by design, and he liked it that way. He kept his women in the smallest, most easily controlled and thus ignored space. It had been many, many years since he'd allowed sex to control his thoughts, much less his life. It was only sex, after all. And what was sex to a man who could buy the world if he so chose? It was a release, yes. Enjoyable, even.

But Achilles couldn't remember the last time he'd woken in the night, his heart pounding, the hardest part of him awake and aware. With nothing in his head but her. Yet it was a nightly occurrence since Valentina had walked onto his plane.

It was bordering on obsession.

And Achilles did not get obsessed. He did not *want*.

He did not *need*. He took what interested him and then he forgot about it when the next thing came along.

And he couldn't think of a single good reason why he shouldn't do the same with her.

"Do you have something you wish to say to me?" Valentina asked, her soft, smooth voice snapping him back to this party that bored him. This victory that should have excited him, but that he only found boring now.

"I believe I said it."

"You misunderstand me," she replied, smiling. From a distance it would look as if they were discussing something as light and airy as that curve to her mouth, he thought. Achilles would have been impressed had he not been close enough to see that cool gleam in her green gaze. "I meant your apology. Are you ready to give it?"

He felt his own mouth curve then, in nothing so airy. Or light.

"Do I strike you as a man who apologizes, Miss Monette?" he asked her, making no attempt to ease the steel in his voice. "Have I ever done so in all the time you've known me?"

"A man who cannot apologize is not quite a man, is he, Mr. Casilieris?" This time he thought her smile was meant to take away the sting of her words. To hide the insult a little. Yet it only seemed to make it worse. "I speak philosophically, of course. But surely the only people who can't bring themselves to apologize are those who fear that any admission of guilt or wrongdoing diminishes them. I think we can both agree that's the very opposite of strength."

"You must tell me if I appear diminished, then," he growled at her, and he had the satisfaction of watching that pulse in her neck go wild. "Or weak in some way."

He wasn't surprised when she excused herself and went back to working the crowd. But he was surprised he let her.

Not here, he cautioned that wild thing inside him that he'd never had to contend with before, not over a woman. And never so raw and bold. *Not now.*

Later that night, they sat in his car as it slid through the streets of Manhattan in the midst of a summer thunderstorm, and Achilles cautioned himself not to act rashly.

Again.

But Valentina sat there beside him, staring out the window with a faint smile on her face. She'd settled beside him on the wide, plush seat without a word, as if it hardly mattered to her if he spoke or not. If he berated her, if he ignored her. As if she was all alone in this car or, worse, as if her mind was far away on more interesting topics.

And he couldn't tolerate it.

Achilles could think of nothing but her, she was eating him alive like some kind of impossible acid, yet *her* mind was miles away. She didn't seem to notice or care what she did to him when he was the one who was allowing her grand deception to continue—instead of outing her the way he should have the moment he'd understood who she was.

His hands moved before he knew what he meant to do, as if they had a mind of their own.

He didn't ask. He didn't push or prod at her or fence more words, forcing some sort of temper or explosion that would lead them where he wanted her to go. He didn't stack that deck.

He simply reached across the backseat, wrapped his hand around the back of her neck and hauled her closer to him.

She came easily, as if she really was made of nothing but light. He pulled her until she was sprawled across his lap, one hand braced on his thigh and another at his side. Her body was as lithe and sweetly rounded as he'd imagined it would be, but better. Much, much better.

She smelled like a dream, something soft and something sweet, and all of it warm and female and *her*. Valentina.

But all he cared about was the fact that that maddening mouth of hers was close to his.

Finally.

"What are you doing?" she breathed.

"I should think that was obvious," he growled. "And overdue."

And then, at last, he kissed her.

He wasn't gentle. He wasn't anything like tentative. He was neither soft nor kind, because it was too late for that.

He claimed her. Took her. He reminded her who he was with every slick, intense slide of his tongue. Or maybe he was reminding himself.

And he couldn't stop himself once the taste of her exploded inside him, making him reel. He wanted more. He wanted everything.

But she was still fighting him, that stubbornness of hers that made his whole body tight and needy. Not with her body, which was wrapped around him, supple and sweet, in a way that made him feel drunk. Not with her arms, which she'd sneaked around his shoulders as if she needed to hold on to him to keep herself upright.

It was that mouth of hers that had been driving him wild since the start.

He pulled his lips from hers. Then he slid his hands up to take her elegant cheekbones between his palms. He tilted her face where he wanted it, making the angle that much slicker. That much sweeter.

"Kiss me back," he demanded, pulling back farther to scowl at her, all this unaccustomed need making him impatient. And testy.

She looked stunned. And entirely too beautiful. Her green eyes were wide and dazed behind those clear glasses she wore. Her lips were parted, distractingly soft and faintly swollen already.

Achilles was hard and he was greedy and he wanted nothing more than to bury himself inside her here and now, and finally get rid of this obsession that was eating him alive.

Or indulge in it awhile.

"In case you are confused," he told her, his voice still a growl, "that was an order."

She angled herself back, just slightly. As if she was trying to sit up straighter against him. He didn't allow it. He liked her like this. Off balance and under his control, and he didn't much care if that made him a savage. He'd only ever pretended to be anything else, and only occasionally, at that.

"I *am* kissing you back," she said, and there was a certain haughtiness in her voice that delighted him. It made him grin, imagining all the many ways he could make her pay for that high-born, inbred superiority that he wanted to lap up like cream.

"Not well enough," he told her.

Her cheeks looked crisp and red, but she didn't shrink away from him. She didn't so much as blink.

"Maybe we don't have any chemistry," she theorized in that same voice, making it sound as if that was a foregone conclusion. "Not every woman in the world finds you attractive, Mr. Casilieris. Did you ever think of that?"

Achilles pulled her even more off balance, holding her over his lap and in his arms, right where he wanted her.

"No," he said starkly, and he didn't care if his greed and longing was all over his face, revealing more to her than he had ever shared with anyone. Ever. "I don't think either of those things is a problem."

Then he set his mouth to hers, and proved it.

* * *

Valentina thought she'd died and gone to a heaven she'd never dreamed of before. Wicked and wild and *better*. So very much better than anything she could have come up with in her most brilliant and dark-edged fantasies.

She had never been truly kissed before—if that was even the word to describe something so dominant and so powerful and so deeply, erotically thrilling—but she had no intention of sharing her level of inexperience with Achilles. Not when he seemed so close to some kind of edge and so hell-bent on taking her with him, toppling over the side into all of this sensation and need.

So she simply mimicked him. When he tilted his head, she did the same. She balled up her hands in his exquisitely soft shirt, up there against the hard planes of his chest tucked beneath his dark suit coat. She was aware of his hard hands on her face. She exulted in his arms like steel, holding her and caging her against him. She lost herself in that desperately cruel mouth as it moved over hers, the touch of his rough jaw, the impossible heat.

God help her, the heat.

And she was aware of that hard ridge beneath her, suddenly. She couldn't seem to keep from wriggling against it. Once, daringly. Then again when she heard that deep, wild and somehow savagely beautiful male noise he made in response.

And Valentina forgot about her vows, old and forthcoming. She forgot about faraway kingdoms and palaces and the life she'd lived there. She forgot about the promises she'd made and the ones that had been made in her name, because all of that seemed insubstantial next to the sheer, overwhelming wonder of Achilles Casilieris kissing her like a man possessed in the back of his town car.

This was her holiday. Her little escape. This was nothing but a dream, and he was, too. A fantasy of the life she might have lived had she been anyone else. Had she ever been anything like normal.

She forgot where they were. She forgot the role she was supposed to be playing. There was nothing in all the world but Achilles and the wildness he summoned up with every drag of his mouth against hers.

The car moved beneath them, but all Valentina could focus on was him. That hot possession of his mouth. The fire inside her.

And the lightning that she knew was his, the thunder storming through her, teaching her that she knew less about her body than he did. Much, much less. When he shifted so he could rub his chest against hers, she understood that he knew her nipples had pebbled into hard little points. When he laughed slightly as he rearranged her arms around his shoulders, she understood that he knew all her limbs were weighted down with the force of that greedy longing coursing through her veins.

The more he kissed her, over and over again as if time had no meaning and he could do this forever, she understood that he knew everything.

When he pulled his mouth from hers again, Valentina heard a soft, whimpering sound of protest. It took her one shuddering beat of her heart, then another, to realize she'd made it.

She couldn't process that. It was so abandoned, so thoughtless and wild—how could that be her?

"If we do not get out of this car right now," Achilles told her, his gaze a dark and breathtaking gold that slammed into her and lit her insides on fire, "we will not get out of it for some time. Not until I've had my fill of you. Is that how you want our first time to go, *glikia mou*? In the backseat of a car?"

For a moment Valentina didn't know what he meant. One hastily sucked-in breath later, she realized the car had come to a stop outside Achilles's building. Her cheeks flushed with a bright heat, but worse, she knew that he could see it. He saw everything—hadn't she just realized the truth of that? He watched her as she flushed, and he liked it. That deeply male curve in the corner of his mouth made that plain.

Valentina struggled to free herself from his hold then, to climb off his lap and sit back on the seat herself, and she was all too aware that he let her.

She didn't focus on that. She couldn't. That offhanded show of his innate strength made her feel...slippery, inside and outside and high between her legs. She tossed herself off his lap, her gaze tangling with his in a way that made the whole world seem to spin a little, and then she threw herself out the door. She summoned a smile from somewhere and aimed it at the doormen.

Breathe, she ordered herself. *Just breathe.*

Because she couldn't do this. This wasn't who she was. She hadn't held on to her virginity all this time to toss it aside at the very first temptation...had she?

This couldn't be who she was. It couldn't.

She'd spent her whole life practicing how to appear unruffled and serene under any and all circumstances, though she couldn't recall ever putting it to this kind of test before. She made herself breathe. She made herself smile. She sank into the familiarity of her public persona, wielding it like that armor she'd wanted, because it occurred to her it was the toughest and most resilient armor she had.

Achilles followed her into that bright and shiny elevator in the back of the gleaming lobby, using his key to close the doors behind them. He did not appear to notice or care that she was newly armored, especially while he seemed perfectly content to look so...disreputable.

His suit jacket hung open, and she was sure it had to be

obvious to even the most casual observer that she'd had her hands all over his chest and his shirt. And she found it was difficult to think of that hard mouth of his as cruel now that she knew how it tasted. More, how it felt on hers, demanding and intense and—

Stop, she ordered herself. *Now.*

He leaned back against the wall as the elevator started to move, his dark gold eyes hooded and intent when they met hers. He didn't say a word. Maybe he didn't have to. Her heart was pounding so loud that Valentina was certain it would have drowned him out if he'd shouted.

But Achilles did not shout.

On the contrary, when the elevator doors shut behind them, securing them in his penthouse, he only continued to watch her in that same intense way. She moved into the great living room, aware that he followed her, silent and faintly lazy.

It made her nervous. That was what she told herself that fluttery feeling was, lodged there beneath her ribs. And lower, if she was honest. Much lower.

"I'm going to bed," she said. And then instantly wished she'd phrased that differently when she heard it echo there between them, seeming to fill up the cavernous space, beating as madly within her as her own frenzied heart. "Alone."

Achilles gave the impression of smiling without actually doing so. He thrust his hands into the pockets of his dark suit and regarded her solemnly, save for that glittering thing in his dark gaze.

"If that is what you wish, *glikia mou.*"

And that was the thing. It wasn't what she wished. It wasn't what she wanted, and especially not when he called her that Greek name that she thought meant *my sweet*. It made her want to taste that word on that mouth of his. It made her want to find out exactly how sweet he thought she was.

It made her want to really, truly be someone else so she could do all the things that trampled through her head, making her chest feel tight while the rest of her... yearned.

Her whole life had been an exercise in virtue and duty, and she'd thought that meant something. She'd thought that *said* something about who she was. Valentina had been convinced that she'd held on to her chastity all this time, long after everyone she'd known had rid themselves of theirs, as a gift to her future.

But the night all around her told her something different. It had stripped away all the lies she'd told herself—or Achilles had. All the places she'd run and hid across all these years. Because the truth was that she'd never been tested. Was it truly virtue if she'd never been the least bit tempted to give it away? Or was it only coincidence that she'd never encountered anything that had felt the least bit compelling in that regard? Was it really holding on to something if she'd never felt the least bit like getting rid of it?

Because everything tonight was different. Valentina was different—or, worse, she thought as she stared at Achilles across the little bit of space that separated them, she had never been who she'd imagined she was. She had never understood that it was possible that a body could drown out what the mind knew to be prudent.

Until now.

She had judged passion all her life and told herself it was a story that weak people told themselves and others to make their sins seem more interesting. More complicated and unavoidable. But the truth was, Valentina had never experienced passion in her life.

Not until Achilles.

"I am your assistant," she told him. Or perhaps she was telling herself. "This must never happen again. If it does, I can't work for you."

"I have already told you that I am more than happy to accommodate—"

"There will be no lateral moves," she threw at him, appalled to hear her voice shaking. "You might lie awake at night imagining what that means and what it would look like, but I don't. I won't."

"Liar."

If he had hauled off and hit her, Valentina didn't think she could have been any more surprised. Shocked. No one had ever called her a liar before, not in all her life.

Then again, chimed in a small voice deep inside, *you never used to lie, did you? Not to others and not to yourself.*

"I have no doubt that you enjoy doing as you please," she spat at him, horrified that any of this was happening and, worse, that she'd let it—when Valentina knew who she was and what she'd be going back to in a few short weeks. "No matter the consequences. But not everyone is as reckless as you."

Achilles didn't quite smirk. "And that is why one of us is a billionaire and the other is his assistant."

"And if we were having a discussion about how to make money," Valentina said from between her teeth, no sign of her trademark serenity, "I would take your advice—but this is my life."

Guilt swamped her as she said that. Because, of course, it wasn't her life. It was Natalie's. And she had the sick feeling that she had already complicated it beyond the point of return. It didn't matter that Natalie had texted her to say that she'd kissed Prince Rodolfo, far away in Murin and neck-deep in Valentina's real life, however little Valentina had thought about it since she'd left it behind.

Valentina was going to marry Rodolfo. That her double had kissed him, the way Valentina probably should have, wasn't completely out of line.

But this... This thing she was doing... It was unacceptable on every level. She knew that.

Maybe Natalie has this same kind of chemistry with Rodolfo, something in her suggested. *Maybe he was engaged to the wrong twin.*

Which meant, she knew—because she was that self-serving—that maybe the wrong twin had been working for Achilles all this time and all of this was inevitable.

She wasn't sure she believed that. But she couldn't seem to stop herself. Or worse, convince herself that she should.

Achilles was still watching her too closely. Once again, she had the strangest notion that he knew too much. That he could see too far inside her.

Don't be silly, she snapped at herself then. *Of course he can't. You're just looking for more ways to feel guilty.*

Because whatever else happened, there was no way Achilles Casilieris would allow the sort of deception Valentina was neck-deep in to take place under his nose if he knew about it. She was certain of that, if nothing else.

"This is what I know about life," Achilles said, his voice a silken thread in the quiet of the penthouse, and Valentina had to repress a little shiver that threatened to shake her spine apart. "You must live it. If all you do is wall yourself off, hide yourself away, what do you have at the end but wasted time?"

Her throat was dry and much too tight. "I would take your advice more seriously if I didn't know you had an ulterior motive."

"I don't believe in wasting time or in ulterior motives," he growled back at her. "And not because I want a taste of you, though I do. And I intend to have it, *glikia mou*, make no mistake. But because you have put yourself on hold. Do you think I can't see it?"

She thought she had to be reeling then. Nothing was solid. She couldn't help but put her hand out, steadying herself on the back of the nearest chair—though it didn't seem to help.

And Achilles was watching her much too closely, with far too much of that disconcerting awareness making his dark gaze shine. "Or is it that you don't know yourself?"

When she was Princess Valentina of Murin, known to the world before her birth. Her life plotted out in its every detail. Her name literally etched in stone into the foundations of the castle where her family had ruled for generations. She had never had the opportunity to lose herself. Not in a dramatic adolescence. Not in her early twenties. She had never been beside herself at some crossroads, desperate to figure out the right path—because there had only ever been one path and she had always known exactly how to walk it, every step of the way.

"You don't know me at all," she told him, trying to sound less thrown and more outraged at the very suggestion that she was any kind of mystery to herself. She'd never had that option. "You're my employer, not my confidant. You know what I choose to show you and nothing more."

"But what you choose to show, and how you choose to show it, tells me exactly who you are." Achilles shook his head, and it seemed to Valentina that he moved closer to her when she could see he didn't. That he was exactly where he'd always been—it was just that he seemed to take over the whole world. She wasn't sure he even tried; he just did. "Or did you imagine I achieved all that I've achieved without managing to read people? Surely you cannot be so foolish."

"I was about to do something deeply foolish," she said

tightly. And not exactly smartly. "But I've since come to my senses."

"No one is keeping you here." His hands were thrust deep into his pockets, and he stood where he'd stopped, a few steps into the living room from those elevator doors. His gaze was all over her, but nothing else was touching her. He wasn't even blocking her escape route back to the guest room on this floor.

And she understood then. He was giving her choice. He was putting it on her. He wasn't simply sweeping her off into all that wild sensation—when he must have known he could have. He easily could have. If he hadn't stopped in the car, what would they be doing now?

But Valentina already knew the answer to that. She could feel her surrender inside her like heat.

And she thought she hated him for it.

Or should.

"I'm going to sleep," she said. She wanted her voice to be fierce. Some kind of condemnation. But she thought she sounded more determined than resolved. "I will see you in the morning. Sir."

Achilles smiled. "I think we both know you will see me long before that. And in your dreams, *glikia mou*, I doubt I will be so chivalrous."

Valentina pressed her lips tight together and did not allow herself to respond to him. Especially because she wanted to so very, very badly—and she knew, somehow, that it would lead nowhere good. It couldn't.

Instead, she turned and headed for her room. It was an unremarkable guest room appropriate for staff, but the best thing about it was the lock on the door. Not that she thought he would try to get in.

She was far more concerned that she was the one who would try to get out.

"One of these days," he said from behind her, his voice

low and intense, "you will stop running. It is a foregone conclusion, I am afraid. And then what?"

Valentina didn't say a word. But she didn't have to.

When she finally made it to her room and threw the dead bolt behind her, the sound of it echoed through the whole of the penthouse like a gong, answering Achilles eloquently without her having to open her mouth.

Telling him exactly how much of a coward she was, in case he hadn't already guessed.

CHAPTER SIX

IN THE DAYS that followed that strange night and Achilles's
world-altering kiss that had left her raw and aching and
wondering if she'd ever feel like herself again, Valentina
found she couldn't bear the notion that she was twenty-
seven years old and somehow a stranger to herself.

Her future was set in stone. She'd always known that.
And she'd never fought against all that inevitability because what was the point? She could fight as much as she
wanted and she'd still be Princess Valentina of Murin,
only with a stain next to her name. That had always
seemed to her like the very definition of futility.

But in the days that followed that kiss, it occurred to
her that perhaps it wasn't the future she needed to worry
about, but her past. She hadn't really allowed herself to
think too closely about what it meant that Natalie had
been raised by the woman who was very likely Valentina's own mother. Because, of course, there was no other
explanation for the fact she and Natalie looked so much
alike. Identical twins couldn't just randomly occur, and
certainly not when one of them was a royal. There were
too many people watching royal births too closely. Valentina had accepted the story that her mother had abandoned her, because it had always been couched in terms
of Frederica's mental illness. Valentina had imagined her

mother living out her days in some or other institution somewhere, protected from harm.

But the existence of Natalie suggested that Frederica was instead a completely different person from the one Valentina had imagined all this time. The woman who now called herself Erica had clearly not wasted away in a mental institution, all soothing pastels and injections and no ability to contact her own child. On the contrary, this Erica had lived a complicated life after her time in the palace that had nothing to do with any hospital—and though she'd clearly had two daughters, she'd taken only one with her when she'd gone.

Valentina didn't entirely understand how she could be quite so hurt by a betrayal that had happened so long ago and that she hadn't known about until recently. She didn't understand why it mattered so much to her. But the more she tried to tell herself that it was silly to be so bothered, the more bothered she got.

It was only when she had gone round and round and round on that almost too many times to count that Valentina accepted the fact she was going to have to do something about it.

And all these years, she'd never known how to go about looking for her mother even if she'd wanted to. She would have had to ask her father directly, the very idea of which made her shudder—even now, across an ocean or two from his throne and his great reserve and his obvious reluctance to discuss Frederica at all. Barring that, she would have had to speak to one of the high-level palace aides whose role was to serve her father in every possible way and who therefore had access to most of the family secrets. She doubted somehow that they would have told her all the things that she wanted to know—or even a few of them. And they certainly would have run any questions she had past her father first, which would have defeated the purpose of asking them.

Valentina tried to tell herself that was why she'd never asked.

But now she was tucked up in a lethally dangerous billionaire's penthouse in New York City, away from all the palace intrigue and protocol, and far too aware of the things a man like Achilles could do with only a kiss. To say nothing of his businesses. What was an old family secret to a man like Achilles?

And even though in many ways she had fewer resources at her fingertips and fewer people to ask for ancient stories and explanations, in the end, it was very simple. Because Valentina had Natalie's mobile, which had to mean she had direct access to her own story. If she dared look for it.

The Valentina who had seen her own mirror image in a bathroom in London might not have dared. But the Valentina who had lost herself in the raw fire of Achilles's kiss, on the other hand, dared all manner of things.

It was that Valentina who opened up Natalie's list of contacts, sitting there in her locked bedroom in Achilles's penthouse. She scrolled down, looking for an entry that read *Mom*. Or *Mum*. Or any variation of *Mother* she could think of.

But there was nothing.

That stymied her, but she was aware enough to realize that the sensation deep in her belly was not regret. It was relief. As if, in the end, she preferred these mysteries to what was likely to be a vicious little slap of truth.

You are such a coward, she told herself.

Because it wasn't as if her father—or Valentina herself, for that matter—had ever been in hiding. The truth was that her mother could have located her at any point over these last twenty-seven years. That she hadn't done so told Valentina all she needed to know about Frederica's maternal feelings, surely.

Well. What she *needed* to know perhaps, but there was a great deal more she *wanted* to know, and that was the trouble.

She kept scrolling until she found an entry marked *Erica*. She thought that told her a great deal about Natalie's relationship with this woman who was likely mother to them both. It spoke of a kind of distance that Valentina had certainly never contemplated when she'd thought about her own mother from time to time over the past nearly thirty years. In her head, of course, any reunion with the woman she'd imagined had been locked away in a pleasantly secure institution would be filled with love. Regret. Soft, sweet arms wrapped around her, and a thousand apologies for somehow managing to abandon and then never find her way back to a baby who lived at one of the most famous addresses in the world.

She wasn't entirely sure why the simple fact of the woman's first name in a list of contacts made it so clear that all of that was a lie. Not just a harmless fantasy to make a motherless child feel better about her fate, but something infinitely more dangerous, somehow.

Valentina wanted to shut down the mobile phone. She wanted to throw it across the small room and pretend that she'd never started down this road in the first place.

But it occurred to her that possibly, she was trying to talk herself out of doing this thing she was certain she needed to do.

Because Achilles might have imagined that he could see these mysteries in her, but what scared Valentina was that she could, too. That he'd identified a terrible weakness in her, and that meant anyone could.

Perhaps she wasn't who she thought she was. Perhaps

she never had been. Perhaps, all this time, she'd imagined she'd been walking down a set path when she hadn't.

If she was honest, the very idea made her want to cry.

It had been important, she thought then, sitting cross-legged on the bed with the summer light streaming in from the windows—crucially important, even—to carry on the morning after that kiss as if nothing had changed. Because she had to pretend that nothing had. That she didn't know too much now. That she didn't think of that kiss every time she looked at Achilles. She'd gone to work, and she'd done her job, and she'd stayed as much in his presence as she ever did—and she thought that she deserved some kind of award for the acting she'd done. So cool, so composed.

So utterly unbothered by the fact she now knew how he tasted.

And she tried to convince herself that only she knew that she was absolutely full of it.

But one day bled into the next, and she'd found that her act became harder and harder to pull off, instead of easier. She couldn't understand it. It wasn't as if Achilles was doing anything, necessarily. He was Achilles, of course. There was always that look in his eyes, as if he was but waiting for her to give him a sign.

Any sign.

As if, were she to do so, he would drop everything he was doing—no matter where they were and what was happening around them—and sweep them right back into that storm of sensation that she found simmered inside her, waiting. Just waiting.

Just as he was.

It was the notion that she was the one who held the power—who could make all of that happen with a simple word or glance—that she found kept her up at night. It made her shake. It polluted her dreams and made her drift off entirely too many times while she was awake, only to be slapped back down to earth when Achilles's voice turned silken, as if he knew.

Somehow, this all made her determined to seek out the one part of her life that had never made sense, and had never fit in neatly into the tidy narrative she'd believed all her life and knew back and forth.

Today was a rare afternoon when Achilles had announced that he had no need of her assistance while he tended to his fitness in his personal gym because, he'd gritted at her, he needed to clear his head. Valentina had repaired to her bedroom to work out a few snarls in his schedule and return several calls from the usual people wanting advice on how to approach him with various bits of news he was expected to dislike intensely. She'd changed out of Natalie's usual work uniform and had gratefully pulled on a pair of jeans and a T-shirt, feeling wildly rebellious as she did so. And then a little bit embarrassed that her life was clearly so staid and old-fashioned that she found denim a personal revolution.

Many modern princesses dressed casually at times, she was well aware. Just as she was even more aware that none of them were related to her father, with his antiquated notions of propriety. And therefore none of them would have to suffer his disapproval should she find herself photographed looking "common" despite her ancient bloodline.

But she wasn't Princess Valentina here in New York, where no one cared what she wore. And maybe that was why Valentina pulled the trigger. She didn't cold-call the number that she'd found on her sister's phone—and there was something hard and painful in her chest even thinking that word, *sister*. She fed the number into a little piece of software that one of Achilles's companies had been working on, and she let it present her with information that she supposed she should have had some sort of scruple about using. But she didn't.

Valentina imagined that said something about her, too, but she couldn't quite bring herself to care about that the way she thought she ought to have.

In a push of a button, she had a billing address. Though the phone number itself was tied to the area code of a far-off city, the billing address was right here in Manhattan.

It was difficult not see that as some kind of sign.

Valentina slipped out of the penthouse then, without giving herself time to second-guess what she was about to do. She smiled her way through the lobby the way she always did, and then she set out into New York City by herself.

All by herself.

No guards. No security. Not even Achilles's brooding presence at her side. She simply walked. She made her way through the green, bright stretch of Central Park, headed toward the east side and the address Achilles's software had provided. No one spoke to her. No one called her name. No cameras snapped at her, recording her every move.

After a while, Valentina stopped paying attention to the expression on her face. She stopped worrying about her posture and whether or not her hair looked unkempt as the faint breeze teased at it. She simply...walked.

Her shoulders seemed to slip down an extra inch or two from her ears. She found herself breathing deeper, taking in the people she passed without analyzing them—without assuming they wanted something from her or were look-ing to photograph her supposedly "at large" in the world.

About halfway across the park it occurred to her that she'd never felt this way in her life. Alone. Free. Better yet, anonymous. She could have been anybody on the streets. There were locals all over the paths in the park, walking and talking and taking in the summer afternoon as if that was a perfectly normal pastime. To be out on their own, no one the wiser, doing exactly as they pleased.

Valentina realized that whatever happened next, this was the normal she'd spent her life looking for and dreaming about. This exact moment, walking across Central Park while summer made its cheerful noises all around her, completely and entirely on her own.

Freedom, it turned out, made her heart beat a little too fast and too hard inside her chest.

Once she made it to the east side, she headed a little bit uptown, then farther east until she found the address that had been on that billing statement. It looked like all the other buildings on the same block, not exactly dripping in luxury, but certainly no hovel. It was difficult for Valentina to determine the difference between kinds of dwellings in a place like this. Apartment buildings, huge blocks of too many people living on top of each other by choice, seemed strange to her on the face of it. But who was she to determine the difference between prosperous New Yorkers and regular ones? She had lived in a palace all her life. And she suspected that Achilles's sprawling penthouse wasn't a far cry from a palace itself, come to that.

But once she'd located the building she wanted and its dark green awning marked with white scrollwork, she didn't know what to do. Except wait there. As if she was some kind of daring sleuth, just like in the books she'd read as a little girl, when she was just…that same old motherless child, looking for a better story to tell herself.

She chided herself for that instantly. It felt defeating. Despairing. She was anonymous and free and unremarkable, standing on a city street. Nobody in the entire world knew where she was. Nobody would know where to look and nobody was likely to find her if they tried. Valentina couldn't decide if that notion made her feel small and fragile, or vast and powerful. Maybe both at the same time.

She didn't know how long she stood there. She ignored the first few calls that buzzed at her from Natalie's mobile tucked in her pocket, but then realized that standing about speaking on her phone gave her far more of a reason to be out there in the street. Instead of simply standing there doing nothing, looking like she was doing exactly what she was doing, which was looming around as she waited for somebody to turn up.

So she did her job, out there on the street. Or Natalie's job, anyway. She fielded the usual phone calls from the office and, if she was honest, liked the fact that she had somewhere to put all her nervous energy. She was half-afraid that Achilles would call and demand that she return to his side immediately, but she suspected that she was less afraid of that happening than she was hoping that it would, so she didn't have to follow this through.

Because even now, there was a part of her that simply wanted to retreat back into what she already knew. What she'd spent her life believing.

Afternoon was bleeding into evening, and Valentina was beginning to think that she'd completely outstayed her welcome. That Erica was in one of the other places she sometimes stayed, like the one in the Caribbean Natalie had mentioned in a text. That at any moment now it was likely that one of the doormen in the surrounding buildings would call the police to make her move along at last. That they hadn't so far she regarded as some kind of miracle. She finished up the last of the calls she'd been fielding, and told herself that it had been foolish to imagine that she could simply turn up one afternoon, stand around and solve the mysteries of her childhood so easily.

But that was when she saw her.

And Valentina didn't know exactly what it was that had

caught her eye. The hair was wrong, not long and coppery like her daughters' but short. Dark. And it wasn't as if Valentina had any memories of this woman, but still. There was something in the way she moved. The way she came down the block, walking quickly, a plastic bag hanging from one wrist and the other hand holding a phone to her ear.

But Valentina knew her. She knew that walk. She knew the gait and the way the woman cocked her head toward the hand holding her phone. She knew the way this woman carried herself.

She recognized her, in other words, when she shouldn't have. When, she realized, despite the fact she'd spent a whole summer afternoon waiting for this moment—she really didn't want to recognize her.

And she'd been nursing fantasies this whole time, little as she wanted to admit that, even to herself. She'd told herself all the things that she would do if this woman appeared. She'd worked out scenarios in her head.

Do you know who I am? she would ask, or demand, and this woman she had always thought of as Federica, but who went by a completely different name—the better to hide, Valentina assumed—would… Cry? Flail about? Offer excuses? She hadn't been able to decide which version she would prefer no matter how many times she'd played it out in her head.

And as this woman who was almost certainly her mother walked toward her, not looking closely enough to see that there was anyone standing down the block a ways in front of her, much less someone who she should have assumed was the daughter she knew as Natalie, Valentina realized what she should have known already. Or maybe, deep down, she had known it—she just hadn't really wanted to admit it.

There was nothing this woman could do to fix anything

or change anything or even make it better. She couldn't go back in time. She couldn't change the past. She couldn't choose Valentina instead of Natalie, if that had been the choice she'd made. Valentina wasn't even certain that was something she'd want, if she could go back in time herself, but the fact of the matter was that there was nothing to be done about it now.

And her heart beat at her and beat at her, until she thought it might beat its way straight out through her ribs, and even as it did, Valentina couldn't pretend that she didn't know that what she was feeling was grief.

Grief, thick and choking. Dark and muddy and deep.

For the childhood she'd never had, and hadn't known she'd missed until now. For the life she might have known had this woman been different. Had Valentina been different. Had her father, perhaps, not been King Geoffrey of Murin. It was all speculation, of course. It was that tearing thing in her belly and that weight on her chest, and that thick, deep mud she worried she might never find her way out of again.

And when Erica drew close to her building's green awning, coming closer to Valentina than she'd been in twenty-seven years, Valentina…said nothing. She let her hair fall forward to cover her face where she leaned against the brick wall. She pretended she was on a serious phone call while the woman who was definitely her mother—of course she was her mother; how had Valentina been tricking herself into pretending she could be anything but that?—turned into the building that Valentina had been staking out all afternoon, and was swallowed up into her own lobby.

For long moments, Valentina couldn't breathe. She wasn't sure she could think.

It was as if she didn't know who she was.

She found herself walking. She lost herself in the tumult of this sprawling mess of a bright and brash city, the noise of car horns in the street, and the blasts of conversation and laughter from the groups of strangers she passed. She made her way back to the park and wandered there as the summer afternoon took on that glassy blue that meant the hour was growing late.

She didn't cry. She hardly saw in front of her. She simply walked.

And dusk was beginning to steal in at last, making the long blocks cold in the long shadows, when she finally made it back to Achilles's building.

One of the doormen brought her up in the elevator, smiling at her as she stepped off. It made her think that perhaps she had smiled in return, though she couldn't tell. It was as if her body was not her own and her face was no longer under her control. She walked into Achilles's grand living room, and stood there. It was as if she still didn't know where she was. As if she still couldn't see. And the huge windows that let Manhattan in all around her only seemed to make her sense of dislocation worse.

"Where the hell have you been?"

That low growl came from above her. Valentina didn't have to turn and look to know that it was Achilles from on high, standing at the top of the stairs that led to his sprawling master suite.

She looked up anyway. Because somehow, the most dangerous man she'd ever met felt like an anchor.

He looked as if he'd just showered. He wore a T-shirt she could tell was soft from down two flights, stretched over his remarkable chest as if it was as enamored of him as she feared she was. Loose black trousers were slung low on his hips, and she had the giddy sense that if he did something like stretch, or breathe too heavily, she would be able to see a swathe of olive skin between the waistband and the hem of his T-shirt.

And suddenly, she wanted nothing more than to see exactly that. More than she could remember wanting anything else. Ever.

"Careful, *glikia mou*, or I will take you up on that invitation written all over your face," Achilles growled as if he was irritated…but she knew better.

Because he knew. He always knew. He could read her when no one else ever had. The masks she wore like they were second nature and the things she pretended for the whole of the rest of the world fooled everybody, but never him.

Never, ever him.

As if there was a real Valentina buried beneath the exterior she'd thought for years was the totality of who she was, and Achilles was the only one who had ever met her. Ever seen her. Ever suspected she existed and then found her, again and again, no matter how hard Valentina worked to keep her hidden away.

Her throat was dry. Her tongue felt as if it no longer fit in her own mouth.

But she couldn't bring herself to look away from him.

She thought about her mother and she thought about her childhood. She thought about the pride she'd taken in that virtue of hers that she'd clung to so fiercely all these years. Or perhaps not so fiercely, as it had been so untested. Was that virtue at all, she wondered?

Or was this virtue?

She had spent all of this time trying to differentiate herself from a woman she thought she knew, but who it turned out she didn't know at all. And for what? She was already trapped in the same life that her mother had abandoned.

Valentina was the one who hadn't left her father. She was the one who had prided herself on being perfect. She was the one who was decidedly not mentally ill, never too overwrought to do the job required of her by her blood and her father's expectations, nothing but a credit to her father in all ways. And she'd reveled in it.

More than reveled in it. It had become the cornerstone of her own self-definition.

And all of it was built on lies. The ones she told herself, and more than that, the lies that had been told to her for her entire life. By everyone.

All Valentina could think as she gazed up the stairs to the man she was only pretending was her employer was that she was done with lies. She wanted something honest. Even—especially—if it was raw.

And she didn't much care if there were consequences to that.

"You say that is if it is a threat," she said quietly. Distinctly. "Perhaps you should rethink your own version of an invitation before it gets you in trouble." She raised her brows in challenge, and knew it. Reveled in it, too. "Sir."

And when Achilles smiled then, it was with sheer masculine triumph, and everything changed.

He had thought she'd left him.

When Achilles had come out of the hard, brutal workout he'd subjected himself to that had done absolutely nothing to make his vicious need for her settle, Achilles had found her gone.

And he'd assumed that was it. The princess had finally had enough. She'd finished playing this down-market game of hers and gone back to her palaces and her ball gowns and her resplendent little prince who waited for her across the seas.

He'd told himself it was for the best.

He was a man who took things for a living and made an empire out of his conquests, and he had no business whatsoever putting his commoner's hands all over a woman of her pedigree. No business doing it, and worse, he shouldn't want to.

And maybe that was why he found himself on his treadmill again while he was still sucking air from his first workout, running as if every demon he'd vanquished in his time was chasing him all over again, and gaining. Maybe that was why he'd run until he'd thought his lungs might burst, his head might explode or his knees might give out beneath him.

Then he'd run more. And even when he'd exhausted himself all over again, even when he was standing in his own shower with his head bent toward the wall as if she'd bested him personally, it hadn't helped.

The fact of the matter was that he had a taste of Valentina, and nothing else would do.

And what enraged him the most, he'd found—aside from the fact he hadn't had her the way he'd wanted her— was that he'd let her think she'd tricked him all this time. That she would go back behind her fancy gates and her moats and whatever the hell else she had in that palace of hers that he'd looked up online and thought looked exactly like the sort of fairy tale he disdained, and she would believe that she'd played him for a fool.

Achilles thought that might actually eat him alive.

And now here she stood when he thought he'd lost her. At the bottom of his stairs, looking up at him, her eyes dark with some emotion he couldn't begin to define.

But he didn't want to define it. He didn't want to talk about her feelings, and he'd die before he admitted his own, and what did any of that matter anyway? She was here and he was here, and a summer night was creeping in outside.

And the only thing he wanted to think about was sating himself on her at last.

At last and for as long as he could.

Achilles was hardly aware of moving down the stairs even as he did it.

One moment he was at the top, staring down at Valentina's upturned face with her direct challenge ringing in him like a bell, and the next he was upon her. And she was so beautiful. So exquisitely, ruinously beautiful. He couldn't seem to get past that. It was as if it wound around him and through him, changing him, making him new each time he beheld her.

He told himself he hated it, but he didn't look away.

"There is no going back," he told her sternly. "There will be no pretending this didn't happen."

Her smile was entirely too graceful and the look in her green eyes too merry by far. "Do you get that often?"

Achilles felt like a savage. An animal. Too much like that monster he kept down deep inside. And yet he didn't have it in him to mind. He reached out and indulged himself at last while his blood hammered through his veins, running his fingers over that elegant cheekbone of hers, and that single freckle that marred the perfection of her face—and somehow made her all the more beautiful.

"So many jokes," he murmured, not sure how much of the gruffness in his voice was need and how much was that thing like temper that held him fast and fierce. "Everything is so hilarious, suddenly. How much longer do you think you will be laughing, *glikia mou*?"

"I think that is up to you," Valentina replied smoothly, and she was still smiling at him in that same way, graceful and knowing. "Is that why you require so much legal documentation before you take a woman to bed? Do you make them all laugh so much that you fear your reputation as a grumpy icon would take a hit if it got out?"

It was a mark of how far gone he was that he found that amusing. If anyone else had dreamed of saying such a thing to him, he would have lost his sense of humor completely.

He felt his mouth curve. "There is only one way to find out."

And Achilles had no idea what she might do next. He wondered if that was what it was about her, if that was why this thirst for her never seemed to ebb. She was so very different from all the women he'd known before. She was completely unpredictable. He hardly knew, from one moment to the next, what she might do next.

It should have irritated him, he thought. But instead it only made him want her more.

Everything, it seemed, made him want her more. He hadn't realized until now how pale and insubstantial his desires had been before. How little he'd wanted anything.

"There is something I must tell you." She pulled her bottom lip between her teeth after she said that, a little breathlessly, and everything in him stilled.

This was it, he thought. And Achilles didn't know if he was proud of her or sad, somehow, that this great charade was at an end. For surely that was what she planned to tell him. Surely she planned to come clean about who she really was.

And while there was a part of him that wanted to deny that what swirled between them was anything more than sex, simple and elemental, there was a far greater part of him that roared its approval that she should think it was right to identify herself before they went any further.

"You can tell me anything," he told her, perhaps more fiercely than he should. "But I don't know why you imagine I don't already know."

He was fascinated when her cheeks bloomed with that crisp, bright red that he liked a little too much. More each time he saw it, because he liked his princess a little flustered. A little off balance.

But something in him turned over, some foreboding perhaps. Because he couldn't quite imagine why it was that she should be *embarrassed* by the deception she'd practiced on him. He could think of many things he'd like her to feel for attempting to pull something like that over on him, and he had quite a few ideas about how she should pay for that, but embarrassment wasn't quite it.

"I thought you might know," she whispered. "I hope it doesn't matter."

"Everything matters or nothing does, *glikia mou.*"

He shifted so he was closer to her. He wanted to care about whatever it was she was about to tell him, but he found the demands of his body were far too loud and too imperative to ignore. He put his hands on her, curling his fingers over her delicate shoulders and then losing himself in their suppleness. And in the delicate line of her arms. And in the sweet feel of her bare skin beneath his palms as he ran them down from her shoulders to her wrists, then back again.

And he found he didn't really care what she planned to confess to him. How could it matter when he was touching her like this?

"I do not require your confession," he told her roughly. "I am not your priest."

If anything, her cheeks flared brighter.

"I'm a virgin," she blurted out, as if she had to force herself to say it.

For a moment, it was as if she'd struck him. As if she'd picked up one of the sculptures his interior designer had littered about his living room and clobbered him with it.

"I beg your pardon?"

But she was steadier then. "You heard me. I'm a virgin. I thought you knew." She swallowed, visibly, but she didn't look away from him. "Especially when I didn't know how to kiss you."

Achilles didn't know what to do with that.

Or rather, he knew exactly what to do with it, but was

afraid that if he tossed his head back and let himself go the way he wanted to—roaring out his primitive take on her completely unexpected confession to the rafters—it might terrify her.

And the last thing in the world he wanted to do was terrify her.

He knew he should care that this wasn't quite the confession he'd expected. That as far as he could tell, Valentina had no intention of telling him who she was. Ever. He knew that it should bother him, and perhaps on some level it did, but the only thing he could seem to focus on was the fact that she was untouched.

Untouched.

He was the only man in all the world who had ever tasted her. Touched her. Made her shiver, and catch her breath, and moan. That archaic word seemed to beat in place of his heart.

Virgin. Virgin. Virgin.

Until it was as if he knew nothing but that. As if her innocence shimmered between them, beckoning and sweet, and she was his for the taking.

And, oh, how Achilles liked to take the things he wanted.

"Are you sure you wish to waste such a precious gift on the likes of me?" he asked, and he heard the stark greed beneath the laziness he forced into his tone. He heard exactly how much he wanted her. He was surprised it didn't seem to scare her the way he thought it should. "After all, there is nothing particularly special about me. I have money, that's all. And as you have reminded me, I am your boss. The ethical considerations are legion."

He didn't know why he said that. Any of that. Was it to encourage her to confess her real identity to him? Was it to remind her of the role she'd chosen to play—although not today, perhaps?

Or was it to remind him?

Either way, she only lifted her chin. "You don't have to take it," she said, as if it was of no import to her one way or the other. "Certainly not if you have some objection."

She lifted one shoulder, then dropped it, and the gesture was so quintessentially royal that it should have set Achilles's teeth on edge. But instead he found it so completely her, so entirely Princess Valentina, that it only made him harder. Hotter. More determined to find his way inside her.

And soon.

"I have no objection," he assured her, and there was no pretending his tone wasn't gritty. Harsh. "Are we finished talking?"

And the nerves he'd been unable to detect before were suddenly all over her face. He doubted she knew it. But she was braver than she ought to have been, his deceitful little princess, and all she did was gaze back at him. Clear and sure, as if he couldn't see the soft, vulnerable cast to her mouth.

Or maybe, he thought, she had no idea how transparent she was.

"Yes," Valentina said softly. "I'm ready to stop talking."

And this time, as he drew her to him, he knew it wouldn't end in a kiss. He knew they weren't going to stop until he'd had her at last.

He knew that she was not only going to be his tonight, but she was going to be only his. That no one had ever touched her before, and if he did it right, no one else ever would.

Because Achilles had every intention of ruining his princess for all other men.

CHAPTER SEVEN

VALENTINA COULDN'T BELIEVE this was happening.

At last.

Achilles took her mouth, and there was a lazy quality to his kiss that made her knees feel weak. He set his mouth to hers, and then he took his time. As if he knew that inside she was a jangle of nerves and longing, anticipation and greed. As if he knew she hardly recognized herself or all the needy things that washed around inside her, making her new.

Making her his.

He kissed her for a long while, it seemed to her. He slid his arms around her, he pulled her against his chest, and then he took her mouth with a thoroughness that made a dangerous languor steal all over her. All through her. Until she wasn't sure that she would be able to stand on her own, were he to let go of her.

But he didn't let go.

Valentina thought she might have fallen off the edge of the world anyway, because everything seemed to whirl and cartwheel around, but then she realized that what he'd done was stoop down to bend a little and then pick her up. As if she was as weightless as she felt. He held her in his arms, high against his chest, and she felt her shoes fall off her feet like some kind of punctuation. And when he gazed down into her face, she thought he looked like some kind of conquering warrior of old, though she chided herself for being so fanciful.

There was nothing fanciful about Achilles.

Quite the opposite. He was fierce and masculine and ruthless beyond measure, and still, Valentina couldn't think of anywhere she would rather be—or anyone she would rather be with like this. It all felt inevitable, as if she'd been waiting her whole life for this thing she hardly understood to sweep her away, just like this.

And it had come into focus only when she'd met Achilles.

Because he was her only temptation. She had never wanted anyone else. She couldn't imagine she ever would.

"I don't know what to do," she whispered, aware on some level that he was moving. That he was carrying her up those penthouse stairs as if she weighed nothing at all. But she couldn't bring herself to look away from his dark gold gaze. And the truth was, she didn't care. He could take her anywhere. "I don't want to disappoint you."

"And how would you do that?" His voice was so deep. So lazy and, unless she was mistaken, amused, even as that gaze of his made her quiver, deep inside.

"Well," she stammered out. "Well, I don't—"

"Exactly," he said, interrupting her with that easy male confidence that she found she liked a little too much. "You don't know, but I do. So perhaps, *glikia mou*, you will allow me to demonstrate the breadth and depth of my knowledge."

And when she shuddered, he only laughed.

Achilles carried her across the top floor, all of which was part of his great master bedroom. It took up the entire top level of his penthouse, bordered on all sides by the wide patio that was also accessible from a separate staircase below. The better to maintain and protect his privacy, she thought now, which she felt personally invested in at the moment. He strode across the hardwood floor with bold-colored rugs tossed here and there, and she took in the exposed brick walls and the bright, modern works of art that hung on them. This floor was all space and silence, and in between there were more of those breathtaking windows that brightened the room with the lights from the city outside.

Achilles didn't turn on any additional light. He simply took Valentina over to the huge bed that was propped up on a sleek modern platform crafted out of a bright, hard steel, and laid her out across it as if she was something precious to him. Which made her heart clutch at her, as if she wanted to be.

And then he stood there beside the bed, his hands on his lean hips, and did nothing but gaze down at her.

Valentina pushed herself up onto her elbows. She could feel her breath moving in and out of her, and it was as if it was wired somehow to all that sensation she could feel lighting her up inside. It made her breasts feel heavier. It made her arms and legs feel somehow restless and sleepy at once.

With every breath, she could feel that bright, hot ache between her legs intensify. And this time, she knew without a shred of doubt that he was aware of every last part of it.

"Do you have anything else to confess?" he asked her, and she wondered if she imagined the dark current in his voice then. But it didn't matter. She had never wanted anyone, but she wanted him. Desperately.

She would confess anything at all if it meant she could have him.

And it wasn't until his eyes blazed, and that remarkable mouth of his kicked up in one corner, that she realized she'd spoken out loud.

"I will keep that in mind," he told her, his voice a rasp into the quiet of the room. Then he inclined his head. "Take off your clothes."

It was as if he'd plugged her into an electrical outlet. She felt zapped. Blistered, perhaps, by the sudden jolt of power. It felt as if there were something bright and hot, wrapped tight around her ribs, pressing down. And down farther.

And she couldn't bring herself to mind.

"But—by myself?" she asked, feeling a little bit light-headed at the very idea. She'd found putting on these jeans a little bit revolutionary. She couldn't imagine stripping them off in front of a man.

And not just any man. Achilles Casilieris.

Who didn't relent at all. "You heard me."

Valentina had to struggle then. She had to somehow shove her way out of all that wild electrical madness that was jangling through her body, at least enough so she could think through it. A little bit, anyway. She had to struggle to sit up all the way, and then to pull the T-shirt off her body. Her hands went to her jeans next, and she wrestled with the buttons, trying to pull the fly open. It was all made harder by the fact that her hands shook and her fingers felt entirely too thick.

And the more she struggled, the louder her breathing sounded. Until she was sure it was filling up the whole room, and more embarrassing by far, there was no possible way that Achilles couldn't hear it. Or see the flush that she could feel all over her, electric and wild. She wrestled the stiff, unyielding denim down over her hips, that bright heat that churned inside her seeming to bleed out everywhere as she did. She was sure it stained her, marking her bright hot and obvious.

She sneaked a look toward Achilles, and she didn't

know what she expected to see. But she froze when her eyes met his.

That dark gold gaze of his was as hot and demanding as ever. That curve in his mouth was even deeper. And there was something in the way that he was looking at her that soothed her. As if his hands were on her already, when they were not. It was as if he was helping her undress when she suspected that it was very deliberate on his part that he was not.

Because of course it was deliberate, she realized in the next breath. He was giving her another choice. He was putting it in her hands, again. And even while part of her found that inordinately frustrating, because she wanted to be swept away by him—or more swept away, anyway—there was still a part of her that relished this. That took pride in the fact that she was choosing to give in to this particular temptation.

That she was choosing to truly offer this particular man the virtue she had always considered such a gift.

It wasn't accidental. She wasn't drunk the way many of her friends had been, nor out of her mind in some other way, or even outside herself in the storm of an explosive temper or wild sensation that had boiled over.

He wanted her to be very clear that she was choosing him.

And Valentina wanted that, too. She wanted to choose Achilles. She wanted this.

She had never wanted anything else, she was sure of it. Not with this fervor that inhabited her body and made her light up from the inside out. Not with this deep certainty.

And so what could it possibly matter that she had never undressed for a man before? She was a princess. She had dressed and undressed in rooms full of attendants her whole life. Achilles was different from her collection of royal aides, clearly. But there was no need for her to be embarrassed, she told herself then. There was no need to go red in the face and start fumbling about, as if she didn't know how to remove a pair of jeans from her own body.

Remember who you are, she chided herself.

She was Princess Valentina of Murin. It didn't matter that seeing her mother might have shaken her. It didn't change a thing. That had nothing to do with who she was, it only meant that she'd become who she was in spite of the choices her mother had made. She could choose to do with that what she liked. And she was choosing to gift her innocence, the virginity she'd clung to as a badge of honor as if that differentiated her from the mother who'd left her, to Achilles Casilieris.

Here. Now.

And there was absolutely nothing to be ashamed about.

Valentina was sure that she saw something like approval in his dark gaze as she finished stripping her jeans from the length of her legs. And then she was sitting there in nothing but her bra and panties. She shifted up and onto her knees. Her hair fell down over her shoulders as she knelt on the bed, swirling across her bared skin and making her entirely too aware of how exposed she was.

But this time it felt sensuous. A sweet, warm sort of reminder of how much she wanted this. Him.

"Go on," he told her, a gruff command.

"That sounded a great deal like an order," Valentina murmured, even as she moved her hands around to her back to work the clasp of her bra. And it wasn't even a struggle to make her voice so airy.

"It was most definitely an order," Achilles agreed, his voice still gruff. "And I would suggest you obey me with significantly more alacrity."

"Or what?" she taunted him gently.

She eased open the silken clasp and then moved her hands around to the bra cups, holding them to her breasts when the bra would have fallen open. "Will you hold it against me in my next performance review? Oh, the horror."

"Are you defying me?"

But Achilles sounded amused, despite his gruffness. And there was something else in his voice then, she thought. A certain tension that she felt move inside her even before she understood what it was. Maybe she didn't have to understand. Her body already knew.

Between her legs, that aching thing grew fiercer. Brighter. And so did she.

"I think you can take it," she whispered.

And then she let the bra fall.

She felt the rush of cooler air over the flesh of her breasts. Her nipples puckered and stung a little as they pulled tight. But what she was concentrating on was that taut, arrested look on Achilles's face. That savage gleam in his dark gold eyes. And the way his fierce, ruthless mouth went flat.

He muttered something in guttural Greek, using words she had never heard before, in her blue-blooded academies and rarefied circles. But she knew, somehow, exactly what he meant.

She could feel it, part of that same ache.

He reached down to grip the hem of his T-shirt, then tugged it up and over his head in a single shrug of one muscled arm. She watched him do it, not certain she was breathing any longer and not able to make herself care about that at all, and then he was moving toward the bed.

Another second and he was upon her.

He swept her up in his arms again, moving her into the center of the bed, and then he bore her down to the mattress beneath them. And Valentina found that they fit together beautifully. That she knew instinctively what to do.

She widened her legs, he fit himself between them, and

she cushioned him there—that long, solid, hard-packed form of his—as if they'd been made to fit together just like this. His bare chest was a wonder. She couldn't seem to keep herself from exploring it, running her palms and her fingers over every ridge and every plane, losing herself in his hot, extraordinary male flesh. She could feel that remarkable ridge of his arousal again, pressed against her right where she ached the most, and it was almost too much.

Or maybe it really was too much, but she wanted it all the same.

She wanted him.

He set his mouth to hers again, and she could taste a kind of desperation on his wickedly clever mouth.

That wild sensation stormed through her, making her limp and wild and desperate for things she'd only ever read about before. He tangled his hands in her hair to hold her mouth to his, then he dropped his chest down against hers, bearing her down into the mattress beneath them. Making her feel glorious and alive and insane with that ache that started between her legs and bloomed out in all directions.

And then he taught her everything.

He tasted her. He moved his mouth from her lips, down the long line of her neck, learning the contours of her clavicle. Then he went lower, sending fire spinning all over her as he made his way down to one of her breasts, only to send lightning flashing all through her when he sucked her nipple deep into his mouth.

He tested the weight of her breasts in his faintly calloused palm, while he played with the nipple of the other, gently torturing her with his teeth, his tongue, his cruel lips. When she thought she couldn't take any more, he switched.

And then he went back and forth, over and over again,

until her head was thrashing against the mattress, and some desperate soul was crying out his name. Over and over again, as if she might break apart at any moment.

Valentina knew, distantly, that she was the one making those sounds. But she was too far gone to care.

Achilles moved his way down her body, taking his sweet time, and Valentina sighed with every inch he explored. She shifted. She rolled. She found herself lifting her hips toward him without his having to ask.

"Good girl," he murmured, and it was astonishing how much pleasure two little words could give her.

He peeled her panties down off her hips, tugged them down the length of her legs and then threw them aside. And when he was finished with that, he slid his hands beneath her bottom as he came back over her, lifted her hips up into the air and didn't so much as glance up at her before he set his mouth to the place where she needed him most.

Maybe she screamed. Maybe she fainted. Maybe both at once.

Everything seemed to flash bright, then smooth out into a long, lethal roll of sensation that turned Valentina red hot.

Everywhere.

He licked his way into her. He teased her and he learned her and he tasted her, making even that most private part of her his. She felt herself go molten and wild, and he made a low, rough sound of pleasure, deeply masculine and deliciously savage, and that was too much.

"Oh, no," she heard herself moan. "No—"

Valentina felt more than heard him laugh against the most tender part of her, and then everything went up in flames.

She exploded. She cried out and she shook, the pleasure so intense she didn't understand how anyone could live through it, but still she shook some more. She shook until she thought she'd been made new. She shook until she didn't care either way.

And when she knew her own name again, Achilles was crawling his way over her. He no longer wore those loose black trousers of his, and there was a look of unmistakably savage male triumph stamped deep on his face.

"Beautiful," he murmured. He was on his elbows over her, pressing himself against her. His wall of a chest. That fascinatingly hard part of him below. He studied her flushed face as if he'd never seen her before. "Am I the only man who has ever tasted you?"

Valentina couldn't speak. She could only nod, mute and still shaking.

She wondered if she might shake like this forever, and she couldn't seem to work herself up into minding if she did.

"Only mine," he said with a certain quiet ferocity that only made that shaking inside her worse. Or better. "You are only and ever mine."

And that was when she felt him. That broad smooth head of his hardest part, nudging against the place where she was nothing but soft, wet heat and longing.

She sucked in a breath, and Achilles took her face in his hands.

"Mine," he said again, in the same intense way.

It sounded a great deal like a vow.

Valentina's head was spinning.

"Yours," she whispered, and he grinned then, too fierce and too elemental.

He shifted his hips and moved a little farther against her, pressing himself against that entrance again, and Valentina found her hands in fists against his chest.

"Will it hurt?" she asked before she knew she meant

to speak. "Or is that just something they say in books, to make it seem more…"

But she couldn't quite finish that sentence. And Achilles's gaze was too dark and too bright at once, so intense she couldn't seem to stop shaking or spinning. And she couldn't bring herself to look away.

"It might hurt." He kept his attention on her, fierce and focused. "It might not. But either way, it will be over in a moment."

"Oh." Valentina blinked, and tried to wrap her head around that. "I suppose quick is good."

Achilles let out a bark of laughter, and she wasn't sure if she was startled or something like delighted to hear it. Both, perhaps.

And it made a knot she hadn't known was hardening inside her chest ease.

"I cannot tell if you are good for me or you will kill me," he told her then. He moved one hand, smoothing her hair back from her temple. "It will only hurt, or feel awkward, for a moment. I promise. As for the rest…"

And the smile he aimed at her then was, Valentina thought, the best thing she'd ever seen. It poured into her and through her, as bright and thick as honey, changing everything. Even the way she shook for him. Even the way she breathed.

"The rest will not be quick," Achilles told her, still braced there above her. "It will not be rushed, it will be thorough. Extremely thorough, as you know I am in all things."

She felt her breath stutter. But he was still going.

"And when I am done, *glikia mou*, we will do it again. And again. Until we get it right. Because I am nothing if not dedicated to my craft. Do you understand me?"

"I understand," Valentina said faintly, because it was

hard to keep her voice even when the world was lost somewhere in his commanding gaze. "I guess that's—"

But that was when he thrust his way inside her. It was a quick, hard thrust, slick and hot and overwhelming, until he was lodged deep inside her.

Inside her.

It was too much. It didn't hurt, necessarily, but it didn't feel good, either. It felt...like everything. Too much of everything.

Too hard. Too long. Too thick and too deep and too—

"Breathe," Achilles ordered her.

But Valentina didn't see how that was possible. How could she breathe when there was a person *inside* her? Even if that person was Achilles.

Especially when that person was Achilles.

Still, she did as he bade her, because he was *inside* her and she was beneath him and splayed open and there was nothing else to do. She breathed in.

She let it out, and then she breathed in again. And then again.

And with each breath, she felt less overwhelmed and more...

Something else.

Achilles didn't seem particularly worried. He held himself over her, one hand tangled in her hair as the other made its way down the front of her body. Lazily. Easily. He played with her breasts. He set his mouth against the crook of her neck where it met her shoulder, teasing her with his tongue and his teeth.

And still she breathed the way he'd told her to do. In. Out.

Over and over, until she couldn't remember that she'd balked at his smooth, intense entry. That she'd ever had a problem at all with *hard* and *thick* and *long* and *deep*.

Until all she could feel was fire.

Experimentally, she moved her hips, trying to get a better feel for how wide he was. How deep. How far inside her own body. Sensation soared through her every time she moved, so she did it again. And again.

She took a little more of him in, then rocked around a little bit, playing. Testing. Seeing how much of him she could take and if it would continue to send licks of fire coursing through her every time she shifted position, no matter how minutely.

It did.

And when she started to shift against him, restlessly, as if she couldn't help herself, Achilles lifted his head and grinned down her, something wild and dark and wholly untamed in his eyes.

It thrilled her.

"Please…" Valentina whispered.

And he knew. He always knew. Exactly what she needed, right when she needed it.

Because that was when he began to move.

He taught her about pace. He taught her depth and rhythm. She'd thought she was playing with fire, but Achilles taught her that she had no idea what real fire was.

And he kept his word.

He was very, very thorough.

When she began to thrash, he dropped down to get closer. He gathered her in his arms, holding her as he thrust inside her, again and again. He made her his with every deep, possessive stroke. He made her want. He made her need.

He made her cry out his name, again and again, until it sounded to Valentina like some kind of song.

This time, when the fire took her, she thought it might have torn her into far too many pieces for her to ever recover. He lost his rhythm then, hammering into her hard and wild, as if he was as wrecked as she was—

And she held him to her as he tumbled off that edge behind her, and straight on into bliss.

Achilles had made a terrible mistake, and he was not a man who made mistakes. He didn't believe in them. He believed in opportunities—it was how he'd built this life of his. Something that had always made him proud.

But this was a mistake. She was a mistake. He couldn't kid himself. He had never wanted somebody the way that he wanted Valentina. It had made him sloppy. He had concentrated entirely too much on her. Her pleasure. Her innocence, as he relieved her of it.

He hadn't thought to guard himself against her.

He never had to guard himself against anyone. Not since he'd been a child. He'd rather fallen out of the habit—and that notion galled him.

Achilles rolled to the side of the bed and sat there, running a hand over the top of his head. He could hear Valentina behind him, breathing. And he knew what he'd see if he looked. She slept hard, his princess. After he'd finished with her the last time, he'd thought she might have fallen asleep before he'd even pulled out of her. He'd held the weight of her, sprawled there on top of him, her breath heavy and her eyes shut tight so he had no choice but to marvel at the length of her eyelashes.

And it had taken him much longer than it should have to shift her off him, lay her beside him and cover her with the sheets. Carefully.

It was that unexpected urge to protect her—from himself, he supposed, or perhaps from the uncertain elements of his ruthlessly climate-controlled bedroom—that had made him go cold. Something a little too close to the sort of panic he did not permit himself to feel, ever, had pressed down on him then. And no amount of controlling his breath or ordering himself to stop the madness seemed to help.

He rubbed a palm over his chest now, because his heart was beating much too fast, the damned traitor.

He had wanted her too much, and this was the price. This treacherous place he found himself in now, that he hardly recognized. It hadn't occurred to him to guard himself against a virgin no matter her pedigree, and this was the result.

He felt things.

He felt things—and Achilles Casilieris did not *feel*. He refused to *feel*. The intensity of sex was physical, nothing more. Never more than that, no matter the woman and no matter the situation and no matter how she might beg or plead—

Not that Valentina had done anything of the sort.

He stood from the bed then, because he didn't want to. He wanted to roll back toward her, pull her close again. He bit off a filthy Greek curse, beneath his breath, then moved restlessly across the floor toward the windows.

Manhattan mocked him. It lay there before him, glittering and sparkling madly, and the reason he had a penthouse in this most brash and American of cities was because he liked to stand high above the sprawl of it as if he was some kind of king. Every time he came here he was reminded how far he'd come from his painful childhood. And every time he stayed in this very room, he looked out over all the wealth and opportunity and untethered American dreams that made this city what it was and knew that he had succeeded.

Beyond even the wildest dreams the younger version of Achilles could have conjured up for himself.

But tonight, all he could think about was a copper-haired innocent who had yet to tell him her real name,

who had given him all of herself with that sweet enthusiasm that had nearly killed him, and left him…yearning.

And Achilles did not yearn.

He did not yearn and he did not let himself want things
he could not have, and he absolutely, positively did not
indulge in pointless nostalgia for things he did not miss.
But as he stood at his huge windows overlooking Manhattan, the city that seemed to laugh at his predicament
tonight instead of welcoming him the way it usually did,
he found himself tossed back to the part of his past he
only ever used as a weapon.

Against himself.

He hardly remembered his mother. Or perhaps he had
beaten that sentimentality out of himself years ago. Either way, he knew that he had been seven or so when
she had died, but it wasn't as if her presence earlier had
done anything to save her children from the brute of a
man whom she had married. Demetrius had been a thick,
coarse sort of man, who had worked with his hands down
on the docks and had thought that gave him the right to
use those hands however he wished. Achilles didn't think
there was anything the man had not beaten. His drinking buddies. His wife. The family dog. Achilles and his
three young stepsiblings, over and over again. The fact
that Achilles had not been Demetrius's own son, but the
son of his mother's previous husband who had gone off
to war and never returned, had perhaps made the beat-
ings Demetrius doled out harsher—but it wasn't as if he
spared his own flesh and blood from his fists.

After Achilles's mother had died under suspicious circumstances no one had ever bothered to investigate in a
part of town where nothing good ever happened anyway,
things went from bad to worse. Demetrius's temper worsened. He'd taken it out on the little ones, alternately kick-

ing them around and then leaving them for seven-year-old Achilles to raise.

This had always been destined to end in failure, if not outright despair. Achilles understood that now, as an adult looking back. He understood it analytically and theoretically and, if asked, would have said exactly that. He'd been a child himself, etcetera. But where it counted, deep in those terrible feelings he'd turned off when he had still been a boy, Achilles would never understand. He carried the weight of those lives with him, wherever he went. No matter what he built, no matter what he owned, no matter how many times he won this or that corporate battle— none of that paid the ransom he owed on three lives he could never bring back.

They had been his responsibility, and he had failed. That beat in him like a tattoo. It marked him. It was the truth of him.

When it was all over—after Achilles had failed to notice a gas leak and had woken up only when Demetrius had returned from one of his drinking binges three days later to find the little ones dead and Achilles listless and nearly unresponsive himself—everything had changed. That was the cut-and-dried version of events, and it was accurate enough. What it didn't cover was the guilt, the shame that had eaten Achilles alive. Or what it had been like to watch his siblings' tiny bodies carried out by police, or how it had felt to stand at their graves and know that he could have prevented this if he'd been stronger. Bigger. *Better.*

Achilles had been sent to live with a distant aunt who had never bothered to pretend that she planned to give him anything but a roof over his head, and nothing more. In retrospect, that, too, had been a gift. He hadn't had to bother with any healing. He hadn't had to examine what had happened and try to come to terms with it. No one had cared about him or his grief at all.

And so Achilles had waited. He had plotted. He had taken everything that resembled a feeling, shoved it down as deep inside him as it would go, and made it over into hate. It had taken him ten years to get strong enough. To hunt Demetrius down in a sketchy bar in the same bad neighborhood where he'd brutalized Achilles's mother, beaten his own children and left Achilles responsible for what had happened to them.

And that whole long decade, Achilles had told himself that it was an extermination. That he could walk up to this man who had loomed so large over the whole of his childhood and simply rid the world of his unsavory presence. Demetrius did not deserve to live. There was no doubt about that, no shred of uncertainty anywhere in Achilles's soul. Not while Achilles's mother and his stepsiblings were dead.

He'd staked out his stepfather's favorite dive bar, and this one in the sense that it was repellant, not attractive to rich hipsters from affluent neighborhoods. He'd watched a ramshackle, much grayer and more frail version of the stepfather roaring in his head stumble out into the street. And he'd been ready.

He'd gone up to Demetrius out in the dark, cold night, there in a part of the city where no one would ever dream of interfering in a scuffle on the street lest they find themselves shanked. He'd let the rage wash over him, let the sweet taint of revenge ignite in his veins. He'd expected to feel triumph and satisfaction after all these years and all he'd done to make himself strong enough to take this man down—but what he hadn't reckoned with was that the drunken old man wouldn't recognize him.

Demetrius hadn't known who he was.

And that meant that Achilles had been out there in the

street, ready to beat down a defenseless old drunk who smelled of watered-down whiskey and a wasted life.

He hadn't done it. It wasn't worth it. He might have happily taken down the violent, abusive behemoth who'd terrorized him at seven, but he'd been too big himself at seventeen to find any honor in felling someone so vastly inferior to him in every way.

Especially since Demetrius hadn't the slightest idea who he'd been.

And Achilles had vowed to himself then and there that the night he stood in the street in his old neighborhood, afraid of nothing save the darkness inside him, would be the absolutely last time he let feelings rule him.

Because he had wasted years. Years that could have been spent far more wisely than planning out the extermination of an old, broken man who didn't deserve to have Achilles as an enemy. He'd walked away from Demetrius and his own squalid past and he'd never gone back.

His philosophy had served him well since. It had led him across the years, always cold and forever calculating his next, best move. Achilles was never swayed by emotion any longer, for good or ill. He never allowed it any power over him whatsoever. It had made him great, he'd often thought. It had made him who he was.

And yet Princess Valentina had somehow reached deep inside him, deep into a place that should have been black and cold and nothing but ice, and lit him on fire all over again.

"Are you brooding?" a soft voice asked from behind him, scratchy with sleep. Or with not enough sleep. "I knew I would do something wrong."

But she didn't sound insecure. Not in the least. She sounded warm, well sated. She sounded like his. She sounded like exactly who she was: the only daughter of one of Europe's last remaining powerhouse kings and the only woman Achilles had ever met who could turn him inside out.

And maybe that was what did it. The suddenly unbearable fact that she was still lying to him. He had this burning thing eating him alive from the inside out, he was cracking apart at the foundations, and she was still lying to him.

She was in his bed, teasing him in that way of hers that no one else would ever dare, and yet she lied to him. Every moment was a lie, even and especially this one. Every single moment she didn't tell him the truth about who she was and what she was doing here was more than a lie. More than a simple deception.

He was beginning to feel it as a betrayal.

"I do not brood," he said, and he could hear the gruffness in his own voice.

He heard her shift on the bed, and then he heard the sound of her feet against his floor. And he should have turned before she reached him, he knew that. He should have faced her and kept her away from him, especially when it was so dark outside and there was still so much left of the night—and he had clearly let it get to him.

But he didn't.

And in a moment she was at his back, and then she was sliding her arms around his waist with a familiarity that suggested she'd done it a thousand times before and knew how perfectly she would fit there. Then she pressed her face against the hollow of his spine.

And for a long moment she simply stood there like that, and Achilles felt his heart career and clatter at his ribs. He was surprised that she couldn't hear it—hell, he was surprised that the whole of Manhattan wasn't alerted.

But all she did was stand there with her mouth pressed against his skin, as if she was holding him up, and through him the whole of the world.

Achilles knew that there was any number of ways to deal with this situation immediately. Effectively. No matter what name she called herself. He could call her out. He could ignore it altogether and simply send her away. He could let the darkness in him edge over into cruelty, so she would be the one to walk away.

But the simple truth was that he didn't want to do any of them.

"I have some land," he told her instead, and he couldn't tell if he was appalled at himself or simply surprised. "Out in the West, where there's nothing to see for acres and acres in all directions except the sky."

"That sounds beautiful," she murmured.

And every syllable was an exquisite pain, because he could feel her shape her words. He could feel her mouth as she spoke, right there against the flesh of his back. And he could have understood if it was a sexual thing. If that was what raged in him then. If it took him over and made him want to do nothing more than throw her down and claim her all over again. Sex, he understood. Sex, he could handle.

But it was much worse than that.

Because it didn't feel like fire, it felt...sweet. The kind of sweetness that wrapped around him, crawling into every nook and cranny inside him he'd long ago thought he'd turned to ice. And then stayed there, blooming into something like heat, as if she could melt him that easily.

He was more than a little worried that she could.

That she already had.

"Sometimes a man wants to be able to walk for miles in any direction and see no one," he heard himself say out loud, as if his mouth was no longer connected to the rest of him. "Not even himself."

"Or perhaps especially not himself," she said softly, her mouth against his skin having the same result as before.

Then he could feel her breathe, there behind him. There was a surprising amount of strength in the arms she still wrapped tight around his midsection. Her scent seemed to fill his head, a hint of lavender and something far softer that he knew was hers alone.

And the truth was that he wasn't done. He had never been a casual man in the modern sense, preferring mistresses who understood his needs and could cater to them over longer periods of time to one-night stands and such flashes in the pan that brought him nothing but momentary satisfaction.

He had never been casual, but this... This was nothing but trouble.

He needed to send her away. He had to fire Natalie, make sure that Valentina left, and leave no possible opening for either one of them to ever come back. This needed to be over before it really started. Before he forgot that he was who he was for a very good reason.

Demetrius had been a drunk. He'd cried and apologized when he was sober, however rarely that occurred. But Achilles was the monster. He'd gone to that bar to kill his stepfather, and he'd planned the whole thing out in every detail, coldly and dispassionately. He still didn't regret what he'd intended to do that night—but he knew perfectly well what that made him. And it was not a good man.

And that was all well and good as long as he kept the monster in him on ice, where it belonged. As long as he locked himself away, set apart.

It had never been an issue before.

He needed to get Valentina away from him, before he forgot himself completely.

"Pack your things," he told her shortly.

He shifted so he could look down at her again, drawing her around to his front and taking in the kick of those wide green eyes and that mouth he had sampled again and again and again.

And he couldn't do it.

He wanted her to know him, and even though that was the most treacherous thing of all, once it was in his head he couldn't seem to let it go. He wanted her to know him, and that meant he needed her to trust him enough to tell who she was. And that would never happen if he sent her away right now the way he should have.

And he was so used to thinking of himself as a monster. Some part of him—a large part of him—took a kind of pride in that, if he was honest. He'd worked so hard on making that monster into an impenetrable wall of wealth and judgment, taste and power.

But it turned out that all it took was a deceitful princess to make him into a man.

"I'm taking you to Montana," he told her gruffly, because he couldn't seem to stop himself.

And doomed them both.

CHAPTER EIGHT

ONE WEEK PASSED, and then another, and the six weeks Valentina had agreed to take stretched out into seven, out on Achilles's Montana ranch where the only thing on the horizon was the hint of the nearest mountain range.

His ranch was like a daydream, Valentina thought. Achilles was a rancher only in a distant sense, having hired qualified people to take care of the daily running of the place and turn its profit. Those things took place far away on some or other of his thousands of acres tucked up at the feet of the Rocky Mountains. They stayed in the sprawling ranch house, a sprawling nod toward log cabins and rustic ski lodges, the better to overlook the unspoiled land in all directions.

It was far away from everything and felt even farther than that. It was an hour drive to the nearest town, stout and quintessentially Western, as matter-of-fact as it was practical. They'd come at the height of Montana's short summer, hot during the day and cool at night, with endless blue skies stretching on up toward forever and nothing to do but soak in the quiet. The stunning silence, broken only by the wind. The sun. The exuberant moon and all those improbable, impossible stars, so many they cluttered up the sky and made it feel as if, were she to take a big enough step, Valentina could toss herself straight off the planet and into eternity.

And Valentina knew she was running out of time. Her wedding was the following week, she wasn't who she was pretending she was, and these stolen days in this faraway place of blue and gold were her last with this man. This stolen life had only ever been hers on loan.

But she would have to face that soon enough.

In Montana, as in New York, her days were filled with Achilles. He was too precise and demanding to abandon his businesses entirely, but there was something about the ranch that rendered him less overbearing. He and Valentina would put out what fires there might be in the mornings, but then, barring catastrophe, he let his employees earn their salaries the rest of the day.

While he and Valentina explored what this dreamy ranch life, so far removed from everything, had to offer. He had a huge library that she imagined would be particularly inviting in winter—not, she was forced to remind herself, that she would ever see it in a different season. A guest could sink into one of the deep leather chairs in front of the huge fireplace and read away a snowy evening or two up here in the mountains. He had an indoor pool that let the sky in through its glass ceiling, perfect for swimming in all kinds of weather. There was the hot tub, propped up on its own terrace with a sweeping view, which cried out for those cool evenings. It was a short drive or a long, pretty walk to the lake a little ways up into the mountains, so crisp and clear and cold it almost hurt.

But it was the kind of hurt that made her want more and more, no matter how it made her gasp and think she might lose herself forever in the cut of it.

Achilles was the same. Only worse.

Valentina had always thought of sex—or her virginity, anyway—as a single, solitary thing. Someday she would have sex, she'd always told herself. Someday she would get rid of her virginity. She had never really imagined that it wasn't a single, finite event.

She'd thought virginity, and therefore sex, was the actual breaching of what she still sometimes thought of as her maidenhead, as if she was an eighteenth-century heroine—and nothing more. She'd never really imagined much beyond that.

Achilles taught her otherwise.

Sex with him was threaded into life, a rich undercurrent that became as much a part of it as walking, breathing, eating. It wasn't a specific act. It was everything.

It was the touch of his hand across the dinner table, when he simply threaded their fingers together, the memory of what they'd already done together and the promise of more braided there between them. It was a sudden hot, dark look in the middle of a conversation about something innocuous or work-related, reminding her that she knew him now in so many different dimensions. It was the way his laughter seemed to rearrange her, pouring through her and making her new, every time she heard it.

It was when she stopped counting each new time he wrenched her to pieces as a separate, astonishing event. When she began to accept that he would always do that. Time passed and days rolled on, and all of these things that swirled between them only deepened. He became only more able to wreck her more easily the better he got to know her. And the better she got to know him.

As if their bodies were like the stars above them, infinite and adaptable, a great mess of joy and wonder that time only intensified.

But she knew it was running out.

And the more Achilles called her Natalie—which she thought he did more here, or perhaps she was far more sensitive to it now that she shared his bed—the more her terrible deception seemed to form into a heavy ball in the pit of her stomach, like some kind of cancerous thing that she very much thought might consume her whole.

Some part of her wished it would.

Meanwhile, the real Natalie kept calling her. Again and again, or leaving texts, but Valentina couldn't bring herself to respond to them. What would she say? How could she possibly explain what she'd done?

Much less the fact that she was still doing it and, worse, that she didn't want it to end no matter how quickly her royal wedding was approaching.

Even if she imagined that Natalie was off in Murin doing exactly the same thing with Rodolfo that Valentina was doing here, with all this wild and impossible hunger, what did that matter? They could still switch back, none the wiser. Nothing would change for Valentina. She would go on to marry the prince as she had always been meant to do, and it was highly likely that even Rodolfo himself wouldn't notice the change.

But Natalie had not been sleeping with Achilles before she'd switched places with Valentina. That meant there was no possible way that she could easily step back into the life that Valentina had gone ahead and ruined.

And was still ruining, day by day.

Still, no matter how self-righteously she railed at herself for that, she knew it wasn't what was really bothering her. It wasn't what would happen to Natalie that ate her up inside.

It was what would happen to her. And what could happen with Achilles. She found that she was markedly less sanguine about Achilles failing to notice the difference between Valentina and Natalie when they switched back again. In fact, the very notion made her feel sick.

But how could she tell him the truth? If she couldn't tell Natalie what she'd done, how could she possibly tell the man whom she'd been lying to directly all this time?

He thought he was having an affair with his assistant. A woman he had vetted and worked closely with for half a decade.

What was she supposed to say, *Oh, by the way, I'm actually a princess?*

The truth was that she was still a coward. Because she didn't know if what was really holding her back was that she couldn't imagine what she would say—or if she could imagine all too well what Achilles would do. And she knew that made her the worst sort of person. Because when she worried about what he would do, she was worried about herself. Not about how she might hurt him. Not about what it would do to him to learn that she had lied to him all this time. But the fact that it was entirely likely that she would tell him, and that would be the last she'd see of him. Ever.

And Valentina couldn't quite bear for this to be over.

This was her vacation. Her holiday. Her escape—and how had it never occurred to her that if that was true, it meant she had to go back? She'd known that in a general sense, of course, but she hadn't really thought it through. She certainly hadn't thought about what it would feel like to leave Achilles and then walk back to the stifling life she'd called her own for all these years.

It was one thing to be trapped. Particularly when it was all she'd ever known. But it was something else again to see exactly how trapped she was, to leave it behind for a while, and then knowingly walk straight back into that trap, closing the cage door behind her.

Forever.

Sometimes when she lay awake at night listening to Achilles breathe in the great bed next to her, his arms thrown over her as if they were slowly becoming one person, she couldn't imagine how she was ever going to make herself do it.

But time didn't care if she felt trapped. Or torn. It marched on whether she wanted it to or not.

"Are you brooding?" a low male voice asked from behind her, jolting her out of her unpleasant thoughts. "I thought that was my job, not yours."

Valentina turned from the rail of the balcony that ambled along the side of the master suite, where she was taking in the view and wondering how she could ever fold herself up tight and slot herself back into the life she'd left behind in Murin.

But the view behind her was even better. Achilles lounged against the open sliding glass door, naked save for a towel wrapped around his hips. He had taken her in a fury earlier, pounding into her from behind until she screamed out his name into the pillows, and he'd roared his own pleasure into the crook of her neck. Then he'd left her there on the bed, limp and still humming with all that passion, while he'd gone out for one of his long, brutal runs he always claimed cleared his head.

It had been weeks now, and he still took her breath. Now that she knew every inch of him, she found herself more in awe of him. All that sculpted perfection of his chest, the dark hair that narrowed at his lean hips, dipping down below the towel where she knew the boldest part of him waited.

She'd tasted him there, too. She'd knelt before the fireplace in that gorgeous library, her hands on his thighs as he'd sat back in one of those great leather chairs. He'd played with her hair, sifting strands of it through his fingers as she'd reached into the battered jeans he wore here on the ranch and had pulled him free.

He'd tasted of salt and man, and he'd let her play with him as she liked. He let her lick him everywhere until she learned his shape. He let her suck him in, then figure out how to make him as wild as he did when he tasted her in this same way. And she'd taken it as a personal triumph when he'd started to grip the chair. And when he'd lost himself inside her mouth, he'd groaned out that name he called her. *Glikia mou.*

Even thinking about it now made that same sweet, hot restlessness move through her all over again.

But time was her enemy. She knew that. And looking at him as he stood there in the doorway and watched her with that dark gold gaze that she could feel in every part of her, still convinced that he could see into parts of her she didn't know how to name, Valentina still didn't know what to do.

If she told him who she was, she would lose what few days with him she had left. This was Achilles Casilieris. He would never forgive her deception. Never. Her other option was never to tell him at all. She would go back to London with him in a few days as planned, slip away the way she'd always intended to do if a week or so later than agreed, and let the real Natalie pick up the pieces.

And that way, she could remember this the way she wanted to do. She could remember loving him, not losing him.

Because that was what she'd done. She understood that in the same way she finally comprehended intimacy. She'd gone and fallen in love with this man who didn't know her real name. This man she could never, ever keep.

Was it so wrong that if she couldn't keep him, she wanted to keep these sun-soaked memories intact?

"You certainly look like you're brooding." There was that lazy note to his voice that never failed to make her blood heat. It was no different now. It was that quick. It was that inevitable. "How can that be? There's nothing here but silence and sunshine. No call to brood about anything. Unless of course, it is your soul that is heavy." And she could have sworn there was something in his gaze then that dared her to come clean. Right then and there. As if, as ever, he knew what she was thinking. "Tell me, Natalie, what is it that haunts you?"

And it was moments like these that haunted her, but she couldn't tell him that. Moments like this, when she was certain that he knew. That he must know. That he was asking her to tell him the truth at last.

That he was calling her the wrong name deliberately, to see if that would goad her into coming clean.

But the mountains were too quiet and there was too much summer in the air. The Montana sky was a blue she'd never seen before, and that was what she felt in her soul. And if there was a heaviness, or a darkness, she had no doubt it would haunt her later.

Valentina wanted to live here. Now. With him. She wanted to *live*.

She had so little time left to truly *live*.

So once again, she didn't tell him. She smiled instead, wide enough to hide the fissures in her heart, and she went to him.

Because there was so little time left that she could do that. So few days left to reach out and touch him the way she did now, sliding her palms against the mouthwatering planes of his chest as if she was memorizing the heat of his skin.

As if she was memorizing everything.

"I don't know what you're talking about," she told him quietly, her attention on his skin beneath her hands. "I never do."

"I am not the mystery here," he replied, and though his voice was still so lazy, so very lazy, she didn't quite believe it. "There are enough mysteries to go around, I think."

"Solve this one, then," she dared him, going up on her toes to press her mouth to his.

Because she might not have truth and she might not have time, but she had this.

For a little while longer, she had this.

Montana was another mistake, because apparently, that was all he did now.

They spent weeks on his ranch, and Achilles made it all worse by the day. Every day he touched her, every day lost himself in her, every day he failed to get her to come clean with him. Every single day was another nail in his coffin.

And then, worse by far to his mind, it was time to leave.

Weeks in Montana, secluded from the rest of the world, and he'd gained nothing but a far deeper and more disastrous appreciation of Valentina's appeal. He hadn't exactly forced her to the light. He hadn't done anything but lose his own footing.

In all those weeks and all that sweet summer sunshine out in the American West, it had never occurred to him that she simply wouldn't tell him. He'd been so sure that he would get to her somehow. That if he had all these feelings churning around inside him, whatever was happening inside her must be far more extreme.

It had never occurred to him that he could lose that bet.

That Princess Valentina had him beat when it came to keeping herself locked up tight, no matter what.

They landed in London in a bleak drizzle that matched his mood precisely.

"You're expected at the bank in an hour," Valentina told him when they reached his Belgravia town house, standing there in his foyer looking as guileless and innocent as she ever had. Even now, when he had tasted every inch of her. Even now, when she was tearing him apart with that serene, untouchable look on her face. "And the board of directors is adamant—"

"I don't care about the bank," he muttered. "Or old men who think they can tell me what to do."

And just like that, he'd had enough.

He couldn't outright demand that Valentina tell him who she really was, because that wouldn't be her telling him of her own volition. It wouldn't be her trusting him.

It's almost as if she knows who you really are, that old familiar voice inside hissed at him. It had been years since he'd heard it, inside him or otherwise. But even though Demetrius had not been able to identify him on the streets when he'd had the chance, Achilles always knew the old man when he spoke. *Maybe she knows exactly what kind of monster you are.*

And a harsh truth slammed into him then, making him feel very nearly unsteady on his feet. He didn't know why it hadn't occurred to him before. Or maybe it had, but he'd shoved it aside out there in all that Montana sky and sunshine. Because he was Achilles Casilieris. He was one of the most sought-after bachelors in all the world. Legions of women chased after him daily, trying anything from trickery to bribery to outright lies about paternity claims to make him notice them. He was at the top of everyone's *most wanted* list.

But to Princess Valentina of Marin, he was nothing but a bit of rough.

She was slumming.

That was why she hadn't bothered to identify herself. She didn't see the point. He might as well have been the pool boy.

And he couldn't take it. He couldn't process it. There was nothing in him but fire and that raw, unquenchable need, and she was so cool. Too cool.

He needed to mess her up. He needed to do something to make all this…wildfire and feeling dissipate before it ate him alive and left nothing behind. Nothing at all.

"What are you doing?" she asked, and he took a little too much satisfaction in that appropriately uncertain note in her voice.

It was only when he saw her move that he realized he was stalking toward her, backing her up out of the gleaming foyer and into one of the town house's elegant sitting rooms. Not that the beauty of a room could do anything but fade next to Valentina.

The world did the same damned thing.

She didn't ask him a silly question like that again. And perhaps she didn't need to. He backed her up to the nearest settee, and took entirely too much pleasure in the pulse that beat out the truth of her need right there in her neck.

"Achilles..." she said hoarsely, but he wanted no more words. No more lies of omission.

No more *slumming*.

"Quiet," he ordered her.

He sank his hands into her gleaming copper hair, then dragged her mouth to his. Then he toppled her down to antique settee and followed her. She was slender and lithe and wild beneath him, rising to meet him with too much need, too much longing.

As if, in the end, this was the only place they were honest with each other.

And Achilles was furious. Furious, or something like it—something close enough that it burned in him as brightly. As lethally. He shoved her skirt up over her hips and she wrapped her legs around his waist, and she was panting already. She was gasping against his mouth. Or maybe he was breathing just as hard.

"Achilles," she said again, and there was something in her gaze then. Something darker than need.

But this was no time for sweetness. Or anything deeper. This was a claiming.

"Later," he told her, and then he took her mouth with

his, tasting the words he was certain, abruptly, he didn't want to hear.

He might be nothing to her but a walk on the wild side she would look back on while she rotted away in some palatial prison, but he would make sure that she remembered him.

He had every intention of leaving his mark.

Achilles tore off his trousers, freeing himself. Then he reached down and found the gusset of her panties, ripping them off and shoving the scraps aside to fit himself to her at last.

And then he stopped thinking about marks and memories, because she was molten hot and wet. She was his. He sank into her, groaning as she encased his length like a hot, tight glove.

It was so good. It was too good.

She always was.

He moved then, and she did, too, that slick, deep slide. And they knew each other so well now. Their bodies were too attuned to each other, too hot and too certain of where this was going, and it was never, ever enough.

He reached between them and pressed his fingers in the place where she needed him most, and felt her explode into a frenzy beneath him. She raised her hips to meet each thrust. She dug her fingers into his shoulders as if she was already shaking apart.

He felt it build in her, and in him, too. Wild and mad, the way it always was.

As if they could tear apart the world this way. As if they already had.

"No one will ever make you feel the way that I do," he told her then, a dark muttering near her ear as she panted and writhed. "No one."

And he didn't know if that was some kind of endearment, or a dire warning.

But it didn't matter, because she was clenching around him then. She gasped out his name, while her body gripped him, then shook.

And he pumped himself into her, wanting nothing more than to roar her damned name. To claim her in every possible way. To show her—

But he did none of that.

And when it was over, when the storm had passed, he pulled himself away from her and climbed to his feet again. And he felt something sharp and heavy move through him as he looked down at her, still lying there half on and half off the antique settee they'd moved a few feet across the floor, because he had done exactly as he set out to do.

He'd messed her up. She looked disheveled and shaky and absolutely, delightfully ravished.

But all he could think was that he still didn't have her. That she was still going to leave him when she was done here. That she'd never had any intention of staying in the first place. It ripped at him. It made him feel something like crazy.

The last time he'd ever felt anything like it, he'd been an angry seventeen-year-old in a foul-smelling street with an old drunk who didn't know who he was. It was a kind of anguish.

It was a grief, and he refused to indulge it. He refused to admit it was ravaging him, even as he pulled his clothes back where they belonged.

And then she made it even worse. She smiled.

She sat up slowly, pushing her skirt back into place and tucking the torn shreds of her panties into one pocket. Then she gazed up at him.

Achilles was caught by that look in her soft green eyes, as surely as if she'd reached out and wrapped her delicate hands around his throat. On some level, he felt as if she had.

"I love you," she said.

They were such small words, he thought through that thing that pounded in him like fear. Like a gong. Such small, silly words that could tear a man down without any warning at all.

And there were too many things he wanted to say then. For example, how could she tell him that she loved him when she wouldn't even tell him her name?

But he shoved that aside.

"That was sex, *glikia mou*," he grated at her. "Love is something different from a whole lot of thrashing around, half-clothed."

He expected her to flinch at that, but he should have known better. This was his princess. If she was cowed at all, she didn't show it.

Instead, she only smiled wider.

"You're the expert on love as in all things, of course," she murmured, because even here, even now, she was the only person alive who had ever dared to tease him. "My mistake."

She was still smiling when she stood up, then walked around him. As if she didn't notice that he was frozen there in some kind of astonishment. Or as if she was happy enough to leave him to it as she headed toward the foyer and, presumably, the work he'd always adored that seemed to loom over him these days, demanding more time than he wanted to give.

He'd never had a life that interested him more than his empire, until Valentina.

And he didn't have Valentina.

She'd left Achilles standing there with her declaration heavy in his ears. She'd left him half fire and a heart that long ago should have turned to ice. He'd been so certain it had when he was seven and had lost everything, including his sense of himself as anything like good.

He should have known then.

But it wasn't until much later that day—after he'd quizzed his security detail and household staff to discover she'd walked out with nothing but her shoulder bag and disappeared into the gray of the London afternoon—that he'd realized that had been the way his deceitful princess said goodbye.

CHAPTER NINE

VALENTINA COULDN'T KEEP her mind on her duties now that she was back in Murin. She couldn't keep her mind focused at all, come to that. Not on her duties, not on the goings-on of the palace, not on any of the many changes that had occurred since she'd come back home.

She should have been jubilant. Or some facsimile thereof, surely. She had walked back into her well-known, well-worn trap, expecting the same old cage, only to find that the trap wasn't at all what she had imagined it was— and the cage door had been tossed wide open.

When she'd left London that day, her body had still been shivering from Achilles's touch. She hadn't wanted to go. Not with her heart too full and a little bit broken at her own temerity in telling him how she felt when she'd known she had to leave. But it was time for her to go home, and there had been no getting around that. Her wedding to Prince Rodolfo was imminent. As in, the glittering heads of Europe's ancient houses were assembling to cheer on one of their own, and she needed to be there.

The phone calls and texts that she'd been ignoring that whole time, leaving Natalie to deal with it all on her own, had grown frantic. And she couldn't blame her sister, because the wedding was a mere day away. *Your twin sister*, she'd thought, those terms still feeling too unwieldy. She'd made her way to Heathrow Airport and bought herself a ticket on a commercial plane—the first time she'd ever done anything of the sort. One more normal thing to tuck away and remember later.

"Later" meaning after tomorrow, when she would be wed to a man she hardly knew.

It had taken Valentina a bit too long to do the right thing. To do the only possible thing and tear herself away from Achilles the way she should have done a long time ago. She should never have gone with him to Montana. She should certainly never have allowed them to stay there all that time, living out a daydream that could end only one way.

She'd known that going in, and she'd done it anyway. What did that make her, exactly?

Now I am awake, she thought as she boarded the plane. *Now I am awake and that will have to be as good as* alive, *because it's all I have left.*

She hadn't known what to expect from a regular flight into the commercial airport on the island of Murin. Some part of her imagined that she would be recognized. Her face was on the cover of the Murin Air magazines in every seat back, after all. She'd had a bit of a start when she'd sat down in the remarkably uncomfortable seat, pressed up against a snoring matron on one side and a very gray-faced businessman on the other.

But no one had noticed her shocking resemblance to the princess in the picture. No one had really looked at her at all. She flashed Natalie's passport, walked on the plane without any issues and walked off again in Murin without anyone looking at her twice—even though she was quite literally the spitting image of the princess so many were flocking to Murin to see marry her Prince Charming at last.

Once at the palace, she didn't bother trying to sneak

in because she knew she'd be discovered instantly—and that would hardly allow Natalie to switch back and escape, would it? So instead she'd walked up to the guard station around the back at the private family entrance, gazed politely at the guard who waited there and waited.

"But the…the princess is within," the guard had stammered. Maybe he was thrown by the fact Valentina was dressed like any other woman her age on the street. Maybe he was taken back because he'd never spoken to her directly before.

Or maybe it was because, if she was standing here in front of him, she wasn't where the royal guard thought she was. Which he'd likely assumed meant she'd sneaked out, undetected.

All things considered, she was happy to let that mystery stand.

Valentina had aimed a conspiratorial smile at the guard. "The princess can't possibly be within, given that I'm standing right here. But it can be our little secret that there was some confusion, if you like."

And then, feeling heavier than she ever had before and scarred somehow by what she'd gone through with Achilles, she'd walked back in the life she'd left so spontaneously and much too quickly in that London airport.

She'd expected to find Natalie as desperate to leave as she supposed, in retrospect, she had been. Or why else would she have suggested this switch in the first place?

But instead, she'd found a woman very much in love. With Crown Prince Rodolfo of Tissely. The man whom Valentina was supposed to marry the following day.

More than that, Natalie was pregnant.

"I don't know how it happened," Natalie had said, after Valentina had slipped into her bedroom and woken her up—by sitting on the end of the bed and pulling at Natalie's foot until she'd opened her eyes and found her double sitting there.

"Don't you?" Valentina had asked. "I was a virgin, but I had the distinct impression that you had not saved yourself for marriage all these years. Because why would you?"

Natalie had flushed a bit, but then her eyes had narrowed. "*Was* a virgin? Is that the past tense?" She'd blinked. "Not Mr. Casilieris."

But it wasn't the time then for sisterly confessions. Mostly because Valentina hadn't the slightest idea what she could say about Achilles that wasn't…too much. Too much and too unformed and unbearable, somehow, now that it was over. Now that none of it mattered, and never could.

"I don't think that you have a job with him anymore," Valentina had said instead, keeping her voice even. "Because I don't think you want a job with him anymore. You said you were late, didn't you? You're having a prince's baby."

And when Natalie had demurred, claiming that she didn't know one way or the other and it was likely just the stress of inhabiting someone else's life, Valentina had sprung into action.

She'd made it her business to find out, one way or another. She'd assured Natalie that it was simply to put her mind at ease. But the truth was a little more complicated, she admitted to herself as she made her way through the palace.

The fact was, she was relieved. That was what had washed through her when Natalie had confessed not only her love for Rodolfo, but her suspicions that she might be carrying his child. She'd pushed it off as she'd convinced one of her most loyal maids to run out into the city and buy her a few pregnancy tests, just to be certain. She'd shoved it to the side as she'd smuggled the tests back into her rooms, and then had handed them over to Natalie so she could find out for certain.

But there was no denying it. When Natalie had emerged from the bathroom with a dazed look on her face and a positive test in one hand, Valentina finally admitted the sheer relief that coursed through her veins. It was like champagne. Fizzy and a little bit sharp, washing through her and making her feel almost silly in response.

Because if Natalie was having Rodolfo's baby, there was no possible way that Valentina could marry him. The choice—though it had always been more of an expected duty than a choice—was taken out of her hands.

"You will marry him," Valentina had said quietly. "It is what must happen."

Natalie had looked pale. "But you… And I'm not… And you don't understand, he…"

"All of that will work out," Valentina had said with a deep certainty she very badly wanted to feel. Because it had to work out. "The important thing is that you will marry him in the morning. You will have his baby and you will be his queen when he ascends the throne. Everything else is spin and scandal, and none of that matters. Not really."

And so it was.

Once King Geoffrey had been brought into the loop and had been faced with the irrefutable evidence that his daughter had been stolen from him all those years ago—that Erica had taken Natalie and, not only that, had told Geoffrey that Valentina's twin had died at birth— he was more than on board with switching the brides at the wedding.

He'd announced to the gathered crowd that a most blessed miracle had occurred some months before. A daughter long thought dead had returned to him to take her rightful place in the kingdom, and they'd all kept it a secret to preserve everyone's privacy as they'd gotten to know each other.

Including Rodolfo, who had always been meant to be part of the family, the king had reminded the assembled crowd and the whole of the world, no matter how. And feelings had developed between Natalie and Rodolfo, where there had only ever been duty and honor between Valentina and her intended.

Valentina had seen this and stepped aside of her own volition, King Geoffrey had told the world. There had been no scandal, no sneaking around, no betrayals. Only one sister looking out for another.

The crowds ate it up. The world followed suit. It was just scandalous enough to be both believable and newsworthy. Valentina was branded as something of a Miss Lonely Hearts, it was true, but that was neither here nor there. The idea that she would sacrifice her fairy-tale wedding—and her very own Prince Charming—for her long-lost sister captured the public's imagination. She was more popular than ever, especially at home in Murin.

And this was a good thing, because now that her father had two heirs, he could marry one of his daughters off to fulfill his promises to the kingdom of Tissely, and he could prepare the other to take over Murin and keep its throne in the family.

And just like that, Valentina went from a lifetime preparing to be a princess who would marry well and support the king of a different country, to a new world in which she was meant to rule as queen in her own right.

If it was another trap, another cage, it was a far more spacious and comfortable one than any she had known before.

She knew that. There was no reason at all she should have been so unhappy.

"Your attention continues to drift, daughter," King Geoffrey said then.

Valentina snapped herself out of those thoughts in her head that did her no good and into the car where she sat with her father, en route to some or other glittering gala down at the water palace on the harbor. She couldn't even remember which charity it was this week. There was always another.

The motorcade wound down from the castle, winding its way along the hills of the beautiful capital city toward the gleaming Mediterranean Sea. Valentina normally enjoyed the view. It was pretty, first and foremost. It was home. It reminded her of so many things, of her honor and her duty and her love of her country. It renewed her commitment to her kingdom, and made her think about all the good she hoped she could do as its sovereign.

And yet these days, she wasn't thinking about Murin. All she could seem to think about was Achilles.

"I am preparing myself for the evening ahead," Valentina replied calmly enough. She aimed a perfectly composed smile at her father. "I live in fear of greeting a diplomat with the wrong name and causing an international incident."

Her father's gaze warmed, something that happened more often lately than it ever had before. Valentina chalked that up to the rediscovery of Natalie and, with it, some sense of family that had been missing before. Or too caught up in the past, perhaps.

"I have never seen you forget a name in all your life," Geoffrey said. "It's one among many reasons I expect you will make a far better queen than I have been a king. And I am aware I gave you no other choice, but I cannot regret that your education and talents will be Murin's gain, not Tissely's."

"I will confess," Valentina said then, "that stepping

aside so that Natalie could marry Rodolfo is not quite the sacrifice some have made it out to be."

Her father's gaze then was so canny that it reminded her that whatever else he was, King Geoffrey of Marin was a force to be reckoned with.

"I suspected not," he said quietly. "But there is no reason not to let them think so. It only makes you more sympathetic."

His attention was caught by something on his phone then. And as he frowned down at it, Valentina looked away. Back out the window to watch the sun drip down over the red-tipped rooftops that sloped all the way to the crystal blue waters below.

She let her hand move, slowly so that her father wouldn't notice, and held it over that faint roundness low in her belly she'd started to notice only a few weeks ago.

If her father thought she was a sympathetic figure now, she thought darkly, he would be delighted when she announced to him and the rest of the world that she was going to be a mother.

A single mother. A princess destined for his throne, with child.

Her thoughts went around and around, keeping her up at night and distracting her by day. And there were never any answers or, rather, there were never any good answers. There were never any answers she liked. Shame and scandal were sure to follow anything she did, or didn't do for that matter. There was no possible way out.

And even if she somehow summoned the courage to tell her father, then tell the kingdom, and then, far more intimidating, tell Achilles—what did she think might happen then? As a princess with no path to the throne, she had been expected to marry the Crown Prince of Tissely. As the queen of Murin, by contrast, she would be expected to marry someone of equally impeccable lineage. There were only so many such men alive, Valentina had met all of them, and none of them were Achilles.

No one was Achilles. And that shouldn't have mattered to her. There were so many other things she needed to worry about, like this baby she was going to be able to hide for only so long.

But he was the only thing she could seem to think about, even so.

The gala was as expected. These things never varied much, which was both their charm and their curse. There was an endless receiving line. There were music and speeches, and extremely well-dressed people milling about complimenting each other on the same old things. A self-congratulatory trill of laughter here, a fake smile there, and so it went. Dignitaries and socialites rubbing shoulders and making money for this or that cause the way they always did.

Valentina danced with her father, as tradition dictated. She was pleased to see Rodolfo and Natalie, freshly back from their honeymoon and exuding exactly the sort of happy charm that made everyone root for them, Valentina included.

Valentina especially, she thought.

She excused herself from the crush as soon as she could, making her way out onto one of the great balconies in this water palace that took its cues from far-off Venice and overlooked the sea. Valentina stood there for a long while, helplessly reliving all the things she'd been so sure she could lock away once she came back home. Over and over—

And she thought that her memory had gotten particularly sharp—and cruel. Because when she heard a foot against the stones behind her and turned, her smile already in place the way it always was, she saw him.

But it couldn't be him, of course. She assumed it was

her hormones mixing with her memory and making her conjure him up out of the night air.

"Princess Valentina," Achilles said, and his voice was low, a banked fury simmering there in every syllable. "I do not believe we have been introduced properly. You are apparently of royal blood you sought to conceal and I am the man you thought you could fool. How pleasant to finally make your acquaintance."

It occurred to her that she wasn't fantasizing at the same moment it really hit her that he was standing before her. Her heart punched at her. Her stomach sank.

And in the place she was molten for him, instantly, she ached. Oh, how she ached.

"Achilles…"

But her throat was so dry. It was in marked contrast to all that emotion that flooded her eyes at the sight of him that she couldn't seem to control.

"Are those tears, Princess?" And he laughed then. It was a dark, angry sort of sound. It was not the kind of laughter that made the world shimmer and change. And still, it was the best sound Valentina had heard in weeks. "Surely those are not tears. I cannot think of a single thing you have to cry about, Valentina. Not one. Whereas I have a number of complaints."

"Complaints?"

All she could seem to do was echo him. That and gaze at him as if she was hungry, and the truth was that she was. She couldn't believe he was here. She didn't care that he was scowling at her—her heart was kicking at her, and she thought she'd never seen anything more beautiful than Achilles Casilieris in a temper, right here in Murin.

"We can start with the fact that you lied to me about who you are," he told her. "There are numerous things to cover after that, culminating in your extremely bad decision to walk out. *Walk out.*" He repeated it with three times the fury. "On *me*."

"Achilles." She swallowed, hard. "I don't think—"

"Let me be clear," he bit out, his dark gold gaze blazing as he interrupted her. "I am not here to beg or plead. I am Achilles Casilieris, a fact you seem to have forgotten. I do not beg. I do not plead. But I feel certain, princess, that you will do both."

He had waited weeks.

Weeks.

Having never been walked out on before—ever—Achilles had first assumed that she would return. Were not virgins forever making emotional connections with the men who divested them of their innocence? That was the reason men of great experience generally avoided virgins whenever possible. Or so he thought, at any rate. The truth was that he could hardly remember anything before Valentina.

Still, he waited. When the royal wedding happened the day after she'd left, and King Geoffrey made his announcement about his lost daughter—who, he'd realized, was his actual assistant and also, it turned out, a royal princess—Achilles had been certain it was only a matter of time before Valentina returned to London.

But she never came.

And he did not know when it had dawned on him that this was something he was going to have to do himself. The very idea enraged him, of course. That she had walked out on him at all was unthinkable. But what he couldn't seem to get his head around was the fact that she didn't seem to have seen the error of her ways, no matter how much time he gave her to open her damned eyes.

She was too beautiful and it was worse now, he thought

darkly, here in her kingdom, where she was no longer pretending anything.

Tonight she was dressed like the queen she would become one day, all of that copper hair piled high on the top of her head, jewels flashing here and there. Instead of the pencil skirts he'd grown accustomed to, she wore a deep blue gown that clung to her body in a way that was both decorous and alluring at once. And if he was not mistaken, made her curves seem more voluptuous than he recalled.

She was much too beautiful for Achilles's peace of mind, and worse, she did not break down and begin the begging or the pleading, as he would have preferred. He could see that her eyes were damp, though the tears that had threatened seemed to have receded. She smoothed her hand over her belly, as if the dress had wrinkles when it was very clear that it did not, and when she looked up from that wholly unnecessary task her green eyes were as guarded as her smile was serene.

As if he was a stranger. As if he had never been so deep inside her she'd told him she couldn't breathe.

"What are you doing here?" she asked.

"That is the wrong question."

She didn't so much as blink, and that smile only deepened. "I had no idea that obscure European charities were of such interest to men of your stature, and I am certain it was not on your schedule."

"Are you questioning how I managed to score an invite?" he asked, making no particular move to keep the arrogant astonishment from his voice. "Perhaps I must introduce myself again. There is no guest list that is not improved by my presence, princess. Even yours."

Her gaze became no less guarded. Her expression did not change. But still, Achilles thought something in her steeled. And her shoulders straightened almost imperceptibly.

"I must apologize to you," she said, very distinctly.

And this was what Achilles had wanted. It was why he'd come here. He had imagined it playing out almost exactly this way.

Except there was something in her tone that rubbed him the wrong way, now that it was happening. It was that guarded look in her eyes perhaps. It was the fact that she didn't close the distance between them, but stayed where she was, one hand on the balcony railing and the other at her side. As distant as if she was on some magazine cover somewhere instead of standing there in front of him.

He didn't like this at all.

"You will have to be more specific, I am afraid," he said coolly. "I can think of a great many apologies you owe me."

Her mouth curved, though he would not call it a smile, precisely.

"I walked into a bathroom in an airport in London and saw a woman I had never met before, who could only be my twin. I could not resist switching places with her." Valentina glanced toward the open doors and the gala inside, as if it called to her more than he did, and Achilles hated that, too. Then she looked back at him, and her gaze seemed darker. "Do not mistake me. This is a good life. It is just that it's a very specific, very planned sort of life and it involves a great many spotlights. I wanted a normal one, for a change. Just for a little while. It never occurred to me that that decision could affect anyone but me. I would never have done it if I ever thought that you—"

But Achilles couldn't hear this. Because it sounded entirely too much like a postmortem. When he had traveled across Europe to find her because he couldn't bear the thought that it had already ended, or that he hadn't picked up on the fact that she was leaving him until she'd already gone.

"Do you need me to tell you that I love you, Valentina?" he demanded, his voice low and furious. "Is that what this is? Tell me what you need to hear. Tell me what it will take."

She jolted as if he'd slapped her. And he hated that, so he took the single step that closed the distance between them, and then there was no holding himself back. Not when she was so close again—at last—after all these weeks. He reached over and wrapped his hands around her shoulders, holding her there at arm's length, like some kind of test of his self-control. He thought that showed great restraint, when all he wanted was to haul her toward him and get his mouth on her.

"I don't need anything," she threw at him in a harsh sort of whisper. "And I'm sorry you had to find out who I was after I left. I couldn't figure out how to tell you while I was still with you. I didn't want to ruin—"

She shook her head, as if distressed.

Achilles laughed. "I knew from almost the first moment you stepped on the plane in London. Did you imagine I would truly believe you were Natalie for long? When you could not perform the most basic of tasks she did daily? I knew who you were within moments after the plane reached its cruising altitude."

Her green eyes went wide with shock. Her lips parted. Even her face paled.

"You knew?"

"You have never fooled me," he told her, his voice getting a little too low. A little too hot. "Except perhaps when you claimed you loved me, then left."

Her eyes overflowed then, sending tears spilling down her perfect, elegant cheeks. And he was such a bastard that some part of him rejoiced.

Because if she cried for him, she wasn't indifferent to him. She was certainly not immune to him.

It meant that it was possible he hadn't ruined this, after all, the way he did everything else. It meant it was possible this was salvageable.

He didn't like to think about what it might mean if it wasn't.

"Achilles," she said again, more distinctly this time. "I never saw you coming—it never occurred to me that I could ever be anything but honorable, because I had never been tempted by anything in my life. Only you. The only thing I lied to you about was my name. Everything else was true. Is true." She shook her head. "But it's hopeless."

"Nothing is hopeless," he growled at her. "I have no intention of losing you. I don't lose."

"I'm not talking about a loss," she whispered fiercely, and he could feel a tremor go through her. "This isn't a game. You are a man who is used to doing everything in his own way. You are not made for protocol and diplomacy and the tedious necessities of excruciating propriety. That's not who you are." Her chin tilted up slightly. "But I'm afraid it is exactly who I am."

"I'm not a good man, *glikia mou*," he told her then, not certain what was gripping him. He only knew he couldn't let her go. "But you know this. I have always known who I am. A monster in fine clothes, rubbing shoulders with the elites who would spit on me if they could. If they did not need my money and my power."

Achilles expected a reaction. He expected her to see him at last as she had failed to see him before. The scales would fall from her eyes, perhaps. She would recoil, certainly. He had always known that it would take so very little for people to see the truth about him, lurking right there beneath his skin. Not hidden away at all.

But Valentina did not seem to realize what had happened. She continued to look at him the way she always did. There wasn't the faintest flicker of anything like revulsion, or bleak recognition, in her gaze.

If anything, her gaze seemed warmer than before, for all it was wet. And that made him all the more determined to show her what she seemed too blind to see.

"You are not hearing me, Valentina. I'm not speaking in metaphors. Do you have any idea what I have done? The lives that I have ruined?"

She smiled at that, through her tears. "I know exactly who you are," she said, with a bedrock certainty that shook him. "I worked for you. You did not wine me or dine me. You did not take me on a fancy date or try to impress me in any way. You treated me like an assistant, an underling, and believe me, there is nothing more revealing. Are you impatient? Are you demanding and often harsh? Of course." She shrugged, as if this was all so obvious it was hardly worth talking about. "You are a very powerful man. But you are not a monster."

If she'd reached over and wrenched his mangled little heart from between his ribs with her elegant hands and then held it there in front of him, it could not possibly have floored him more.

"And you will not convince me otherwise," she added, as if she could see that he was about to say something. "There's something I have to tell you. And it's entirely possible that you are not going to like it at all."

Achilles blinked. "How ominous."

She blew out a breath. "You must understand that there are no good solutions. I've had no idea how to tell you this, but our... What happened between us had consequences."

"Do you think that I don't know that?" he belted out at her, and he didn't care who heard him. He didn't care if the whole of her pretty little kingdom poured out of the party behind them to watch and listen. "Do you think that I would be here if I was unaware of the consequences?"

"I'm not talking about feelings—"

"I am," he snapped. "I have not felt anything in years. I have not wanted to feel. And thanks to you all I do now is feel. Too damned much, Valentina." She hadn't actually ripped his heart out, he reminded himself. It only felt as if she had. He forced himself to loosen his grip on her before he hurt her. "And it doesn't go anywhere. Weeks pass, and if anything grows worse."

"Achilles, please," she whispered, and the tears were falling freely again. "I never wanted to hurt you."

"I wish you had hurt me," he told her, something dark and bitter, and yet neither of those things threaded through him. "Hurt things heal. This is far worse."

She sucked in a breath as if he'd punched her. He forged on, throwing all the doom and tumult inside him down between them.

"I have never loved anything in my life, Princess. I have wanted things and I've taken them, but love has always been for other men. Men who are not monsters by any definition. Men who have never ruined anything—not lives, not companies and certainly not perfect, virginal princesses who had no idea what they were signing up for." He shook his head. "But there is nothing either one of us can do about it now. I'm afraid the worst has already happened."

"The worst?" she echoed. "Then you know...?"

"I love you, *glikia mou*," he told her. "There can be no other explanation, and I feel sorry for you, I really do. Because I don't think there's any going back."

"Achilles..." she whispered, and that was not a look of transported joy on her face. It wasn't close. "I'm so sorry. Everything is different now. I'm pregnant."

CHAPTER TEN

ACHILLES WENT SILENT. Stunned, if Valentina had to guess.

If that frozen astonishment in his dark gold gaze was any guide.

"And I am to be queen," she told him, pointedly. His hands were still clenched on her shoulders, and what was wrong with her that she should love that so much? That she should love any touch of his. That it should make her feel so warm and safe and wild with desire. All at once. "My father thought that he would not have an heir of his own blood, because he thought he had only one daughter. But now he has two, and Natalie has married Rodolfo. That leaves me to take the throne."

"I'm not following you," Achilles said, his voice stark. Something like frozen. "I can think of no reason that you have told me in one breath that I am to be a father and in the next you feel you must fill me in on archaic lines of succession."

"There is very strict protocol," she told him, and her voice cracked. She slid her hands over her belly. "My father will never accept—"

"You keep forgetting who I am," Achilles growled, and she didn't know if he'd heard a word she'd said. "If you are having my child, Valentina, this conversation is over. We will be married. That's an end to it."

"It's not that simple."

"On the contrary, there is nothing simpler."

She needed him to understand. This could never be. They could never happen. She was trapped just as surely as she'd ever been. Why couldn't he see that? "I am no longer just a princess. I'm the Crown Princess of Murin—"

"Princess, princess." Achilles shook his head. "Tell me something. Did you mean it when you told me that you loved me? Or did you only dare to tell me in the first place because you knew you were leaving?"

That walloped Valentina. She thought that if he hadn't been holding on to her, she would have staggered and her knees might well have given out from beneath her.

"Don't be ridiculous." But her voice was barely a whisper.

"Here's the difference between you and me, princess. I have no idea what love is. All I know is that you came into my life and you altered something in me." He let go of her shoulder and moved his hand to cover his heart, and broke hers that easily. "Here. It's changed now, and I can't change it back. And I didn't tell you these things and then leave. I accepted these things, and then came to find you."

She felt blinded. Panicked. As if all she could do was cower inside her cage—and worse, as if that was what she wanted.

"You have no idea what you're talking about," she told him instead. "You might be a successful businessman, but you know nothing about the realities of a kingdom like Murin."

"I know you better than you think. I know how desperate you are for a normal life. Isn't that why you switched places with Natalie?" His dark gaze was almost kind.

"But don't you understand? Normal is the one thing you can never be, *glikia mou*."

"You have no idea what you're talking about," she said again, and this time her voice was even softer. Fainter.

"You will never be normal, Valentina," Achilles said quietly. His fingers tightened on her shoulder. "I am not so normal myself. But together, you and I? We will be extraordinary."

"You don't know how much I wish that could happen." She didn't bother to wipe at her tears. She let them fall. "This is a cage, Achilles. I'm trapped in it, but you're not. And you shouldn't be."

He let out a breath that was too much like a sigh, and Valentina felt it shudder through her, too. Like foreboding.

"You can live in fear, or you can live the life you want, Valentina," he told her. "You cannot do both."

His dark gaze bored into her, and then he dropped his other hand, so he was no longer touching her.

And then he made it worse and stepped back.

She felt her hands move, when she hadn't meant to move at all. Reaching out for him, whether she wanted to or not.

"If you don't want to be trapped, don't be trapped," Achilles said, as if it was simple. And with that edge in his voice that made her feel something a little more pointed than simply restless. "I don't know how to love, but I will learn. I have no idea how to be a father, but I will dedicate myself to being a good one. I never thought that I'd be a husband to anyone, but I will be the husband you need. You can sit on your throne. You can rule your kingdom as you wish. I have no need to be a king. But I will be one for you." He held out his hand. "All you have to do is be brave, princess. That's all. Just be a little brave."

"It's a cage, Achilles," she told him again, her voice ragged. "It's a beautiful, beautiful cage, this life. And there's no changing it. It's been the same for untold centuries."

"Love me," he said then, like a bomb to her heart. What was left of it. "I dare you."

And the music poured out from the party within. Inside, her father ruled the way he always did, and her brand-new sister danced with the man Valentina had always imagined she would marry. Natalie had come out of nowhere and taken her rightful place in the kingdom, and the world hadn't ended when brides had been switched at a royal wedding. If anything, life had vastly improved for everyone involved. Why wasn't that the message Valentina was concentrating on?

She realized that all this time, she'd been focused on what she couldn't do. Or what she had to do. She'd been consumed with duty, honor—but none of it her choice. All of it thrust upon her by an accident of birth. If Erica had taken Valentina instead of Natalie, she would have met Achilles some time ago. They wouldn't be standing here, on this graceful balcony, overlooking the soothing Mediterranean and her father's kingdom.

Her whole life seemed to tumble around before her, year after year cracking open before her like so many fragile eggs against the stones beneath her feet. All the things she never questioned. All the certainties she simply accepted, because what was the alternative? She'd prided herself on her serenity in the face of anything that had come her way. On her ability to do what was asked of her, always. What was expected of her, no matter how unfair.

And she'd never really asked herself what she wanted to do with her life. Because it had never been a factor. Her life had been meticulously planned from the start.

But now Achilles stood before her, and she carried their baby inside her. And she knew that as much as she wanted to deny it, what he said was true. She was a coward. She'd used her duty to hide behind. She could have stayed in London, could have called off her wedding. But she hadn't.

And had she really imagined she could walk down that aisle to Rodolfo, having just left Achilles in London? Had she really intended to do that?

It was unimaginable. And yet she knew she'd meant to do exactly that.

She'd been saved from that vast mistake, and yet here she was, standing in front of the man she loved, coming up with new reasons why she couldn't have the one thing in her life she ever truly wanted.

All this time she'd been convinced that her life was the cage. That her royal blood trapped her.

But the truth was, she was the one who did that.

She was her own cage, and she always would be if she didn't do something to stop it right now. If she didn't throw open the door, step through the opening and allow herself to reach out for the man she already knew she loved.

Be brave, he'd told her, as if he knew she could do it. As if he had no doubt at all.

"I love you," she whispered helplessly. Lost somewhere in that gaze of his, and the simple fact that he was here. Right here in front of her, his hand stretched toward her, waiting for her with a patience she would have said Achilles Casilieris did not possess.

"Marry me, *glikia mou*. And you can love me forever." His mouth crept up in one corner, and all the scars Valentina had dug into her own heart when she'd left him seemed to glow a little bit. Then knit themselves into something more like art. "I'm told that's how it goes. But you know me. I always like to push the boundaries a little bit farther."

"Farther than forever?"

And she smiled at him then, not caring if she was still crying. Or laughing. Or whatever was happening inside her that was starting to take her over.

Maybe that was what it was to be brave. Doing whatever it was not because she felt it was right, but because it didn't matter what she felt. It was right, so she had to do it.

"Three forevers," Achilles said, as if he was promising them to her, here and now. "To start."

And he was still holding out his hand.

"Breathe," he murmured, as if he could see all the tumult inside her.

Valentina took a deep breath. She remembered lying in that bed of his with all of New York gleaming around them. He'd told her to breathe then, too.

In. Out.

Until she felt a little less full, or a little more able to handle what was happening. Until she had stopped feeling overwhelmed, and had started feeling desperate with need.

And this was no different.

Valentina breathed in, then out. Then she stepped forward and slid her hand into his, as easily as if they'd been made to fit together just like that, then let him pull her close.

He shifted to take her face in his hands, tilting her head back so he could fit his mouth to hers. Though he didn't. Not yet.

"Forever starts now," Valentina whispered. "The first one, anyway."

"Indeed." Achilles's mouth was so deliriously hard, and directly over hers. "Kiss me, Valentina. It's been too long."

And Valentina did more than kiss him. She poured herself into him, pushing herself up on her toes and winding her arms around his neck, and that was just the start.

Because there was forever after forever stacked up in front of them, just waiting for them to fill it. One after the next.

Together.

CHAPTER ELEVEN

ACHILLES MADE A terrible royal consort.

He didn't know who took more pride in that, he himself or the press corps, who finally had the kind of access to him they'd always wanted, and adored it.

But he didn't much care how bad he was at being the crown princess's billionaire, as long as he had Valentina. She allowed him to be as surly as he pleased, because she somehow found that charming. She'd even supported him when he'd refused to allow her father to give him a title, because he had no wish to become a Murinese citizen.

"I thank you," he had said to Geoffrey. "But I prefer not to swear my fealty to my wife by law, and title. I prefer to do it by choice."

Their wedding had been another pageant, with all the pomp and circumstance anyone could want for Europe's favorite princess. Achilles had long since accepted the fact that the world felt it had a piece of their story. Or of Valentina, certainly.

And he was a jealous bastard, but he tried not to mind as she waved and smiled and gave them what they wanted.

Meanwhile, as she grew bigger with his child she seemed to glow more by the day, and all those dark things in him seemed to grow lighter every time she smiled at him.

So he figured it was a draw.

She told him he wasn't a monster with that same deep certainty, as if she'd been there. As if she knew. And every time she did, he was more and more tempted to believe her.

She gave birth to their son the following spring, right about the time her sister was presenting the kingdom of Tissely with a brand-new princess of their own, because the ways in which the twins were identical became more and more fascinating all the time. The world loved that, too.

But not as much as Valentina and Natalie did.

And as Achilles held the tiny little miracle that he and Valentina had made, he felt another lock fall into place inside him. Maybe they could not be normal, Valentina and him. But that only meant that the love they would lavish on this child would be no less than remarkable.

And no less than he deserved.

This child would never live in the squalor his father had. He would never want for anything. No hand would be raised against him, and no fists would ever make contact with his perfect, sweet face. His parents would not abandon him, no stepfathers would abuse him, and it was entirely possible that he would be so loved that the world might drown in the force of it. Achilles would not be at all surprised.

Achilles met his beautiful wife's gaze over their child's head, lying with her in the bed in their private wing of the hospital. The public was locked outside, waiting to meet this latest member of the royal family. But that would happen later.

Here, now, it was only the three of them. His brand-new family and the world he would build for him. The world that Valentina would give their son.

Just as she'd given it to him.

"You are mine, *glikia mou*," he said softly as her gaze met his. Fiercely. "More now than ever."

And he knew that Valentina remembered. The first vows they'd taken, though neither of them had called it that, in his New York penthouse so long ago.

The smile she gave him then was brighter than the sun, and warmed him all the same. Their son wriggled in his arms, as if he felt it, too. His mother's brightness that had lit up a monster lost in his own darkness, and convinced him he was a man.

Not just a man, but a good one. For her.

Anything for her.

"Yours," she agreed softly.

And Achilles reckoned that three forevers would not be nearly enough with Valentina.

But he was Achilles Casilieris. Perfection was his passion.

If they needed more forever they'd have it, one way or another.

He had absolutely no doubt.

* * * * *

MILLS & BOON

MODERN

Power and Passion

Prepare to be swept off your feet by sophisticated, sexy and seductive heroes, in some of the world's most glamourous and romantic locations, where power and passion collide.

Julia James

Heiress's
**PREGNANCY
SCANDAL**

MILLS & BOON
MODERN

Jennie Lucas

Chosen as the
**SHEIKH'S ROYAL
BRIDE**

MILLS & BOON
MODERN

Kim Lawrence

A WEDDING
or the
ITALIAN'S DEMAND

MILLS & BOON

Sharon Kendrick

The
**SHEIKH'S
SECRET BABY**

MILLS & BOON
MODERN

Eight Modern stories published every month, find them all a

millsandboon.co.uk/Modern

MILLS & BOON
Desire

Indulge in secrets and scandal, intense drama and plenty of sizzling hot action with powerful and passionate heroes who have it all: wealth, status, good looks... everything but the right woman.

JOIN US ON SOCIAL MEDIA!

Stay up to date with our latest releases, author news and gossip, special offers and discounts, and all the behind-the-scenes action from Mills & Boon...

 millsandboon

 millsandboonuk

 millsandboon

It might just be true love...